Harlequin's Romance Library invites you to enjoy three romantic adventures superbly created by author Hilary Wilde

The Golden Maze... The sight of Claife Castle brought back a rush of childhood memories. Only then, Cindy's mother had been alive and engaged to Robert Paxton. The marriage never took place and they'd left the lovely Lake District. Now Cindy was back—remembered in the will of a man *she* could barely recall. (#1624)

The Fire of Life... Rayanne knew she had to get out from under her family's thumb if she was to overcome her inferiority complex. But coming to the Jefferson Wild Life Reserve had been a mistake. Now she was under the even firmer thumb of authoritarian Cary Jefferson! (#1642)

The Impossible Dream... Meg had a hard time making her boss, Craig Lambert, believe she'd had no idea her brother was working for Craig's archrival. It seemed such an obvious plot. How could she convince him that she'd never stoop to such trickery—at least, not knowingly? (#1685)

**Another collection
of Romance favorites...
by a best-selling Harlequin author!**

In the pages of this specially selected anthology are three delightfully absorbing Romances—all by an author whose vast readership all over the world has shown her to be an outstanding favorite.

For those of you who are missing these love stories from your Harlequin library shelf, or who wish to collect great romance fiction by favorite authors, these Harlequin Romance anthologies are for you.

We're sure you'll enjoy each of the engrossing and heartwarming stories contained within. They're treasures from our library... and we know they'll become treasured additions to yours!

The first anthology of 3 Harlequin Romances by

Hilary Wilde

Harlequin Books

TORONTO • LONDON • LOS ANGELES • AMSTERDAM
SYDNEY • HAMBURG • PARIS • STOCKHOLM • ATHENS • TOKYO

Harlequin Romance anthology 58

Copyright © 1977 by Harlequin Enterprises Limited. Philippine copyright 1982. Australian copyright 1982. All rights reserved. Except for use in any review, the reproduction or utilization of this work in whole or in part in any form by any electronic, mechanical or other means, now known or hereafter invented, including xerography, photocopying and recording, or in any information storage or retrieval system, is forbidden without the permission of the publisher, Harlequin Enterprises Limited, 225 Duncan Mill Road, Don Mills, Ontario, Canada M3B 3K9.

All the characters in this book have no existence outside the imagination of the author and have no relation whatsoever to anyone bearing the same name or names. They are not even distantly inspired by any individual known or unknown to the author, and all the incidents are pure invention.

These books by Hilary Wilde were originally published as follows:

THE GOLDEN MAZE
Copyright © 1972 by Hilary Wilde
First published in 1972 by Mills & Boon Limited
Harlequin edition (#1624) published September 1972

THE FIRE OF LIFE
Copyright © 1972 by Hilary Wilde
First published in 1972 by Mills & Boon Limited
Harlequin edition (#1642) published December 1972

THE IMPOSSIBLE DREAM
Copyright © 1972 by Hilary Wilde
First published in 1972 by Mills & Boon Limited
Harlequin edition (#1685) published May 1973

ISBN 0-373-20058-7

First edition published as Harlequin Omnibus in June 1977

Second printing March 1982

The Harlequin trademark, consisting of the words HARLEQUIN ROMANCES and the portrayal of a Harlequin, is registered in the United States Patent Office and in the Canada Trade Marks Office.

Printed in Canada

Contents

The Golden Maze 9

The Fire of Life 189

The Impossible Dream 369

The Golden Maze

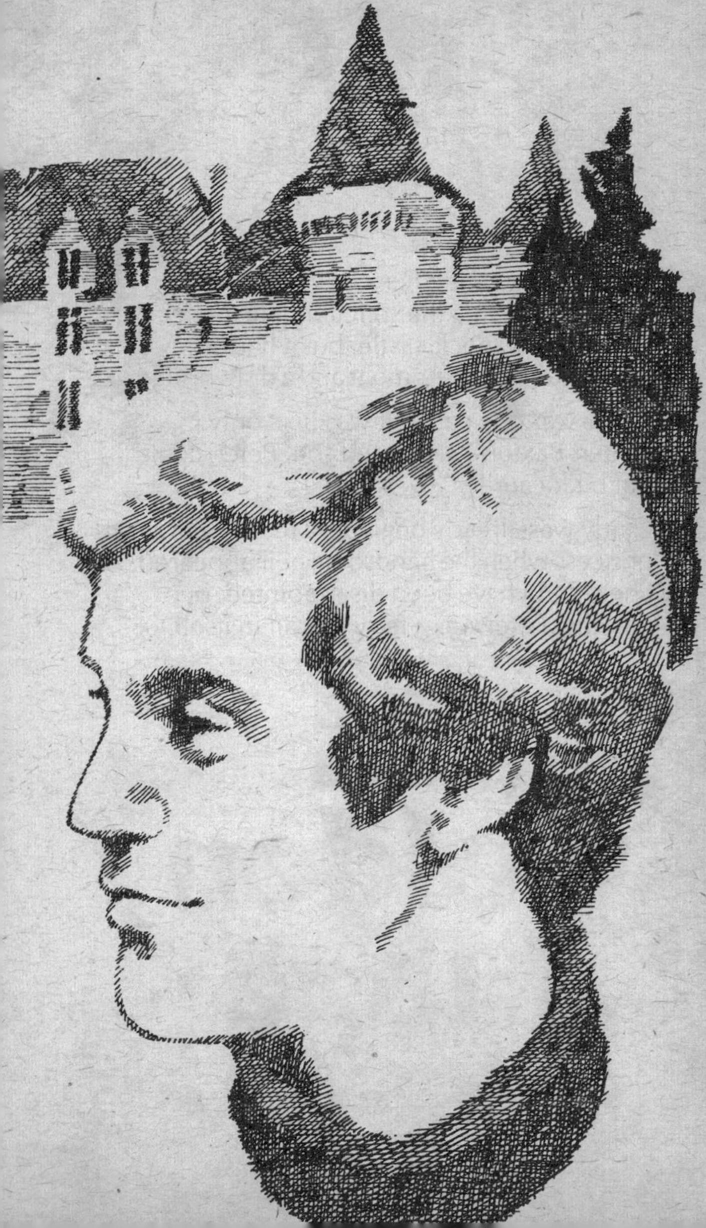

Somebody had left her a castle? Cindy Preston stared at the solicitor in disbelief. Well, only a mock castle, but it had an honest-to-goodness moat and a drawbridge.

There was one catch. It was hers only if Robert Paxton's estranged son, Peter, could not be located.

Cindy was already beginning to feel like a princess when the handsome heir appeared. She should have been disappointed, but meeting Peter was a fairy tale all in itself.

CHAPTER ONE

CINDY FROWNED as she gazed up at the names on the board, high up on the wall, that she could not see properly. She had almost run up from Ludgate Circus, hardly hearing the roar of traffic, for all she could think of was the castle.

The castle of her dreams!

And now here she was to learn all about it and she couldn't even see which floor the solicitors were on!

"Having trouble?" A deep masculine voice interrupted her thoughts. Startled, she swung around and saw the man standing by her side. She couldn't see his face clearly, but he was tall, with broad shoulders and blond hair. He towered above her.

"Why not wear glasses?" he asked, sounding amused. "Then you could see."

"I do, usually." She gave an excited little laugh. "But I was in such a hurry to get here, I forgot them. I mean, it isn't every day you inherit a castle!"

"A castle?" He sounded surprised, then paused before continuing. "You've inherited a castle?"

The condescension in his voice irritated her, but she answered, "Yes, a real castle." Then she corrected herself, "At least it will be mine if his son doesn't turn up."

"His son? So there's a son." For some odd reason,

the man sounded more amused than ever, so Cindy frowned.

"It's quite simple. If the son can't be found after three years' searching, I'll inherit the castle."

"If there's a son alive, where do you come into it?"

"Well, you see, they don't know. I mean, if the son is alive or not. It seems he quarreled with his father years ago and walked out and—well, I suppose the father was sorry. Anyhow, he left everything to his son. But if the son isn't traced for three years, then it comes to me. I honestly don't know why." Cindy shook her head thoughtfully, her long chestnut brown hair swinging. "I hardly knew him—Mr. Baxter, I mean. I was about seven when mummy, who was a widow, met him and we were asked there for a holiday. She hated the quietness. I loved it." Remembering, Cindy half closed her eyes. "It was absolutely super. A real castle! Of course I had the usual absurd dreams." She laughed and then looked grave. "They weren't just dreams at the time. I persuaded myself that I was a princess and that my so-called parents had found me in a dustbin and that one day the truth would be discovered and I would live in the castle and it would be mine." As she spoke, her voice rose excitedly. "And now this—this has happened."

"The son might turn up," the stranger said dryly.

Cindy nodded. "Of course he might, but they've been hunting for him for three years and the solicitor's letter said only three weeks were left of the search."

"Where is this wonderful castle?"

"Cumberland—in the Lake District. I can just remember the lakes and the mountains and the—"

"Castle." He gave a funny little laugh. "How will you run it? Castles cost money, you know."

The Golden Maze

Cindy tossed her head, her hair swinging. "I'll find a way." She twisted her hands together, her brown handbag hanging from her shoulder, her little oval face framed by the pale pink woolen cap. "It's so wonderful, you see. I woke up this morning feeling... feeling so unhappy. So... well, rejected. No one cared for me. I was all alone, and then—then this letter came. I couldn't believe it. Uncle Robert—that's what he made me call him—hadn't forgotten me. He said he wanted the castle to go to someone who loved it as he did. Just think, he hadn't forgotten me all these years. Ever since I was seven."

"How long ago is that? Eight years?"

Cindy's eyes blazed, for she hated this kind of joke. Just because she had a young look! Her cousins were always teasing her about it, too, just as they did about her miserable five feet two inches in height.

"I'm nineteen years and ten months," she said with dignity as well as anger.

"Is that so? You don't look it. Well, I'm thirty-three and seven months."

"Well, you—" she began indignantly, and stopped, having to laugh instead. "I'm afraid I can't see you properly," she admitted, and looked at her watch. "Help! I must hurry and see the solicitor. I told my boss I'd be as quick as I could."

"I thought you only got your letter this morning?"

"I did, but I rang my boss at once. He's always late at work himself, so I rang his home and he quite understood. He told me to be as quick as I could, so I must be."

"How can you have a castle in Cumberland and a job in London? Rather an expensive distance to commute," the stranger said dryly.

Cindy laughed. "Oh, I'll give up my job, of course. Could you tell me which floor Ayres & Bolton are on?"

"Certainly. Third floor. The lift's over there. Do you think you can reach the button?"

Her faced flamed. "Of course I can," she said angrily.

"Well, watch your way. You're moving in a golden maze."

Even as she started to turn, she paused. "A golden maze?" she repeated, puzzled.

He smiled. "Dryden. 'I think and think on things impossible, and love to wander in that golden maze.'"

"Oh." Cindy hesitated. "You mean dreams. What's wrong with dreams?" she asked defiantly.

"Nothing—except that you get hurt when the balloons burst."

"This one isn't going to," she told him, and hurried to the lift.

Inside it, she wondered at herself. How could she have talked so easily to a complete stranger? Why? She must have bored him terribly. That was another thing her cousins were always telling her: that she talked too much. What must he think of her, she asked herself as the lift stopped and she hurried down the carpeted corridor to a door with the names Ayres & Bolton on it. Please Walk In, she read underneath them.

Obeying, she went through a glass door that swung open as she touched it. A girl with blond hair piled high on her head looked up.

"My name is Lucinda Preston," Cindy said. "I rang Mr. Ayres early this morning in reply to his letter."

The girl smiled. "Of course. Please sit down and I'll see if Mr. Ayres is ready."

Cindy obeyed, looking around her curiously. It was

The Golden Maze

all very modern and luxurious, so it must be a reliable firm, she decided.

The girl returned. "Mr. Ayres will see you now. This way."

Cindy followed her down the carpeted corridor and into a large room with an enormous picture window that showed St. Paul's Cathedral in all its dignified glory. But Cindy was looking at the lean handsome man who came to meet her, holding out his hand. His hair was dark but graying at the temples, his eyes were dark, too, and he had a pleasant friendly smile. She liked him at once.

"How good of you to contact me so quickly," he said, shaking her hand, leading her to a chair, then sitting opposite her on the other side of the large walnut desk. He ruffled through some papers and then looked up with a smile. "You are Miss Lucinda Preston, daughter of the late Bartholomew Preston and of Winifred, his wife? You are, I understand, an only child? Your father died when you were very young and your mother when you were ten years old?"

Cindy nodded, her eyes misting. Would she ever forget the awful loneliness when her mother died, the knowledge that she was a nuisance to her cousins and an unwelcome burden to their parents, for she had been tossed from one aunt and uncle to another. Maybe she had been stupidly sensitive, but she still inwardly squirmed at the memories of her older cousins' teasing: "Goggly-eyed Cindy"; "Tiny Cindy"; "Brainless Cindy." Her height had been a handicap, for they were all tall, all bright at school, flowing effortlessly through exams, while she, working like mad, just managed to squeeze past the final posts. That was why, as soon as she could, she had learned shorthand and typing, got herself a good job and a bed-sitter in Earl's

Court. Living sensibly, she had saved enough money to buy herself a car—small, gray and efficient. It made all the difference in the world to her life, for every weekend she could slip away to the quietness of the country she loved.

She realized with a shock that she hadn't been listening to the solicitor. Her cheeks hot, she apologized. "I am sorry. I was thinking."

He smiled. "That's all right. I asked if you could remember Mr. Baxter."

Cindy shook her head slowly. "Not really. Just as a big man with a kind voice. I know he was a friend of mummy's. They met somewhere, and he asked us to visit him. I loved it, but mum hated it, so we never went back again."

"You loved it?"

Her eyes shining, Cindy nodded. "It was super. The most exciting and romantic thing that ever happened to me. Living in a castle!" She sighed ecstatically.

Mr. Ayres smiled. "It's not a real castle, you know. It's what is called a mock castle—built years after real castles were built."

"It may be mock or real, but I remember it as a castle. It looked just like one, with a drawbridge and a moat and vaults and—" Cindy stopped. "I expect you've seen it."

"No, I haven't. My uncle was alive at that time and Mr. Robert Baxter was his client."

"I'll never forget it, ever. There were mountains and a great lake and then this lovely castle. Mummy had always read me fairy stories and of course I felt like a princess in her castle, waiting for my handsome prince to come."

"It certainly made an impression on you." Keith

Ayres smiled. "As I told you in my letter, Mr. Baxter never forgot your love of the place."

"I can't understand how he could have remembered me all those years." Cindy spread out her hands expressively.

"He was old and lonely. It was a pity about his son. Mr. Baxter was devoted to the boy. These family quarrels are sad things. Fathers so easily forget how they felt when they were sons."

"Well, if you build up a big business, surely you're building it for your son, too?" Cindy asked. "Not that that means the son must automatically follow on, of course."

Keith Ayres smiled ruefully. "It's so easy to judge. I'm not married, so I can't talk from experience, but I'm building up this firm from the mess it was in when my uncle died, and I must confess, I'd like a son of mine to benefit as a result of my hard work."

"It's funny, isn't it, as you grow older, everything seems to reverse," Cindy began, and stopped abruptly. It was when she said stupid things like that that her cousins called her a bore. "You...you haven't found Mr. Baxter's son?"

"No, but there are still three weeks...." Keith Ayres hesitated before continuing. "Actually, we fear he is dead. We traced him to Australia, then Canada and finally South America. There was some turmoil there and he just vanished. We have advertised...are still advertising." He frowned. "Your mother didn't like the castle?"

"It wasn't that—it was the loneliness. Mummy liked people and bright lights and...and life, as she called it. I'm more like my dad, an introvert."

Keith Ayres laughed. "I'd hardly call you that. You can't remember anything about Mr. Baxter?"

Cindy looked around the luxurious office and half closed her eyes. "What you said about a mock castle — that does seem to ring a bell." She clapped her hands excitedly. "I've got it! I remember how mummy told me that. She said it wasn't a real castle and... and I remember crying and then...." Cindy frowned thoughtfully, her eyes narrowed. "Yes, I am beginning to remember. This man I had to call Uncle Robert gave me a big white hankie and said it would always be a real castle to him, and that made me awfully happy, because it was *his* castle, so he had to be right. It *was* real!"

Keith Ayres looked thoughtful. "What you liked when you were seven years old may look different now, Miss Preston. Er, did your mother, er, I don't want to sound impertinent, but have you a private income?"

Looking surprised, Cindy shook her head. "No, mummy had an annuity that died with her. I lived with aunts and uncles and I got a job as soon as I could and — well, I'm not doing too badly. I have a car and — "

Keith Ayres smiled. "Very commendable, Miss Preston, but I doubt if it would be enough to enable you...." He paused. "Mr. Baxter was not a rich man when he died. Locals believed him to be wealthy, but he had many troubles, financially as well as physically. I'm afraid after all the death duties and taxes, et cetera, there won't be much money left. The reason I wished to contact you before the three years were up was that at the moment you view this inheritance with romantic eyes, but it could become a pain in the neck. The castle is large and expensive to keep in repair. In addition, there is a housekeeper and her son, the gardener, who have been there ten years. Efficient, I gather, but expecting and getting generous salaries. The estate pays

The Golden Maze

this at the moment. You may find it advisable to sell the castle."

Cindy's eyes widened in horror. "Sell it? Sell the castle?"

Keith Ayres tried not to smile. "Well, until I wrote to you you had forgotten it, so it can't mean all that much."

"Oh, but it does, and I hadn't—" Cindy leaned forward, her hair swinging on either side of her face. "It's always been a wonderful dream to me. If things got bad, I could cheer myself up by thinking of the castle that would one day be mine. It was a dream that had somehow come true, if you know what I mean."

"Yes, I do, but all the same.... Look, I think it would be a good idea for you to visit it as soon as possible, Miss Preston."

Cindy's eyes brightened. "I'd love to visit it."

"Good. I suggest you talk things over with your boss and get a week off. Let me know the date you can go up to Cumberland and I'll arrange with Mrs. Stone—she's the housekeeper—to expect you. You can go by train or coach."

"I'll drive up. I don't know that part of England, so it will be fun," Cindy told him eagerly.

Keith Ayres hesitated. "You're rather young to drive around alone." He saw the frown on her face and hastily added, "I was thinking, if the car broke down, some of those roads in the Lake District in winter can be very isolated. Do you have a friend who could go with you?"

It was Cindy's turn to hesitate. "Yes," she said slowly, which wasn't the whole truth but half of it. She had *friends* at the office, but the friendship ended at five o'clock each day. Somehow she wasn't one of them. She had found London lonely, but with the weekends in the country to look forward to, she had learned to live with loneliness.

"Good." Keith Ayres stood up and smiled. "Let me know which day you're free to go up to the castle and I'll contact Mrs. Stone." He hesitated. "I hope you won't be too disillusioned, Miss Preston."

She shook hands with him at the door and her eyes were bright with excitement. "I'm never disillusioned, Mr. Ayres," she said gaily. "Mummy used to say, 'When one door closes, another opens.' Something good always happens to me."

Look at today, she told herself as she hurried down toward the large block of offices where she worked. She had woken up that morning feeling depressed, dreading the hours at the office, where she could see mirth mixed with sympathy in the girls' eyes because she had been dropped by Oliver Bentley. And then the letter had come! The letter that had opened a whole new exciting world for her.

Now, as she hurried down the corridor in the office building, she smiled through the glass walls of the typing pool and waved to the girls gaily. She had the most wonderful news imaginable to tell them. What did Oliver matter after all? True, he was a charmer, and she had enjoyed the two evenings he'd taken her out. He had been attentive, had kissed her; and then next day she had been cut dead by him. Later, meeting in the canteen, he had paused by her side and said, "It was nice knowing you, Cindy, but not half as nice as I'd hoped."

One of the typists close behind Cindy had giggled. Cindy hadn't understood what Oliver meant, thinking it must be because she was—as her cousins had frequently told her—an awful bore. That she was a *nothing*. That no man with any sense would look at her! As Oliver had hurried by, Maggie, the girl behind Cindy, had squeezed her arm.

"It's not your fault, Cindy; you're just not with it," she had said sympathetically, which had made it worse. But today—why, a castle was better than all the Olivers in the world put together!

As soon as Cindy had hung up her winter coat and little hat, carefully looked at her face and wondered why she looked so different, her cheeks flushed, her eyes shining, she hurried to her boss's office, her notebook in hand, half a dozen pencils ready.

"Well?" Patrick Jenkins looked up. A tall lean man with reddish hair and green eyes, he was a hardworking boss whom most of the girls disliked but whom Cindy enjoyed working for.

"I told you it was a castle!"

Patrick Jenkins grinned. "You know, I was half-asleep when you phoned this morning, and you should know by now that I can't think properly until twelve o'clock, so please tell me slowly and in detail what happened."

She obeyed, sitting opposite him, her hair swinging as she kept nodding her head and her voice rising excitedly. When she had finished, he frowned.

"Oh, dear, just as I've bullied you into being the perfect secretary! I suppose I must let you go. Will you postpone it for a week and train one of those idiots in the pool? Last time you were ill, I nearly went mad. The girl I had couldn't even spell, and as for the filing cabinet—"

The phone bell shrilled loudly. It was a long-distance call and Cindy waited while he talked. Her thoughts were racing around in circles like a little trapped mouse. A mixture of beautiful lakes, mountains topped with snow and a castle—a real castle!

When Patrick Jenkins replaced the receiver, he looked at Cindy. He sighed dramatically, but she saw the twinkle in his green eyes.

"When will you grow up?" he asked sadly. "You've forgotten your glasses again and you walk around with your head stuck forward like an ostrich's, your eyes screwed up."

Cindy's cheeks burned. "I know. I forgot them because I was so excited."

"You're always *forgetting* them. A subconscious refusal to wear them, I imagine. Now, why?"

"Well...." Cindy wriggled around on the seat uncomfortably. Put into words it sounded so stupid. "My cousins used to tease me a lot. I was called Goggly-eyed Cindy, and they said—they said I looked pretty awful in them because I was so ugly in the beginning. I—well...." Her voice tailed away weakly.

He looked grave. "What utter tripe! I find you extremely pretty, and I think you're even prettier when you're wearing glasses."

"You do?" Cindy looked so startled, Patrick Jenkins found it hard not to laugh.

"I do. Now—" he glanced at his watch "—maybe we'd better get some work done. You can go next week, but come back quickly." He smiled. "I shall miss you," he said so pathetically that they both laughed. "Now, this Drinkwater firm, for instance. Ready?"

Cindy nodded, pencil poised, as she tried to concentrate on the job at hand.

CHAPTER TWO

THE WEEK CRAWLED BY for Cindy, impatient as she was to get to the castle that might be hers. She had phoned Mr. Ayres, and he had sent her a letter of instructions and had repeated his fears that she would find it too expensive to run *if* the real heir didn't materialize.

Now, on the cold wintry day, with the sun trying to peep out from behind the clouds, Cindy started on her journey and tried to think of how she *could* find the money required. Whatever happened, she wouldn't sell it. She was used to London traffic, and her little gray car slipped in and out until the slow-moving crowded roads of London were left behind and she was on the highways. Here she could settle in the lane she had chosen and let the speed-crazy race by, for she was in no hurry, looking at the countryside with interested eyes. The first part of the journey she found dull, for she loathed flat country. Mountains and lakes and forests, she thought happily, were what she loved. Claife Castle would be so different from this flat uninteresting land. Mr. Ayres had told her the word *claife* meant "steep hillside with path," so there must be a special path. Her boss, Mr. Jenkins, had chuckled and said there'd been a lot of smuggling in that part of the world in days gone by—maybe this special path led to a hideaway, as he called it.

Would she ever marry, she wondered. According to her cousins, no man would look twice at her, but Mr. Jenkins had said.... Suddenly she was laughing happily. He really was a pet, so kind and understanding. Of course he had said that to boost her morale, and it certainly had.

The scenery began to change, the roads to curve, the hills to appear, and she sang gaily as she drove along. She had a feeling that everything was going to be all right.

Then the fog came down without warning. A frightening moment as the cars vanished in the swirling mist. It grew worse, and while still in the fast lane cars whizzed by, Cindy crawled along, nose to tail in the long line of cautious drivers as they felt their way. The sight of a motel loomed up through the mist, so Cindy turned off and decided to spend the night there if the fog didn't lift. She tried to phone Claife Castle but was told the line was out of order. Probably the fog had reached them, so Mrs. Stone would understand, she thought as she sat pretending to read a magazine and finding her thoughts going back again and again to that morning when she had heard from the solicitors and had stood in the hall trying to read the names that she couldn't see. And then that stranger had spoken to her. That was the amazing thing. She didn't know him, but he kept coming into her thoughts. If only she had not forgotten her glasses and had seen him properly. Somehow she couldn't forget him. He seemed to haunt her. Had it been his voice? Deep and—what was the word? Oh, yes, *authoritative*, a favorite word used frequently by her boss! It was amazing how easy she had found it to talk to the stranger and—she had to smile—how cross he had made her by teasing her about her age and

The Golden Maze

height, as well as her glasses. Yet he had done it nicely, not rudely.

She walked around the room restlessly. Why must she keep thinking of this man she would never see again? Had she bored him terribly, she wondered. Yet if she had, surely he could easily have ended the conversation and walked away.

The fog was still thick, so she must definitely spend the night there at the motel. She dined early to go to bed and sleep, for she was tired. But whether it was excitement about the castle or fear lest the fog persist for days and so shorten her stay in Claife Castle, for she must remember the real heir might turn up, Cindy didn't know, but she could not sleep that night. Lying awake, tossing and turning, plumping up the pillows, her mind returned time and again to the stranger she could not forget.

Why had he made such an impression on her, she wondered. It was absurd, because she hadn't even seen his face properly, nor did she know the color of his eyes.

The fog had gone in the morning. Relieved, and with the excitement flooding her veins, she ate a hasty breakfast and then, with Mr. Ayres's painstakingly careful descriptions of how to find the castle by her side, Cindy set off. Now the mountains she loved appeared as the roads wove around the lakes and through the sleepy stone-house villages. It was absurd, she knew, but she felt that she was going home. Yet how could it be home simply because when she was seven, she had spent a few weeks there?

The beauty seemed to grow the farther she drove. The mountains with their golden brown bracken and the clumps of trees reflected in the quiet stillness of the water seemed to be welcoming her. This was the life she loved, Cindy thought happily. Quietness, serenity—that was a good word. She felt serene here, free from troubles, far from the humiliation Oliver had caused her, far from the loneliness of life in big cities, far from the squabbles at the office, the pettiness she hated. Maybe she was what is called a loner, Cindy thought as she drove carefully along the twisting roads, enjoying the glimpses of blue water or a quick look at a square-towered church tucked away in a small village.

At last she was getting near Claife Castle. She knew because a large beautiful lake was Windermere. Of course the quiet roads would be very different in the summer months, but then, tucked up in the castle, she needn't see them.

If the castle is yours, she told herself quickly. After all, the real heir might suddenly turn up at any moment.

Ambleside! She recognized the name on the signpost and knew that she could not be far. Slowing up by the side of the road, she read the directions.

"After Ambleside, you'll see a crossroads. Take the sharp turn to the left. After about ten miles, you'll see a white signpost on the right. This leads to the castle."

She drove on slowly. Mr. Ayres was right. The crossroads, then farther on, the white post with the words Claife Castle painted on it.

It was only a track, with deep corrugations, so she drove slowly up the side of the hill and around it until she found herself on a plateau. Far below was a lake, a strange-looking one absurdly the shape of a heart. Grassy slopes went down to the water's edge, while clumps of trees, their bare branches like animated fingers of a ballet dancer, were silhouetted against the bright sky. Then she saw the entrance to the castle. This she had not remembered, and it took her breath away. An old stone lodge with small windows, while on one side were two castellated towers with heavy wrought-iron gates between them that were closed.

Cindy hooted and a short fat man with a cap pulled over his eyes, wearing a thick pullover and corduroy breeches and Wellingtons, came hobbling out and gave her a quick look.

"I'm Miss Preston," Cindy called. "Mrs. Stone is expecting me."

He came close to the car, his weather-beaten face sour, his eyes suspicious. "Has ta been afore?"

"No, this is my first visit," Cindy told him, and smiled.

He pursed his mouth and nodded slowly. "I'll be seeing you now," he told her, and moved off to open the gates.

"Thanks," Cindy called, but he had turned his back, as if glad to see the last of her. She wondered why.

Feeling a little shattered at his unfriendly welcome, she drove on more slowly down a curving narrow drive hemmed in by tall bushes she thought might be rhododendrons. Down below, through gaps in the bushes, she could see a small village, the houses huddled together near the lake, but then as she drove around a corner, she had eyes only for what lay ahead.

The castle! It was even more fabulous than she had remembered. She slowed down to look at it—a huge square collection of castellated towers joined together by gray stone blocks, with narrow slits of windows and heavy wooden doors. Farther around the building the windows were larger. There was a narrow moat and a drawbridge down.

She just could not believe it. They called it a mock castle! It was exactly the kind of castle you thought of for fairy stories where the princess is rescued by the handsome prince. Beautiful time-kissed gray stone and far below, the blue of the lake. What more could you want?

A car was parked on the gravel square before the castle, so Cindy parked alongside, took out her suitcase and walked over the drawbridge to the front door. She had to keep turning to look at the lake below or up at the trees that made a pretense of protecting the castle from the winds that must blow fiercely at times.

A huge carved brass lion's head was on the door, so Cindy knocked. Silence. It seemed endless, so she knocked again. The door groaned and squeaked but slowly opened. Cindy caught her breath as she and the woman facing her stared at one another. Cindy found it hard to believe her eyes, wondering if this were some kind of joke, for the woman looked like a tall scarecrow, her gray hair drawn tightly back from her forehead and neck with wisps of hair that had escaped. Her high cheekbones made her face almost like a skull, the skin taut and gray, her mouth drooping at the corners, her chin spotty, and her eyes...! Her eyes were a strange gray and cold with hatred.

"Mrs. Stone," Cindy said politely, smiling a little nervously. "I'm Miss Preston."

"You were to come yesterday," the shrill impatient voice accused.

"I know, Mrs. Stone, but there was a bad fog and I had to spend the night on the way."

"You could have let me know."

"I tried to, but I was told the phone at Claife Castle was out of order."

Mrs. Stone frowned. "Is it?" she said accusingly, almost as if it were Cindy's fault. "I'll get Paul to go down

The Golden Maze

to the village and complain." She turned away, putting her hands to her mouth and bellowing, "Paul... Paul!"

Cindy fidgeted a little and put down her case, for what else could she do? Short of pushing her way past the housekeeper, she had to wait.

In a moment, a long-legged man in blue jeans and a pullover came running. His fair hair curled on his shoulders; his eyes as he looked at Cindy were angry.

"So she's here now," he said.

"Paul, the phone isn't working. Go down to the village," Mrs. Stone told him.

Paul looked Cindy up and down, his eyes narrowed.

"I'll go now."

He bounded off to the car Cindy had seen parked and, with a great roar and strange hooting, went off down the drive. Mrs. Stone looked at Cindy.

"The phone was working in the morning."

"Well, it wasn't in the late afternoon," Cindy said, trying not to be annoyed, though Mrs. Stone's voice had almost implied that she was a liar. "At least that's what the exchange said."

Mrs. Stone didn't answer and then turned away. "You'd better come in," she said reluctantly, almost as if she wished she could think of an alternative.

Cindy followed, carrying her suitcase. In the hall she paused, looking up at the lofty rafters, the stationary soldiers in armor that stood about, the wide curved staircase.

Mrs. Stone paused on the stairs, looking around. "Are you coming, now?" she asked crossly.

"Of course." Cindy followed the older woman up the uncarpeted stairs, looking around curiously. Everything was old but also very shabby, she noticed, as if no money had been spent on the castle in years. Perhaps it hadn't been, for according to Keith Ayres, Uncle Robert had had financial troubles.

Mrs. Stone opened a door, stood back dramatically to let Cindy in, staring at her as if wondering what Cindy's reaction would be.

Cindy gasped, because it was like going into a museum—a huge four-poster bed with a torn but clean apricot-colored silk bedspread, a dark brown carpet, heavy dark green curtains hanging on either side of a big window. Cindy acted impulsively. Dropping her suitcase, she ran across the room. It was indeed a beautiful view, for they were above the trees and she could see the whole steep slope down to the lake, with the gentle mountains on the other side. It was so beautiful.

"The bathroom is down the passage. The door is open," Mrs. Stone said, but Cindy only heard her as from a long distance. "Lunch will be served at one o'clock." Then there was a pause and Mrs. Stone's voice rose so shrilly that Cindy was jerked back to the present. She turned around to meet the cold suspicious eyes that glared at her. "And how long will you be staying, now?" Mrs. Stone demanded.

"A week, Mr. Ayres suggested," Cindy told her, wondering at the animosity she saw.

"Ugh!" Mrs. Stone grunted, turned away and left the room, closing the door with a gentle bang that was far more expressive of her temper than a loud slam might have been.

But why is she so mad at me, Cindy wondered as she hastily unpacked. Glancing at her watch, she saw she had an hour to spend before lunch. She decided to stroll around, hoping to keep out of Mrs. Stone's way.

The castle was every bit as fascinating as Cindy had

remembered, and yet it was different, not less beautiful or exciting, but sadly shabby, as if no one had bothered about it for years. It was clean, the beautiful antique furniture well polished, so Mrs. Stone was not to be blamed. It was as if the owner of the castle had either ceased to care or had given it up as hopeless, knowing he had not the money needed to revive it. Another favorite expression of Mr. Jenkins's, Cindy thought with a smile, wondering how he and Maggie, who was relieving for her, were getting on.

Wandering around the castle, Cindy found it difficult not to feel some dismay. She now understood what Keith Ayres had meant when he talked of money. It would need thousands of pounds to bring the castle back to what it once was. And where could she find thousands of pounds? Perhaps the antiques could be sold and the money raised could be spent on new curtains and carpets, as well as repairs to the cracks in some of the walls.

Coming to an open door, Cindy stepped outside. The crisp cold air stung her cheeks, but she stood still, breathing deeply. There must be a way—there had to be. But where was she to find it?

Walking around the garden, she decided that Paul Stone was not the hard worker his mother was, nor was he as conscientious. Cindy knew little about gardening, but it seemed to her that this garden was in a shocking state. Long tough grass, weeds everywhere, trees and bushes that needed pruning. Surely Uncle Robert must have noticed.

Glancing at her watch, Cindy had to hurry, for she didn't want to give Mrs. Stone more reason for her hostility.

The lunch was delicious, well cooked and served.

Cindy congratulated Mrs. Stone and was repaid with an angry glare.

"So I ought to be—a good cook, I mean. The years I've cooked should have taught me. Ever since Paul's father died I've cooked for others, I have," Mrs. Stone said angrily, almost as if she blamed Cindy for it.

"I'm sure Mr. Baxter appreciated your cooking," Cindy told her.

"I don't think he ever noticed anything much. A sad man brokenhearted by his wicked son," Mrs. Stone said as she whipped off the plates.

"Was he wicked?" Cindy ventured to ask.

Mrs. Stone scowled. "Of course he was wicked—ungrateful, cruel. Lets his father give him a good education and then walks out—just when his father needed help because he wasn't well. This was before I came, of course. Never came back—the son, I mean. Just walked out. Proper broke the old man's heart. He could never forgive the boy. And quite right, too! Well, I must be getting on with my work now. Dinner at seven. Will you be wanting tea now?"

Cindy hesitated. She had just had coffee! Then she realized it was just Mrs. Stone's habit of adding the word *now* on to most sentences.

"No, thank you." She stood up. "I thought I'd drive around."

"Better to do so while the sun is out. 'Tisn't often sunny here. Fearful lot of rain for weeks on end," Mrs. Stone said depressingly as she lifted the tray and disappeared.

Cindy wandered around the dining room, with its long walnut table. She wondered how long it had been since a dinner party had been held there. In the big glass-fronted sideboard she could see beautiful glasses of every shape and size. Once upon a time this must have been a beautiful room. Now it was sad—sad for the loss of beauty that time and lack of money had caused. But it could be put right. If the drab walls were repainted and cheap curtain material bought....

Upstairs, she put on her thick coat and a scarf around her head. Where should she go? Maybe just wander around. No, perhaps the local village at the bottom of the hill was a good place to start.

She drove through the wide-open gates slowly, then ignored the track by which she had come and drove down a track that seemed to be going straight down the hillside. It wasn't, of course. Instead it went sideways in a series of twists, rather like the way a snake moved, Cindy was thinking as she glanced around. Far below she could see the spire of a church. From behind a clump of trees came rising the smoke from a cottage. Every now and then she saw the lake below as the branches of the trees moved. She wondered where the path from which the castle got its name was.

At last she saw the village ahead. Here the fields were gently separated by the fascinating dry stone walls, each one a miracle to Cindy as she wondered how they stayed put for so many centuries. Now she could see the church with its long pointed spire, the old timbered house by its side and what was obviously a school, then a cluster of houses, all made of gray stone. She drove over a humped bridge made of mellow stones, and then there was a space in the cottages and she saw the lake.

How peaceful it looked with the bushes and trees clustering around the edge. Not a ripple on it. Just so still.

She parked the car in an open space and then walked

along, looking for a post office. She had promised both Keith Ayres and Mr. Jenkins that she would let them know she had arrived safely, so maybe postcards showing the beautiful countryside would be a good idea. Finding the post office, she turned and stopped dead, almost bumping into a tall man as he came out.

Cindy recognized him instantly. But today with her glasses on, she could see his face clearly. A handsome face if you like a square chin, a rather long nose and cold blue eyes.

Cold eyes that looked at her and halted the smile of recognition she was giving him. She had already started to speak.

"Fancy meeting you here!" she began.

"Excuse me," he said coldly, moving her to one side and walking by her, paying no attention as he walked fast down the side of the street.

It was as if he had slapped her in the face. Never had she felt such a shock. She turned around and walked down the road in the opposite direction. It was absurd, of course, but even her legs were trembling. Why had he been so rude? Cutting her dead, worse still, implying that she was trying to pick him up!

How could he do such a thing to her? But he had.

CHAPTER THREE

SOMEHOW CINDY WALKED ALONG the narrow pavement, her mind in a whirl. Why had he been so rude to her? Maybe he hadn't recognized her in her glasses? Perhaps *he* was shortsighted. She found herself making excuses for his behavior, yet it all boiled down to one thing and that was what shocked her so. He hadn't wanted to see her again. It was a real brush-off.

She noticed a small tea shop and went in and sat down. It was empty, but Cindy didn't mind. She wanted to be alone so that she could think. What could she have done to annoy him so? For annoyed he had been. She shivered as she remembered the coldness in his eyes.

Though perhaps his eyes were always cold. After all, she reminded herself, she hadn't seen his eyes before. Yet his voice had been so different. Here it had been so curt.

"Excuse me," was all he had said.

Yet in London he had teased her, joked and even been sarcastic, but there had been no curt coldness in her voice.

Suddenly a tall girl came from the back of the shop. Cindy gazed in amazement. Why, she was beautiful! A real model type, tall, with long slender legs well revealed by the elegance of her sea-green skirt and pale cream tunic. She had high cheekbones and surprisingly dark eyes as compared with her blond hair, which was beautifully curled.

"I'm sorry I didn't hear you come in," the girl said. "Would you like some tea?"

"Please," said Cindy.

When the tea came, the tall girl smiled. "Mind if I join you? One gets so bored here with never a new face. You're Miss Preston now?"

Cindy looked startled. "Yes, how did you know?"

The girl laughed. "Everything is known in the village. The castle will be yours if Peter Baxter doesn't turn up. Right?"

"Yes, but—"

"He still may, though I doubt it. I'm Johanna Younge." She smiled ruefully. "Believe it or not, I was once a beauty queen. Then like an idiot, I fell in love with a country boy, and here I am." She waved her hand vaguely. "Thirty-five and stuck in this dump—a widow looking for a rich husband. Thought I'd found one but it seems he's not as wealthy as I thought." She laughed. "Nor as interested."

Cindy stirred her tea slowly. "Why stay here?" she asked.

Johanna shrugged. "Because I'm a fool. I love him."

"Oh," said Cindy. She couldn't think of anything else to say. What *did* one say? A startling frightening thought struck her. Was *she* in love? In love with a man she'd only met once—no, twice, if you could count today's a meeting. If not, why was she so upset? If he were just an ordinary man, would she care?

"This place does well in the summer, but in the winter—well, you can see for yourself. Every year I swear that next year I'll go to London, but I stay here. I know I'm a fool."

In the distance the telephone bell shrilled. Johanna

The Golden Maze

Younge quickly drank her tea and stood up. She smiled at Cindy.

"The village is coming to life, I think. You're the second southerner we've had here in the past week. Both interested in the castle, too. The castle! What a farce—it's no more a castle than I'm a beauty!" Johanna shrugged as she walked away.

Cindy drank her tea slowly and ate the delicious scones with jam and cream. She glanced at her watch. The sun was still shining—should she drive around or....

Johanna joined her again. "Sorry about that. Wrong number as usual. Look, if you want to know anything about the castle—and you'd be very odd if you didn't—I suggest you go along and see old Mrs. Usher. She's lived here all her life. Never been outside the village and, hard as it is to believe, never wants to go anywhere else. She'll tell you about the castle and the Baxters." Her voice was bitter.

"You don't like them?"

Johanna shrugged. "I met Peter once or twice and liked him. But of course David, his cousin, and he never hit it off. I don't know why. The old man I never knew—bit of a recluse, you see. Didn't like visitors—at least, according to his housekeeper." Johanna chuckled. "Now there's a broken heart for you!"

"Mrs. Stone?" Cindy was startled.

The phone bell shrilled again. Cindy stood up, hastily paid for her tea and left.

Outside she looked up and down. There was not a soul in sight. Somehow she didn't feel in the mood for driving around, and she had an absurd urge to learn more about the castle. What was the old lady's name? Usher! That was it!

Cindy went into the post office, chose two postcards

with lovely pictures of Windermere, wrote quickly on each to say she was fine, and then got stamps. The postmistress, fat and cheerful, beamed.

"Did Mr. Baxter knock you down?" she asked.

"Mr. Baxter?" Cindy echoed, puzzled. Mr. Baxter is dead, she nearly said.

"I saw it happen. You were coming into the shop now and out he went, storming like a madman because the telegram he was expecting hadn't arrived. Not my fault, and I told him so."

"Was that Mr. Baxter who bumped into me?" Cindy blinked her eyes, shaking her head, for her mind felt muzzy. "But—"

"Yes, David Baxter, the late Robert Baxter's nephew." The postmistress chuckled. "I bet he's feeling mad. Did you have a cup of tea? I guessed that was where you were now. What do you think of our local beauty queen?" she chuckled again.

"I thought she was very beautiful."

"So she is, but he just doesn't see her."

"He?" Cindy said, puzzled.

"David—David Baxter. Johanna is crazy about him; seems like he prefers to be a bachelor."

Cindy drew a long deep breath.

"Mrs. Younge is in love with David Baxter?" Cindy said slowly. Gone was her last hope. How could a short ugly girl who wore glasses compete with such a beauty?

The postmistress gave her the stamps with another chuckle.

"We all thought once they were going to wed, and then he changed. It's ever since his uncle died that he's been so bitter. Not that I'm surprised, mind." Her eyes narrowed. "Are you Miss Preston?" she asked, her voice losing its friendliness suddenly.

The Golden Maze

Cindy felt uncomfortable. Now what had she said to upset the postmistress? Why had her attitude changed so suddenly? At that moment the doorbell clanged, and two elderly women came in chatting. Both stopped talking as they saw Cindy. She hurried past them, uncomfortably aware that they were staring at her.

In the street she hesitated, looking up and down. An elderly man in breeches and a jacket, his cap pulled over one eye, paused.

"Where's ta gaan?" he asked sympathetically.

Cindy smiled. "I'm looking for Mrs. Usher."

"She'll be there anytime. Fourth cottage on the left—a dog in t'garden. He don't bite now." He smiled, touched his cap and hobbled by her.

Hurrying down the street, Cindy found the cottage. A typical Lake District cottage, she was to learn in the days ahead, with a door and four windows. A beautifully cared-for garden, with snowdrops in flower and some of the bushes showing green buds. A spaniel lying on the white doorstep stood up and wagged his tail friendly.

The door opened instantly, and a tiny woman stood in the doorway. A thin woman whose dark gray woolen frock hung loosely on her narrow shoulders. Her skin was perfect, rosy pink, as though the crisp air acted as a tonic. Her eyes shone.

"Miss Preston," she said with a warm welcoming smile. "I hoped you'd come and see me."

"I...it..." Cindy began. "The village knows everything."

"But of course, and you are news. Do come in. I hope you aren't allergic to cats, dogs or budgies, because I've got the lot!" She opened the door wider, and Cindy walked in.

The main room was surprisingly big, with a huge log fire crackling merrily and a tray of tea and cakes waiting. As Cindy went in, several cats stood up, stretched, took one look at her and lay down again. Two dogs came racing, one a gracefully slender greyhound, the other a corgi, who gave Cindy a good look up and down, then turned away and lay down. Pushed gently into a deep comfortable armchair, Cindy was given a cup of tea and induced to eat some of the delicious homemade cakes.

Mrs. Usher never stopped talking. She had an attractive voice with a sort of Welsh lilt. "I'm so glad you've come, dear. I hoped you'd be here earlier, but I suppose it was the fog, because we expected you yesterday. And how do you like the castle? Rather sad, isn't it. Poor Robert was a generous man, and the castle suffered for it."

She poured out another cup of tea and then sat back in her chair, folded her hands and smiled at Cindy. "Now what do you want to know, dear?"

Cindy didn't know what to say. After all, what did she want to know? She grabbed at the first thing that came into her mind.

"Why is David Baxter so bitter? The postmistress told me how he'd changed after his uncle died and—and I met Mrs. Younge and she said he had changed—and what I can't understand is that I met him by chance in London and... we talked. You see, it was like this." Cindy told the white-haired old lady the whole story. "He was so different in London. Not rude and... cold, as he was here," Cindy finished.

"I didn't know he'd been to London lately," Mrs. Usher said thoughtfully. "But you travel so fast these

The Golden Maze

days that you're often back before you know you're going."

They laughed together.

"He is bitter, but it's natural like. You see... you see, he always thought he'd be his uncle's heir."

"Oh, he thought he'd get Claife Castle?" Cindy frowned. "But why didn't he tell me when I told him about the castle? He must have known it would be the same one."

Mrs. Usher shrugged. "The Baxters have always been a funny lot. I've known them all my life."

Driving home to the castle an hour later, Cindy thought of all Mrs. Usher had told her: how Robert Baxter had been a domineering man and his wife very quiet and biddable. Peter had been like his father, yet different: where his father knew he was always right, Peter Baxter queried it and was willing to accept advice. The one thing he had been adamant about, though, had been his refusal to go into his father's business. Peter wanted to be an engineer. So they had quarreled.

"Very sad indeed," Mrs. Usher had said. "I think poor Robert often regretted his own obstinacy, and probably poor Peter wished they could have seen eye to eye. Peter was a nice lad. I was fond of him and sorry, too. He hated hurting anyone, but sometimes you have to. Then David took over the job that should have been Peter's. When Robert grew older and was suffering from gout, he sold his business to David at a very reasonable, almost absurd figure. A generous man, Robert, but sometimes foolish. David was certain he would inherit the castle and everything. When he heard about you, an unknown stranger...."

And yet, Cindy thought as she drove carefully up toward the castle, David had shown no anger or coldness in London. He must have known she was the girl who had literally stolen the castle from him, though without knowing it.

One thing, she told herself, this settled her stupid dream about him. No wonder he didn't want to know her!

She drove the car around behind the castle and parked it in one of the open garages. Paul was in the yard, but he ignored her. Cindy was tempted to go to him and say how sorry she was. Yet could she say that truthfully, she wondered. Mrs. Usher had explained Mrs. Stone's animosity.

"She hoped that Robert would leave Paul the castle. Why she should think that, I don't know. After all, they'd only been with him ten years. Again Robert was too generous. He paid for a good education for Paul, but look what the boy's like now—a typical hippie, lazy as they come. Adored by his mother, of course, who sees no fault in him."

Cindy had sighed. "It makes me feel pretty miserable. I didn't want to hurt all these people."

Mrs. Usher had smiled. "Not to worry, dear child. Robert often talked to me of you. He loved your mother, you see. That's why you were asked to stay here. Unfortunately your mother said no, and that was that. But he never forgot how you loved the castle. He knew, you see, that both the Stones and David would sell the castle. Only Peter wouldn't—or you."

Now, as Cindy hurried to her bedroom to change into another frock, she wondered just *how* she was going to keep the castle going—always, of course, allowing for the fact that Peter didn't turn up. How David must hate her, she thought unhappily. Why, oh, why had she to meet a man she liked so much on sight, only to find he hated her?

CHAPTER FOUR

CINDY WAS VERY QUIET as Mrs. Stone served dinner. She had never felt so uncomfortable before in her life. She had no desire to hurt the Stones or David Baxter; indeed, she herself had nothing to do with it. But perhaps they didn't realize that. What was there she could say? Unable to answer that question, Cindy decided it might be wiser to keep quiet.

Afterward she sat alone in the huge cold drawing room before a log fire that crackled and sparkled. How quiet everything was. If she ever lived there, Cindy decided, she would certainly have a dog, or several even, and some cats. How wonderful to have a real home—not just a boxlike bed-sitter where you had to ease your way around the furniture that took up what little space there was. Suddenly restless, she got up and wandered down the lofty dark hall, dimly lit by a very old chandelier that looked as if it might fall at any moment.

The click-clack of her heels on the polished floor sounded absurdly loud and echoed and reechoed as she went from room to room. There was little difference in them, for they were all full of old antiques—each article amazingly clean and polished. Mrs. Stone certainly worked hard, Cindy thought. Poor Mrs. Stone—her dream demolished.

The library was the most interesting, even though it

The Golden Maze

was so cold. Cindy walked past the crowded bookshelves, looking for something to read.

After she had collected several books that looked interesting, all biographies, she paused by the huge old desk, then opened it. There were a few papers in it, neatly folded, so obviously whoever had gone through Uncle Robert's papers had taken everything of value. It was a fascinating desk, with so many drawers and shelves of different sizes. She had a job getting one drawer shut, and as she pushed and pulled it, a small doorlike board swung open.

"A secret drawer!" she said slowly, her eyes wide with excitement. Of course many of those old desks had secret drawers, she knew. She put in her hand and slowly pulled out a long thin flat book. Opening it, she peered at the incredibly tiny neat writing. It was hard to read.

Suddenly she heard footsteps—angry ones, she thought—as they went clomp, clomp, clomp, along. It could only be Mrs. Stone!

Hastily Cindy closed the desk, pushed the flat book under her cardigan and moved to the bookshelves.

"What do you think you're doing now?" Mrs. Stone demanded. Standing in the doorway, her hands on hips, cheeks flushed, hair more wispy than usual, her eyes were angry.

"I was getting something to read," Cindy explained, gathering the books up.

"You've not the right to meddle about with Mr. Baxter's things," Mrs. Stone said angrily. "The castle ain't yours, yet; nor may it ever be, if Mr. Baxter turns up."

"I'm sure Mr. Baxter wouldn't object to my reading some of his many books," Cindy said, lifting her head and returning, glare by glare, Mrs. Stone's angry looks. "I was thinking how wonderfully clean you've kept the castle," she added.

Mrs. Stone sniffed. "Someone has to, haven't they? Not easy, mind, nor appreciated. Mr. Baxter never saw if it was clean or t'dirt was around."

Somehow Cindy managed to escape and went back to sit by her fire. She looked through the books, keeping the long flat book under a cushion. She wondered why she had hidden it so quickly. After all, whoever went through Mr. Baxter's things must have known of the secret drawer. Yet something had told her to keep it from Mrs. Stone. Cindy realized with a shock that not only did she dislike Mrs. Stone but she distrusted her—and disliked and distrusted the son, Paul, even more.

The quietness was so oppressively still—the only sound being the occasional crackle of a twig fallen off the log as it was burned through—that Cindy found herself looking constantly over her shoulder. In the end she went to bed, propped up by pillows, and began to read the long flat book she had found.

It was very hard to read the tiny neat writing. Cindy tried both with and without her glasses. She read enough to realize it was Robert Baxter's diary. Not a very, very old one, as she had hoped. One dating back to the eighteenth century would have been more exciting!

Yet in a way she wanted to know more about the man who had never forgotten her, who had remembered how, as a little girl of seven, she had wept because her mother said the castle wasn't *real*. As Cindy read, she realized it was not a diary but more a collection of notes he had made.

"Sometimes I feel I cannot survive unless I have

The Golden Maze

someone to talk to. This is why I am writing this,'' Cindy read. ''The quiet emptiness is the most devastating experience I have ever known. If only Peter would write! Just a few words, so that I know he is well. How can I write to him when I have no idea where he is?''

Cindy closed the book with a sigh. As Mrs. Usher had said, how terribly sad. Yet surely Peter Baxter *could* have written to his father. Or was the quarrel too bitter to allow a proud man to make the first move?

At breakfast next day, Mrs. Stone told Cindy that Mr. Fairhead wished to speak to her.

"He manages the estate," Mrs. Stone explained. "A mean man if ever there was one."

Cindy wondered what sort of man he was that she went out to meet. He was standing in front of the castle, frowning as he looked down at the lake below. As she joined him, she saw she hadn't realized just how high up the castle stood. Now she could see the winding narrow track. Two cars that looked like toy cars scuttling along were going along it.

The man turned to look at her, his eyes narrowed thoughtfully. He was a big burly man with a slight tummy bulge and gray tufty hair. He held out his hand.

"I felt I'd like t'know you, Miss Preston. Seems like you may be my boss." His grin split his weather-beaten face in two. He shook her hand firmly and frowned. "You're younger than I expected."

Cindy's chin tilted. "I'm nearly twenty."

He grinned. "You remind me of my daughter. She's nearly sixteen." Luke Fairhead had a dog beside him. "This is Bessie, a farmer's best friend."

The sheep dog looked up as Cindy stroked her ears.

"You're lucky," Luke Fairhead said. "The sun isn't always with us."

"I don't mind if it rains, Mr. Fairhead. I think this is so lovely."

He beamed again. "You like it here?"

"So much. I never forgot it, you know."

"It's gone to seed badly. You...." Mr. Fairhead looked embarrassed. "We know nought about you, Miss Preston. If you do inherit the castle, will you be able to—"

"Finance it?" Cindy looked at him. "I don't know. There must be some way. Other beautiful old places manage."

"But, Miss Preston, Claife Castle is different. It isn't really *old*."

"I know. Mr. Ayres, the solicitor, told me so. Yet there must be a way."

"I'd like you to come to my office and then let me show you around, Miss Preston. I think it's only fair for you to see the bad side as well as the good of your inheritance."

"But Mr. Fairhead—" Cindy put out her hand and touched his arm "—I think you're forgetting that I'm not the *heiress* to the castle. There's still time for the son to turn up."

"No, Miss Preston, that I haven't forgotten. Peter was a strange lad with a habit of turning up unexpectedly. Real sad, that quarrel with his dad. The old man was always sure he was right, and Peter had the same kink, but differentlike, if you know what I mean. It was some years after he'd walked out, and I saw the lad arrive. He knocked on the door and spoke to Mrs. Stone. She closed the door in his face and kept him waiting. Then when she came back, she told him something and then slammed the door. I never seen Peter look like that. White as a sheep turning sick, that was

The Golden Maze   47

what he looked like, as if his face had been slapped. He didn't see me.... He just drove off like a madman."

"I wonder what she said."

Mr. Fairhead shrugged. "I can only guess that the old man refused to see him."

"But he wanted—" Cindy began, and stopped, for the front door behind had opened with its usual squeaks and groans. Mrs. Stone stood there.

"Paul'd like to see you now, Mr. Fairhead."

Luke Fairhead frowned. "Tell him I'm busy. I'll see him later. Come on, Miss Preston," he said, and strode away, Cindy following, trying to keep up with his long strides, straightening the glasses that were sliding down her nose.

It didn't make sense somehow, she was thinking as she hurried. Peter coming to see his father—then the old man refusing to see him. Yet in the notebook she was reading....

"Ah, come inside, Miss Preston." Mr. Fairhead led the way into an immaculately neat office. "Let's get down to business."

Two hours later he shook Cindy warmly by the hand. "Well, you now see the position, Miss Preston. I'm glad you feel as you do. Maybe if we sold the farm.... Your uncle would not hear of it, but then he didn't realize that he was running it at a loss. Colin Pritchard is too old to manage it, really, but Mr. Baxter wouldn't turn him out. A kind man, Mr. Baxter, for all his tempers. His nephew David takes after him for the last. Now there's a bitter young man what's had too much done for him. His uncle was generous."

"I understand Mr. David Baxter expected to inherit the castle," Cindy said.

Mr. Fairhead grunted. "David may have thought it,

but not me. Robert Baxter always meant Peter to have it. David would sell the lot tomorrow, and that was something Robert Baxter didn't want."

"Well... well, if I do get it," Cindy said awkwardly, "I'll do my best to keep it."

"I know you will, Miss Preston, and you can count on me for help. Now where's that young layabout, Paul? Around the back, I've no doubt. Another sign of Robert's generosity that goes wrong. Young Stone has been given everything and what does he do in return? Nothing! Bye for now."

He strode off around the castle, Bessie following him. Cindy knocked on the door. She was startled when, after the usual squeaking and groaning, Paul Stone opened it.

He held out an envelope. "Letter for you, Miss Preston." He looked down at it, turning it over. "Funny thing—it's got a London postmark, but the address on the back is American."

"So?" Cindy took it, looking down at the address. "This isn't for me," she said. "It's addressed to the owner of Claife Castle. I'm not—"

"Yet!" Paul Stone's mouth curled. "But you will be, eh? Open it and see what it says." He leaned against the door, making it impossible for her to go into the hall.

"I've got no right to open it. I'm not the owner," she repeated.

"Don't be square, Miss Preston," Paul Stone laughed scornfully. "I bet you're longing to open it just as much as me. What can an American have to do with Claife Castle?"

Cindy shook her head. "I have no right to open it. I shall send it at once to the solicitor. Please let me pass."

The Golden Maze

He shrugged, standing back. "Okay, if you feel stuffy. I'm going down to the village. Want me to bring you up a newspaper?"

"No, thanks, I'm going down myself." Cindy told him. "By the way, Mr. Fairhead is looking for you."

"Let him look," Paul said with a grin. "He made me wait; now it's my turn." He strode over the gravel toward his bright red car.

Cindy hurried to her bedroom, found an envelope and hastily wrote to Mr. Ayres.

"I've no right to open it, so think it best to send it to you."

Quickly she put on her thick coat, tied a green scarf around her head and looked in the mirror. She had thick dark rims to her glasses. Did they seem to hide her face, she wondered. Mr. Jenkins had said they made her look prettier, but then he was only being kind. Perhaps she'd meet David Baxter in the village and he might be in a better mood.

CHAPTER FIVE

CINDY DROVE DOWN to the village by the lake, parked her car and hurried to the post office. It had struck her that the letter might be about the missing heir—whoever it was might not know that Robert Baxter was dead but merely that the heir was being sought. As she opened the shop door and entered, the babble of voices stopped with an abruptness that startled her.

How crowded the small shop seemed, for that was what it really was: a stationer's, newsagent's and sweet shop, with a side made over to be a subpost office. Now it seemed full of women, talking again as they turned their backs on her and she made her way to the post office counter.

She caught words here and there, words spoken loudly, as if the speaker hoped they'd be overheard.

"No right t'it, has she?"

"Jumping the bridge afore it's built...."

"Of course she musta seen the paper now...."

Trying to ignore the crowd, Cindy bought a stamp. The postmistress looked at her with cold eyes.

"Reckon you're pleased with yourself, Miss Preston," she said. "A good day to you now."

Puzzled, Cindy hesitated. What had she to be pleased about? The talk with Mr. Fairhead had been depressing and even alarming, for she could see no solution to the

The Golden Maze

problems she'd have to face if the castle were hers. How could it be a good day? Perhaps she meant the weather.

So Cindy smiled. "Yes, it is a lovely day, isn't it?"

There was another silence, and she felt a cold wave of anger go through the small shop. She hurried outside as fast as she could, almost forgetting to stick the stamp on the envelope and drop it into the letterbox.

Once outside, she almost ran to her car. She had to get away. Somehow or other she had angered the villagers. But how? Or why? Maybe it was absurd, she thought unhappily, but it frightened her. It was like walking on the edge of a volcano here—she was never sure when or how she might anger the local people.

As she started the car, she remembered a holiday she had once spent in Cornwall. There, an old inhabitant had laughed.

"Take no notice of them," she had said. "I've lived here fifty year and I'm still a 'furriner.' You have to be born here to be accepted."

Maybe it was the same in the Lake District, Cindy thought as she drove down a road she had never been along. Soon she was driving along a wider road, not sure where she was going, not really caring. Passing a public call box in a small village, she stopped and put a call through to the castle. Mrs. Stone answered it.

"Oh, it's you now, is it?" she said, her voice impatient. "Has ta something to tell me?"

Cindy stifled a sigh. "Just that I shall be out to lunch, Mrs. Stone."

"Is that so now? I'm not surprised. Celebrating with champagne, I don't doubt!" she said, and slammed down the receiver.

Putting down the receiver, too, but slowly, Cindy

went out into the cold crisp mountain air. So Mrs. Stone was also mad! What on earth was wrong with them all?

Back in her car, Cindy started to drive. She had no idea where to go, but probably she would find herself in a town at lunchtime and could eat there. She felt she could not face Mrs. Stone's cold anger or Paul's cheekiness.

The road lay along the side of the hill, going slowly downward. One side was covered with heather, the other with huge boulders perilously balanced, or so they looked, while clumps of trees kept hiding the lake that was, as could be expected here, in the valley below. Here it was peaceful, she thought, as she drove through a tiny village. The church was outside, alone in dignified solitude. Nearer the village, a house that had to be the vicarage and a church school—then just a row of small shops and a few cottages huddled together as if whispering secrets.

Turning a corner, she found herself suddenly on a level with the lake. She saw it was a waiting place for a ferry and already two cars were parked, waiting as the flat-bottomed ferry slowly made its way toward them across the sun-sparkled lake. She might as well go across, she thought, and parked behind the cars.

Looking up at the sky, she saw the sun was about to be temporarily hidden by a strangely gray cloud and that behind it darker gray clouds looked ominous. Perhaps the sunny period was over and the rain near. Well, it matched her mood, she thought unhappily, for suddenly everything seemed to have gone wrong and the excited happiness that had filled her ever since she had received Keith Ayres's letter had vanished.

The lake water rippled gently as the ferry came to-

The Golden Maze

ward them with a strange slow dignity, almost as if the journey were effortless. On the opposite bank was a large white house down near the water. In the middle of the lake, a small island. If there was a cottage on it, it was hidden by the dense cluster of trees.

Cindy drove on the ferry with the other cars. It was only when she chanced to turn her head she saw that in the car next to hers David Baxter sat!

Had he seen her, she wondered. He was sitting, his arms folded, his head turned to look the opposite way. Was it on purpose, she asked herself. Then he turned suddenly and caught her staring at him. She half smiled nervously, feeling perhaps she should make the first move; he lifted a newspaper that lay by his side and waved it angrily.

For a moment she thought he was going to throw it at her. Then he dropped it down on the seat and deliberately turned his back on her.

She turned away, too, shocked and bewildered. Now what on earth could she have done to have so offended everyone? She stared, without really seeing them, at the masses of gulls that were swooping down to dive into the water. Suddenly she saw that the white house had become a great deal bigger than before, and she realized that the ferry was nearing the opposite shore. Several swans swam slowly past, looking at the ferry arrogantly, almost as if defying it to run them down, Cindy thought, as she tried to forget the look of anger on David Baxter's face as he waved the newspaper at her.

She drove ashore and straight up the hill, concentrating on looking at the scenery to distract her thoughts. She saw a squat little church with a square tower that stood in a churchyard and seemed guarded by a row of dark dignified cypresses that appeared determined to shut out the world. Suddenly she was on a straight road, running alongside the lake but much higher. The gray clouds had moved and the sun shone. How yellow the fields looked, but she knew it was only golden bracken. Up here, on the other side of the road, she saw the flag walls that Mr. Fairhead had told her about. In the quiet fields sheep were grazing, while a few small lambs were gamboling about, having what looked like a lot of fun.

As she drove on, she reached Ambleside. Startled because she had thought herself much farther from the castle, Cindy stopped and had lunch. She also bought a booklet of colored pictures of the different parts of the Lake District and decided to drive up past Langdale and toward Keswick. She had no desire to go back to the castle, though she knew she would have to—no matter how long she postponed it.

Now, as she drove, she found herself in a totally different countryside. The mountains seemed larger, and they were no longer covered with trees and grass. Bracken, yes, but mostly they were bare rocks. Suddenly it was eerie—the huge gray and green mountains standing high above the quiet lakes threateningly, while the distant view was of mountains going away in their curving beauty. She shivered, for now the sun had vanished again and the gray coldness seeped through her warm coat. Realizing how late it was, she turned to drive home. Maybe things would be better next day, she thought. She had liked Luke Fairhead; perhaps she could ask him what she had done to offend the local villagers and then she might be able to put the matter right.

Turning a corner, she slowed up instinctively, driving off the road onto the grass verge to stare at the

The Golden Maze

scene before her. It was horribly desolate, yet had a beauty she had never seen before. The mountains had grown dark as the sun fell. Now they were silhouetted against a sky of weird loveliness, a sky of pale gray with streaks of palest mauve and a wonderful clear yellow of the remains of the sunshine—all this reflected in the still lake. Down by the water stood some trees, their bare branches spread upward as if appealing to the darkening sky, their delicate twigs looking like fine crochet against the light.

She sighed. How she loved this beauty—if only she could find a way to keep the castle—if, that is, the castle was going to be hers.

It was dark when she reached Claife Castle. She saw a car parked outside but drove on around the back to the garages. She walked around to the front of the castle, thinking again that there must be a way to find the money to rejuvenate it. Would a bank manager consider her old enough—or reliable enough—to be loaned the money? If she ran it as a hotel....

She knocked on the front door. It opened immediately, as if Mrs. Stone had been waiting for her. Now she stood back, her face bright with triumph.

"You're late, Miss Preston. I thought you might be lost now. There's a gentleman waiting to see you."

"A gentleman?" Cindy was startled. Whom did she know who'd be visiting her? A sudden rush of hope filled her. Could it be David Baxter? Come to apologize for his strange and rude behavior?

She pulled off her coat and scarf, running her hands through her hair, and went to the big drawing room.

A tall man stood by the fire. Now he turned to look at her. It was David Baxter! In his hand was a newspaper.

CHAPTER SIX

HE CAME TOWARD HER with no smile or sign of friendliness on his face.

He lifted the newspaper. "How do you explain this?" he asked.

She stared at him, startled, indeed bewildered. He had changed! His voice was much deeper, his face more suntanned, his fair hair shorter. How could he have changed in so short a time?

"You *are* Mr. Baxter?" she said uncertainly.

"Of course I am. Why else should I be here? I want an explanation of this." He lifted the paper again as he spoke curtly.

Something seemed to snap inside her. "About what? I haven't seen a paper today, but I'm absolutely sick of your rudeness. Waving the paper at me on the ferry like that!"

"What on earth are you talking about? What ferry? I drove up from London as soon as I read the article." Suddenly she knew! It was the voice she had been unable to forget, the voice he had used in London as he teased her about her eyes and her height.

"You *are*..." she hesitated. "You are David Baxter?"

He frowned, his thick eyebrows almost meeting.

"David Baxter? Of course I'm not. I'm Peter Baxter."

The Golden Maze

"Peter!" Without thinking, Cindy put out her hand vaguely and the next moment the man had her by the arms and was gently pushing her into an armchair.

"Let's get this straight," he said briskly. "You seem to have had a shock. What made you think I was David Baxter? Incidentally, he's my cousin."

"I can see now you're so different. I thought when I saw him that it was you."

"If you remember, you'd left your glasses behind, so you didn't really know what I looked like."

"No, I didn't. He was big and tall and fair and...." Cindy shook her head slowly, her long hair swinging. "I'm beginning to understand."

"Understand what?"

"His behavior. I spoke to him and he—"

"Was rude? He's not noted for his good manners. Has a foul temper, too. What's all this about waving a paper at you?"

"I—I was on the ferry. I wanted to get away. They were all so unfriendly, I couldn't understand it... and then I turned my head and he was in the next car and he looked furious. I thought he was going to throw the paper at me and—"

"I see." Peter pulled up a small straight-backed chair and straddled it, looking at her thoughtfully. "You haven't read the paper today?" He passed it to her. "I suggest you read the front-page article. It might explain a lot of things."

Cindy opened the paper and stared at the headlines.

TEENAGER PLANS TO SELL MOCK CASTLE
SHE MAY INHERIT FOR
TWENTY THOUSAND POUNDS

Underneath it said.

> A nineteen-year-old girl who may become heiress to a mock castle in Cumberland has been offered twenty thousand pounds by an American who plans to demolish the castle and rebuild it, stone by stone, in America. A distant ancestor of his lived in the castle soon after it was built and he has always wanted to live in it himself—but in his own country. Of course there is always the possibility that the real heir—the son of the deceased—may appear. No one seems to know why this girl, who is no relation to the Baxter family, should have been made heiress at all. She said that if the castle is hers, she will sell it to the American. Local people are angrily against the project. It is their castle, they say, not hers.

Cindy looked up as she finished reading. "But it isn't true!" she said, her voice shocked. "No American has offered me twenty thousand pounds." Her hand flew to her mouth. "Today, just before lunch, there was a letter for me. But it wasn't really for me—it was addressed to the owner, so I sent it to Mr. Ayres."

"After opening it?"

Cindy frowned. "I didn't open it. I am—was not the owner, so I went straight down from the village and posted it off."

"Paul Stone says you opened it and smiled."

Cindy was on her feet. "Paul is lying." She glared at the man. "Of course if you prefer to believe him...." She turned and walked to the door, but Peter Baxter was quickly on his feet, grabbing her by the arms, turning her around.

"Where do you think you're going?"

"To pack my clothes and drive back to London. I have no right to be here now."

"I agree." Surprisingly, he smiled. "All the same, I'm not allowing a slip of a girl like you to drive back to London alone in the dark. You stay here tonight," he said quietly—very quietly, so quietly that she looked at him quickly. It had been an order, not a suggestion.

"Why should I?"

He smiled. "Because I say so, and I'm a lot stronger than you." He bent one arm, pretending to flex his muscles.

She found herself laughing. "Are you threatening me?"

"Not really. Now I'll ask you politely: please stay the night. It's going to be foggy and Keith Ayres would never forgive me if anything happened to you."

"Keith Ayres?" She was puzzled. "You mean the solicitor?"

"Who else?" Peter Baxter chuckled. "Don't tell me you didn't notice? He fell for you, hook, line and sinker." He laughed. "He thinks you're—well, quite something."

"But I only met him once!" Cindy was startled. "I liked him, but—"

"There was no 'but' about his liking for you. Although he was pleased to see me, he was equally disappointed because you wanted the castle and he knew I didn't."

"You don't!" Cindy took a step backward and his hand fell off her arm.

"No, I've always hated it, but...." He led her back to the chair. "Sit down and let's talk about this sanely."

She sat down. "Look, Mr. Baxter—"

"Please call me Peter and you're...?"

"Cindy—Lucinda Preston." She leaned forward. "Mr.—I mean, Peter, I just don't understand. You met me in London and I told you all about the castle and the missing son. You must have known it was Claife Castle."

"Of course I did. I'd seen the advertisement and wasn't very keen to claim the heritage. I knew it would probably cost me more than it was worth. My memories of this place are not particularly happy, but I was persuaded that it was my duty." He smiled ruefully. "An example of the power of a woman being underestimated. In a way, she was right. I went there, met you and realized how much the castle meant to you, so I decided not to make a claim but to let you have it."

"You were going to let me have it?" Cindy stared at him in amazement. "But it's yours!"

"Then let's see it as a gift to you. At least—" his voice suddenly changed "—it *was* to be a gift. I didn't realize the first thing you'd do would be to sell it. Seeing that my father left it to you because he believed you loved it—well, it made me change my mind about you."

"But I knew nothing about the sale. How could I sell something that wasn't mine?" Cindy twisted her hair around one hand. "Look—" she leaned forward "—I only got that letter before lunch. This article was in the morning's paper. I knew nothing about it."

"That, of course, would be your story," he said. Again his voice was cold and unfriendly. "The letter today might have been an acknowledgment of your acceptance of the offer."

She let go of her hair, shook her head and leaned back.

"You think I'm that sort of person?"

"No, I didn't think so. I don't. All the same, I gathered from Keith Ayres that you have no money of your own, only the pittance you earn." He smiled suddenly. "I gather you're a careful saver and have your own car, but as he said, that's hardly enough to run a castle this size. I know he arranged for you to see Luke, as well. I'm sure he depressed and frightened you about the money needed. It is a heavy burden to put on a teenager's shoulders. In fact, my father should have known better. Of course Ayres wanted you to sell it."

"But why?" Cindy was bewildered. Keith Ayres had seemed so nice.

Peter Baxter chuckled. "Because he wants you in London, of course." He stood up. "Look, I fancy a drink, and I expect you can do with one. I suggest you go and have a quick wash and change into a pretty frock and then we'll have a drink and something to eat. We might as well enjoy this evening."

She stood up. "Enjoy?" she said slowly. "Enjoy?"

Peter turned and looked at her. "Please don't do anything dramatic and run away. My car is faster than yours, so I would soon catch you. Besides, the fog has come down pretty badly. See you in ten minutes," he said, and left the room.

She moved very slowly. Her limbs felt heavy and tired. Somehow she walked upstairs and into her ice-cold bedroom. Rather like a robot she moved, washing, finding her pale green trouser suit and changing, brushing her hair and pinning it up on her head. She looked anxiously in the mirror. Should she wear her glasses or not, she asked herself. She decided she had better wear them, or else it would give him an opportunity to tease her. What a funny face she had! Her cousins were right.

What man in his senses would look twice at her? Peter's jokes about the solicitor liking her just proved it. He—Peter, that is—was only being kind, just as Mr. Jenkins had been. How small her face was, with the strange oval look and the big round glasses. She pulled them off, but then her reflection was blurred. Maybe that was why she thought she was better-looking without them, she told herself, and put the glasses on again.

She looked around her. Her last night in what she had thought was—or might be—her own castle. She went to the window. The fog was thick, curling itself around in the darkness like the cloak of a witch who was flying by on her broomstick.

The long flat book she had found in the secret drawer was safely locked in her suitcase. She would read it that night, she decided, and then give it to Peter. It was his by rights; yet she wanted badly to read it, for there were several things that puzzled her.

For one thing, Mrs. Stone saying that Peter had never come to see his father. Yet Luke Fairhead had said he had *seen* Peter come and also seen him turned away *by* Mrs. Stone, "his face white as a sheep being sick." Cindy would have trusted Luke Fairhead any day before Mrs. Stone. And why had Paul Stone lied about the letter? He had been the one who wanted her to open it. He must have lied deliberately. But why? What for?

In addition, there were the nice things Mrs. Usher had said about Peter Baxter. And she knew him well. As Mrs. Stone implied, if Peter so hated his father, would he deliberately shoulder what he had called the "burden" of the castle simply because he had believed Cindy was prepared to sell it, which was something his father would have hated?

The Golden Maze

It didn't make sense. There were too many contradictions. Perhaps reading Uncle Robert's notes might give her the answer.

She went downstairs. Peter was waiting for her, the armchairs drawn up close to the flaming fire, a drink ready. He sat by her side and they talked, lightly, amusingly as he told her of his interesting life and incidents that had happened to him during his working years abroad. It was a pleasant evening, marred only by Mrs. Stone's behavior. The dinner was delicious, but she didn't say a word to Cindy. Cindy might just as well not have been there, she was so completely ignored, while Mrs. Stone almost crawled at Peter's feet, determined to please him.

Afterward, as they drank their coffees by the fire, Peter looked at Cindy and grinned.

"Poor Mrs. Stone! Afraid of losing her job."

"I suppose she is." Cindy hadn't thought of that.

"What about your job? Have you lost it?"

"Oh, no," Cindy said eagerly. "Mr. Jenkins said I could have a week off. I had some holiday time due."

"A week? How long have you been here? One day to come up, two days here, so why not stay the whole week? As my guest, of course."

Cindy stared at him. "But why? I mean—"

"Because you love the Lake District and the castle. It may make your disappointment a little less painful. Besides, I'd be glad of your advice. Something must be done to make the castle habitable—new curtains and carpets and.... Your advice would be of great help," he added, and then smiled. "Doesn't that sound pompous? Sorry, but I'd like you to stay."

Cindy looked around the room wildly. Part of her longed to stay, while the other part told her to run. And fast, too! This was the man she had fallen hopelessly in love with, the man she could not forget, and there could only be one result—heartache. Yet she wanted so badly to stay.

She was startled when he leaned forward and put his hand on hers. The touch of his warm fingers sent a tingling through her. "Please!" he said quietly. "It's years since I've been here, and I'd enjoy driving around the lakes with you. It's not much fun on your own."

Staring at him, as if mesmerized, Cindy swallowed.

"I'll stay," she said. "Just for the rest of the week."

He let go of her hand. "Good! That calls for another drink."

Later that night, in bed, Cindy read some more of Robert Baxter's notes. He blamed himself for losing his son, wished he could contact him and say how sorry he was. But the son never gave him an address, never approached him. Yet Luke Fairhead had said he'd seen Peter there! And Mr. Fairhead would not lie, Cindy thought.

Peter was already in the dining room when Cindy went down for breakfast. He greeted her with a smile.

"Don't look as if you're on the way to the guillotine," he said. "I'm not going to eat you, you know."

As usual, Cindy found herself laughing with him. "I'm sorry. I didn't intend to look scared."

Mrs. Stone came in with a big plate of sausages, bacon and eggs. She gave Cindy a strange look.

"You'll be packing to go now?" she asked. But it was more of a statement than a question.

Peter spoke before Cindy could. "On the contrary, Mrs. Stone, Miss Preston has consented to stay for the rest of the week as my guest."

Mrs. Stone looked startled. "Is that so now?" she said, and almost scuttled from the room.

"Was Mrs. Stone here before you—" Cindy began, and then stopped, feeling her cheeks burn, for it was no business of hers and she had no desire to awaken sad memories.

But Peter didn't seem to mind. "No," he said, "we had a dear old ex-nannie. You know the kind I mean. Unfortunately she died, and I suppose my father engaged Mrs. Stone because he was sorry for her. My father was a stange man," he went on as they ate their breakfast. "The essence of compassion and understanding, except where his son was concerned."

Cindy looked at him quickly. "Perhaps that was because he loved you."

"Loved me? I doubt it," said Peter. "More coffee? Sleep all right?"

"Fine." Cindy hesitated. Should she tell him about the diary she had found? Surely that would make him realize how much his father had loved him and how greatly he regretted the quarrel. But Mrs. Stone came hustling back with some crisp hot toast.

"I hope it's all to your liking, Mr. Baxter," she said.

Peter smiled at her. "Splendid, Mrs. Stone, thanks."

Mrs. Stone made a quick exit, giving a strange look in Cindy's direction.

"Why doesn't she like me?" Cindy asked.

Peter laughed. "You're not as dumb as that, surely, Cindy. In the first place, she obviously expected the castle to be taken over by some wealthy person, so she hoped she could stay on. Then you turn up, a bit of a girl without a penny, so she sees the sack. Then she hears the castle is to be demolished. And then I turn up. She must feel very confused and has to blame someone, and you happen to be handy."

"I suppose that's one way of explaining it, but she hated me from the beginning... as they all do," Cindy said wistfully.

"Can you blame them?" Peter frowned, rubbing his chin. Cindy realized suddenly that that was a habit of his. She saw there was a cleft in his chin, or was it a dimple? He was looking at her with ill-concealed amusement and she felt her cheeks go hot.

"It wasn't my fault," she said defiantly. "Uncle Robert chose me. I didn't ask him to make me his second heir."

"It wasn't that. It was the thought of the castle being pulled down and moved to another land."

"That had nothing to do with me, either!" Cindy's voice rose angrily. "I know you don't believe me, but it's the truth. I had no idea until you showed me the newspaper."

He went on, half smiling at her in that hateful way.

"Is that so," he said slowly.

Cindy's hand closed around the marmalade jar she happened to have in her hand. Never before had she so felt like throwing something at someone. She put it down, stood up and said, "I think it would be best if I left at once."

He stood up, too. "I agree, provided we leave together in the same car."

They stared at one another, Cindy clenching and unclenching her hands. It wasn't right or fair for any man to be so handsome, to have that kind of eyes, that mouth....

"You did promise to stay," Peter said gently.

The Golden Maze 67

Cindy swallowed. "All right. I'd—I'd like to see Mrs. Usher."

"Dear old Mrs. Usher. Is she still here?" Peter sounded pleased. "I'd like to see her, too. Look, I'll drop you there and go into the village, as I have business to attend to, and then I'll come back and pick you up. Okay?"

"Okay," Cindy agreed, and went up to her room, changing into a pale yellow woolen frock, looking worriedly at her face, half-hidden by her hair and glasses. He was being very pleasant, but at the same time she was conscious of this curtain between them, the curtain he had dropped because he could not—or would not—believe her.

Peter was waiting in front, wandering around. He looked up as she joined him.

"I don't think much of Paul Stone as a gardener, do you?"

"Well, I did think it looked pretty scruffy. But then I know nothing about gardening," Cindy admitted as they got into the car.

"I'll have to talk with Luke Fairhead when we get back. Seems to me my father just gave up caring and the whole place has—well, gone to the dogs, you might say."

Cindy looked at him quickly. There was an impatient note in his voice. He was probably a hardworking perfectionist and expected everyone else to be the same. In that respect he reminded her a little of her boss, Mr. Jenkins.

"I think Mrs. Stone has done a wonderful job," she said quickly. "It can't be easy to keep a place as big as the castle so clean and polished."

Peter looked at her, his mouth curling a little. "Yes, she's made a good job of it. But that doesn't excuse her son's laziness. Why do you want to see Mrs. Usher?" he asked abruptly.

"Because... because I like her."

"That's not the truth, is it? You're a bad liar, Cindy," Peter said, driving down the winding road toward the village. On the other side of the lake, lofty hills stood out boldly in the clear blue sky that promised a perfect day.

"No," Cindy agreed. "I want to ask her advice."

"Why not ask mine?"

Cindy turned toward him. "Because you think I lied."

"You didn't lie. I know that. I know you didn't write the article. But you could have known of the offer and accepted it—if the castle became yours—before you ever came here. It was so obvious to me that Ayres was determined to make you sell the castle."

"But he wasn't. He knew I wanted to live here."

"Is that so?" Peter spoke slowly. "You must admit he made it plain that it would be impossible for you to afford it, didn't he?" He snapped the question at her.

Startled, Cindy said, "Yes, but—"

"Look, there are too many 'buts' for my liking. Ayres wanted you to see the castle—that we're agreed on, right? Well, maybe Ayres arranged to sell it for you and someone sneaked out the news, right?"

"No, definitely not right," Cindy said quickly. "Mr. Ayres isn't like that. He knew I was going to try everything to keep the castle."

"And what, may I ask, is 'everything'?"

Cindy's cheeks were hot. "I thought perhaps it would make a hotel."

"Ye gods and little fishes!" Peter nearly exploded.

The Golden Maze

"Just how naive and stupid can you be? Have you any idea how much it costs to convert an old rundown place like this into a hotel?"

"We could have kept it as it is. People love to stay in a castle, and they don't expect modern conveniences. I believe they did it successfully in Ireland. People like to live as they did *then*!" Cindy fought back. "And with the staff dressed in period clothes!"

He turned to look at her and laughed.

"Honestly, I didn't think people like you were still born. Where were you going to get the money?"

"That was what worried me," Cindy said gravely. "I wondered if the bank would loan it."

They were near the village now, the blue water very still, the small snowdrops pushing up their white little heads above the soil. Peter left her at Mrs. Usher's cottage.

"I'll be along in about an hour, tell her," he said, and drove away.

There was no answer to Cindy's knock. She waited, uncertain what to do, not wanting to go back to the village and the curious condemning eyes. Suddenly someone on a bicycle came along the road, stopped at the little wicket gate. It was the little old lady who got off, waving a hand. She wore a trouser suit, a thick anorak and a scarf around her head.

"Well, dear, this is nice," she smiled, lifting out her shopping. "I had to go down along the lake to get my mushrooms. Do come in; the kettle will be boiling now."

"I'm afraid it's very early."

Mrs. Usher's face shone. "The earlier the better, dear. Sit you down now and be comfy while I get around."

In ten minutes the tea was ready, the fire crackling, as Mrs. Usher looked at Cindy sympathetically.

"I thought maybe you'd come down now. 'Twas a nasty shock for you, I would say, seeing that in the paper."

"Oh, Mrs. Usher!" For one awful moment, Cindy thought she was going to cry. "You believe me, then? You know I had nothing to do with it?"

"Of course I do, child. 'Twouldn't be like you t'do such a thing. That's what I told them all. No judge of character, that's their trouble, as I said now. Tell me about it."

Gratefully Cindy obeyed, starting with David Baxter waving the paper on the ferry.

"I thought he was the man I'd seen in London. But it seems he wasn't, because Peter Baxter is quite different. Yet they do look alike."

"You thought David was Peter?" Mrs. Usher chuckled. "I doubt if t'either would be flattered. Never did get on, those two."

Then Cindy told Mrs. Usher of the scene in the post office.

"I could feel their anger, and I didn't know what I'd done wrong." She described her dismal day and how frightening the mountains and quiet lakes had been.

"I know, dear," Mrs. Usher agreed. "They can give you the creeps now. Real eerie, they are. So you went home."

"Back to the castle, and... and he was there."

Mrs. Usher's face dimpled as she tried not to laugh.

"And who, might I ask, is *he*?"

"Peter, of course."

"Of course. Go on."

So Cindy did, telling her how Peter had implied that

she was lying, had said he had planned to let her have the castle until he saw the article in the paper.

"It isn't fair," Cindy nearly wailed. "I had nothing to do with the article. You know I would never sell the castle."

"Unless you had no choice," Mrs. Usher said dryly. "Sometimes it's impossible to do what we want to. All the same, it is sad. You could have had the castle and Peter not had to come up. Is he sad about it? Memories?"

"He was and he isn't, if you know what I mean," Cindy tried to explain. "He's—well, not easy to understand. He's a mass of contradictions."

Mrs. Usher poured them out more tea. "He always was a strange one anytime. So what happens now?"

"Well, I wanted to pack and go, because I have no right here now he's here, and he wouldn't let—"

"Wouldn't let you?" Mrs. Usher looked shocked. "You mean, he stopped you?"

"In a way." Cindy told the little old lady what had happened and was startled when Mrs. Usher laughed.

"The same old Peter—turns on the charm." Suddenly she was serious. "My dear child, don't tell me you've...?"

Cindy knew instantly what she meant. "I—I...."

"Am afraid so?" Mrs. Usher finished the sentence. "Oh, my poor child! Peter isn't the marrying kind, you know."

"I don't know, but I—well, I know he would never see me," Cindy sighed.

"And why not?" Mrs. Usher's voice changed again; now it was sharp. "You're a rare good-looking girl, my child, and don't forget it! There's a fey look about your face and dreamy eyes that has a charm all its own and—"

A knock on the door interrupted her and she got up to open it.

"Peter, my dear boy!" she exclaimed, putting her arms around him.

"Aunt Rhoda—it is good to see you!" he said warmly.

He came to sit by the fire while Mrs. Usher fluttered around like an anxious hen. "I knew you'd be coming, Peter, " she said. "And I cooked those crumpets you like. I'll go and fetch them now. I know you'll eat them anytime."

"You bet!" he grinned, and settled himself comfortably, stretching out his long legs, smiling at Cindy. "Isn't she a pet?" he said softly.

Cindy nodded, her face grave. This was a different Peter from the one she knew. How relaxed he was, how... how happy.

Mrs. Usher joined them, and she was full of questions. Where had Peter been; had he found the heat too much for him; any good adventures? How well he was looking, and it was wonderful to have him back....

"Not that you were ever overfond of this part of the world, Peter," she said a little sadly. "Nor was your mother, for that matter. It was your dad the castle meant so much to."

"I know. That's why I'm here," Peter said, looking across at Cindy, his eyes narrowed.

"Peter, I've known you since you were a small wee baby, so I can ask you certain things." Mrs. Usher's face was concerned as she leaned forward. "Tell me, Peter, why didn't you write to your father?"

"But I did," Peter said at once, leaning toward the old lady. "That was the worst part of it. He returned every one of the letters. Unopened! Then I heard he

The Golden Maze

was ill and I came across from Africa, came straight here. Mrs. Stone went to tell him I was there and she came back again and said he had told her he never wanted to see me again. Mrs. Stone was upset and—and so was I." He smiled ruefully. "What more could I do, Aunt Rhoda? He just didn't want to have anything to do with me. That's why I was surprised when I heard he'd left everything to me."

"Peter—" Cindy turned to him quickly, unable to keep quiet "—the other day I found—"

There came a pounding on the door and Mrs. Usher went to open it. Peter stood up as a tall girl came in. Cindy recognized her at once—Johanna Younge from the little tea shop, the onetime beauty queen who had said jokingly that she was looking for a wealthy husband.

Now she held out her hands. "Welcome back, Peter. You won't remember me—we only met a few times."

Peter smiled. "Of course I do—the beauty queen. We all envied Jim and wondered how he'd done it."

"You're back for good?" Johanna asked eagerly.

"In a sense. I'll be here some time, anyhow," Peter told her.

Johanna smiled at Cindy. "Tough luck, Miss Preston; but the castle needs a man. It'll be nice having you around, Peter. One gets very bored here." She gave him a brilliant smile, then looked at Mrs. Usher. "Just thought I'd pop in and welcome him back."

"Very sweet of you, dear, most thoughtful," Mrs. Usher said, her voice dry. She closed the door and smiled at Peter. "Well?"

"She hasn't changed at all, has she?" he said, and laughed. "Once a beauty queen, always a beauty queen, I suppose. Well, Cindy, it's a lovely morning. I suggest we drive around and share the beauty."

"A good idea," Mrs. Usher said warmly. "It really is nice to have you back, Peter."

He bent and kissed her lightly. "Know something, Aunt Rhoda? It's nice to be back, too."

Once in the car, he looked at Cindy.

"I meant it," he said. "I wasn't happy here before—perhaps that's why I hated the place. Today I can see its charm."

It was a pleasant morning. Peter took her to see all the beauty he found himself remembering. They stopped at Ambleside and looked at the quaint little cottage perched on the bridge. He showed her Cray Castle and then the cottage where Wordsworth lived, the rock on which he was supposed to have sat as he composed his poems, as well as the church where he and so many of his family were buried. Finally Peter drove into the more bleak mountains, explaining that screes were where rocks had broken into small fragments and that they were dangerous to walk on. He showed her the majestic beauty of Honister Pass and the gloomy frightening grayness of Wastwater. As they drove back to Claife Castle, Cindy felt sad, for she had an intuition that this would be their last morning alone together. She didn't know why, but she had a feeling that something unpleasant was about to happen....

As they went into the castle, Mrs. Stone came hurrying, her face concerned.

"You're late now, and a young lady phoned you, Mr. Baxter, asked you to pick her up at the station."

"A young lady?" Peter sounded perplexed and then he laughed. "Was her name by chance Miss Todd?" he said.

"That's right."

"Well, we're starving, so please serve lunch, Mrs. Stone. Paul can fetch the young lady."

"But she won't have had anything to eat."

"I expect she's eaten there. In any case, she's on a diet, so it won't hurt her to starve for once. Or if she's hungry when she arrives, I'm sure you can toss up a delectable omelet." He smiled as he spoke, but Cindy shivered. She knew—how, she had no idea—but she knew he was angry, that he was battling to control his temper.

Who was this Miss Todd, Cindy wondered as they ate their lunch almost in silence. He didn't seem to want to talk, so she sat quietly.

They were drinking coffee when they heard the sound of a car. Peter frowned and looked at Cindy.

"Women!" he said scathingly. "Why were they ever invented? They're nothing but a nuisance!"

CHAPTER SEVEN

THEY SAT IN SILENCE, listening to the impatient hammering on the front door, then the squeak as it was opened.

Cindy had no idea what sort of person she expected Miss Todd to be, but it seemed obvious that she was someone Peter didn't like particularly, for he had sent Paul to meet her and had also told Mrs. Stone they wouldn't wait for lunch! So, as Cindy heard the sound of heels pattering on the polished floor, an impatient voice and Mrs. Stone's shrill answer before the dining-room door was flung open and Miss Todd stood there, she didn't expect what she saw!

Cindy caught her breath; for a moment she could not believe her eyes or that this slim, tall, beautiful girl could possibly be Miss Todd.

But she obviously was, for Peter was on his feet.

"Hullo, Yvonne."

She practically charged into the room, glaring at him, her black-and-white fur coat swinging, her small white fur hat perched on top of short curly dark hair.

"I just can't understand you, Peter Baxter!" she almost shouted, her cheeks flushed with rage. "A fine way to treat me! I had to wait on that beastly cold platform, I'm starving, and then, to add to it, you haven't the decency to come and meet me yourself!" She looked around the room and as she saw Cindy she seemed to freeze with shock. Then she swung around to look at Peter.

"What's *she* doing here? I'd have thought she'd have had the decency to go after the way she's behaved!" Yvonne Todd demanded.

Peter's face was suddenly hard. "Miss Preston was a good friend of my father's, and I hope she will be my friend, too, so kindly stop behaving like a fishwife and being so rude!"

Peter and the lovely girl just stood and stared at one another—almost as if it were the start of a duel, Cindy thought as she stood up. Or perhaps two angry cats about to fight.

Yvonne gave a little grunt, then smiled politely. "How do you do, Miss Preston. Delighted to meet you," she said sarcastically before turning back to Peter. "What some people can get away with amazes me. You're just like your father—soft to the wrong people. Is that boy bringing in my luggage?"

Peter raised an eyebrow. "You've come to stay?"

"Of course. You'll need a woman's hand here." She looked around the lofty cold room and at the big oil paintings on the wall. "It has gone to seed, hasn't it? I can't wait to explore it." She turned swiftly to Cindy, her eyes bright with suspicion. "I suppose you've been over it from top to toe with a magnifying glass," Yvonne Todd added bitterly.

"Naturally Cindy was interested in what she believed might be her castle," Peter said quietly.

Cindy wondered what she should do. Her inclination was to rush out of the room, for why should she stand there to be insulted? Yet Peter was defending her. It was puzzling. Yvonne Todd was everything Cindy wished she could be—tall, slim, those huge dark eyes, the high cheekbones, the husky voice....

"Mrs. Stone will show you to a room," Peter said, turning to the tall thin silent woman who was still standing just outside the door, her eyes bright with curiosity. "I'm sorry at such short notice, Mrs. Stone, but I wasn't expecting Miss Todd."

Cindy saw the color flame in Yvonne's cheeks and the quick intake of breath she gave. So Yvonne Todd *had* come up uninvited.

"Yvonne—" Peter swung around "—if you're hungry, I'm sure Mrs. Stone will make you an omelet. I understood you were on a diet." He looked at his watch. "I must go. I have an appointment with Mr. Fairhead." He glanced at Cindy. "I'm sure you can find plenty to do and I imagine Yvonne will be busy unpacking her incredible amount of luggage, so I suggest we all meet for tea."

He walked past Yvonne, who took a step back, showing her surprise. Cindy hurried after him, trying to get to the stairs. She was going to start packing immediately, and while Peter was with Mr. Fairhead, she could quietly slip away.

But at the foot of the stairs, Peter caught her by the arm. "I'm sorry, Cindy, for her rudeness. Yvonne believes in calling a spade a spade."

Cindy looked at him. "She doesn't just call a spade a spade, she—" She stopped herself in time. What was the good of losing her temper? It wouldn't help. She looked up at him. "Look, Peter, I think it would be better for us all if I went back to London. I can always sleep on the way if it gets foggy, as I did coming up."

He looked at her, his thick eyebrows moving together.

The Golden Maze

"You promised," he said gently. "I had an idea you always kept your word."

"But—but you don't need me now. You have her."

"Suppose I don't want her?"

Cindy managed to laugh. "Please! Look, I'm sure I'll only be in the way."

His hand tightened on her arm. "Please," he echoed.

She sighed, "All right."

"Good girl! See you later." Peter smiled and hurried out of the front door while Cindy, giving a quick glance at the five enormous suitcases piled up in the hall, fled up the stairs. How long did Yvonne Todd propose to stay, she wondered. How close were Yvonne and Peter? He had been almost rude and she had been angry in a possessive way. It seemed to be a strange sort of—well, relationship.

Alone in her bedroom, Cindy locked the door, got out Uncle Robert's diary, curled up on the windowsill, the electric fire switched on and a blanket around her shoulders, for the rooms were too big to heat quickly.

She read the beautifully written words slowly because the handwriting was so tiny. It seemed odd that a successful businessman, who was, apparently, rather a tyrant, could have written with such care, obviously thinking about each word before he wrote it.

It was sad reading. He admitted frankly that he regretted so much of his past. He wrote of his wife, "so gentle that it irritated me immensely," of his son, "too much like me. Maybe that is why we constantly clashed."

Cindy was searching for the mention of his illness, of the day his son had come to see him and he had rejected him, telling Mrs. Stone to tell his son that he never wanted to see him again.

Somehow it didn't make sense—unless this *diary* was supposed to be a satire. Could it be that he had written it as a joke? Pretending to be the opposite of everything he was? Or was this his real self?

He had marked down the dates he had written, so perhaps if she could find out *when* Peter had come to see his father, she could trace the entry Uncle Robert would surely have made? Mrs. Stone might know, but she was the last person Cindy wanted to ask. Peter? Definitely not. That left her Luke Fairhead. He had said he had *seen* Peter—even if it wasn't the actual date, he might remember the year and the season, which would help.

Quickly Cindy locked away Uncle Robert's diary, brushed her hair, put on a warm yellow jersey over blue trousers. If she was quick, she might catch Mr. Fairhead after his talk with Peter. She would wait in the car... from there she could see Mr. Fairhead's office. He was sure to be there before going home.

The castle was very still as Cindy went down the curving staircase as quietly as she could, for she had no desire to meet Yvonne Todd. The drawing room was empty, so she let herself out through one of the French windows onto the paved terrace that ran down the sides of the castle. Even as she did, a man came out from the shadow of a clump of trees and came to meet her.

A short man, not much taller than herself, Cindy noticed. He had a pointed black beard, sideburns and even thicker black eyebrows than Peter.

"Miss Preston?" he asked politely.

"Yes." She was startled. There was no sign of a car, so how had he got up there? Unless he had parked the car farther down the road and come up quietly, not wanting to be seen. But if so....

The Golden Maze

"I understand you are inheriting this castle," he went on.

Cindy stared at him and frowned. "I am not. Mr. Baxter's son is."

"I understand he can't be traced."

"He's been found. He's here now," Cindy told him. "Look, I'm afraid I can't stop now...."

The man moved forward, blocking her way. "Please, Miss Preston. You say Peter Baxter has been found? This is news. So the castle and its treasures are no longer yours. Is Mr. Baxter here?"

"Yes. Look, I can't—"

"Mr. Baxter is staying here and so are you?" The short man grinned, his big white teeth flashing. "Oh, maybe you and he will marry and share the castle." He gave a funny little laugh.

"It's most unlikely," Cindy said angrily. "We don't know one another. Besides, he has a friend also staying—" She stopped abruptly. She shouldn't be answering questions. It would only mean more news in the papers and more trouble.

"I see—the eternal triangle!" he chuckled, and Cindy's cheeks burned.

"Look, please get out of my way. I don't wish to be interviewed."

"I understand. You've found yourself in a very embarrassing position, Miss Preston. I understand you arranged to sell the castle to an American. Will Mr. Baxter do the same?"

"What the—" Peter had come around the side of the castle and towered above them. "Just who are you?" he asked angrily. "You know Miss Preston?"

The little man swung around. "She spoke to me on the phone in London."

"I did not!" Cindy cried.

Both the men looked at her.

"Excuse me, Miss Preston, but you did. You rang my newspaper and told me about the castle you were about to inherit and that you'd been made an offer by an American that you were going to accept if the deceased's son did not turn up..." the little man said quietly.

Cindy stared at him, bewildered. Suddenly she thought of something. "I gave you my name?"

He shook his head. "I asked, but you said you'd prefer not to...."

"Why should I have said that? What would it matter if you had my name?" Cindy asked quickly. "You could easily have found out from the solicitor...."

"Ah, the solicitor," Peter said.

Cindy looked up at him. "Peter, I didn't phone the newspaper. Why should I? It just doesn't make sense...."

It certainly didn't. Peter soon got rid of the polite little reporter, who told them that his name was Neil Gifford and that he was sorry if he had embarrassed them but... news was news and it was his job. He finally went and Cindy looked at Peter, who looked back at her, an odd expression on his face.

"You don't believe me, do you?" Cindy said. "This is the end. I'm going!"

He caught her by both arms. "Oh, no, you're not," he said quietly. "Not until I say so."

She tried to free herself, but his grip was tight.

"There's something funny here," he told her. "And you're not going until I find out...."

"Peter!..." A demanding voice broke the stillness as they looked at one another. "Peter—where are you?"

Yvonne came around the corner, elegant in her white trouser suit. "Oh, there you are," she said, her voice disapproving. "What's going on?"

"I've just persuaded Cindy to stay on. She's eager to get back to London, but I said we would prefer her to stay." Peter gave an odd smile. "We need a chaperon."

He let go of Cindy and they walked back to the front of the castle. Mrs. Stone must have seen the French window open, for now it was closed and locked and they heard the tinkle of a gong through the open front door.

"Tea," said Peter. "I don't know about you two, but I could do with a cup." He looked at Cindy. "Things are worse than I expected them to be according to Luke Fairhead. I imagine you saw that, too."

Yvonne, leading the way, spoke over her shoulder.

"Surely your father was a rich man. I understood—" She stopped abruptly. "Who was that little man I saw walking down the drive?"

"Only a reporter," Cindy said.

"A reporter?" There was a sharp note in Yvonne's voice. "What was he doing here?"

"Asking questions, of course. That's what reporters always do," Peter told her, his voice amused.

"I know that," Yvonne snapped. "But what about?"

"The American who wants to buy the castle and take it, stone by stone, to rebuild in his own country," Peter said slowly, sounding bored.

"Well, that's off now, isn't it?" asked Yvonne. "So it isn't news."

"Isn't it?" inquired Peter as they reached the open front door, where Mrs. Stone stood, tall, dignified and disapproving, the gong in her hands. "I wonder..." he added as he led the way indoors.

CHAPTER EIGHT

TEA WAS NOT A VERY PLEASANT MEAL for Cindy, as Yvonne completely ignored her, talking to Peter all the time, while Peter kept including Cindy in the conversation. Afterward, Peter looked at Yvonne.

"Like me to show you around the castle?" he asked casually.

"I have been all over it, but maybe you'll show me things I missed," Yvonne said with a sweet smile.

"Good—let's go now." Peter got up and they left the room. Cindy sat very still, trying to reassure herself that Peter hadn't just forgotten her, that he might have done it thoughtfully, in believing that it would be kinder not to show her the castle she had lost.

Mrs. Stone came in to collect the tea things. She gave Cindy a quick disapproving glance but said nothing. Cindy went up to her bedroom and got out Uncle Robert's diary. If only she knew the date of the day Mr. Fairhead had seen Peter come to see his father! Suddenly she knew what she must do. Quickly she put away the notes, pulled on her anorak, because it would be chilly outside, and hurried out to Mr. Fairhead's office.

He wasn't there. But Paul Stone was. He looked up from some bushes he was clipping and asked her what she wanted.

"I want to see Mr. Fairhead."

"Why?" he asked.

Cindy bit her lip. "That's my business."

"No longer," Paul Stone said with a grin. "How do you feel now?" He laughed. "Serves you right, that's what I say."

"Look Mr. Stone—" Cindy kept a grip on her temper "—I want to see Mr. Fairhead. Where would he be at this time?"

Paul Stone made a great show of looking at his watch. He took as long as he could over it, even lifting it to his ear to see if it was ticking. Cindy forced herself to wait. She had to see Luke Fairhead; otherwise she would have walked off.

"Reckon that at this hour, he'll be home with his missus. It's other side of the village. You can't mistake it—t'roof is going green with age."

"Thank you," Cindy said politely. "I'll wait and see him tomorrow."

Paul grinned. "He won't be coming tomorrow, neither the next day. He has his own farm to run."

"I see." Cindy hesitated for a moment, then went and backed her car out. It was fast growing dark, but that didn't worry her.

She had soon driven through the village. There was an open space of fields coming down to the lakeside and then she saw a large square-looking farmhouse. She couldn't see if the roof was green or not, but she pulled up outside and went through the little white gate to the front door. She pulled the bell and the door opened. A tall woman with a large plump face and a friendly smile stared at her. She wore a bright blue frock.

"Who's ta wanting?" she asked.

"Is this Mr. Fairhead's farm?" Cindy was relieved

when the woman nodded. "I wonder if I could see him."

"Of course." The door was opened wider and she was invited into a tiled hall. "You must be Miss Preston. Luke is just having tea. Come and join us, Miss Preston."

"That's very good of you."

"A pleasure, I'm sure. I'm Mrs. Fairhead, Maidie Fairhead. Born in this house, and so was my grandfather," she said as she led the way down the hall and to a huge warm kitchen where a kitchen range blazed cheerfully.

Mr. Fairhead stood up. He was in his shirt sleeves and looked a little embarrassed. Two children were also at the table and turned to stare at Cindy.

"Come in, Miss Preston," Luke Fairhead said warmly. "Sit down and have something to eat."

"No, thanks. I've just had tea," Cindy smiled at him. "I tried to see you before you left the castle, but I got held up."

Luke Fairhead grinned. "The press, I hear. Peter Baxter wasn't amused, eh?"

Cindy laughed. "Nor was I. Why can't the press leave us alone?" She sat back in the high-backed chair and ran her hand over her face. "You know, Mr. Fairhead, sometimes I wish Uncle Robert *had* forgotten me."

Mrs. Fairhead leaned forward eagerly. "I remember when you stayed at the castle with your mum. A lovely woman, she. You were but a little lass."

"I loved the castle. It was so, er, so—"

"Romantic," Luke Fairhead said dryly.

Cindy looked at him ruefully. "I still find it fascinating. Will... will Peter be able to save it?"

The Golden Maze

"I think so. Shrewd, that lad's become. And bright. I always thought he was. Eeeh, Miss Preston, maybe I shouldn't ask you anytime, but—but is he and that... well...." Luke Fairhead seemed embarrassed and looked at his wife. She came to the rescue.

"We were wondering, like, if he was going to marry Miss Todd anytime."

Cindy looked at them both and shook her head. "I don't know. She practically told me they were."

"And what did he say, Peter himself?" Luke Fairhead asked.

"He wasn't there. I don't know him very well. I mean, we've only just met and—"

Maidie Fairhead nodded her head wisely, her dark hair slightly streaked with gray. "A good-looking lad is our Peter. 'Twas a sad day when he left. I always wished he and his dad could have made it up. Fair broke his dad's heart, it did."

Cindy drank the cup of tea she had been given, then turned to Luke Fairhead. "Can you remember when it was that Peter came to see his father and was turned away?"

Luke's weather-beaten face wrinkled as he frowned.

"Ah'll think. Maidie, you're the one for remembering. Let's see, he died three years ago, and 'twas about a year before."

"It was September, four years ago. I remember how upset you were, Luke. Fair broke your heart."

"Well, the look on that lad's face—"

"It couldn't have been easy for Mrs. Stone to have to give Peter the message," Cindy said, and saw the quick look the two Fairheads gave one another. "You said the quarrel broke his dad's heart; yet he refused to see Peter. It doesn't make sense."

"You're right. We couldn't understand it. Mrs. Stone, none of us liked her anytime. Just crazy about that boy of hers, out to get all she could from the poor old man."

"Do you think..." Cindy began cautiously. "Do you think Mrs. Stone could have made it up and actually never told Uncle Robert that Peter had come to see him?"

Again Mr. and Mrs. Fairhead glanced at one another.

"Wouldn't put it past her," said Mrs. Fairhead. "We never did trust her. Luke's always saying the money she spent on running the castle and we couldn't see where t'had gone."

"You'll be leaving us soon?" Luke Fairhead asked. "I'm sorry."

Cindy smiled at him. "Thanks very much. I'm sorry, too, but I always did know that if Peter turned up, the castle wouldn't be mine. You know, it's strange. I just can't understand it, but—but Peter was going to let me have the castle, he said, because he didn't want it and he knew I did. But—but then there was that article in the paper. You saw it, of course?"

The children had raced away with Bessie, the dog, and now there were only Cindy and the two Fairheads around the table.

"I didn't give that information to the paper. I knew nothing about it," Cindy said almost desperately. "And today that horrible little reporter came and asked questions and told Peter I'd phoned him and told him about the American offer. I knew nothing about it."

Luke Fairhead leaned forward and patted her hand. "Don't fret so, lass. We know that."

"Peter doesn't believe me." Cindy heard the desperate note in her voice and stopped.

The Golden Maze

"Another cup of tea, love?" Mrs. Fairhead asked tactfully, rising to take the cup and fill it.

"That doesn't sound like our Peter," commented Luke.

"Well, as I said, the reporter told Peter *I* had phoned him and told him that if I inherited the castle I would sell it to the American, and I didn't," Again Cindy heard her voice rise.

Mrs. Fairhead put the cup of tea on the table. "There, love, don't let it fret you. I'm sure no one with sense would believe you'd do a thing like that."

"Peter does," said Cindy, and sipped the hot sweet tea gratefully.

Afterward she told them about the diary she had found.

"I felt rather awful about reading it, but—but I wanted to know more about Uncle Robert and—and honestly, he seemed awfully upset about Peter and blamed himself."

"Has Peter read it?" Luke asked.

"Not yet. I'm giving it to him when I leave at the end of the week because I haven't finished it. It's terribly tiny writing, and I'm afraid Peter might be too impatient to read it and miss the important parts. About the letters, I mean. Peter told me that he got back all the letters he wrote to his father. They were returned unopened. Yet Uncle Robert says how he longs for a letter. And I want to see if I can trace the entry of September, four years ago, and see what he says then about Peter's visit. I can't understand why he refused to see Peter when he kept writing about him."

"*If*... he refused," Maidie Fairhead said slowly. "I never did trust that Stone woman."

"You think she may have—" Cindy looked at them.

"I want to be able to say to Peter, 'Read these dates and see what your father really felt.' As I said, the writing is terribly small and Peter can be impatient." She smiled. "Oh, I can't tell you how wonderful it is to have you both on my side. I wanted to leave, but Peter persuaded me to say. And yet I feel horribly in the way and...and unwanted. It hurts when someone you...when someone just refuses to believe you," she added wistfully.

"We're behind you all the way," Luke Fairhead said gravely. "Maybe you've mistaken Peter. 'Twasn't the impression I got."

The grandfather clock in the hall chimed noisily.

"I'd better go." Cindy jumped up. "If I'm late for dinner, it'll just give them something else to blame me for."

Both Fairheads went out to see Cindy off in her little gray car.

"Thanks...thanks for everything," Cindy called.

Driving back to the castle, she felt happier than she had for days, for at least the Fairheads were on her side.

Peter was in the hall and opened the door after she had knocked.

"Where have you been?" he asked angrily. "You had me worried."

"I wanted to see Mr. Fairhead."

"Was it important?" Peter demanded.

Cindy looked up at him. Should she tell him now, she wondered. Or would it be better to wait until she could give specific facts and dates to look up?

"Yes, it was," she said coldly, and walked by him. "I think I'll have an early night. I'm tired."

"Come and have a drink," he said, taking her anorak off and leading the way to the drawing room.

The Golden Maze

Yvonne glanced up from where she sat by the fire.

"I thought you'd gone," she said, her voice implying that it was a pity Cindy hadn't.

The Fairheads' loyalty and belief in her had heightened Cindy's courage, so she laughed.

"I promised Peter I'd stay till the end of the week."

Yvonne frowned. "It seems daft to me. It can only hurt you more."

"On the contrary," Cindy said almost lightheartedly, "I'm thoroughly enjoying it."

After dinner, they were having coffee in the drawing room and talking when Mrs. Stone opened the door and said, her voice stiff, "Mr. Baxter... Mr. David Baxter."

Cindy looked up, startled, staring at the man she had mistaken for Peter. Now that she saw the two of them together, she could see how foolish she had been.

"David!" Peter stood up and went over to him, hand outstretched. The two men stood side by side, so alike and yet so completely different. Peter's skin was suntanned, whereas David's was florid. Peter's hair was cut short, whereas David's was much longer, curling slightly. Peter's smile was friendly—David's sour.

"I thought I'd better look in and welcome you home," he said.

"I'm glad you did. Look, Yvonne, I want you to meet my cousin, David."

David smiled more graciously as he nodded to Yvonne, whose face had brightened when she saw him.

"And this is Cindy. I think you've met." Peter's voice rippled with laughter.

"Met?" David frowned. "Not exactly."

Peter had to laugh. "She thought you were me."

"She did?" David looked startled. "That explains—"

Cindy pushed her glasses up a little. "Yes, I thought you were Peter that day you bumped into me at the post office."

"We're not alike," David told her quickly.

"We are in a way," said Peter. "Cindy, when she first met me, wasn't wearing her glasses, so she didn't really know what I looked like."

David began to laugh and the two men, looking at Cindy, laughed together. Yvonne sat quietly, looking away from Cindy disdainfully, as if Cindy had done something offensive.

"I forgot them that day."

"I know," said Peter. "You were so excited. Anyhow, what about a drink, David? Sit down. It's been a long time."

"You knew I bought your father's business?" David asked, sitting next to Yvonne but looking at Peter, who was handling the bottles.

"I didn't, but I was told since I got back."

"Your father aged fast. I think he was relieved when I took over."

"How's it doing?"

"Fine, just fine," David said, but the bitterness in his voice shocked Cindy.

"Yvonne here is a good businesswoman," said Peter, coming to sit in the circle. "She started off with one boutique in Sydney—we met in Australia—did so well, she had one in every city, then moved over here. Already she's got three going in England, haven't you, Yvonne?"

David was looking impressed.

"You came over together?"

"No, but we're old friends, aren't we, Yvonne?"

The Golden Maze

Peter said with a strange smile. "Always meeting by chance."

Cindy wondered why Yvonne was frowning. Peter went on, "Actually, Yvonne has lucky fingers. Everything she touches succeeds. Remember the old legend of Midas? How everything he touched turned to gold? Yvonne is like that. But it isn't all luck; she has brains and the ability to judge characters."

"Better than you, Peter," said Yvonne, almost snapping as if he was annoying her.

"She should have been a man," Peter went on. "She'd have ended up as a business tycoon, a millionaire. I'm not sure she isn't headed that way already. She's a real genius—she has the gift of choosing the right people for the jobs and keeping an eye on them so that things don't go wrong."

David looked even more impressed. "You like England?"

"I think there are terrific opportunities for anyone who works hard and has a bit of initiative," Yvonne said, giving Cindy a quick glance; almost, Cindy thought, as if suggesting that Cindy lacked the latter and so could never be a success.

"I'm thinking of giving a party, David. I hope you'll come," Peter announced.

"I'd like to, thanks. When?"

"It has to be this week, because we're losing Cindy," Peter said casually. "Make it Friday?"

"Fine." David stood up. "I must be going now. Nice meeting you," he said, smiling at Yvonne.

Cindy seized the opportunity to slip away to her bedroom as Peter walked out with David to his car. Hurriedly she undressed and got into bed, Uncle Robert's diary in her hand.

September, four years ago.... It was difficult to find, but she finally got near the mark. September 28.

> Sometimes Mrs. Stone is a menace. She is convinced I have bronchitis threatening and insists I stay in bed. I am not feeling well and very exhausted, so instead of losing my temper, I agreed, just to keep the peace. I find it very lonely, for I miss my chats with Luke. He never attempts to see me, nor do I have any visitors at all. Mrs. Stone has a poor opinion of my neighbors, such as they are. She says that not even in the village does anyone inquire after me. I suppose one must expect this as one grows older and of less use. At the same time, it hurts.

Cindy sighed with relief. She had found what she wanted to find. She scrambled out of bed, hunting for pencil and paper, finally finding it, writing on the paper:

> Dear Peter, you never believe me, so you may not believe me now, but please read page 33. This was the time you came to see your father. I don't believe Mrs. Stone ever told him you were here. If you can read it all, you'll see he never got your letters. I think Mrs. Stone may have sent them back to you. Ask Mrs. Usher. She'll tell you that Mrs. Stone hoped your father would leave the castle to Paul—perhaps that was why she kept you apart.

She sighed, folded it and put it in the notebook. She would give it to Peter as she left and leave him to decide what to do....

The Golden Maze

As she fell asleep she felt happier. At least when Peter read the notes he would realize that his father had not stopped loving him, as he had thought.

CHAPTER NINE

When Cindy awoke, the sun was shining. She rose early and hurried down to be the first at breakfast. When Yvonne and Peter joined her, she was finishing her second cup of coffee.

"Isn't it a lovely day," she said, smiling at them. "I'm going for a long walk."

Peter looked skeptical. "Watch out for the screes, and don't get lost. If a mist comes down—"

"Really, Peter," Yvonne interrupted, "she isn't a child!"

Cindy stood up. One of these days she knew she was going to lose her temper with Yvonne. "See you at lunch," she said, and hurried away, going to her room to change into jeans and her warm anorak, brushing back her hair and tying it loosely with ribbon.

Then she set off. It was so beautiful that she was glad she was alone, for such beauty required you to sit and enjoy it without interruption. Perched on a boulder, she looked down at the castle below. How huge it seemed from here, with its tall square castellated towers, the funny little slits of windows in them, the courtyard in the middle. For a moment tears stung her eyes. She wished she had never seen the castle again. Before it had been a child's dream; now it was real.

Yet in a way she was glad she had come. Despite the

The Golden Maze

unhappy moments, she would never forget her week up here.

Was it because of Peter, she asked herself. Each time she saw him, she loved him more. How could she ever get over it? Did people get over broken hearts, or did the pain stay forever?

She began to walk again, finding the paths that wound around the hillside, pausing to look at the streams trickling down toward the lake. She walked over to the other side, where she could no longer be tempted to stop and stare down at the castle, and found something beautiful. It was an immense waterfall, the water sliding abruptly over the side of huge polished boulders, falling far below into a pool. There the water frothed before escaping into a brook that weaved its way between small trees and foliage, yet still made its way to the lake. Above the waterfall was a huge erect boulder and a flat one before it on which one could stand and gaze down the long drop into the white-frothed water.

Sitting down, she looked at it. How quiet everything was save for the distant cries of the gulls and the sound of water. When she heard a scraping noise, she turned, startled.

Peter!

"Hi," he said, lifting his hand. "Mind if I join you?"

"Of course not." She was puzzled. "Yvonne?"

"Didn't feel like walking. Wants to go over the castle again." He frowned. "I can't understand her interest in it. I mean, it isn't as if it were a *real* castle—that would be understandable because of its age and association with people dead for hundreds of years—but why *this* castle? I think she's been right through it several times already, yet she's still fascinated. Now she's down in the vaults. She says they would make good playrooms—billiards, table tennis, etc."

"But wouldn't that spoil the atmosphere? I mean, if people come to live in an *old* castle, surely they won't expect modern games and things."

Peter shrugged. "I agree with you. Of course, on the other hand, Yvonne is right. We have to think of the financial side of it. Why did you want to see Luke?" he asked abruptly. "Was it about me?"

Startled, Cindy looked at him, then away. "Not really."

"Then why did you want to see him?"

"It was something he'd told me about Uncle Robert.... I wanted to make sure I'd remembered right."

"Look, let's get things in proportion. You met my father when you were seven or eight. How long did you stay here?"

"I don't know. It didn't seem long enough to me."

"Why did he ask you?"

"Mrs. Usher said he wanted to marry my mother. She... she didn't like the castle and nothing would have made your father move."

Peter laughed. "Odd to think that I might have been your stepbrother."

Cindy gave him a quick glance. Perhaps it would have been better that way; then she wouldn't have loved him. Or would she have? It might have made it even more complicated.

"Anyhow, Cindy, let's face it. You were only with my father for a few weeks. You can't be so interested in him."

Cindy swung around. "But I can! Don't you see, Peter, how wonderful it was to me to know your father had never forgotten me? I mean, it probably doesn't worry a man, but—but I was very much alone after mummy died, and I was miserable living with my aunts, uncles and cousins. Then... then just before I got the letter, I'd been given the brush-off."

"Brush-off?"

"Yes, Oliver.... Oh, I know it wasn't anything much, but he seemed to like me and took me out and then dropped me. I was—well, pretty upset, and... and I felt no one cared what happened to me, and then this letter came and Uncle Robert had never forgotten me. He cared... he knew I would love the castle and look after it for him."

"I see." Peter was silent for a moment. "You do love this part of the world. I'd forgotten how beautiful it was."

Cindy, glad that the subject had been changed, turned to him again. "There are so many words I don't understand. What is a fell?"

"I suppose you could call it a mountain, or large hill. Dales are the valleys. Mere means water. Windermere and all the other names come from that."

"I saw a strange name the other day—Ings."

Peter chuckled. "It does sound crazy, doesn't it? Actually, it means fields with water."

"Everything is so quiet here—no people, no mad rush of cars."

"That's because it's winter. I bet it's very different in summer. Tourists pour in. Then of course there are masses of climbers and walkers. The place is packed with young walkers and lots of hostels for them. Then the birds.... It isn't nearly so quiet then."

"But even that couldn't change its beauty," Cindy persisted.

Peter laughed, "You have got the bug all right! What

do you think of this waterfall? Did you stand on the rock?"

"No, I'm not good at heights. It's terrific, though."

"There's a legend about it. Apparently in 1806 a young girl came to stay in the village. She was alone, and in those days young women rarely traveled or lived on their own. Her landlady asked questions, but the girl evaded them all. Every day she went to walk on the fells. Always she wore a white dress with broad pink ribbons tied around the waist, with two long ends dangling at the back and reaching to her feet. Then she would stand on a rock and let the wind blow the ribbons around her. This was her favorite place and she would stand on that rock, gazing down at the water below, the ribbons fluttering in the wind." He laughed. "You can imagine the gossip in the village. But she ignored it. Then one day a carriage was seen, but it vanished almost as fast. The girl never came home that night from the fells, nor was she ever seen again or her body found. No one knew what had happened. Some people said that someone must have come in the carriage to fetch her; others, that she had jumped into the water in despair. It was even suggested that someone who came in the carriage had crept up behind her and pushed her in. Mrs. Usher used to tell me that story when I was very young. I could never understand why she wept. Maybe it was an ancestor of hers."

Cindy stared at the huge erect pillar of rock, imagining the girl standing there, leaning against it, looking down at the water foaming so far below. Had she jumped to escape the sorrow she couldn't bear anymore? Maybe she had felt, as Cindy did, the hopeless pain of loving a man who loved another.

She shivered. "What a sad story! Perhaps we should

be going back." She jumped up. He did the same, standing by her side.

"Cindy," he said abruptly, "could you be a little more friendly to Yvonne?"

She was so startled that she nearly lost her balance, but he caught her by the arm.

"Watch out! You could have fallen in."

They walked slowly down the path that led back to the castle's track.

"Yvonne is hurt by your behavior," he began, and when she looked up at him, frowning, her eyes puzzled, he burst out laughing. "Sorry, I did sound pompous, didn't I? Yvonne has that effect on me. She should have been born a hundred years ago."

"I think if anyone could be hurt, it should be me," Cindy said angrily. "She isn't exactly friendly, so why should I be?"

"Because she can't help it. Jealousy is a disease, something that isn't her fault. We should feel sorry for her."

"Jealous?" Cindy almost laughed. "Of whom? Certainly not me."

"You're wrong. She *is* jealous of you—bitterly."

Cindy stopped dead and turned to face him. "But how can she be when she has everything I would like? She's so tall and graceful and beautiful and—"

"Boring," Peter ended. "All Yvonne thinks about is money."

"How can you say such a horrible thing when she's your—"

"Maybe because I know her so well. That's not her fault, either. She needs financial security. You're different."

"I haven't got financial security, only what I earn."

"Exactly. But it doesn't worry you, does it? To you there are other things in life. There aren't for Yvonne. Money is the beginning and end of everything. As soon as she heard about the castle, she started planning how to make it earn money."

"Was it Yvonne who persuaded you to go to the solicitor?"

Peter laughed. "In a way. She nagged like mad, and of course I ignored it. Then it struck me that I owed it to dad to look after it. Then, as you know, I met you and changed my mind."

"Then that article was published and you changed your mind again," Cindy put in. "I wish I knew who phoned the newspaper. I didn't." She looked up at him angrily. "You think I'm a liar, but I'm not," she said, and began to run down the slope.

"Watch out!" Peter shouted, chasing after her, catching up, grabbing her hand and running with her.

As she ran, Cindy looked straight ahead. She was afraid if she turned to look at him, he might see the truth in her eyes. Why must she love this man, she asked herself miserably. If only it were possible to control love! If only....

They were both a little breathless as they reached the castle. The sun shining on it seemed to increase its majesty. Some of the trees had a few green buds, and the snowdrops were pushing their way bravely through the cold soil as usual.

"Spring won't be long," Cindy said gaily.

"Spring comes late here," Peter began.

"Do you have to be so depressing?" Cindy asked laughing.

"I'm a realist, not a dreamer like you."

"Remember what you said that day? Something

The Golden Maze

about a golden maze," Cindy asked as they went inside the castle.

"Peter!" Yvonne came storming down the hall, her cheeks bright red, her eyes flashing. "You must speak to that impossible creature, Paul Stone. Impudent! I've never heard such cheek in all my life, or such bad language—and I thought I'd heard most. There he was—down in one of the vaults, digging. 'What are you doing?' I asked. He told me to mind my own business. I said it was my business, and then he was rude and said it had no right to be my business...." She stopped, glaring at Peter, who was laughing. "I don't see anything funny in that." She turned to Cindy. "Do you?"

"No, I don't," Cindy agreed.

Peter stopped laughing. "Sorry, Yvonne, but you get so involved with the word *business* I couldn't help laughing. That young man has got to pull up his socks. He's been able to do just what he likes too long. Why was he digging?"

"He wouldn't tell me."

Mrs. Stone appeared, banging the gong. She, too, looked angry.

"I'm hungry, aren't you, Cindy?" Peter asked, leading the way. "Walking gives one an appetite."

Yvonne sulked all through lunch, hardly saying a word. Cindy felt uncomfortable, particularly as Peter was obviously finding it hard not to laugh. But as they drank coffee, Peter said, "Cheer up, Yvonne; it isn't the end of the world. I'll speak to Stone."

Her face changed. "You will? And find out why he was digging, Peter. That's most important. You won't forget, will you?"

"No, I won't forget," he promised.

It amazed Cindy, but Yvonne's whole attitude

changed. She turned to Cindy and began to talk in a friendly voice, asking questions about her work, and it was only as they finished their coffee that she turned to Peter again and asked him in a casual voice, a voice so casual that it caught Cindy's attention, "By the way, Peter, doesn't Claife mean a steep hillside with path? I can't find the path. There must have been one to give the castle its name. That Paul Stone knows where it is. He told me so and refused to tell me where it was." Her voice shook angrily. "Perhaps you know the path?"

"The path?" Peter looked puzzled. "I never thought of there being one."

"Oh, dear, it is so annoying. Look, Peter, you find out from Stone. You're his boss. He'll have to tell you."

Peter stood up. "I can hardly twist his arm, can I? But I'll do my best. It's time he realized who's the boss around here. I'm afraid he's done what he likes too long."

He left them and Cindy wondered how she could get away tactfully. Yvonne stood up and wandered around the room, then turned.

"Cindy, I wonder what would be the best color for the curtains in here. We ought to have it centrally heated, too."

"I thought Peter wanted it to be furnished in the way it would have been in the period this castle represents."

"Does he? We've got to consider the best way to make money, not some sentimental idea.... We shall only live here part of the year because London must be our headquarters. I'll have to get a good manager, for Peter is hopeless at judging characters. He's too much of a romantic."

The Golden Maze

"A romantic?" echoed Cindy, and began to laugh.

Peter came in. "What's the joke?" he demanded.

"Yvonne says you're a romantic, Peter."

He gave her an odd look. "You don't think I am?"

"Most certainly not," Cindy said firmly.

"Did you see Paul Stone?" Yvonne demanded.

"I did."

"And what did he say?"

"Nothing. Precisely nothing," said Peter, sounding amused.

"But, Peter, he must have said something!"

"My dear Yvonne, he did. He talked for a long time and at the end he said precisely nothing. I gather the digging in the vaults was because of the rats."

"Rats?" Yvonne sounded worried. "I didn't see one down there."

"It seems they roam at night. Stone is putting down poison or something."

"And the path?" Yvonne asked eagerly.

"He says he's heard of it—folk talk of it in the village. He doesn't know where the path is exactly, but reckons it would start from the lake but grew over long ago."

"I thought you said he had told you nothing?" said Cindy.

Peter smiled. "Well, what I've just told you took an awful long time to say. A sort of intelligentsia type, using long words whose meaning he probably doesn't know himself. Anyhow, I made it clear that he mustn't be rude to you. He said you were rude to him, that he wasn't a serf—that was the word he used." Peter sounded amused. "Apparently you were rather arrogant, Yvonne."

"Arrogant? Me? I merely told him that he was your

employee and had no right to dig in the vaults without your permission."

Cindy, murmuring something, slipped away from the two of them and escaped to her room. Somehow their wrangling made it all much worse, for they had sounded like a couple who had been married for years and who enjoyed a quarrel because of the fun of making up afterward! The more Cindy saw them together, the more convinced was she that they would one day marry, for Yvonne seemed so sure of herself, so possessive of Peter.

If only the week would end, Cindy thought miserably, and she could go miles away, never to see them again. Yet, inconsistently, the idea made her want to cry, for how *could* she say goodbye to Peter, knowing she would never see him again.

In the morning, soon after breakfast, Yvonne vanished. Peter asked Cindy if she would like to walk around the castle with him, giving him her ideas of what they should do to turn it into a profitable business.

"I'd love to," she said, her face glowing with surprised pleasure before she had time to hide it. "Yvonne says, though, that—"

Peter smiled. "Let's forget Yvonne; she's full of ideas. I still prefer yours. I think a lot of people, particularly from abroad, would enjoy the feeling that they were living in a replica of an old castle. We wouldn't fool them; we'd just make it as much like it would have been in the old days. I'm afraid you'll have to do a lot of research on it for me."

Cindy caught her breath. So Peter was not going to walk out of her life. Or perhaps it would be more accurate to say he was not going to let her walk out of his.

The Golden Maze

"I'll enjoy it," she said breathlessly.

They took their time, wandering up and down the different flights of stairs, going into the lofty cold rooms, many of them filled with furniture that was covered with sacking.

"When mother was alive, everything was different," Peter said wistfully.

"I imagine in those days you had quite a big staff?"

"Actually, we did. I suppose dad, on his own, didn't need them. I wonder why he took on Mrs. Stone?"

"Ask Mrs. Usher," Cindy suggested. "She knows everything."

Peter laughed, "I will, too!"

They went down into the vaults. No sign of Paul Stone anywhere. It was dark and cold and Cindy shivered, imagining the days long gone by when in real castles these horrible places might be full of prisoners.

"I wonder where Yvonne is," she said as they went back to what Peter called the civilized part and Mrs. Stone brought them coffee.

Peter gave Cindy an odd look. "She's a perfectionist. She has some idea that the imaginary path—for that's what I think it is—holds some secret and that it must be discovered if we're to get the castle's full value." He laughed. "Honestly, Cindy, she amazes me. That girl has a one-track mind: money! She can't bear to be cheated or fooled."

Cindy sat silently, listening as Peter tried to make her understand Yvonne. He did it in a surprisingly gentle way, almost as if he were a father talking of a difficult child he loved. For it seemed to Cindy that Peter's love for Yvonne showed all the way through.

Yvonne joined them just before lunch. She looked tired and bad-tempered.

"You'd think some of the locals would know about the path," she grumbled. "Or is it just that they won't tell me?"

"Why not go and ask Mrs. Usher?" Cindy suggested. "She's very helpful."

"Where does she live?" Yvonne asked, so Cindy told her. "I'll go down this afternoon."

"Mrs. Usher likes an after-lunch nap, Yvonne," Peter pointed out.

Yvonne frowned. "So what?"

"Why not go about half-past three," said Cindy. "She'll give you a marvelous tea."

Cindy went walking that afternoon, but first she drove down to the village and parked her car before walking along the side of the lake. Here she was under the shadow of the mountain behind her, but she could just see the castle through the groups of trees. It was cold and she shivered; yet anything was better than staying in the castle and listening to Yvonne laying down the law as to what should be done to make the castle a financial success. Peter must really love her, Cindy thought, to have the patience to listen to her all the time. It was odd, because Peter was *not* a patient man. Nor was he—what was the word—biddable. He did what he liked. Yet he often seemed to give way to Yvonne. It could only mean one thing: he loved her.

That evening, the guests arrived for dinner: Luke and Maidie Fairhead, Mrs. Usher, David Baxter and Johanna Younge. Mrs. Stone cooked a delicious dinner of roast duckling and the conversation was easygoing. Cindy sat next to Luke Fairhead, with David on her other side. David hardly spoke to her, but that didn't matter, for Luke Fairhead had plenty to say. Yvonne, of course, was very much the hostess, but afterward, as they all went to the drawing room to have coffee around the huge log fire, David Baxter went to sit by Yvonne, Cindy by Mrs. Usher, and Johanna was left with the Fairheads and Peter.

Not unnaturally, both the Fairheads had a lot of questions to ask Peter, for both were interested in his adventures since he had left. Johanna sat still, looking attractive, her hands folded almost meekly as she looked at Peter. But Cindy noticed that she kept glancing to where David and Yvonne were talking seriously.

Poor Johanna, Cindy thought, *loving David, and now Yvonne has walked in.* For despite Johanna's beauty, she was nothing in comparison with Yvonne, who was years younger and much more beautiful. Cindy sighed, glad she had Mrs. Usher to talk to, for Cindy knew she herself was the plainest of them all.

"It must be wonderful to be so beautiful," she said wistfully to Mrs. Usher.

The little old lady chuckled. "They pay a price later. Can you imagine how ghastly it must be to look in the mirror and say, 'My, can that be me?' in horror?"

Cindy laughed, "I say that all the time!"

Mrs. Usher looked at her. "Your trouble, child, is that you believe what those naughty cousins of yours said. You mustn't. Can't you see they wouldn't have said it if they weren't jealous?"

Cindy was startled. "They were jealous of me?"

"Why not? Your face has an unusual charm, a sort of fey look. Heart-shaped with huge dark eyes and the prettiest of hair. You look kind of cute with your glasses on."

"Oh, Mrs. Usher, that's just what Mr. Jenkins—he's my boss—said."

"Did he now? Shows the man had some sense. Tell me what he said."

It was quite early when Johanna said she had to go. Peter took her to her car, and when he came back he had a puzzled look, Cindy noticed.

Gradually everyone went, the last being David, who seemed unwilling to leave.

"That'll be fun, David," Yvonne said gaily. "I'll meet you for lunch tomorrow. Peter will drive me in."

As Cindy went to her room, she realized with a shock that her week was nearly up. On Sunday she could go back to London. How swiftly the past few days had gone. The best way would be to slip off early on Sunday, before breakfast, perhaps, leaving the diary and a letter for Peter. No doubt they'd be glad to go down and find she had gone—for good.

But the diary had to be somewhere safe, Cindy thought worriedly. Whatever happened, Peter had to see it. Maybe it would be safer if she took it back to London and then posted it to him? If she registered it, he'd have to get it, because it could be traced.

At breakfast next morning, Peter looked at Cindy.

"Yvonne's lunching with my cousin. Care to come along and we can lunch somewhere? Good idea? Looks as if it's going to be a nice day after all."

Yvonne buttered her toast and looked up. "You don't mind my lunching with David, Peter?"

He looked surprised. "Of course not, Yvonne. I'm afraid we've never got on well."

"So I gathered. I wonder why? He seems intelligent, easy to talk to, full of good ideas."

"That invariably fail and he rushes to someone with a soft heart for help. I gather from Luke that David practically bled dad, always asking for money."

The Golden Maze

"Oh, Mr. Fairhead!" Yvonne said scornfully. "These narrow-minded country people! No doubt your father saw David as the son who'd let him down."

A dull flush filled Peter's cheeks, and Cindy wondered what he'd say. To her surprise he merely smiled. "Is that David's line? Well, I've some work to do, but I'll pick you both up around about twelve. Okay?"

"Okay," they agreed, and he left them.

Yvonne glanced at Cindy. "You don't like David?"

"I don't know him. I think he was—well, very unlike Peter when I could really see him."

"It must be an awful bind having to wear glasses," Yvonne said sympathetically. "It makes you lose all your real personality."

Cindy managed a laugh. "I loathed them when I was younger, but I'm beginning to get used to them. My boss told me that I was even prettier in them."

Yvonne laughed. "Some boss! He likes you, I take it."

"Actually, he's very sweet. None of the other girls can stand him because he loses his temper and shouts at them."

"And not at you?" Yvonne poured herself out some more coffee.

"Oh, yes, he yells at me more than at them. But I know he doesn't mean it. You see, he can never forgive himself if he makes a mistake. And he makes lots, so he has to yell at someone who happens to be handy."

"It sounds as though you're in love with him," commented Yvonne. "Rather surprises me, because I thought—"

Peter came into the room. "Yvonne, David's on the phone and wants to speak to you."

"Oh, no! I hope he doesn't want to cancel our lunch,

because I've a lot of questions to ask him. I was wondering if a boutique would pay off in Keswick."

"I think there are several already," Peter said dryly.

"That means there's a market." Yvonne gulped down the remains of her coffee and hurried from the room.

Peter stayed, leaning against the door. "What were you two talking about?" he asked.

Cindy hastily finished her coffee, too. "About my boss."

"Are you in love with him?"

"Well, not really," she said slowly. "I do like him very much. He's thoughtful and kind."

"These are important traits to you?"

"Traits?" Cindy wrinkled her face as she tried to understand, and then she nodded, her hair swinging. "Oh, yes. I think one wants to be loved by someone kind."

"He loves you? He's said so?"

"Oh, no, of course not," Cindy said hastily. "There's never been any question. I mean, I don't really know him."

"He's never taken you out to lunch?" Peter said dryly.

"Lunch? Goodness, no! Oh, once he did take me out to dinner, but that was different."

"Why was it different?" Peter came and straddled a chair, looking at her curiously.

"Well we'd been working very late. He'd been away ill and everything had just piled up. There was just Mr. Jenkins and me in the office, and we both had a shock when we saw the time. It was nine-thirty! 'I'm starving,' he said, 'so must you be. Let's get something to eat.'" Cindy laughed. "We were both so tired he

The Golden Maze

yawned all through the meal, and then he paid for a taxi to take me home."

"Home?"

"I have a bed-sitter in Earl's Court."

"Did you ask him in for a drink?"

Cindy looked startled. "Of course not! I could hardly stay awake. Besides, he didn't come with me, just put me in the taxi and gave me a pound note. He said I could give him the change next day—which I did."

"Very thoughtful of him. I expect he'll be glad you're going back."

Cindy laughed. "He told me I mustn't stay away more than a week or he'd go mad. None of the other girls can stand him, nor he them. He says they can't spell and the files get in a mess."

"And you can spell and the files don't get in a mess?" Peter asked, a strange smile on his face.

"Yes, I am lucky that way," Cindy said gravely. "It's just having a photographic memory."

"Useful." Peter looked at his watch. "I must go. I want to talk with Johanna Younge. She was very strange last night when I saw her out to her car. She said she was sure she'd seen Yvonne before, yet she couldn't place her. Then she said she might remember it in the night and would I look in to see her." He laughed. "She's very amusing as a rule, but I don't know what was wrong last night, because I've never known her so quiet. Not that I ever really *knew* her. I think we actually met once. But she used to go to the club quite a lot and I saw her there—the life and soul of the party. Last night she was very... well, not herself."

Cindy hesitated. Should she tell him that Johanna was in love with David and that he'd had eyes only for Yvonne? Peter was in one of his gentle moods but was just as likely to change, and he might accuse her of being unkind to Yvonne, so Cindy decided to say nothing.

Peter drove them to Kendal, where Yvonne was meeting David, and then he drove Cindy around. The sun shone, the snow on top of the mountains sparkled, the lakes looked placid, the villages were huddled together. Together they admired Windermere, with the distant mountains and the trees sheltering the little stone houses.

"I imagine that lake would be packed in the summer," Peter said dryly. "Steamers and launches."

They went to Thirlmere, to Derwentwater, finally lunching at Keswick. Cindy had been quiet all the way; indeed, she had little chance to talk, for Peter seemed full of life and kept her amused with tales of the first time he went climbing and how once, when camping, he had crawled into his sleeping bag to find it full of water. He really seemed cheerful and she was glad, for it meant she would have a happy memory of this, their last day together.

At lunch he startled her by saying abruptly, "I expect you're looking forward to being back at work on Monday."

"Well, I . . . ." Cindy wasn't sure what to say.

"You must have missed your friends and found life rather boring up here, as well as lonely."

Cindy stared at him in amazement. All those things were the very last she could have felt up here. Everything had happened so fast, so much had happened.

"I've... I've thoroughly enjoyed my stay here. I certainly wasn't bored."

"Good. Only it's a drab life for the very young."

"I'm not the very young," she said slowly.

The Golden Maze

He laughed, and she saw he was teasing her and she had, as usual, risen to the bait.

"Anyhow, your boss'll be glad to have you back," Peter said cheerfully, as if that finalized everything.

Afterward he drove her around the lakes again, showing her what they had missed. He showed her the Langdale Pikes, even taking her to the Dungeon Ghyll Force, where the waterfall plunges sixty feet into a basinlike valley between huge cliffs. At Blea Tarn they looked back at Great Langdale. It was all so beautiful, even though parts of the bleak mountains were eerily depressing and this would be her last view, for she knew that she would never come up here again. Once she had gone out of Peter's life, she must never return. That was the only way to avoid heartache... if it was to be avoided, which she doubted.

Finally they drove back to the castle.

"Enjoy the trip?" Peter asked her cheerfully.

"Very much," Cindy said brightly. It meant nothing to him at all that she was going away, nothing whatsoever. He had met her, and now she was going. It was as simple as that.

In any case, why should he miss her when he had Yvonne to be his companion?

Yvonne looked up to greet them. She was sitting at the table, papers before her and a pen in her hand.

"I've got a wonderful idea, Peter. David and I think it would work," she said eagerly. "Now if we were to build on at the back of the castle...."

Cindy escaped to her bedroom and reached it just in time before the tears came. She stood in the middle of the room, her hands pressed against her eyes as she tried to stop crying. The castle was Yvonne's—Yvonne's and Peter's—and it looked as if David was easing his way in and she was the one left out. This was a fact Cindy had to accept—the hardest she had ever known.

The evening seemed endless. Yvonne chatted away, while Peter listened patiently and Cindy twisted her hair around her hand until Yvonne told her to stop fidgeting.

"You're not a child, Cindy. Do grow up!" she said in the patient voice of an exasperated adult.

"I'm sorry, I didn't realize," Cindy said, and stood up. "I think I'll have an early night."

"Good idea!" Yvonne smiled sweetly. "You have a long journey tomorrow."

Both Yvonne and Peter, though neither had mentioned it, had remembered that that day was Cindy's last. Both probably were pleased, Cindy thought miserably.

She carefully packed her clothes, putting Uncle Robert's diary under everything. The first thing she would do in London would be to post it back and register it! At least in that way she could repay Uncle Robert a little for his remembering her.

It was hard to sleep. She hugged her pillow, almost like a child hugging her teddy bear for comfort. How could she bear it, she asked herself. How could she look at Peter and calmly say goodbye?

Next morning, she awoke early and she got up soon after six, washed, dressed and hastily scribbled a note for Peter: "Thanks for everything, Cindy."

She crept down the stairs of the quiet castle, left the note on the silver platter in the hall, and then, hoping the heavy wooden door's squeaks and groans wouldn't wake anyone up, she let herself outside, her suitcase in hand.

Quickly she walked around the back to the garages.

The Golden Maze

As she backed the car out, Paul Stone walked out of the kitchen.

"Where are you off to?" he asked.

"Home," she said simply, and drove away.

It was still very dark, the sky starting to brighten, and Cindy drove carefully along the track back toward the main road. But suddenly it began to rain. It was only a drizzle, but it blotted out the fells, and now the depressing mistiness came down to shut out the new light and everything else. Cindy felt a strangely frightening feeling of finality—almost as if she were in a small oasis of isolation. Again she felt the terrible depression she had known before she heard of her chance to own the castle—the awful feeling of belonging to no one, of knowing that no one cared about her.

She had to drive slowly, for it was difficult to see, but as she reached the main road, the mist lifted and everything was for a brief moment beautifully clear. Then the rain fell and really fell. A great gray curtain of water was before her and her windscreen wipers seemed inadequate to do their job. Suddenly the car skidded, and though she tried to save it, it went off the road, bouncing against a tree and stopping dead.

For a moment she sat stunned. Luckily she had been crawling along, so she had not been flung forward through the windscreen; she had only bumped her head badly. She moved her legs, arms and hands nervously. Nothing was broken!

She heard a car draw up and someone shouting and turned as a man came running toward her. Dimly she saw his face but did not know him, and then everything went black....

When she came around, something hot was stinging

her throat. She opened her eyes to see the man bending over her, a flask at her mouth as he gently eased down a little brandy.

"Nasty shock," he said tersely. "Skidded, eh? Lucky thing you were going so slowly. I was behind you. Could hardly see a thing."

"It...it was a bit of a shock," Cindy whispered. "I...I think I'm all right."

"But your car isn't. We'll have to get it towed. I'm taking you to a hospital."

"But I'm all right," Cindy said quickly.

"Is that so?" he asked, amused. He was a man of about Luke Fairhead's age, Cindy saw. "You should see the bulge on your head! Reckon by tomorrow your eyes will be black. No, I'm taking you along to have an X ray. Can't be too careful about bumps on the head. Come along, see if you can walk to my car. I'll bring your suitcase and lock your car; then I'll phone a garage for you."

Cindy managed to get out of the car. Her legs felt absurdly shaky and yet she felt quite well.

"Where were you off to?" he asked as he helped her walk along slowly.

"London. I've got to go—I must be at work tomorrow."

The man chuckled. "A likely story! You can ring your boss and explain. Reckon he wouldn't want you around with two black eyes. You been on holiday?"

"I've been staying...staying at Claife Castle."

"Oh, there," the man laughed. "It's certainly been in the news lately. You must be Miss Preston."

"Yes." A spurt of energy filled Cindy. "And I did *not* promise to sell the castle to any American!" she said angrily.

"Of course you didn't," the man said soothingly, helping her into his car. "If you'd promised, you'd not have been such a fool as to tell the world, now would you?"

Cindy hadn't thought of it from that angle. She wondered why Peter hadn't.

The man hurried and got the suitcase, which he put in the trunk, then handed her the car keys.

"This is very good of you, Mr.—" said Cindy. She was beginning to feel better. Gently she touched her forehead. He was right; there was a swelling there.

"Eastwood. Tony Eastwood. A married man with six children, five girls and a boy," he said cheerfully. "Now I'm taking you to the hospital for an X ray."

"I don't think—"

He turned and smiled. Now she could see that he was a big man with a double chin and dark eyes and practically bald. She put her hand to her glasses. How easily she could have broken them!

"Your nose is a bit cut," he told her with a grin. "Don't think your beauty will be harmed."

"My beauty?" Cindy found herself laughing. "This is good of you!"

"Pleasure. Think what a wonderful dinner story this will be. By the way, I gather the real heir turned up, so the castle isn't yours. Bad luck. A rare old monstrosity, but you can't help being fond of it. What'll the real heir do? Sell it?"

"Oh, no, he's got lots of plans—" Cindy stopped abruptly. After all, she didn't know the truth. She had no idea just what Peter's future plans would be. Would he follow her suggestion and make it into a mock-medieval castle, or Yvonne's and turn it into an up-to-date hotel?

They stopped outside a long building and Mr. Eastwood took Cindy in, handing her over to the casualty doctor.

"I'll come back for you," he promised. "Meanwhile I'll arrange for your car to be towed to a garage."

"Will it take long? The repairs, I mean," Cindy asked worriedly.

"Not more than a few days, I reckon."

"A few days?" Cindy caught her breath with dismay. "Then I'd better stay at a hotel near the garage...."

"Don't you worry—just leave it all to me," Mr. Eastwood said, striding away, leaving Cindy sitting in the chair, waiting for her X ray.

CHAPTER TEN

CINDY HAD JUST BEEN TOLD that the X ray showed no damage had been done when a little nurse came and said, "The gentleman is waiting outside, Miss Preston."

Following the nurse to the square in front of the hospital, Cindy stopped still, staring unbelievingly before her.

"It's you!" she gasped.

Peter came forward with a grin. "Who else? I've got your suitcase in the car."

"But, Peter, I asked Mr. Eastwood to find me a hotel while the car's repaired."

"Mr. Eastwood had enough sense to know I wouldn't allow that. You're coming back to the castle with me and going to bed. It must have been quite a shock." He gripped her arm firmly and led her to the car. "He told me you were driving very carefully, or it could have been what he called a nasty business."

"But, Peter, I've got to get to London and—"

"You can phone your boss. I'm sure a kind man will understand," he said sarcastically.

Cindy looked at him quickly. "I'd really rather not come back."

"I'm afraid you have no choice," he said casually. "As I said once before, I'm much bigger and stronger than you."

"Oh, Peter..." Cindy began, and then, just as before found herself laughing. "What do you propose to do? Drag me by my hair?"

He glanced at her as he drove through the High Street, past the impressive cross in the middle of the road.

"Well, it's long enough. The X ray was okay?"

"Yes, nothing's wrong with me."

"Good. The car won't take long. Probably be ready by Wednesday."

"Wednesday?" Cindy almost wailed.

"Your boss can always cut it out of your holiday time if he feels like it."

"He wouldn't!"

"Of course not. I was forgetting what a fine man he is," Peter said, again in an odd voice that made Cindy glance at him. "Why did you go off without saying goodbye, Cindy?"

"I left a note. I hate goodbyes."

"As it turned out, it wasn't."

She wondered what Yvonne would say and wasn't at all surprised when they reached the castle to have Yvonne look at her and declare, "I might have known it! You castle maniacs just can't stay away. It's in your blood, like some virus."

"I hardly think Cindy's so addicted to the castle as to risk her life," Peter said dryly, for which Cindy was grateful.

She went to bed—not because she felt ill, but because she felt exhausted, limp, unable to face up to Yvonne's accusing eyes or Mrs. Stone's disapproving face. On Monday she stayed in bed, too, pleading nervous exhaustion and no doubt pleasing both Yvonne and Peter, she thought. He had sent up quite a few

The Golden Maze

books for her to read from the library, so she was quite happy—except now and then, when she realized Peter was downstairs and that she was deliberately denying herself the pleasure of his company. But was it pleasure, she wondered, when it hurt so much? Her eyes were black, as her rescuer had expected.

Next day Cindy decided she couldn't pretend any longer to be ill, so she went down for breakfast.

"Had a good rest?" Yvonne greeted her. "My word, your eyes!"

Cindy smiled. "I feel fine, thanks. I must phone my boss. Is that okay, Peter?"

"Of course, be my guest," he said.

"Isn't that what she is?" Yvonne asked sweetly.

"Not a very willing one," Peter said with a chuckle. "I had to practically force her to come back."

Yvonne looked skeptical.

"How long will the car be, did you say, Peter?" Cindy asked. "I could go up by train...."

"That's absurd. You'd have to come back to fetch the car. I think it'll be ready tomorrow or the next day."

"Then I *could* be back at work on Thursday...."

"Depends on the weather. If the fog comes down, better make it the following Monday," Peter said with a grin.

The telephone was in the library, so after ten o'clock, remembering her boss's late appearance at the office, Cindy phoned him.

"You've what?" he said. "Had a car accident? Are you all right?"

"I'm fine. I had to have an X ray, as I hit my head, but everything's okay. It's the car. It got rather badly damaged and may take a few days to be put right. You do understand? Oh, thanks so much, I knew you would. Thank you very much indeed. That's lovely," Cindy finished warmly, and replaced the receiver.

Peter stood in the doorway, an odd look on his face. "He took it all right?"

"Oh, yes," Cindy smiled. "He was quite worried. Told me to rest, as delayed shock often happens days later. He says I'm not to go back to work until next Monday. But all the same, Peter, I'd like to go as soon as the car is ready."

"Of course, I understand your eagerness to return to your job," he said curtly, and walked out of the room.

The next thing was to write to Keith Ayres. Not that there was much to say—just that now that Peter, the real heir, had turned up, she was leaving as soon as she could. She began:

> I expect you saw the article in the paper. I imagine it had something to do with the letter I posted you. No one here—or at least only a couple—will believe me when I say I didn't phone the newspaper, in fact didn't know *anything* about the American's offer. It hasn't been very nice for me—being practically called a liar—and I shall be glad to be back in London. It was maddening to have the accident just as I was on my way back. I'm all right, but the car needs repairing and I don't think I'll be back much before Thursday or Friday.

She sealed the envelope and drove down to the village, borrowing Peter's car. Not eager to get back to the castle, she went into Johanna's tea shop.

Johanna came to greet her. "Nice to see you. Sure you're all right? Your poor eyes!"

"You heard about the accident." Cindy pretended to sigh. "One can't do anything in this village without everyone knowing."

Bringing two cups of coffee, Johanna sat down opposite Cindy.

"She's very beautiful," Johanna said abruptly.

Cindy looked at her sympathetically. "I know."

"I hear she had lunch with David next day."

"Yes."

There was a silence while they both looked at one another. "I thought it was her and Peter," said Johanna.

"I still think so," Cindy told her quickly, and saw the relief in Johanna's eyes. "I think she was talking business with David. Something about opening a boutique up here."

"Is that all?" Johanna seemed to relax. "You know, it's a funny thing, Cindy, but I'm sure I've met her somewhere. I can't place it, and yet I have this strange feeling. Maybe it's her voice. I don't know, I just don't know. I told Peter so."

"And what did he say?"

"He looked amused and said he doubted it very much, that this was Yvonne's first trip to Cumberland and he doubted if she'd be likely to have a double."

Cindy laughed, "I'd doubt it, too!"

"And yet I feel certain I've met her somewhere," Johanna mused.

Back at the castle, Cindy saw it was time for lunch. But only Peter was there. He looked puzzled.

"I thought Yvonne was with you," he said, almost accusingly. "I've been with Luke Fairhead all the time."

"She wasn't with me."

Peter shrugged. "Maybe she's gone to see David."

"But how could she without a car?"

"That's a point—or he could have called for her. Mrs. Stone," he asked as the tall thin woman brought in the bowls of tomato soup, "any idea where Miss Todd is? Did she ask Paul to drive her anywhere?"

Mrs. Stone looked quite offended. "She did not. I saw her go off wandering down the slope—beyond t'end of the garden."

"What would she be doing there?"

Showing off her sharp teeth in a grimace, Mrs. Stone shrugged.

"Maybe looking for that path she's so interested in."

"Well, we'll have lunch, but keep something hot for her, will you?" Peter asked. "She'll probably turn up soon."

But Yvonne didn't. At three o'clock, when there was still no sign of her, Peter went in search of Cindy.

"We're going to look for her. You stay here, Cindy. I'll take Paul and Luke."

"I'll come, too," Cindy said quickly.

"No, you won't."

"Yes, I will," Cindy said firmly. "She might have fallen and hurt herself, so I'll bring some brandy."

"Look, you'll be nothing but a nuisance—" Peter began, when there was a hammering at the front door.

It was Luke Fairhead and Paul Stone.

Luke spoke first. "Ah, good, Miss Preston. You come with me and we'll drive down to the lake and start from there. Peter, you and young Stone start from the top and work your way down...."

"I'm going to help Mr. Fairhead, Peter," she said firmly.

"Okay. Not so dangerous working your way up," he said abruptly. "Come on, Stone."

The Golden Maze

Mr. Fairhead drove Cindy down to the lake's edge.

"I can't think what Yvonne could be doing down here. She's looking for that mystery path, but—"

Mr. Fairhead chuckled. "Women are queer cattle, Miss Preston. I gather she's always searching for some way or other to make money."

"I suppose money is important."

"It's a great help when you're very young or very old. However, 'twould not be so important to me as having work I love. You got a job you like?"

"I'm a secretary to a very nice man."

"That's good. Look, we'll park this way along here, now. There are some caves just above this spear of land."

"Caves?"

"Yes, mostly grown over by grass and dangerous. Only a fool would go into them," he said, giving her a hand as they went up the steep grass-covered side of the mountain.

They reached a small flat surface. Tall grass and matted fern covered the outside of the caves.

"Miss Todd!" he shouted, holding his hands over his mouth to form a funnel. "Miss Todd!"

A faint sound replied and he turned to look at Cindy.

"I think we've found her already. You wait here," he ordered, and broke down some of the long bracken. "I'm coming..." he shouted. Then he vanished into the dark opening of the cave.

Cindy waited. All was still. She wondered if she should follow him into the cave. But then, if he didn't come out, who would there be to tell Peter? She decided to wait, as Mr. Fairhead had said.

Then she heard shouts from above and she made out Peter's tall body leaning over a boulder and looking down.

"We think we've found her... in the caves!" Cindy shouted.

"Tell Luke to stay out. He's too fat!" Peter yelled back. But it was too late!

It was five or more minutes before Peter and Paul Stone slid to the ground by her side. Paul, grumbling under his breath, dived into the cave. Peter looked at Cindy.

"Give me your word you won't go in," he said curtly.

Something seemed to snap inside her. "What's the good, when you think me a liar?"

His hands closed on her arms and he shook her. "Look, cut out this childish nonsense. I do *not* think you're a liar. If you go in there.... Look..." he began again. "It can be pretty dicey in these caves. If none of us gets out, you'll have to call for help. If you're in, as well, no one will know. Is that clear?"

"Yes, that's clear. I give you my word," she said. "But, Peter—" her voice shook a little "—be careful, won't you?"

He gave her a strange look. "Of course I will."

Then he let go of her and pushed his way through the bracken into the cave. Cindy stood trembling. Three men and Yvonne in there. Why were they so long? Surely the caves weren't so big....

And then Luke Fairhead came out, scrambling on his knees. He stood up, brushing down his corduroy breeches and smiling at her.

"It's all right. She was caught in a narrow turn. Silly young fool, she shoulda known better."

"Peter?" Cindy asked.

"He's coming. He and Paul are easing her along. Seems she's a bit hystericallike. Not that I blame her.

Fair gives you a fright, being stuck in those dark caves."

"Why did she go in there in the first place?" Cindy asked.

A question that Peter repeated an hour later after they had carried Yvonne to the car, driven her back to the castle and got her propped up in a chair, sipping some brandy.

"Why on earth did you go in alone, Yvonne?" he asked angrily, impatiently pacing up and down. "Any fool knows these caves aren't safe."

"Well, this fool didn't," said Yvonne. She was apparently over her shock and fear. "I find caves fascinating, and when I saw this big cave with the high roof, I thought I could squeeze around the corner. I was too fat...." She looked at her watch. "You left it pretty late, Peter," she said accusingly. "Why didn't you come and look for me before?"

"Hadn't a clue where you were. I thought you might have sneaked off for lunch with David," he grinned. "Then Mrs. Stone told me you'd gone for a walk down the garden and I thought maybe you'd got down to the lake, decided to have lunch there."

"A fine story!" Yvonne's eyes were angry. "I suppose the truth is you just couldn't be bothered."

"Why should I be bothered, Yvonne? You're not a child. I credited you with enough sense not to do such a crazy idiotic thing. What were you looking for in those caves?"

Yvonne looked startled. "Looking for? Why—well, nothing really. I just find caves fascinating and...."

Cindy slipped out of the room unnoticed. Obviously they were about to start another of their friendly "quarrels," and she wanted to have nothing to do with it.

At dinner, the quarrel seemed to have been over and forgotten, for when Cindy joined them in the drawing room for a drink, Peter was telling Yvonne about the castle. He looked up with a smile when Cindy arrived.

"You might be interested in this, too, Cindy," he said as he went to pour her out a drink. "Yvonne asked me when and why the castle was built." He gave Cindy the glass and sat down by the huge log fire. "It was some time in the eighteenth century that a man called Penn lived in the village. He was a farmer and through clever breeding and a stroke of luck, his sheep were exceptionally good and bought by people from overseas who were building up their farmlands. He did well and fell in love with a girl of a good family who also happened to be wealthy. Penn felt ashamed, for he had so little to offer her save money, so he had the castle built, copying some famous castle—which one, I've no idea. He hoped it would make the world treat him like an aristocrat. I don't know if it worked. Anyhow, years later, a Penn married a Baxter, and that's how *we* got here. Actually, Caterina—a local Gypsy you'll probably see, she tells fortunes—has it that the castle is cursed because its women have been so timid. The Mrs. Penn I was talking about is said to have been as timid as a mouse, and so was the Penn daughter who married a Baxter." He gave a little grunt. "So was my mother another quiet little mouse."

Yvonne laughed. "Would you like a quiet little mouse for a wife, Peter?"

"Most certainly not," he said, getting up to refill the glasses. "It would be intolerably boring."

Cindy looked at Yvonne, who smiled at her. Yvonne looked pleased with herself, Cindy thought. One thing, when Peter married Yvonne, he would not be married to a "quiet little mouse," so perhaps the legend of the family curse would end.

When Cindy woke up next day, she was amazed at the rain that was coming down heavily. The clouds seemed to have split, and it was hard to see the lake, even as the mist curdled and then cleared for a moment before shutting out the view again. She dressed quickly and hurried downstairs. It was the same on every side. The dales looked as black as tar, and the whipping wind was tossing the peaceful lake, forcing the water up in the air in waves. She was glad to see Mrs. Stone had lit fires in both the dining room and drawing room, for it was bitterly cold.

Yvonne was irritable. "It would rain now, just when I'm getting somewhere!"

Peter looked interested. "Somewhere?"

"Yes, this mysterious path that no one seems to know about or where it is. It must be somewhere, and I'm determined to find it. How long will the rain last?"

"Ask me!" Peter laughed. "It can go on for days or weeks." He smiled at Cindy. "Don't look so depressed; I don't think it will. Anyhow, I have a lot to discuss with Luke, so see you both at lunchtime. Don't go doing too much, either of you, because I don't want two invalids on my hands." He smiled and left them.

"Men!" Yvonne said with a sigh. "They treat everything so casually. If they succeed—well, it's their good luck; and if they fail, it most certainly isn't their fault. A woman attacks a problem quite differently. Don't you agree, Cindy?"

"I honestly don't know. Well, yes, in a way I do agree," Cindy said, remembering how hard she had worked at school and then at shorthand and typing so that she could escape from her unfriendly family.

"Good. We see eye to eye about a lot of things, Cindy, don't we?" Yvonne's smile was so sweet that Cindy felt nervous. Now what was Yvonne planning? It seemed it was nothing, for Yvonne merely announced that she had letters to write and would be in the library if anyone came to see her.

That could only be David Baxter, Cindy thought, as she curled up on the rug before the log fire and read the newspapers. She was leaning against an armchair and must have dozed off, for she awakened suddenly to a loud voice.

"I said get out and I mean get out! We don't take tramps in here!"

It could only be Mrs. Stone, Cindy thought at once, and scrambled to her feet. Maybe she needed help.

In the hall Cindy stopped with surprise. It was no tramp who stood on the doorstep asking to come in. Two walkers stood there, wearing thick dark blue trousers, bright red anoraks, with matching woolen caps, and colossal packs on their backs. They were dripping with water, and both had long hair that hung over their faces so that you could hardly see their eyes.

"Just to get dry, please," the girl begged, almost in tears.

"You heard what I said: we don't take in tramps anytime."

Cindy walked toward the door. "Mrs. Stone, I'm sure Mr. Baxter wouldn't want you to turn them away. Please come in. You poor things, you certainly are wet!"

Mrs. Stone was white with fury. "You've no right... just you wait." She mumbled the words, but Cindy gathered that she was furious. Then Mrs. Stone said loudly, her shrill voice echoing in the lofty hall, "All that water on my polished floor! In any case, we don't want no hippies anytime."

The two of them were sliding the huge bundles off their backs and taking off their wet anoraks, shaking the water off them.

They ignored Mrs. Stone and turned to Cindy.

"It began to rain just after we started walking. We didn't think it would be much. I'm Martin Haynes, and this is Roxanna Webster."

"I'm Cindy Preston."

Now she could see they were both about her age. Martin might even be younger, in his bright yellow shirt and thick white sweater as he tossed back his long brown hair. Roxanna had long black hair that she swept back with a dramatic gesture to smile at Cindy.

"You've saved our lives. I don't think I could have walked another step!"

"Nonsense, Roxanna," Martin said with a smile.

Cindy turned to the tall silent angry woman by her side.

"Would you please make some hot chocolate for us all, Mrs. Stone; then could you dry their clothes in the kitchen? Would you take off your boots, too?" Cindy asked the two walkers. "Then come and sit by the fire. You'll soon dry."

Mrs. Stone's mouth was like a tightly closed purse, but she did what Cindy asked: carried the wet clothes and boots to the kitchen and made them all hot chocolate. Sprawling on the rug by the roaring fire, they chatted.

"I don't know how you can enjoy walking when you have to carry everything. . . . It must be a weight," said Cindy.

"You get used to it." Martin was warming his fingers by holding the mug in both hands. "Must say, it was pretty bad today."

"They did warn us at the hostel, Martin," Roxanna said gently.

He laughed. "If we took notice of all the weather reports, we'd get nowhere. Must say, I didn't think it could be so bad."

"Where are you making for?"

Martin shrugged. "Just anywhere. This is our favorite part of the world, especially in winter, when no one's around."

"You know this part well?" Yvonne asked.

Startled, Cindy turned around, for she hadn't heard Yvonne come in. Now Yvonne came eagerly to sit down by them.

"Yvonne, Roxanna, Martin." Cindy quickly introduced them and stood up. "I'll just go and check that Mrs. Stone is drying your clothes," she promised, and left them alone.

Mrs. Stone was stiff with fury as she let fly at Cindy.

"I have to keep the place clean, and no easy job is it anytime, and with them dripping water everywhere! Never did like that kind of hippie. Shouldn't wonder if 'tain't really burglars having a good look-see before breaking in!"

"If they make a mess, Mrs. Stone, I'll clear it up," Cindy promised. "But it's such a terrible day. Do you often get it like this?"

"Anytime it comes down like so, it stays for days, even weeks." Mrs. Stone looked almost triumphant. "How long will you be here?"

"Only until my car is repaired." Cindy looked out of the kitchen window at the gray curtain of misty rain.

"Though I can't see myself driving through this sort of weather."

Mrs. Stone was busy at the stove, stirring something. Now she looked up. "When will she be going?" Mrs. Stone jerked her head and Cindy knew she could only mean Yvonne.

"I don't know." Cindy hesitated, and Mrs. Stone put Cindy's thoughts into words.

"Maybe she won't ever go now?"

"Well, I honestly don't know." Cindy wandered around the kitchen. "You see, I don't really know either of them, Mrs. Stone. What a gorgeous smell! You really are a wonderful cook."

Mrs. Stone sniffed. "Have to be when you've a living to make and a son to rear. 'Twasn't easy when my husband died and I had a child and never'd done nothing but housework. Mr. Baxter—Mr. Robert Baxter, that is—he gave me this job. I knew 'twould be hard work, but I didn't mind. We had a home and...I thought," she added bitterly, "a future."

Cindy hesitated. Should she stay and let Mrs. Stone weep on her shoulder? Or—

The bell above the kitchen door rang. Mrs. Stone hastily wiped her hands, pulled her apron straight.

"That front door," she grumbled. "Maybe life'd be easier working in a house rather than t'castle."

Joining the others in the drawing room, Cindy found Yvonne enthralled with what Martin was saying. He was leaning back on his hands, his long hair swinging as he talked dramatically. Roxanna stood up and went to meet Cindy.

"Do you think I could have a quick bath?" she whispered. "I'm still frozen and I feel—well, messy."

"Of course, come up with me." Cindy led the way to

the curving staircase. "I know how you feel. The water is always marvelously hot."

She could see Mrs. Stone at the door talking to a tall woman.

"It won't take more than a few moments anytime." The woman was half-hidden in an enormous loose-hanging mackintosh, with a purple scarf twisted around her head.

"You be off. We want no Gypsies here!" Mrs. Stone snapped, and slammed the door.

Turning, she saw Cindy standing there.

"Only Caterina," Mrs. Stone explained. "Always wanting to tell fortunes, but we won't have nothing to do with such folk anytime. Just layabouts. Too lazy to work, that's what I say." She gave Roxanna a suspicious look. "Remember what I said, Miss Preston, now."

"Yes, Mrs. Stone."

"Who's she? Proper dragon!" Roxanna commented as they went up the stairs.

"Actually, I'm very sorry for her," said Cindy, leading the way to her bedroom. "She was Mr. Baxter's housekeeper for ten years and her son grew up here, and somehow she thought the old man would leave the castle to the son."

"But he didn't. Never does to count your chicks before they're hatched. My mum used to say that and I got real mad with her. But she was right, you know."

"Do you really like all this walking?" Cindy asked curiously.

Roxanna gave her a quick smile. "It isn't the walking...."

Cindy laughed. "It's Martin?"

The Golden Maze

"It's always someone, isn't it?" Roxanna sighed. "It's the only way I can get to be with him. But oh, how my feet hurt!"

Cindy showed her to the bathroom and went to wait in her bedroom, content that Yvonne should be keeping Martin occupied. As she sat there, Cindy read some of Uncle Robert's diary again. The items really were so sad—sometimes cheerful, but always with that wistfulness, that disappointment that things had turned out as they had, always blaming himself for a terrible mistake. In one case, he had written: "I should have realized that Peter is like me. He has to be a person—not someone's shadow."

How right Uncle Robert was, Cindy thought, curled up on the floor before the electric fire. Now David was much more of a shadow—Peter was definitely a person.

The rain was still pelting down when Peter came in for lunch. He looked annoyed but was pleasant to the "guests."

"Real bad luck," he agreed. "Where were you making for? I'll run you over this afternoon, if you like."

Roxanna's eyes glowed. "Would you?" she said eagerly.

"Why not? In the morning the sun may be shining and you won't have wasted a day after all. Care to come, Yvonne?" he asked casually.

"No, thanks." She smiled "I have some phone calls to make. Perhaps Cindy would like to."

"I took that for granted," Peter told her, and looked at Cindy and then at Roxanna. "We won't go until teatime; then you'll get to the hostel in time for your evening meal and bed."

"Thanks a ton," Roxanna said happily. She looked quickly at Cindy and away again. Cindy understood—a whole wonderful day without having to walk! What a girl will do for love, she thought sympathetically.

The rain was still pouring down as Peter drove them to the long gray hostel. Cindy was startled when Peter abruptly asked Martin, "What was Yvonne talking to you about?"

Martin pushed back his hair. "She's interested in folklore; so am I. I told her all the local legends and things."

"She was interested?" Peter sounded amused.

"Yes, particularly anything I knew about the castle. I didn't know much, because it isn't one really, is it? I mean, everyone knows it's a mock castle."

"I agree. Yet she wanted to know all you could tell her about the castle? Was there much?"

"No, very little. The usual tales of the smuggling days. But every old house around the lakes and sea up here has those stories. Seen that old farmhouse near the coast with seven chimneys? Said to have been built by an old man so that each of his jealous daughters could have a chimney. Who'd want a chimney?" Martin chuckled. "Anyhow, the legend is that only two of those chimneys have fireplaces and that the other chimneys were used to hide their smuggling treasures."

"She was interested in that?"

"Very... even asked me where the house was, and when I told her it was for sale—well, she got real excited like."

"I bet she did!" Peter laughed.

They stopped at the hostel, which was comfortably settled at the foot of a mountain and facing the lake, where the wind rippled the water into tiny patterns.

"Thanks a ton," Roxanna said to Cindy. "If it hadn't been for you...."

The Golden Maze

Cindy smiled. "Good luck!"

Roxanna whispered in her ear, "I just hope it goes on raining!" and chuckled as she and Martin left with their heavy packs, turning at the door of the hostel to wave.

Peter drove away. "Funny, that," he commented.

"What's funny?"

"Yvonne's interest in the house with seven chimneys. Surely she wouldn't be mug enough to believe that nonsense about smugglers' treasure? I mean, if there were any there, it would have been found years ago."

Suddenly Cindy had an idea. She opened her mouth and then closed it again. Peter wouldn't believe her. He might even accuse her of cattiness or childishness. Yet she'd had a thought—perhaps that was why Yvonne was so keen to find the mysterious path that had given the castle its name and why she was so concerned about the vaults and Paul Stone digging there. Did she think there was treasure hidden in the castle? Yet it might all be coincidences. It was best to keep quiet, Cindy decided.

"Was it really necessary," Peter asked without warning, "to be quite so abrupt with Mrs. Stone?"

"Abrupt?" Cindy, jerked from her thoughts about Yvonne, turned in surprise. "Was I abrupt?"

"She asked me who was the mistress here, as she didn't know whose orders to obey. She seemed pretty mad."

"I had to rescue them. It was the two...." Quickly she told him how Mrs. Stone had been turning them away, refusing them a chance to dry. "They were wet through and looked half-drowned. She was very rude to them."

"I'm afraid she has an unfortunately abrupt manner," said Peter, his voice suddenly cold. "On the other hand, you have to draw the line somewhere. We can't give hospitality to every Tom, Dick and Harry."

Cindy's cheeks burned. "Under which heading do I come?"

"You know very well I didn't mean you!" he almost snapped at her. "I agree you did right in asking them in. Only a couple of kids," he said almost scornfully. And Cindy, remembering that Roxanna and Martin had been about her age, felt her cheeks burning still more. "Shouldn't be out trekking alone. They could easily get lost. The girl didn't look as if she enjoyed it much."

"She hates it."

"Then why do it?"

Drawing a deep breath, Cindy turned to him. "Are you men blind? She loves him, that's why she does it, and he's too... too selfish to see it!"

"You mean, she walks these miles, gets half-drowned, her feet painful, just because she loves that...? She must be crazy!"

"Most females are. I suppose no man would do such a thing for a girl he loved," Cindy said bitterly. "He'd expect her to mold her life the way he wanted it."

"Well, that's right, isn't it?" he asked, his voice casual.

"No, it is not!" Cindy retorted angrily. "There should be compromise. It shouldn't all be for one to have his own way."

"But you're as bad as the rest of them, Cindy. Look how eager you are to get back to your boss, and I bet he whistles the tune and you do what he says, even when you don't like it."

"The boss—" she began, and stopped. "He never asks me to do anything I don't want to."

Peter whistled softly. "Well, well, well, aren't we a lucky girl!"

She clenched her hands, fighting the desire to smack his face. Instead she turned her back and looked out at the rain-drenched world. Where had the beauty of the mountains and lakes gone? The stark loveliness of the leafless trees had vanished in the mist. Now everything was gray sheets of rain and the maddening tick-tock-tick-tock of the windscreen wipers.

CHAPTER ELEVEN

IT WAS NOT UNTIL they were near the castle that Peter broke the silence, and then only casually, almost as if unaware it had existed.

"Cindy, as I said, I would be grateful if you'd do some research for me about the castle. I think it was designed to be like the castles built in the eleventh and twelfth centuries, but I'm not sure as to the date. I'd like to know what sort of furniture they had in that period and the clothes, so that the staff could wear them. Wasn't it your idea in the first place? After all, as you said, in Ireland it's successful, and there are quite a lot of people who'd get a kick out of living in the past. But, as I say, I want it to be the *right* background."

Cindy turned around a little. She was tempted to refuse, yet knew she never could.

"I'll go to some of the museums and libraries. You are going to run it as a hotel?"

"I can think of no other way. It would cost the earth to have it as a mere home, and it's far too big. I did think of it as a school, but can't imagine it somehow, can you?"

"No." Cindy had to laugh, imagining the swarms of little boys or girls racing up the stairs. "Actually, I think it would be rather dangerous. They'd have to rail off the garden."

"You're right. It's a bit too close to danger."

"You're selling the farm?"

"Yes. I've persuaded old Colin Pritchard to come and be my head gardener. There's a cottage on the fell that he can have, so he'll be quite happy. I'm only keeping ground enough for a flower and vegetable garden, and of course somewhere the guests can sit in the sun.... I might even build a little folly—you know, those comic little sort of summerhouses they built."

"That's a good idea," Cindy said warmly. "You'll want a lot of staff."

"I thought of keeping Mrs. Stone as housekeeper, in charge of the staff. She was good to the old man and seems very efficient."

"She is. And Paul?"

Peter frowned as he turned off the main road and they began to jolt and slide on the muddy track. "I'm not sure. I'll have a good talk with him. He's done absolutely nothing to the garden, but he's a good driver and quite a good mechanic, so I might keep him for that."

"You oughtn't to have cars, but coaches," Cindy pointed out.

"Help! You're right. But can you imagine a coach going down that narrow winding road to the village?"

"Yet it must have done once."

"You're right, you know." Peter sounded surprised.

The rain seemed to have lessened a little as they came in sight of the castle. Cindy gave it a desperate look; she loved it so much. It seemed to her that she was always saying goodbye to it. When would she finally go?

"When will my car be ready?" she asked.

"Ready? Oh, about Thursday or Friday."

"It's taking longer than we expected," she said, dismayed.

Peter shrugged. "So it seems."

Cindy pleaded a headache as an excuse to go to bed early, and after coffee in the drawing room, she left them talking. Halfway upstairs, she remembered she had left her book there, so she went back. As she began to open the door, she heard Peter ask, as if amused, "Planning to buy a house with seven chimneys?"

"So what if I am?" Yvonne snapped back.

Cindy pulled the door to gently. Were they going to start another of those wrangles that depressed her so much? She went up to her bedroom; she would read Uncle Robert's diary instead. There were so many notes and the handwriting so small that there was still quite a lot she hadn't read yet.

It was teatime next day that Keith Ayres arrived. Peter and Yvonne were having tea with Cindy. It was a chilly dismal day, though the rain was less severe. Yvonne was in a strange mood, hardly talking, constantly looking at Cindy as if she wanted to say something but was hesitating.

Mrs. Stone ushered him in. "Mr. Keith Ayres," she announced.

He stood in the doorway, staring at them. They were startled and showed it. Then he went straight to Cindy.

"Miss Preston? Good to see you again." He turned to Peter and held out his hand. "Mr. Baxter, I came up to settle some small details." He looked at Yvonne and waited for Peter to introduce her, which he did promptly.

"Sit down. Have a cup?" Peter asked.

"No, thank you. I had rather a big lunch on the way. I can only stay for a night and if you can't put me up I

The Golden Maze

can go to a hotel somewhere, but there are a few things we have to clear up."

He sat down, speaking curtly, as if angry. Cindy wondered why, for he had been so different before. He was a good-looking older man, with slightly graying hair and a friendly smile when he looked at her.

"Of course you can stay here. I'll tell Mrs. Stone to get your room ready," said Peter, leaving them.

There was a little silence. "You are the solicitor?" Yvonne asked.

Keith Ayres looked at her. "Yes, I am," he said, his words clipped.

Peter returned and sat down. "Was it a bad journey up? I mean much fog?"

"Pretty unpleasant, but it got better when I got nearer here." He looked around. "It's quite some place, isn't it? I'm not surprised Miss Preston liked it." He smiled at Cindy. Then he looked at Peter. "I have an important thing to tell you, which I believe may be of interest. You know all that hullabaloo about the American who wanted to buy this castle?" He waited until they had nodded; then he folded his arms and looked from face to face. "Well, the whole thing was a hoax. There was no American."

"But then—" Cindy began.

"No American?" Peter echoed slowly. "Then why was it in the paper?"

Keith Ayres looked at Yvonne.

"That's absurd," she said. "There was a letter from him."

"I know. Miss Preston sent it to me—unopened." He looked at Peter thoughtfully. "One point was rather interesting. The letter had been posted several days earlier and should have reached the castle *before* the article in the newspaper appeared. Something went wrong and the letter was delayed."

"Paul Stone said the letter *was* opened," Yvonne put in, looking at Cindy. "Why should he lie?"

"Because he hates Miss Preston, and Mr. Baxter. His mother brought him up to believe that Robert Baxter would treat him as a son and leave him the castle and a good sum of money. When the will was read, Paul was furious. I was not there at the time, but my uncle was. He said he thought the boy would have a fit and that Mrs. Stone was extremely rude and wanted to fight the will. But my uncle persuaded her that she had no hope of winning. Probably the boy said the letter was opened by Miss Preston out of sheer malice." Keith smiled at Cindy. "Personally I should have thought that anyone knowing Miss Preston would unhesitatingly believe anything she said."

"The reporter said she rang him up," Yvonne chimed in.

Keith looked at her, his eyes narrowed. "Voices, as doubtless you are aware, can sound very different on the telephone. That sort of evidence would never be accepted in court."

"But who else would do it? I mean, there's no point in it, is there?" Yvonne asked.

Cindy found her voice. "But why should *I* do it? All that happened was that I lost the castle." She stood up, suddenly unable to bear it. "Excuse me," she murmured, hurrying out of the room. They were talking about her as if she weren't there, as if she didn't exist. Why hadn't Peter leaped to her rescue, she wondered. But then, of course, he must be on Yvonne's side. Now who would make up an American buyer?

Suddenly she thought, *Mrs. Stone!* Knowing the local people, she knew there would be an outcry because their precious Claife Castle was to be demolished and removed to America, another land. Perhaps Mrs. Stone hoped that through the noise and arguments, Cindy's right to the heirdom would be queried, for if the castle was left to her only because she *loved* it, wouldn't her apparent willingness to sell it prove she had no right to have it?

Cindy stayed upstairs as long as she could and then went down, for she didn't want to give them a chance to say anything. She hoped they would all have left the drawing room. But they hadn't, though Peter and Keith Ayres were obviously making for the library to talk business. Yvonne saw Cindy coming and stood up.

"You do know, of course, Cindy, that your car has been ready in the garage for two days," she said in her husky voice.

"Two days?" Cindy was startled. "But I was told it wouldn't be ready until Thursday or Friday."

"That's your story," Yvonne said coldly. "The plain truth is that you intend to stay here as long as you can despite the fact that you should have gone long ago. You have no right to be here."

Peter looked startled. "Yvonne, you have no right to say that. I am the host. I asked Cindy to stay. I knew her car was ready, but—"

Cindy was suddenly so angry she could hardly speak. She swung around to stare at Peter.

"You knew? Yet you knew very well I wanted to get back to London. You lied!" she exclaimed angrily.

He smiled and, for a moment, she hated him. He looked so...so *complaisant*, which was not a word used generally, though it was one of her boss's favorites.

"For your own good, Cindy. I didn't think it wise for you to start work again so soon after your near accident.

Besides, I knew you loved the castle and I didn't want to deprive you of the pleasure of being here."

"Oh, you...you...." She was battling between anger and tears. She turned to Keith Ayres and caught hold of his arm. "Would you drive me right away to the garage? I'll pick up my car and I can stay at a hotel. I don't want to be here another moment!"

"Calm down, Cindy," said Peter, and his condescending voice was the last straw. "Mr. Ayres and I have business to talk over. You can leave tomorrow morning, but not before. Come along, Ayres," he said, leading the way.

Cindy rushed by him and stood for a moment on the stairs. "Please ask Mrs. Stone to bring my dinner up," she said. "I never want to speak to either of you again." She turned and ran up the stairs, stumbling, as the tears ran down her cheeks.

In her own room, she stood still, her hands to her eyes. How dared he speak like that? As if she were a small child! How dared he lie like that—telling her the car wasn't ready, making it look as if she were the liar, she the one who wanted to stay....

An hour or so later, there was a knock on Cindy's door and she heard Peter's voice.

"Cindy, I want to speak to you," he said firmly.

She slid off the bed, hastily brushed her hair and went to the door.

"May I come in?" he asked with that slightly pompous air he put on often and that invariably made her want to laugh.

"It's your castle," she muttered, standing back.

He came inside, closed the door and looked at her.

"Isn't it time you behaved like an adult and not like a spoiled child?" he asked her.

The Golden Maze

She was completely taken aback. She wasn't sure what she had expected him to say, but it certainly wasn't what he had.

"Why should I stay there and let Yvonne insult me? She implied that I lied about the car and—"

He smiled. "It was me. I apologize. But honestly, Cindy, it was for your good. However, that's the past. We're now involved in the present. I've invited David and Johanna to dinner as I don't want Keith Ayres to be too utterly bored tonight. Somehow he and Yvonne don't hit it off."

"I'm not surprised," Cindy said bitterly.

Peter laughed. "Oh, it's just her way. If you knew her as well as I do, you'd take no notice." He opened the door. "You'll be down, then?"

"Yes," said Cindy, closing the door quickly, leaning against it. Now why had she agreed? Why should she go and be a sitting duck for Yvonne to aim at? Was she getting like the rest of the females in the Baxter world? A "meek little mouse," dutifully saying yes all the time?

She dressed carefully, wearing her long pale green dress with the high waist. It was the only party dress she had, for she so seldom went out! But with Yvonne and Johanna looking so beautiful, she had to look her best. At the dinner party, Mrs. Usher had mentioned how well she thought it suited Cindy.

"Charming color with your hair, my dear."

A little nervous, Cindy went downstairs. David and Johanna were already there, talking and laughing with Peter over their drinks.

Johanna welcomed her with a smile, but David with only a stiff jerk of his head. Cindy wondered why he disliked her so much. Then Yvonne came in with a flourish, looking ravishing in a shimmering gold maxi-dress.

"David!" she said, holding out both her hands. "I'm so glad you could come. Peter and Keith will talk shop all the time and one gets so unutterably bored." She flung a quick vague smile at Johanna and ignored Cindy completely.

Dinner was pleasant; as usual, Mrs. Stone had proved what a competent cook she was. Afterward, as they sat in the drawing room with coffee and liqueurs, Yvonne sat next to David, as she had done at dinner, talking and laughing with him, while Johanna talked stiffly to Keith and Cindy found herself with Peter.

"I wonder where Roxanna and Martin are," said Cindy, more for something impersonal to talk about than because she was interested.

"At least the rain is ceasing, so they should start walking soon," he said casually.

Suddenly he leaned forward, speaking so loudly that everyone automatically looked at him, so that there were no longer three groups of two people talking but one large group.

"Have you heard the latest, Johanna?" he asked with a laugh. "Yvonne has fallen for the old story about the house with seven chimneys. I think she's even trying to buy it!"

As he spoke, he glanced at his cousin David, who immediately looked uncomfortable, fidgeting a little in his chair.

"Well, why not? These legends can't last for years without there being some truth in them," Yvonne defended herself quickly.

Suddenly Johanna clicked her fingers. "I've got it!" She looked triumphant and amazingly beautiful in her

The Golden Maze

straight white silk dress. Now her face seemed to glow; her eyes sparkled. "I remember where I met you!" Johanna pointed a finger at Yvonne. "It was a few days before Cindy came. You came into my tea shop and—"

"That's absurd, Johanna," Peter said with a smile. "Yvonne had never been in the Lake District before she came here."

Johanna swung around to him. "Oh, yes, I *know* she was here. It was something she said to me that day. You had a blond wig on," Johanna said accusingly to the startled Yvonne. "And you looked fatter and much—well, less with it. Also, you wore dark glasses. As soon as you started asking questions about Claife Castle, I knew you were from the south. I thought, *what a lot of idiots you must be to believe that after all these years the smugglers' treasure would still be hidden.* It so happened I was pretty bored that day, so I played you up. I told you a lot of codswallop about the treasure in the castle, which could only be discovered by finding the mysterious path that gave this castle its name. And you said," Johanna went on triumphantly, "just as you said just now—that's how I recognized your voice—'These legends couldn't last for years without there being some truth in them.'"

Yvonne's face had gone very white, but now her cheeks were flaming with anger.

"You lied to me? Why, you...you...." She nearly exploded.

Johanna laughed. "Why not? Only a sucker like you would have fallen, so I laid it on good and thick."

"You...you...." Yvonne half rose from her chair, looking as if she were going to fly at Johanna in her fury.

Peter spoke quietly, very quietly, so that Cindy's heart seemed to skip a beat.

"You came up here at once to find out about the castle, Yvonne? You made up the yarn about the American buyer because you wanted me to claim the castle?"

"Of course I did. It was for you." Yvonne turned toward him, her face still flushed. "I had to do something, because you were so stubborn. I came up to see if the castle was worth having. I decided it wasn't because of what it would cost to modernize it. Then this—this—" she bit back her angry words and glared at Johanna, who was sitting back, her hands folded demurely, her eyes bright with triumph "—lied to me. I thought when I heard about the treasure that had been hidden for centuries it might be found by modern methods. I thought it worth trying as an investment."

"You phoned the newspaper to get publicity and make me believe that Cindy was—" Peter began, still with that ominous quietness that made Cindy shiver but that Yvonne didn't seem to notice.

She even smiled. "Of course I did. I had to do something to make you claim the castle. You were being so impossible, giving away the castle—and perhaps a hidden treasure—to a bit of a girl we didn't even know. The treasure was yours by right, and I was determined you should have it. Yes, I wrote the letter, which was, unfortunately, delayed. It should have been here before the article in the newspaper. Not my fault. I phoned the newspaper, yes, and it worked," she went on triumphantly. "You claimed the castle and... and...." Her words began to die as she looked at Johanna. "You... you..." Yvonne spluttered.

Cindy sat hunched up, words growing inside her, angry, accusing, ugly words. How could Yvonne be so mean, so greedy, so money-mad? It didn't make sense.

It was something she just couldn't understand. It would have been easier to understand if it had been who Cindy had thought: Mrs. Stone. At least she had her love for her son to excuse her. But Yvonne....

There was a strange silence in the room. David was leaning back in his chair, arms folded, a dismayed look on his face. Johanna was obviously delighted at the way she had fought her rival. Keith Ayres looked puzzled, glancing from Yvonne to Peter and then back to Yvonne.

It was Peter who spoke first, quietly but so firmly that no one could argue with him. "This is something we'll discuss tomorrow, Yvonne," he said coldly. "Now let's forget it. No one wants to see his dirty washing hanging on the line. Mr. Ayres, I would like you to meet Luke Fairhead tomorrow," Peter said, his voice conversationally casual as he turned to the solicitor. Then he looked at Johanna. "It can't be true that you're thinking of selling your tea shop and leaving us?"

"I was... maybe I won't go now," said Johanna, looking quickly at David, whose face was flushed, as if annoyed.

But Yvonne was not content to leave it at that. She stood up, glared at Johanna and then at Peter.

"A fine way to treat a friend, I must say," she said angrily. "*I did it for you*. I'll see you in the morning," she added, and flounced out of the room.

There was another strange silence, and then Johanna looked at Peter. "I'm sorry if I put my foot in it," she said, her voice sincere. "It just came out. I had no idea it was Yvonne until she said those same words and I recognized her at once."

He smiled; a little wearily, Cindy thought.

"Not to worry, Johanna. I had thought it was Yvonne because I know how crazy she is about making money, but I had no way of proving it. I'm glad it came out this way."

How brave he was, Cindy was thinking. She longed to comfort him, for how hurt he must be that the girl he loved could behave so meanly. Yet she knew there was nothing she could say. She turned to Keith Ayres, by her side.

"Have you never been here before?" she asked, her voice a little shrill, which startled her. "It's very lovely."

Keith Ayres looked at her thoughtfully. "So I've heard. You don't mind the rain and the cold?"

Somehow the evening dragged by, with everyone obviously doing his or her best to behave normally; yet undoubtedly the memory of Yvonne Todd, with her flaming cheeks and flashing eyes as she defended herself with the words "I did it for you," could not leave them. At last Peter went outside into the damp night to see Johanna and David off, and Keith was alone with Cindy.

"I'm sorry you should have been involved in all this unpleasantness," he said in his rather nice deep voice. "It must have been an ordeal."

Cindy shivered. "It has been. I thought it was Mrs. Stone. I can't understand Yvonne. She's so clever and—"

"A gambler," Peter said as he joined them.

Cindy felt her cheeks burn as she looked at him apologetically. "I...I...."

Peter smiled at her. "That's all right, Cindy. I owe you an apology, if anything. Yvonne is a brilliant financier, but her one weakness is gambling. I imagine it's

The Golden Maze

like a disease. Perhaps you'd agree?" Peter turned to Keith Ayres, who nodded.

"Absolutely. The bug bites them and they lose their senses. I can quite see how she felt, though I do rather...." Keith hesitated, looking at Cindy.

Peter nodded. "So do I. Well, Cindy, so you'll be off tomorrow," he said cheerfully. "I'll be seeing Yvonne in the morning, and then we can have a chat with Luke, but—"

"Mr. Ayres will drive me to the garage to pick up my car," Cindy said quickly. *Why prolong the agony,* she asked herself, and although she knew the words sounded melodramatic, at least they were the truth. Why did love have to hurt one so, she wondered.

"Good," said Peter, still cheerful. "See you in the morning," he said, and walked toward the library, looking back. "I wonder if you could spare me a moment here, Ayres. It might be an idea if we looked at these figures now—save time in the morning. I know Cindy is eager to get off."

Cindy went upstairs slowly. It meant nothing to Peter that tomorrow she was going. Really, this time! Alone in her room, she looked at Uncle Robert's diary. Should she hand it to Peter tomorrow? Would he impatiently toss it aside? Would it have more weight with him if it came by post together with an explanatory letter, she wondered. He could be so impatient at times; he might not give her a chance to tell him what he had to know.

The door handle turned. Hastily she tucked the book under her pillow and wondered if she had done it fast enough as Mrs. Stone appeared, a hot-water bottle in her hand. Every night she put a bottle in each bed, but surely tonight she was rather late.

"It's very good of you, Mrs. Stone" said Cindy, uncomfortably aware that Mrs. Stone was looking at her curiously. This wasn't the first time Mrs. Stone had nearly caught her reading Uncle Robert's notes, Cindy realized. Anyhow, only tonight left, she comforted herself. This time tomorrow she would be miles away....

Alone. Alone in her miserable little bed-sitter. How was she going to bear it?

Simple, she told herself as she quickly undressed. She had no choice. It was as simple as that.

CHAPTER TWELVE

IN THE MORNING Cindy found only Keith in the dining room. Mrs. Stone was telling him that Mr. Baxter and Miss Todd had gone off some time before—and that Miss Todd had taken all her luggage with her. This, Mrs. Stone said almost triumphantly, and she glanced silently at Cindy as if thinking, *well she'll be gone soon, too!*

As they ate the well-cooked bacon and eggs, Keith Ayres looked at Cindy.

"I think you took it very well yesterday. Most girls would have been furious with Miss Todd."

Cindy smiled. "I was—terribly angry. There were lots of things I wanted to say, but what was the good? The damage was done."

"I still think you're being very generous. The castle would have been yours all right. Peter Baxter didn't want it."

Cindy poured out some more coffee. "I'm afraid you were right, you know." She sighed. "I had a long talk with Mr. Fairhead—you'll like him, a very nice man—and quite honestly, I don't know *how* I was going to keep the castle going, so maybe it's better this way. At least Uncle Robert would be happy knowing Peter was here."

Keith Ayres passed her the toast, then the butter and marmalade. "Mrs. Stone is a good cook."

"Isn't she?" Cindy gave a little laugh. "I had a feeling that it was Mrs. Stone who'd told the newspaper all those lies. I never once thought of Yvonne."

"It's certainly more understandable from Mrs. Stone's point of view," Keith Ayres agreed. He glanced at her thoughtfully. "Is it true, Miss Preston, that you're in love with your boss?"

"In love with my boss?" Cindy was startled. "What makes you ask that?"

"Just that Peter Baxter is rather annoyed because you're so eager to get back to London. He said you were crazy about your boss."

Cindy laughed. "Of course I'm not! I only said he was a good thoughtful boss and I liked him. Peter jumped to conclusions, that's all."

"I see." He smiled. "Then you're not bespoken for."

"Goodness, no," Cindy said quickly, and wished Keith Ayres would not look at her so intently. She began to twirl a spoon on the tablecloth, concentrating on it.

"Not by anyone?" Keith Ayres asked quietly.

"Not by anyone." After all, that was the truth, Cindy thought. She loved Peter, but that didn't mean he loved her!

"I wonder when he'll be back." Keith Ayres sounded impatient. "I want to get to London and I know you do, too. I wonder if it might be a good idea to go and get your car now."

"Oh, no," Cindy said quickly. "Peter will have arranged for you to meet Luke Fairhead and he—well, he would be annoyed if you weren't here when he got back. It sounds as if he was driving Yvonne to the station, but it wouldn't surprise me in the least if she came back with him."

"You think he'd let her?"

Cindy shrugged. "They're always quarreling—you should hear them—and the next moment smiling at one another. It's just the sort of quarreling some married people seem to enjoy."

"For the making up again?" he suggested.

"Yes."

"So you think they'll... marry?"

Shrugging again, Cindy said, "I honestly don't know. She seems to think so. She said they would only live up here a part of the year but usually they'd be in London."

"And he—what did he say?"

"Oh, he wasn't there. He's never said anything about marriage, but he's—well, I would say he is in love with her, because he lets her nag him and he finds it funny. Now if I tried to do that...."

"He wouldn't find it funny?"

"He'd tell me to stop acting like a child," Cindy said ruefully.

They finished breakfast and went to stand outside the castle. The sun was not out, but at least it was not raining. Cindy waved her hand toward the lake.

"Isn't it beautiful?"

Keith Ayres gave her a quick look. "You'll miss it. Very different from London's traffic and noise."

"I know," Cindy said wistfully. "However, I do get out in the country at weekends. Having a car makes that easy."

They walked toward the cliff edge where the grass slid down toward the water and turned to look at the castle.

"I must confess," Keith Ayres said slowly, "to me it's just a castle—a big one and in good condition, admittedly, but all the same a mock castle. No history, nothing to make it stand out."

"But it's beautiful!" Cindy turned to him. "Don't you love all those towers and the funny chimneys at the back and... and...."

"Everything? You love it because it was a childhood dream. I think we all remember certain times when we were very happy when young."

Cindy didn't answer for a moment. She was staring at the castle, taking in the beauty of the battlements, the aged drawbridge, the water that still trickled through what had once been the moat. How many times must she say goodbye to the castle, she wondered sadly, for each time it was harder than before.

A car came up the drive. They turned and saw Peter, who waved, and as soon as he was out of the car, came striding across to them. He looked pleased with life.

"Here I am. Sorry to have kept you waiting," he said cheerfully. Then he looked at Cindy and his voice changed. "I imagine you'll want to pack. You can have your chauffeur in an hour's time. Come on, Ayres, Luke will be waiting for us."

The two men walked away. Cindy looked up at the majestic facade of the castle once again and then went into the hall and up to her room. She finished packing, locked the suitcase and took it down to the hall. Then she went into the library to look through the many books in order to pass the time. She found one that interested her—it was to do with the future of castles and questioned how much longer castles would be protected and paid for by the state.

Curled up on the window seat, Cindy was reading

The Golden Maze

this when she heard a noise in the hall. She began to get up and then sat back, for it was probably Mrs. Stone polishing the beautifully carved banister and Cindy was in no mood for Mrs. Stone's icy glare.

When Cindy heard the men's voices in the hall, she hurried to join them. They were talking seriously, but both smiled as they saw her.

"A cup of coffee," Peter said cheerfully, "and then you can be on your way. I've phoned the garage, Cindy, and the car is ready for you. Luckily not too much damage was done. I'll just tell Mrs. Stone."

"No, I will," Cindy said, and ran down the hall to the baize door that shut off the kitchen area. "Mrs. Stone!" she called, and heard a drawer slam. Mrs. Stone came to meet her, her face flushed, her hair more wispy than usual.

"What is it now?" she asked crossly.

"Mr. Baxter would like coffee for the three of us, please," Cindy said, and hurried back to the men, who were still talking in the drawing room.

The coffee came—delicious, as usual, and very hot. As they drank it, Cindy listened to the two men discussing the castle's finances.

"Admittedly, it means a good deal would have to be invested, but I agree that it should pay in the long run. It could be the sort of hotel that would attract tourists." Keith Ayres grinned. "Why not ask Miss Younge to be receptionist? Her tales of hidden treasure might encourage even more visitors!"

A cloud seemed to pass over Peter's face, but it was soon gone. "A good idea—if she stays here. I think she's getting rather fed up with life."

"She's lonely," said Cindy.

Keith Ayres turned at once. "Aren't we all? I don't

know about you, Miss Preston, but I reckon one of the loneliest places in the world is a bed-sitter in London."

Cindy nodded. "I should know," she agreed. "I'd have thought you'd make friends more easily here."

"I agree all the way," said Peter, "but it might not be friends who talk your language, share your interests. I think that's the trouble with Johanna. She feels she's growing old before her time. Maybe a difficult job in London would boost her morale a bit. She's still a very attractive person."

Everyone was attractive to Peter except herself, Cindy thought unhappily. Keith Ayres, glancing at his watch, stood up.

"I'll just go up to my room and check that I've left nothing out. I see your suitcase is already down," he said to Cindy.

"Yes."

And then they were alone, she and Peter. Peter stirred his coffee slowly, looking intently at it.

Suddenly Cindy could bear it no more. Poor Peter, he was so miserable and so bravely hiding it.

"I'm sorry about Yvonne," she said gently. "Some people are made like that."

Peter looked up. "Don't be sorry for her, Cindy, she needs a good spanking. It was the meanest, most disgusting trick to play. And all because she wants more money. She's already incredibly wealthy. She inherited a fortune from her grandfather."

"I...." Cindy hesitated, but she had to know. "Are you going to marry her?"

"What? Me?" Peter was obviously amazed. "What on earth made you think that?"

Cindy twirled a spoon, avoiding his eyes. "She...

she told me that you—well, she said, '*We* will only live here part of the year.'"

"Yvonne was always implying that we should marry, but no... my word, Cindy! Imagine being married to her!" He laughed suddenly. "I wouldn't wish it on my worst enemy. I've known her for years, met her in Australia first. We always seem to be meeting by chance—that is, by chance where I'm concerned. I sometimes wondered if she wasn't there with a purpose. You see, her father's a stockbroker and she's really good about stocks and shares and advises me. Marriage? Never!" he said scornfully.

He stood up, as if eager to be rid of her, Cindy thought, so she stood up, too. Then Peter startled her as he said, almost wistfully, "I just wish dad knew that I was doing what he wanted me to do...."

She knew in that moment that Peter was in a receptive mood.

"Peter," she said, catching hold of his arm, "will you promise to let me say something without jumping down my throat or telling me to grow up?"

He looked amused. "Okay, but what's it all about?"

"Your father, Peter. Please... please don't interrupt. I'll be as quick as I can, but... but you must let me tell you," she said breathlessly, unaware that she was clinging to his arm. "I found your father's diary in a secret drawer in his desk. Maybe I shouldn't have read it, but I wondered what sort of a man he was. Peter, he never got *one* of your letters. He kept saying in the notes that if only you would write a few lines to let him know you were well.... That time you came to see him, he was ill. Not very, but Mrs. Stone refused to let him have visitors. He said she fussed and he was lonely, but he was too tired to fight her. Peter, I believe Mrs. Stone kept those letters from your father, that it was she who told you to get out, and not your father at all." Cindy stopped, completely breathless as she stared at the man standing silent by her side.

"You've got the diary?" he asked gruffly, his face looking grave.

"Yes, in my suitcase. I've got the key here. I was afraid you wouldn't listen to me. I've made notes of the dates to look at, because your father wrote terribly small and it's hard to read. I was so afraid your impatience would make you toss it to one side, but you should read it; you must...."

"Well, let's get it."

They went to the hall. Cindy bent over the suitcase, then looked up, her face startled. "The lock's been broken!"

Peter bent down by her side to look at it. "Been forced open," he said curtly. "We'd better see Mrs. Stone."

Keith Ayres came down the stairs. "Trouble?" he inquired.

"It seems Cindy found some notes my father had written and she thought I should read them. She left them in here, but the lock's been broken."

"Better make sure they're not inside."

Cindy looked up. "They won't be." She was nearly in tears. It was so terribly important that Peter should see his father's words, to know his father had forgiven him and wanted to be forgiven in turn. However, she opened the suitcase. "I left them on the top."

They weren't there!

Peter was down the hall in a moment. Cindy hurried after him, Keith Ayres close behind.

The Golden Maze

Mrs. Stone was stirring a saucepan on the stove and looked startled to see the three of them coming out.

"You want some coffee now?" she asked.

"No, Mrs. Stone," Peter said quietly. "I want my father's diary."

"Your father's diary? What's t'do with me? I don't know anything about your father's notes," she said.

"The lock on Miss Preston's suitcase in the hall has been broken and the diary taken out."

Mrs. Stone looked indignant. "She's accusing me, is she now? Well, maybe you'd better look at her. No doubt she broke the lock so that she could accuse me and make trouble."

"Mrs. Stone," Peter said even more quietly, "this is a serious matter. Did you or did you not break open Miss Preston's suitcase and remove a book?"

"I...did...not!" Mrs. Stone almost shouted.

Suddenly Cindy remembered something. When she had hurried out to Mrs. Stone to ask her for some coffee, she'd heard a drawer slam.

"Peter," she said, "it's in one of the drawers."

She knew she was right, for Mrs. Stone's face turned almost purple. "You've got no right t'open the drawers. They're my private property!"

"They are not, you know," Keith Ayres said gently. "We have every right to look in them."

"You—Mr. Baxter, now, it's not fair...." Mrs. Stone waved a wooden spoon at them. "Never before has anyone accused me of theft!"

"Mrs. Stone—" Cindy felt she could no longer hold her tongue "—you didn't want those notes read because you knew Mr. Baxter would say he'd never received a letter; nor did he ever know his son had been to see him."

Mrs. Stone's cheeks were bright red now, her eyes flashing vindictively. "Ever since you came here, you've tried t'cause trouble, anytime. I am not a liar or a thief, and I—"

"Careful, Mrs. Stone," said Keith Ayres, turning from a drawer in the dresser. "I've found the diary!"

He handed the long flat book to Peter, who opened it, frowning a little as he saw the tiny neat print, then unfolded a piece of paper. "You worked hard on this, Cindy," he said. "It means a lot to you?"

"I want you to know that your father did love you," she said earnestly. "It's so terrible when you feel no one loves you."

He turned to Mrs. Stone. "Did you send the letters back to me, Mrs. Stone? Was it a lie when you told me my father never wanted to see me again?" He patted the book in his hands. "I have the evidence here."

It was as if something exploded in Mrs. Stone, for suddenly she was screaming at him.

"Of course I did! I had to keep you away from him. 'Twasn't fair, and that's the truth. You go off to live your own life and I look after him—then up you turn and expect to start again. What about the work I did? What about my son, Paul? A proper son to the old man, he was. And what do I get for my ten years' work? A paltry thousand quid and nothing for my poor Paul, who'd been a-counting on it.... I had to think of Paul, and I knew you didn't really care...."

Peter took Cindy by the arm and bent over, whispering to her.

"Please go, Cindy, I'd rather handle this on my own. Look after this, though." He gave her the diary.

She obeyed and went to stand in the drawing room, by the French window, looking through blurred eyes at the serene blue lake below. The sun had thrust the clouds on one side; the distant mountains were almost blue in the strange light. Poor Mrs. Stone, Cindy was thinking. It was understandable when Mrs. Stone loved her only child so much. Cindy hoped Peter would be charitable.

When the two men rejoined her, she saw that Peter was the cheerful one.

"Don't look so worried, Cindy," he said. "I'll see that she's looked after financially. They'll have to go, of course, but I'll give her a good reference."

"But what will you do?" Cindy's eyes widened with dismay. "You can't cook and clean the castle, Peter."

He laughed, "Not to worry, Cindy. I have friends. Probably Luke's wife will come and lend a hand or find someone from the village. It'll be better without the Stones on the property. She gives me the creeps and he makes me want to box his cheeky ears." He smiled as he turned to Keith Ayres. "Sorry to land you in my domestic troubles like this." He took the book from Cindy. "Thanks, Cindy, for going to so much trouble. I'll read every word if it takes me the rest of my life," he promised with a smile.

"I found a magnifying glass helpful. I've got one in my suitcase."

"There's one in the library, thanks. Well—" Peter looked at them both "—you want to be on your way, I suppose. Let's take the luggage out to the car. One thing, the weather is good."

Silently Cindy followed as Peter carried her suitcase. She gave one last look around the huge lofty hall and then walked across the gravel to the car, trying not to look back at the castle but failing at the last moment. She stared up at it as it towered above her. The castle where she had known both sadness and happiness. She would never forget it, she knew that.

"Cindy," Peter urged, and she looked around. He was standing by the car, holding the door open. She realized with a shock that he was eager to get rid of them.

"Thanks," she said as she got in by Keith Ayres's side.

Peter closed the door, tested it to make sure it was shut, then spoke through the window. "You won't forget the research you promised to do for me, Cindy?"

His face was so near and yet so far. Her hand ached as she fought the longing just to stroke his cheek once. The tears seemed to be gathering, but she managed a watery smile.

"I won't forget, Peter," she said, and as the car moved forward, she added quietly, "Anything."

"A nasty business for Peter Baxter," Keith Ayres observed as the track neared the main road.

"Horrible," Cindy agreed, grateful that he had kept silent for so long. She had fought and overcome the desire to look back at the castle. After all, she didn't really need to look at it—she had only to close her eyes and she could see it again, with all its mock majesty. In a way it was a farce, something to make people laugh. Just as her love for Peter was... a farce.

"Poor Mrs. Stone," she sighed. "She only wants to help Paul."

"Actually, she's doing the worst thing she can do for the boy. He's a cheeky layabout, that's all. Do him good to have to work."

"But will he ever work?"

"That's her problem. Tell me, what do you think of Peter Baxter?" Keith Ayres asked suddenly.

"Peter? Well, I like him...very much," Cindy said without thinking. "Don't you?" She turned to look at her companion.

"I do and I don't," he said as they turned off the track onto the main road. "He's either extremely self-disciplined or very callous. He seems to take everything in his stride—his girl friend's behavior, the housekeeper who hurt his father so much by holding back those letters and not letting the old man see his son.... Yet Peter Baxter—well, I don't know what to make of him."

"He told me he wasn't in love with Yvonne. He said there was nothing like that—just that they've known one another for years and she advised him about stocks and shares."

"I gathered she was very bright. Honestly, though, how she fell for that tale about treasure in the castle! I suppose that once a gambler, always a gambler. You say you like Peter Baxter. He seems to like you. He's paying all your expenses for your trip up here. I've been given instructions to send you a substantial check."

What was Peter doing, Cindy thought unhappily. Paying her off?

"There's no need for him to do that," she said aloud.

"There is. The estate would have paid your expenses anyhow. I just wondered how you saw him."

"Well, it's difficult," Cindy said slowly. "He's kind and thoughtful, and yet he can be very cruel. He was always saying I was so young and a child and—"

"I suppose to a man of thirty-three, a girl of nineteen is rather young."

"I suppose so," Cindy said miserably. "Almost a different generation."

"He's very—well, let's say authoritative. I suppose he's been in executive positions?"

"I don't know, really. He's an engineer and has been in Africa, Australia, Canada, practically everywhere."

"Somehow I can't see him settling down to a cabbage existence in the castle."

"Why should that be a cabbage existence?" Cindy asked quickly.

Keith Ayres shrugged. "Sooner him than me. The countryside is lovely, but—"

"But...?" Cindy was almost aggressive at the thought of anyone attacking her beloved Lakeland.

"What sort of people will he meet? The Fairheads—but they're years older. Of course there's always Johanna," Keith Ayres chuckled. "Maybe she'll get her fangs in him now that Miss Todd is away."

"Johanna is in love with David."

"But David is obviously not in love with Johanna," Keith Ayres said with equal haste. "So where will Johanna look now?"

Cindy was glad they had reached the garage then, so that she need not answer. But it was the seed of a thought he had tossed into her brain, a seed that was to grow with alarming speed in the next few days.

She could see her little gray car waiting for her and pointed it out to her companion. He looked rather amused.

"You won't want me driving on your tail all the time, so I suggest we meet for lunch. I'll drive ahead and book a table." He told her the name of the place he suggested and of a good hotel he knew there.

"If you don't turn up," he promised, "I'll come and look for you."

"I shall be all right," she said stiffly.

He smiled. "I'm sure you will, but at the moment you're a little trouble-prone. Everything you have to do with seems to go wrong."

How right he was, Cindy thought as she watched the large dark green car pull out and she went to find the garage owner.

"What do I owe you?" she asked him, a little nervous, for she was afraid it might be more than the cash she had with her.

"Nothing, miss." The manager, a tall thin man with a cap pulled over one eye, smiled. "Mr. Baxter, he paid for it."

"Oh!" Cindy frowned. "It's... it's all right now?"

"Fine... goes like t'little bomb, it does, anytime," the man told her with a smile.

Driving along the roads, Cindy had little time to think; yet at the back of her mind gnawed several unhappy thoughts. Peter's obvious eagerness to get rid of them. Who was he expecting? Had he merely left Yvonne somewhere and promised to fetch her back when the others were safely out of the way? Or was it Johanna? Keith Ayres's suggestion was growing fast in her mind. Peter had obviously liked Johanna... and Johanna? Caught on the rebound, she could easily mistake liking for love.

Cindy was quite relieved when she reached the hotel Keith had told her about and he was waiting for her. There was no doubt but that he was a very nice man. She felt so relaxed when she was with him, for he talked interestingly and made her laugh a lot.

They were having coffee when Keith took her breath away, without warning, as he said abruptly, "It's Peter, isn't it?"

To Cindy's horror, the tears stung her eyes. She nodded silently. Keith leaned forward and put his hand over hers.

"You poor darling," he said tenderly.

CHAPTER THIRTEEN

CINDY'S RETURN TO LONDON was like a nightmare. Her small square bed-sitter, with its narrow bed, curtained corner that was a wardrobe, small table and chair and dismal lime green curtains, was such a contrast to the huge rooms of the castle that she found herself constantly comparing them. She realized she had also been spoiled, taking it for granted her meals would be prepared, whereas now she forgot her evening meal and did no shopping.

She couldn't have returned at a worse time, for after she and Keith Ayres had parted after lunch, they ran into rain and the last part of her journey was a miserable one, with the rain pounding down mercilessly. There was, of course, no one to greet her after she had parked her little car and carried her suitcase back up to her bed-sitter on the fourth floor. Somehow, that evening, she missed the welcome she had never known before her stay at the castle. It was so still—not even Mrs. Craddock, her landlady, in sight as she trudged up the steep narrow staircase, her suitcase dragging her back. Then she opened the door and the awful dull impersonality of the room hit her.

She closed the door, leaning against it, looking around at the smallness. There was no possible way of calling it "home." She knew, though, that it was mostly her own fault. She had wanted to save up for a car so much that nothing else mattered; hence, she was paying as low a rent as she could. Nor had she spent money on bright posters or gay bedcovers, as others had. She shuddered at the thought of what Peter would say if he ever saw this dingy cell, for that was what it was. The cell in which she was a prisoner....

Hastily she unpacked. Realizing she had no food, she unearthed a box of water biscuits and some honey and made herself a cup of coffee. An early night would be a good idea.

But was it? She tossed and turned in the narrow bed, moving quickly several times and nearly falling out! Sleep was far away. No matter how hard she tried to push the castle and Peter out of her thoughts they returned again and again, refusing to be forgotten.

How kind Keith Ayres had been, she mused, grateful for a different thought. She had nearly cried, but after he had comforted her, he had changed the subject and even made her laugh. Was it so obvious, Cindy found herself wondering anxiously. If Keith Ayres could see her love for Peter so plainly, then could...?

She squirmed in the narrow bed. Was that why Peter was so eager to see them go? Why he had almost pushed them out of the castle. Because he thought she was *after* him!

Tears finally helped her and she fell asleep with her cheeks wet. In the morning she awoke and faced the truth. She had to accept it! There was nothing else she could do.

She had a warm welcome at the office on Monday when she began work, the girls crowding around to hear what had happened. Cindy hesitated about telling them everything, for she had no desire to cause more trouble.

The Golden Maze

"The real heir, Mr. Baxter's son, was found," she explained simply.

But the girls weren't prepared to leave it at that.

"What about that article in the papers? Were you really going to get twenty thousand pounds for the castle?" Maggie asked eagerly.

"I knew nothing about that until someone showed me the paper," Cindy could say truthfully. "It was all a hoax."

Maggie looked disappointed. "You mean, it wasn't true? There wasn't an American?"

"No, someone did it for a—"

"Joke? Funny kind of joke," Maggie declared, and Cindy silently agreed with her.

Yvonne's "joke" had lost Cindy the castle; yet Cindy knew in her heart that she could never have kept the castle, for how could she, a girl of nineteen, ever raise the money required? It was different for a man of Peter's age and finances.

Mr. Jenkins was more discerning. As he dictated the letters, he sighed and Cindy looked up. Her boss's face was grave.

"Miss Preston," he said slowly, "I see you have your glasses on today, so that can't be used as an excuse. What have you in mind?"

Cindy's forehead wrinkled as she stared at him. "I... what—what have I in mind?"

He nodded. "Yes, what excuse today have you for the fact that I've dictated for ten minutes and you haven't done a single one of those little squiggles you seem so efficient in reading back," he said dryly.

Cindy looked at her notebook in dismay. He was right. She had neither heard nor realized she wasn't listening. She had been thinking of Peter... wondering how he was managing with no Mrs. Stone there. Had Johanna taken him under her wing, or was it Mrs. Fairhead?

"I'm sorry," she said sincerely.

Mr. Jenkins gave an odd smile. "That's good of you. So am I. Before you went to see your castle, Miss Preston, you were extremely on edge, making foolish mistakes that were unlike you, but which I forgave, as I know what heartache can do. Then this excitement about the mock castle and off you go, thrilled. Now you come back, even less aware of what's going on around you than before. We seem to be back to square one. Just what has happened? You've fallen in love?"

"Yes," Cindy admitted.

"I see. And he?"

"Sees me as a child and...and...."

Mr. Jenkins smiled. "Well, it's hard not to, Miss Preston. I suppose you'll get over it if I bear with you?"

Cindy blinked. "Of course. I have no choice."

"Very sensible of you, Miss Preston. I suggest you type the letters you've got down and maybe tomorrow you'll be feeling better. Meanwhile, send Maggie in to me; she can do the rest of the letters."

"Yes, Mr. Jenkins." Gratefully Cindy escaped to her little office, pausing to tell Miss Point what Mr. Jenkins had said.

That night Cindy went home, having been to the supermarket and bought a "meal in a bag" that she could heat up on her gas ring. Her depression was, if anything, greater than ever. The drabness of the room seemed even more stark than before. How could she bear to go on living in this...this.... She couldn't find a word to describe it.

As her dinner slowly cooked, she read the evening paper—not really reading, her eyes skimming over the words—because it was better to do something than just sit there and think.

It was the word America that caught her eye and made her start to really read the short article about an employment agency that made a speciality of finding efficient British secretaries for jobs in the States. The pay was good, though the qualifications demanded were high.

Was that the answer, Cindy wondered. It was unusual for her to buy an evening paper. Why had she done so tonight? Was it to find a way to escape? A completely new life, different people, a challenge to her?

Wouldn't that be wiser than sitting here in this... this... and fretting? Surely the only way to overcome painful memories was to lead so busy a life you had no time to sit and mope, she told herself.

She made a note of the name and address of the agency. Would she have time to go in her lunch hour, she wondered. Or perhaps they weren't open at that time. She decided to write to them and ask when it would be convenient to call.

One thing, Mr. Jenkins would give her a good reference, she knew that, and maybe he would be glad to see her go if he was finding her, as he said, "not with it" at the moment. She wrote several letters before she was satisfied with one. Maybe she should have typed it, she thought. Yet she could remember Mr. Jenkins saying that the best way to read a person's character was to look at his handwriting! Cindy studied hers worriedly and then went over the spelling carefully. Luckily, she thought, she was a natural speller.

She addressed the envelope and sealed it. In the lunch hour next day, she'd get a stamp and post it.

Her dinner was bubbling fiercely. She only hoped it was not overdone. Eating it, she found herself looking ahead.... Suppose she was sent to New York. What would it be like? Salaries were very high there, but so was the cost of living, she reminded herself. But it would be nice to meet new people.

She pushed the empty plate on one side, flung herself down on her bed and wept. There was one person she could not fool. Herself!

NEXT DAY she was determinedly bright at the office. Mr. Jenkins made no comments, but she got through all his letters in record time. In the lunch hour she posted the letter to the employment agency.

It was absurd how miserable she felt. Yet she knew she was doing the right thing. *If you can't overcome pain, ignore it; fill your life full,* she told herself sternly.

Mr. Jenkins sent for her that afternoon.

"Miss Preston, full marks for your behavior today," he said with a smile. She smiled back. "Now as a reward, how about having dinner with me tonight?"

She was really startled. Perhaps it showed in her face, because he chuckled.

"My eldest daughter is about your age. She's meeting me with her latest boyfriend. I thought four would be a more comfortable group than three."

"It's very kind of you," Cindy began, and suddenly knew she could not go. Mr. Jenkins's eldest daughter and her latest boyfriend, both probably looking gooey-eyed at one another, which would only make everything much worse. "I'd love to, but—but I have a date."

Mr. Jenkins smiled. "Good—so long as you're not sitting at home alone weeping. It makes your eyes swell, you know."

"Does it?" Cindy's hand flew to her glasses.

Back at her desk she was busy filing when the phone rang. It was a private call for her.

Peter, she thought instantly, her heart seeming to leap with joy.

But it wasn't. It was Keith Ayres.

"How are things going, Cindy?" he asked, his voice concerned. "I guess it must be pretty tough." Actually, he had told her at the lunch they had shared that he felt guilty about her unhappiness and that he should have waited until the three years were up before telling her of the castle.

Cindy managed a little laugh. "It's not exactly easy, Keith, but—"

"I know. Look, I've got tickets for a concert at the Festival Hall and wondered if you'd care to come."

Music! Cindy swallowed. That would be the last straw. She could just see herself, sitting by Keith's side, the tears running down her cheeks. If anything could make her cry, it was music.

"I'm awfully sorry, but I've got a date," she lied.

"I see. Another time?" he spoke cheerfully and she wondered if he knew she wasn't telling the truth. "Be seeing you," he added, and rang off.

She put down the telephone slowly. Was she being stupid, she asked herself. Should she have accepted one of the invitations? It was no good just sitting in that awful little room.... Funny, because until she'd been to the castle, the little room hadn't seemed awful. It was as if the castle and Peter had changed her entire outlook on life.

On the way home, she was tempted to go to a cinema, yet felt that would be just as bad. Just give herself a few days and everything would be better, she tried to comfort herself.

The hall door was always left unlocked. She walked up the steep stairs wearily, thinking of the long lonely hours ahead, and then, as she turned the corner for her last flight, she stopped dead.

It couldn't be true, she thought. It must be a dream. But it wasn't.

Peter was sitting on the stairs, reading a newspaper. He must have heard her gasp, for he put it down and smiled at her.

"Hullo," he said cheerfully.

"But—Peter, what are you doing here?" And then she understood, or thought she did. "I'm afraid I haven't had time to do any research yet," she added.

He folded the paper neatly, stood up and came down the stairs to stand on the small landing by her side.

"I came to ask you to dinner," he said with a smile. Just as if it was the most natural thing in the world, Cindy thought. Somehow it riled her, so she lifted her chin.

"That's funny—you're the third man today who's asked me out," she told him.

"Is that so?" Peter began to laugh. "Looks as if I'm a bit late. Some other time?" He began to turn away and she knew she couldn't do it.

"I said no to the others," she almost whispered.

Peter nodded as he turned back. "I'm glad. I'm really here," he went on, chatting lightly, "to fight your boss. I admit it's hardly fair, for you haven't been working until nine-thirty tonight; nor will we, I hope, both spend the evening yawning." It was the pompous

The Golden Maze

tone she knew so well and loved. As usual, it made her laugh.

"I'd better change," she began.

He looked her up and down thoughtfully—at the white laced boots, the unbuttoned long green coat, the little matching hat perched on the chestnut brown hair that hung to her shoulders.

"I like you as you are," he said lightly, taking her arm. "Come on. No wonder you're so slim—climbing up and down these stairs so often!"

His car was parked close by. As usual, it was difficult to find a parking place in the West End, but he finally succeeded—as he always succeeded, Cindy thought. She hardly talked, glad to leave it to him; yet all the time she was wondering what this was all about. Why had he driven all this way to take her out to dinner? Was he feeling guilty? Was this to be a compensation for Yvonne's behavior? Or was he just being kind?

Despite her tenseness and her knowledge that being with him like this would only make it worse when the parting came again, Cindy enjoyed the evening—a good dinner, then dancing.

She had never been in Peter's arms before. He was much taller than she was, so she was not tempted to put her cheek against his! He danced the old way and actually she preferred it, perhaps because it meant she was in his arms, she thought, and could fool herself for a while.

The evening fled by, with Cindy wishing it would not end, and then Peter took her back to the bed-sitter. In the hall he looked down at her.

"Well?" he asked.

"Well?" she echoed, puzzled.

"Was I as kind and thoughtful as he is?"

"As who?"

Peter chuckled. "Your boss, of course. You were always praising him. Was I? I mean, how am I as a rival? Have I any hope?"

Cindy was tired and suddenly not in a mood for jokes.

"A hope of what?" she asked crossly.

Peter took hold of her shoulders and looked down at her. "Have I a hope of being a more suitable husband than your beloved boss?"

She stared up at him. Her throat seemed to tighten, her nose prickled. How could he be so cruel, taunting her, she wondered.

"Is this some kind of a joke?" she asked angrily.

"A joke?" Peter sounded shocked: "Look, Cindy, I knew your boss meant a lot to you. I could tell that from the way you wanted to get back to London. But then—well, after you'd gone, it was so quiet and lonely and I had time to think. It was then I realized just how stupid I'd been. Maybe it was seeing Caterina, the Gypsy, who reminded me of the family curse. I think I told you about it—that the family would never be free of the curse until the castle owner's wife ceased to be a meek little mouse. I realized then that *I* was acting like a meek little mouse."

Cindy found herself laughing, for he looked so odd, so solemn. "You—a meek little mouse? Oh, Peter!"

"I mean it." He didn't even smile. "I asked myself why I had been willing to accept the fact that you loved your boss. Why hadn't I asked you? So here I am. Cindy, do you love your boss?"

"Of course I don't! I never did." Cindy was getting confused again. What did Peter mean? He couldn't—

But it seemed he could, for he suddenly put his arms

around her, his face near hers as he said quietly, "Then you mean—there is some hope for me?"

"Oh, Peter!" Maddeningly the tears slid down her cheeks, but Peter took no notice.

"You really mean—" he asked, his arms tightening around her.

"Of course I do. It was always you," Cindy told him. Now her arms were around his neck, her cheek against his. "Peter—I just can't believe it."

"Neither can I," he said, and kissed her.

THE FIRE OF LIFE

The Fire of Life

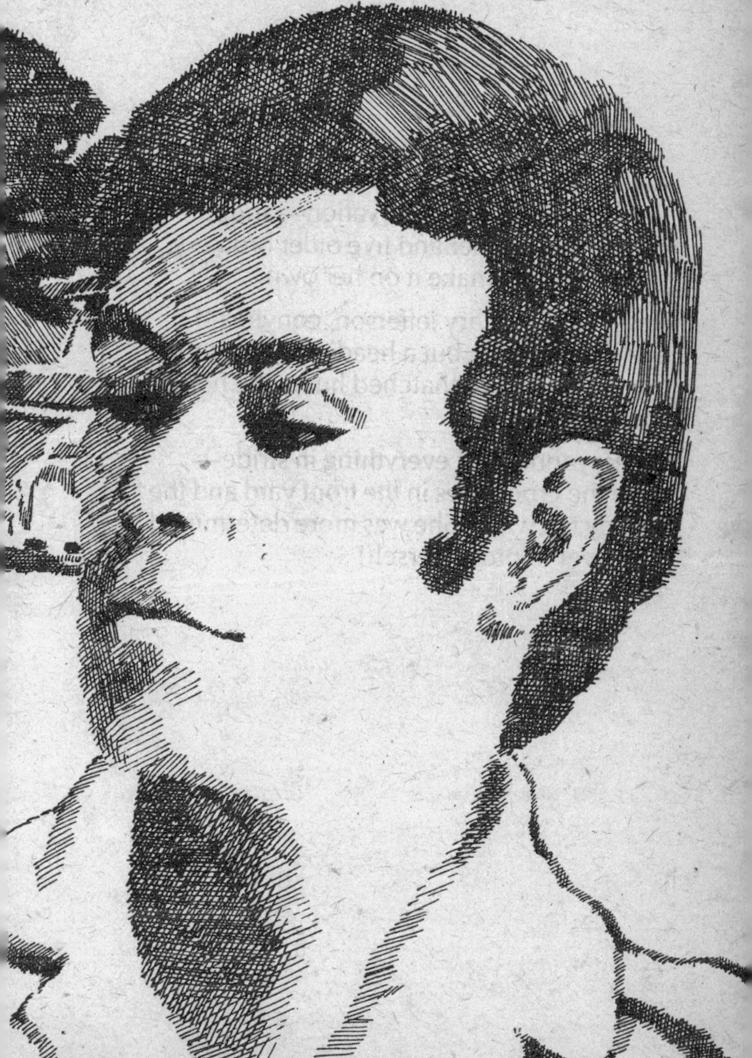

Rayanne Brisco went to Africa to write a thesis on wildlife conservation—and to prove to her father and five older brothers that she could make it on her own.

Reserve chief Cary Jefferson, convinced she'd be nothing but a headache, housed her in a primitive thatched hut in the hope she would leave.

But Rayanne took everything in stride—even the crocodiles in the front yard and the muddy tap water. She was more determined than ever to prove herself!

CHAPTER ONE

As Rayanne sank into the chair with a sigh of relief, Mike Crisp, a suntanned man with fair hair and a pointed beard, smiled sympathetically. He was chief warden of the Jefferson Wildlife Reserve and had driven to the small African airport to meet her.

"Tired?" he asked. "You've come a long way in a short time. You're here, I understand, to write a thesis on wildlife conservation?"

Rayanne nodded wearily. "Yes..." and wondered if she was quite mad to have flown more than six thousand miles to do so. Even if she succeeded, which she doubted, what would it really prove?

She felt a mess, hot and sticky. Her short, curly, honey-colored hair was thick with dust, her leaf-green linen coat and dress both crumpled. She found it hard to breathe, the air was so humid, and she just longed for a cold drink and to be able to relax in a hot bath.

"I saw Mr. Jefferson's Rover outside, so he must be in my office," Mike Crisp said. "I'll tell him you're here."

He went through the door that led into the single-floored house from the wide *stoep* running all around it. The garden outside was ablaze with crimson, yellow and blue flowers. Rayanne closed her eyes wearily.

"I was a fool to agree to have her." A deep impatient masculine voice jerked her awake. "These girls are nothing but headaches."

Her sleepiness vanished and became dismay as she realized she had unwittingly gone into the same atmosphere she had known and hated at home. An atmosphere in which she was just a *dumb blonde*, a stupid moron with no brains, and now she was "nothing but a headache." She had hoped that leaving home might land her in an environment where girls were accepted as equals, but it seemed she had failed. She wanted to get up and run away, but how could she? Driving through the reserve in the Land Rover, she had seen enormous elephants strolling along, swinging their huge trunks, and the lions were looking up as they passed. She was caught...for how could she escape?

The door swung open and two men stood there. She stared at them. They stared at her. She had no idea what she had expected to see, but Cary Jefferson was completely different from what his angry, impatient voice had suggested. He was tall, much taller than Mike Crisp, as broad-shouldered, with the same deeply tanned skin, his black hair cut short, his eyes dark.

A smile lit up his grave face. "I hope you're not too tired, Miss Briscoe," he said gently as he stared at the quaint three-cornered face. There was fear—or was it hostility in her eyes, he wondered. "It can be a tiring journey and I gather the road through the reserve was pretty bad." He turned to Mike. "I'll leave Miss Briscoe in your efficient hands, Mike. The hostels are closed, so she'd better go in one of the rondavels."

Rayanne saw the quick dismay on Mike Crisp's face. "But...."

"It's the only answer, Mike." There was a new note in Cary Jefferson's voice, a note of authority, perhaps arrogance, Rayanne thought. "Please apologize to Samantha for not letting her know earlier." He turned to the girl waiting, her mouth dry, her eyes smarting. "You need a good rest, Miss Briscoe. I'll come along tomorrow and show you around."

This time Mike Crisp turned to him. "When will Mrs. Jefferson be back?" he asked.

"Any moment now." Cary Jefferson shrugged. "You know what she's like—here today and gone tomorrow. I expect her when I see her."

"You'll be glad to have her back," said Mike. It was a statement, not a question.

"I most certainly will," Cary Jefferson laughed. "I try not to worry about her, but she does such stupid things."

Rayanne stiffened. What a strange man he was! He could be charming, and apparently considerate, and the next moment making fun of his wife. Of course he must be married, for anyone as attractive and handsome as Cary Jefferson would be married before his mid-thirties. He turned to speak to her. "You need a hot bath, a cool drink and a long sleep, Miss Briscoe, and you'll feel a different person. I'll see you in the morning. Cheers, Mike. I'll phone you later."

"Yes," Mike said slowly. The screened door closed with a sharp little bang and Mike smiled ruefully. "Better sit down, Miss Briscoe. I must go and break it to the wife."

"Break it?" Rayanne began, but Mike had vanished into the house. Rayanne sat down slowly and sighed. What was the corny old phrase? *Out of the frying pan into the fire?* She had escaped from her home only to land where women were, obviously, a "headache." But how could Mr. Jefferson speak like that about his wife? It didn't make sense, because he was polite, so... she sighed. She knew she should never have come, never have listened to Uncle Joe.

She wondered what Mike Crisp's wife would be like. He had said some funny words: "break it." Break what? The news that she had an unwanted guest? Rayanne moved uncomfortably. She really had got herself in a mess.

Then she heard voices. A female voice.

"It's all very well for him to apologize, but I'm getting sick and tired of this! He must have known she was coming. Yes, I know *we* knew, but I took it for granted she'd either stay with Miss Macintyre or Miss Horlock, if not in the hostel. Why she has to go into one of those ghastly rondavels...."

The door opened and Rayanne looked up nervously. Mike Crisp had seemed nice and friendly, but his wife...?

Again, Rayanne had a surprise. She certainly had not expected to see such an elegant, beautiful girl as Mike Crisp's wife was, with her long legs in crimson slacks, a white blouse, and her blond hair piled elaborately on her head, and surprisingly dark eyes.

Rayanne stood up. "I'm sorry if I'm being a nuisance."

Surprisingly, Samantha Crisp laughed. "You are, but I don't blame *you*. It's the boss—he expected us to do the impossible. Anyhow, not to worry; I've told the boy to switch on the geyser. I'll show you to your rondavel. This way."

Mike Crisp smiled rather ruefully, almost apologetically, at Rayanne, so she smiled back before she followed his wife. Through a long, narrow hall that went the length of the building, then out through a stable door, the top half open to the glaring heat of the

The Fire of Life

sun. Through the door, down six steps and along a path that led to a group of round cottages with thatched roofs.

"You're an intellectual, I take it," Samantha said over her shoulder. "Come straight from university to study for your thesis? Where's it going to get you?"

"I...." Rayanne hesitated and then was honest. "I don't know."

Samantha laughed. "As good an excuse as any! Lucky you had an uncle like Sir Joe Letherington or you'd never have got here. The boss is selective."

"I gather he sees women as a headache," said Rayanne.

Samantha laughed again. "That's what he says!"

"I hear Mrs. Jefferson is away."

"Yes, she's an old darling. Fusses like mad, but it slides off the boss's back like water off a duckling."

An old darling, Rayanne was thinking, shocked and surprised, for Cary Jefferson wasn't the type of man to marry an older woman, surely?

Samantha went on, still talking over her shoulder, as the path was too narrow for two to walk abreast. "Of course she's going on for eighty, now, though you wouldn't think it the way she prances around."

Rayanne began to laugh. "I didn't know we were talking about his mother. I thought it was his wife."

"His wife?" Samantha snorted. "He'll never marry. He's too clever. Not that we're ever short of girls chasing him and finding excuses to come here." She turned her head and narrowed her eyes as she looked at Rayanne. "Is that why you're here? If so, you're wasting your time. You haven't a hope."

Rayanne's face burned. "Of course it isn't! I had no idea.... I mean I thought Mr. Jefferson was an older man, the way Uncle Joe talked. Incidentally, he's my godfather, no real relation."

Samantha chuckled. "I've heard that story before. No idea! This first one is yours. All the other rondavels are empty at the moment."

The unusual-looking round little one-room cottage was clean. It had a thatched roof, stable door, and was freshly painted. Samantha opened the door and led the way inside. It was cool and quite light with two windows, mosquito netted, a single bed, a table and a chair and a foldup garden chair.

"There's a communal bathroom just along here," Samantha explained, leading the way.

"It's a...a bit lonely," Rayanne said diffidently, not wanting to admit fear.

Her companion chuckled. "Not to worry, we have a very good night watchman with a ferocious dog. Scares the liver out of anyone who comes near. Now watch out for snakes. Don't for heaven's sake walk into that long grass."

They were standing outside the communal bathroom now. The glare made Rayanne's eyes smart. The long grass seemed to surround them, coming close to the narrow path. The land sloped gradually down in front of them and she could just see the turgid brown water through the trees that lined the river.

"Snakes," Samantha went on cheerfully. "Not that they attack you—only the dangerous kind. Just never walk through long grass, because if you frighten them or step on them, they'll bite you. If they do, race like mad for the house and we'll give you an injection quickly. Has to be fast or it could be fatal."

"I won't go in the grass," Rayanne said quickly, trying not to shiver. "No wild animals about?"

The Fire of Life

Samantha laughed. "No. We're safely fenced off. Oh, except for the crocodiles." She waved her hand dramatically toward the river. "We have crocodiles at the bottom of our garden," she chanted.

"Not really?"

"Yes, really. You're in no danger, though, unless you go for a swim, and if you did a stupid thing like that you deserve to be caught."

"Do... do people get caught?"

"If they're fools. The children play in the water sometimes or their mothers wash their clothes and don't watch out. Well, I'll leave you to unpack. I see Moses has brought down your luggage. The bath should be hot in twenty minutes. Then have a sleep. Better come up to the house about five and we'll have a drink before we eat. Mike will bring you home, because it can be pretty scaring in the dark."

And that's no lie, Rayanne thought miserably as Samantha hurried back toward the house. *It's pretty scaring in daylight!*

Once inside her rondavel, she unpacked, keeping an eye on her watch. She longed to lie in the hot water, to wash her dusty hair, her aching limbs. When twenty minutes was up, she seized her dressing gown and put it on and made her way to the small, immaculately clean bathroom. She locked the door and turned on the tap, then froze with horror. She could not believe her eyes.

The water was brown. *Muddy river water.* How could she ever wash her face in that?

LATER, AFTER RAYANNE HAD BATHED reluctantly, then drunk gratefully the iced lemonade Samantha had sent down to the rondavel, and had slept for several hours, Samantha, greeting Rayanne in the doorway, confessed that she had forgotten to warn her about the muddy water.

"Sorry about that," Samantha said briskly. She had changed into a many-colored caftan; now her hair hung down her back in soft curls. "I should have warned you. Fair makes you sick, doesn't it? By the way, don't ever drink it, will you? That way you could only get bilharzia. A nasty illness, that... can kill you. I'll send down a jug of drinking water in case you get thirsty in the night."

She led the way indoors. It was quite an attractive house, Rayanne thought, but she wondered if she would like to live in it—perched above the muddy river, gazing out onto trees of every kind and long grass, with a small garden fighting for existence and in the distance, the mountains, changing color as the sun began to go down slowly. The lounge was newly decorated, the walls a pale lilac shade; the chairs and couch had yellow silk covers. Samantha poured them each a sherry and they sat down.

"Nice to have someone who's not a ghastly intellectual to talk to," she began, then her face screwed up. "I forgot—*you're* an intellectual, too. Straight from university with all the long words, I don't doubt."

Rayanne laughed. "Some of them do really go to extremes, don't they? I can't bear that kind of talk."

"Nor me, neither," Samantha laughed. "How would you like to live here?"

Rayanne hesitated, looking around. "It's a very nice house...."

"Exactly," Samantha said triumphantly. "That's all that can be said. It's a nice house, it's a nice house! 'You're lucky, you are, my girl'; that's what they say. No, 'my *dear* girl,' of course. 'Lots of women would be

The Fire of Life

grateful,' but I'm not lots of women. I want to live, not vegetate. I'd never have married Mike if I'd known life was to be like this. Tricked me, he did, all right. I thought he was interested in trees—forests, you know. I guessed we'd be off to Canada—British Columbia, or somewhere exciting like that, but oh, no, oh, dear me, no," she said bitterly. "Mike meets up with the boss and before you can say, 'Bob's your uncle,' we were on our way out here."

Mike came in, yawning. "Oh, dry up, darling," he said. "You're boring Miss Briscoe to tears. You know it's not as bad as you make out. I'm earning good money; we're not spending it."

"You're telling me, Mike! Never a gay moment do I have. No one to talk to...."

Mike straightened, his glass in hand. "Look, Samantha, you know very well you can go to any of the socials. You refuse, but...."

"And why? You know why. All those girls with their hoity-toity words and that condescending grin. They talk all the time. I never get a chance to say a word." She swung around to look at Rayanne. "It'll be interesting to see how you get on with them, Miss Briscoe. You'll have to be tough or they'll just swamp you."

"Samantha, please! Miss Briscoe isn't a student. She need have nothing to do with them."

"Well, if she's got any sense, she'll keep away from them or they'll finish her off all right," Samantha said angrily. "I must go and see how the dinner's going. Dorcas has no idea at all...."

Alone, Mike and Rayanne smiled at one another. "Poor Samantha," Mike said. "She really does hate it here. Trouble is, I love it. This is my work and, as I said, I get good money and am saving for our future.

Samantha would like me to drop everything and walk out and find another job. I can't help feeling that wherever we go, she'll be fed up with it."

"I should think it could be very lonely," Rayanne said carefully.

Mike jumped up, took her empty glass to refill it. "I don't find it so," he said cheerfully. "But then I'm the type that can adjust. Unfortunately, Samantha can't."

"Talking about me?" Samantha asked, coming in quickly, looking alert.

"I was just saying, darling, that you and I are different types," Mike said soothingly. "That's why we get on so well. We complement one another."

"Compliment? You never pay me compliments," Samantha said bitterly, and Rayanne saw that Samantha had got hold of the wrong word.

"I expect if you always look as you are tonight, he just expects it of you. How do you manage to be so glamorous?" Rayanne asked.

Samantha's face relaxed. "You like my hair down?" She turned in a circle, her hair swinging. "I've got to keep myself up to my standards or else I'll just... well, go to bits. Yes, Mike, another drink, please."

Slowly the evening dragged by, or so it did to Rayanne, though Samantha seemed to enjoy it, talking away, constantly speaking angrily about "the boss." At last Rayanne, pleading a headache, was taken down through the dark night by Mike, who had two torches.

"I'll leave you with one, because at midnight your electricity is switched off automatically. If you hear someone outside, don't worry. It's the watchman. He may look rather alarming, but I assure you he's to be trusted. He has a dog with him that sometimes growls or barks."

The Fire of Life

"Do crocodiles walk ashore?" Rayanne asked as he led the way, the torch throwing a beam of light on the narrow path ahead. It was a hot humid night with small insects buzzing around her face.

"Only up on to the sandbanks. Samantha told you about them?" Mike sounded annoyed. "She delights in scaring people. I can assure you that no crocodile could get up to this height."

"Or... or snakes?"

"Very unlikely. Maybe you noticed that there was a wide band of small stones around the rondavel. This keeps away snakes. It's where people allow creepers or shrubs to grow up close to the windows that snakes get in. You scared?"

Rayanne managed a laugh. *The understatement of the year!* It was another corny phrase, yet it described the words exactly. "In a way. It's all so strange."

"You'll adjust. It's amazing what you can get used to when you have no choice," Mike said cheerfully, unlocking her rondavel, opening the door, switching on the light.

After he had left her, first checking that a tray with iced water, a thermos of boiling water, a cup and saucer, coffee, sugar and milk was on the table by her bedside, Rayanne thought of his words.

"It's amazing what you can get used to when you have no choice." How right he was: *when you have no choice!* Had Cary Jefferson deliberately put her in this horrible rondavel in order to scare her, she wondered. Was this his sly method of getting rid of her? He had said she was a "headache." Perhaps this was part of his plan.

Well, if so, his plan was going to fail, she told herself as she undressed, carefully putting the torch under her pillow, for after midnight there would be no light.

Once in bed, she switched off the light and lay hugging the torch as if it were the proverbial teddy bear. How quiet it was! She could hear the mosquitoes banging against the screens on the windows. Perhaps they could scent her, for there was no light to attract them. Some frogs began croaking. Then quiet again. Then suddenly a loud buzzing, rather like a hive of bees let loose. The cicadas, of course! She was nearly asleep when a nerve-shattering howl broke the quietness. In a moment, the howling came again. It was closer. Another howl and again it was even still closer. Her hand shaking, Rayanne fumbled for the bedside lamp switch. Nothing happened. Only the darkness stayed. She switched on the torch....

Again, nothing happened. The batteries must have run out, for there was only darkness still.

CHAPTER TWO

IN THE MORNING, Rayanne looked at her reflection anxiously. It had been a terribly frightening night in which she had hardly slept, hugging the useless torch, listening to the strange night cries. She was sure she had heard a lion roaring...and an elephant trumpeting anger. A flash of light had shone through her windows several times, frightening her until she heard a dog bark and knew it was the night watchman. Not that he was much comfort, for he was only walking by and soon gone. Never in all her life had she been so frightened.

And it showed in her pale face, her red tired eyes with the dark shadows below them. Somehow she must hide that. Cary Jefferson must not be allowed to win, or even know how near winning he had been! In the night, she had sworn she would leave in the morning. But now the sun was bright and warm, making the brown river sparkle as she looked out of the window and saw the huge red flowers on the flamboyants and could smell the delicious scent from the white gardenias behind the rondavel, and she knew that somehow or other, she must stick it out. She could just imagine her brothers' teasing if she went home the day after she arrived at the reserve.

"We knew you'd never make it," they'd say triumphantly.

And her father would shake his head sadly. "I told you this was no life for a girl. It's work for a man with his strength and brains."

And perhaps her mother would say very quietly, "I don't blame you, Rayanne. I'd have been scared stiff, too."

No, she had to stay; Rayanne knew that. Maybe Mike was right and in a little while she would adjust. She had to. She had no choice.

Half an hour later she made her way to the house, where breakfast was waiting. Samantha smiled, her eyes amused.

"Well, what sort of a night did you have? Manage to sleep?"

Rayanne forced a bright smile. "It took a while to get to sleep, but then I slept like a log."

"Heard the hyenas howling? They were really bad last night," Mike said, helping himself to toast.

Rayanne mentally made a note of that hopeful, helpful news. So the hyenas didn't howl every night. One blessing.

It was at ten o'clock that Cary Jefferson called for her. He was wearing what she had learned was known as a safari suit. He looked incredibly handsome, even more so when he smiled, yet she was on her guard. He had deliberately put her in the hateful rondavel to try to frighten her. No doubt he was waiting to enjoy his victory. Well, he could wait, she told herself, as she smiled sweetly at him and said she had slept well.

"A most comfortable rondavel and Samantha looked after me," Rayanne said brightly.

Cary smiled. "I'm glad. Samantha is a wonderful hostess."

The Fire of Life

He led the way to the Land Rover and helped her in. Before he started the engine, he turned to her.

"You'll be given a Rover and can go wherever you like for the research you plan to do—but there's one thing, Miss Briscoe, and on this I must insist." He looked down at her gravely. "You are not to go out in the Land Rover alone. Is that clearly understood? I'll let you have one of the rangers and he must always go with you."

"But why?" she asked quickly, sensing patronage in his words. "I mean, I'd never get out of the Rover, of course. Does everyone have to take a ranger with him?"

A slight movement of Cary's mouth made her think he was amused. "No, not everyone," he said gently. "Only girls."

"But why girls? I don't need protection. I promise you I'd do nothing stupid."

He turned his body around on the seat so that he could look down on her more comfortably.

"Look, Miss Briscoe, suppose the Rover broke down. Would you enjoy getting out in the midst of a crowd of lions to cope with the problem? That's why you're to take a trained mechanic who is also a ranger with you. Is that understood?"

Rayanne frowned as she looked at him. Yet he was right.

"I understand," she said reluctantly.

It seemed to be his turn to frown as he looked at her. She was wearing white jeans and a vividly striped black-and-white blouse.

"Very attractive outfit," he said thoughtfully, "but hardly suitable for this. I suggest you run along to your rondavel and change into something else—brown, black, navy blue or khaki."

Instantly she was on the defensive. "What's wrong with what I'm wearing?"

He smiled. "Nothing, but it's not for *now*. I quite sympathize with you, Miss Briscoe. A small person has to wear something strikingly startling or else she—or he—will never be noticed, but I would prefer a little less publicity this time. The monkeys are attracted by bright colors and can be a darned nuisance. Do you mind?"

She hesitated. He had no right to criticize...yet he had, in a way. After all, he knew more about the reserve than she did.

"I'll be as quick as I can," she promised.

She almost tripped up as she ran fast to her rondavel, hastily changing into a pair of dull dark blue jeans and a matching blouse. She looked in the mirror and saw that some of her whiteness had gone. Anger, obviously, was doing her good.

As she hurried back to the Land Rover she wondered if she had a right to be angry. After all, Cary Jefferson was right about the danger of a Land Rover breaking down. She shivered at the thought of it happening and a great crowd of enormous elephants coming along the road toward her! This would be a time in which she would need a man, not only able to make the engine go, or change the tire but to protect her, as well. As for the clothes...! She hadn't been sure what sort of appointment she would have with Mr. Jefferson, and thinking he might be going to introduce her to the rest of the staff, some of whom sounded ghastly, according to Samantha, she had thought she should dress up.

As she reached the Land Rover, Cary smiled. "You were quick!"

"Well trained," she said. "Five brothers."

"Help!" he laughed as he started the engine. "No sisters?"

"None. Dad wanted six sons. I was a disappointment." Without her realizing it, her voice was wistful. It had always hurt her, the knowledge that she had disappointed her parents. They made no secret of it. She had disappointed them in so many ways, for she had only just scraped through her exams while her brothers had got honors. All five were lawyers. Only she was drifting, not knowing what she wanted to do. It had been Uncle Joe's suggestion that she write a thesis on wildlife conservation that had seemed the answer.

Glancing quickly at the man by her side, she was no longer sure that it was. The Land Rover bumped over the earth road and went through the gate of the wire fence to the main road.

"I'll introduce you to the staff first," Cary Jefferson said cheerfully, and Rayanne knew dismay. It was just as she had thought! He had made her change into these drab clothes and look a fright and then let her meet the staff members that Mrs. Crisp disliked so much! What would they think of her? Had he done it on purpose? To cut her down to size, she wondered.

Again she quickly glanced at him. His profile was almost more handsome than his full face, with that square chin, the rather large nose and the arrogant lift to his head. He was whistling softly. She seemed to know the tune but could not name it.

Was he resenting her, she wondered. Was she wasting his precious time? Yet why had he to show her around? Surely Mike Crisp could have done it? Or was Uncle Joe's influence on Cary Jefferson so strong?

Later she was to realize that she had been so wrapped

up in self-pity and resentment that she hardly noticed the beauty of the house they reached, a long L-shaped white house with the usual wide *stoep*. She could see the river below, much closer than at the rondavel where she had slept, or rather tried to sleep! There was a sloping lawn down to the water, shaded by tall red-flowered flamboyant trees, and she could see sandbanks on the side of the still, dark brown water. Something on one of them moved!

"Are there crocodiles there?" she asked, as Cary Jefferson stopped the car before the house.

He turned and looked at her, his eyes amused. "Of course there are. Scared?"

"Of course not," she said indignantly.

"Well, I am. Scared of people taking foolish risks." He opened the door of the Land Rover. "I've got to fetch some keys. Won't be a moment," he said, and left her.

She looked around curiously. This was obviously his home, where he lived, apparently, with his mother. Now she could see it was a beautifully designed house with large windows shaded against the hot glare of the sun by venetian blinds. Several Africans were working in the garden and glanced at her without interest.

Cary Jefferson joined her and started the engine, driving around the tall weeping willow that grew in the center of the circular parking space.

"Know what the croc does to his victim?" Cary said cheerfully as they left the garden and were back on the main road, trees and bushes growing closely on either side. He did not wait for her answer. "They drag him under water to a shelf at the side of the river they've prepared, then leave the body there until it rots before they eat it."

The Fire of Life

Before she could control it, a shiver passed through Rayanne.

"Oh, no!" she said.

Cary Jefferson chuckled. "Oh, yes. I'm surprised you didn't know that!" His voice changed suddenly. "Just what interest have you in nature conservation?" he asked sternly.

Rayanne was startled. "Well, I... I was always interested in wildlife, biology, conservation... and when Uncle Joe told me of the wonderful job you were doing out here, he suggested...."

"It was his suggestion, not yours?" Cary Jefferson asked curtly.

"Oh, yes. You see... you see I didn't know what I... well...." Rayanne stumbled over the words, trying not to sound too stupid, wishing she had never left the shores of England.

Again he startled her, for he smiled. "I see. You were just at that stage we all go through when we've gone so far and can't be sure where to go on. I went through it. Can you imagine it? I was a stockbroker originally."

"You weren't?" Rayanne turned to stare at him, at his dark suntanned skin, his safari suit with open collar and short sleeves. "I can't see you in an office!"

He laughed. "You're so right. That's how I felt. Then as a kid, I'd always been interested in the fast-diminishing wildlife of this country and used to spend all my money going to the game reserves. At one time I wanted to be a game warden, but my father was ill and I didn't want to leave home. Then he died, so I told my mother I wanted to start my own wildlife reserve and finally persuaded her I had to do it or be a crazy mixed-up kid for the whole of my life. So we came up here, built the house and slowly everything else."

Ahead of them was a tall narrow building. "That's Jefferson Hall," Cary Jefferson told her. "That's where we lecture."

He drove past it and she saw three square two-storied houses in a row, joined by glassed-in corridors. He stopped the Land Rover and she slid out so that she was ready when he came to her side.

"This middle house is where they eat, have games and study. On the left is the hostel for boys, on the far right the hostel for girls. Actually, we get a surprising number of girls interested in conservation. I've often wondered why."

"And why shouldn't they be interested?" Rayanne asked quickly.

She saw the smile playing around his mouth as he stared down at her. "And why should they?"

"Oh!" She tried to control her quick anger, but the Irish blood in her was coming out. "Why must you men always differentiate between men and women? Why shouldn't a woman be interested in wildlife?"

"Two simple reasons, my dear child."

Rayanne's hand ached as she kept it from smacking his smug face.

"Name them," she challenged.

"Well, first men and women are physically different. Man is much stronger—"

"That's absolute tripe! We're as strong as you. How many men could have six children and run a house without breaking down? I wonder how many men would have the second child. Once would be enough!"

He was obviously trying not to laugh. "It might be the answer to the problem of the world's fast-growing population. My second reason is that it's a lonely life, hard work, and not very well rewarded financially."

"You think women work only for money?" Rayanne was having a hard fight with her temper, but she tried to steady her voice.

Cary threw back his head and laughed. "My, my, Ray, you do bite the bait! I was only teasing you. In any case, let's be honest—don't you think women require financial security more than men?"

She wasn't sure whether to be angry with him or share in his laughter. Why hadn't she recognized the signs? He had only been teasing her—just as her brothers did. And just as she did with them, she had risen to the bait!

"I don't know. I've never been very poor," she said thoughtfully. "I think if I had children, I would want financial security."

"You want children?"

Startled, Rayanne looked at him. "Of course I do. I'd like four, but I'll be content with two. One of each."

"Are you engaged—or in love?"

She stiffened, because it was none of his business. She glared at him. "No, I'm not engaged..." she began angrily, and then hesitated. As she stared at him his face seemed to blur for a moment and then came back, each item on his face brilliantly outlined. Her hand ached again, but this time to touch his face gently, to trace those thick dark eyebrows, the prominent nose, the square chin, his ears with their slightly big lobes but that lay flat against his head. "No," she said unsteadily, "I'm not in love...at least...."

"Good, so you won't be getting long phone calls from your beloved," Cary said, taking her arm. "We'll go to the clinic first."

Stumbling a little, for though it was absurd, Rayanne knew, her legs felt weak and she longed for a cup of tea or even something stronger. Perhaps it was the altitude, the different climate. It was so humid, so still the air!

The clinic consisted of a small room with a couch, a waiting room that was much bigger, and the nurse's office and locked cupboard of drugs, et cetera.

A tall slim girl with dark hair came to meet them. "Cary, how nice to see you," she said eagerly. "I've got a quiet morning for a change." Then she stopped, staring at Rayanne, her eyes narrowing. "This is...?"

"Yes, I want to introduce Rayanne Briscoe. I told you mother's close friend, Sir Joe Letherington, wrote and asked if Miss Briscoe might come here to study our work for her thesis." Cary Jefferson's voice was friendly yet impersonal. "Mind if I show her around?"

"Of course not. Glad to meet you, Miss Briscoe," Nurse Daphne Macintyre said in her husky attractive voice, but Rayanne knew that the nurse was not in the least bit glad to see her! She could see Nurse Macintyre's eyes noting the drab jeans and dark shirt, and for a moment Rayanne knew hatred of Cary Jefferson. The nurse was beautiful, elegantly dressed in a pale pink nylon overall, and Rayanne felt horribly plain.

She followed Cary Jefferson around the clinic, listening to his description of the sort of casualties they had.

"More often it's the boys who come to study. They're so keen to prove their strength, they'll do the craziest things and turn up with broken legs or arms."

"Do you get many injuries from...from the animals?" Rayanne asked.

Cary Jefferson looked amused. "Very few, and those we do are the patients' own fault. Occasionally we get a snake bite, of course."

The Fire of Life

Next he took her to what he called "the lab."

"I think you'll like Christine Horlock," he said as he led the way. "She's beautiful, but plenty of brains. She isn't suffering from the inferiority complex that Nurse Daphne is."

Startled, Rayanne almost gasped. "Why should she have an inferiority complex? She's beautiful, and...."

"And uneducated. Oh, I'm not saying she isn't educated, but she's the only one of the staff who didn't go to a university, and this smarts. She hates us all."

"That's absurd! I thought she was very nice," Rayanne said quickly, as usual leaping to the defense of anyone attacked.

Cary Jefferson chuckled. "You're a bad liar, Ray," he said, and pushed open two swinging doors. "Here we are. Christine!" he called. "We've come to see you!"

It was a very modern, efficient-looking laboratory Rayanne saw instantly, and the girl who came to meet them was the same—tall and blond, with blue eyes and a friendly smile as she held out her hand.

"Welcome, Miss... Miss Briscoe. Is that right?" she said, and turned to Cary. "Not often we see you at this hour, Cary."

"I'm just showing Ray Briscoe around," he told her with a smile.

Rayanne stood silently. They seemed to have forgotten her as they stared at one another, both smiling. It was almost as if they were talking, as if through their eyes a message could pass.

Then Cary Jefferson turned to Rayanne. "Well, we mustn't waste any of our precious time or that of Christine.... I won't be a moment, Ray."

It was odd—and yet strangely nice—that he called

her *Ray*. It was a name no one had ever called her before, Rayanne was thinking as she waited while Cary Jefferson and Christine Horlock looked through a microscope and earnestly discussed something.

What a mixture of different people he was, Rayanne thought. A real Jekyll and Hyde, only instead of being two people he was about a dozen. She was never sure which one he was going to be: one moment, so relaxed and friendly, then accusing, then understanding, and the next almost condemning her. She felt horribly drab and plain in her clothes. Miss Horlock was wearing a sleeveless white overall and still managed to make it look as if it came from Paris.

Back in the Land Rover again, Cary explained something of the problems.

"Nature conservation isn't only a case of keeping wild animals alive, but it is an applied science," he began, sounding rather pompous, Rayanne thought as she sat meekly, hands folded, as the Land Rover bounced about the bad earth roads. "We're continually engaged in observation and research. We leave the academic type to research institutes. Soil conservation means the soil must be protected against exposure as well as erosion and must be chemically treated or it may become impoverished. Dead trees and other vegetation should be allowed to rot rather than be burned. Water, of course, is another problem. The depth and stability..." he went on gravely.

Rayanne listened. At least, she tried to, but she found her thoughts going constantly back to the way Christine Horlock and Cary Jefferson had looked at one another. Were they in love? Perhaps they were without knowing it? Christine Horlock was very beautiful, she also had brains and obviously a deep interest in conservation, so she would make Cary Jefferson a good wife.

They paused as they came to a big double gate that divided the eight-foot-tall wire fence and the African came running to open it, lift his hand in greeting and give a big smile as Cary Jefferson spoke to him.

"Why don't you like women visitors?" Rayanne asked as they drove through. She was as startled as he, because she had not meant to ask the question. She felt her cheeks go red. "I...I couldn't help hearing you in the next room."

Cary laughed. "Sorry if I sounded inhospitable, but it's happened so often in the past."

"What's happened?"

He chuckled. "Well, females can be a headache, because they complain about the heat, the dust, the water. They also talk of their own home with nostalgic reverence, saying what a beautiful place it is, what a fine social life they lead, how very different from this life—this boring, lonely life."

"It must be boring and lonely for the wife." Once again, Rayanne leaped to the defense of Samantha Crisp.

"I agree. That's why wardens should be careful before they marry—or cease to be wardens. The trouble is, it's a kind of bug. Getting involved, I mean. You may have heard of a poet called Landor. I don't know if he's well-known, but I always remember a poem I learned at school.

"I strove with none, for none was worth my strife.
Nature I loved, and next to Nature, Art;
I warmed both hands before the fire of life.
It sinks and I am ready to depart."

He laughed. "You must think I'm mad, but that's how I feel about nature. It's so amazingly wonderful, so fascinating to study. Do you know...?"

As the Land Rover jolted and jerked, going through the well-shrubbed hillocks and sudden little valleys, giving Rayanne glimpses of distant zebras or wildebeests, he talked to her about his work, what he had learned, what he hoped to learn. She listened entranced, for she had never thought of nature conservation in this light before. Finally he paused and sounded apologetic.

"Sorry, I must have bored you to death."

Rayanne looked at him gravely. "On the contrary, you've given me an entirely new slant on conservation. I'm afraid I had no idea...."

He glanced down at her. "Good. It means so little to a lot of people. What's the sense in keeping these animals alive, they say."

"Mike Crisp feels as you do."

"I know. I wish Samantha could settle down. That's another reason why I don't welcome female visitors, Ray," Cary went on, using his abbreviation of her Christian name as if it was the most natural thing in the world, as it would be with some men, yet it had not seemed to her that Cary Jefferson was the type of man to call a girl by her Christian name without first asking permission. He had that rather old-fashioned but very nice courtesy you so seldom saw. But she was glad. Every time he called her Ray, a kind of warmth swept through her body, almost as if he were caressing her.

"If she had a baby..." Rayanne said slowly.

"That would be the answer, of course. I gather they want one, but..." Cary said slowly.

"Do you want children?" Rayanne asked abruptly. After all, he had asked her!

He looked startled. "Honestly, I don't know. Never thought about it. In fact, I doubt if I shall ever marry. I want to be free."

"Free? But lonely?" Rayanne felt suddenly bleak as if the sun had gone behind a cloud.

"Well, yes, maybe as you grow older you need someone around, but I think when you're young and have work you love, that's all you need. I'm talking about men, of course. Women are different."

Rayanne looked up. There was a wild canary balanced on a slightly swaying branch, its golden breast so bright, the brown body flecked with gold as he sang sweetly.

"What makes you say that? Why do you always say we're different?"

"Because you are." Cary was driving slowly past a herd of rhinos, but Rayanne was too engrossed in the conversation to pay wild animals much attention. She was amazed at the ease with which she could talk to Cary Jefferson, and the way he was talking to her. Somehow she had not expected it.

"In what way?"

His powerful hands gripped the steering wheel as he deftly negotiated the Rover from the deep ruts.

"In every way. The average woman needs love. A man doesn't. He can sublimate his need by being engrossed in his work. A woman never could. She has this mother streak in her, this protective desire to have someone need her, someone she can be kind to, can... well, can make dependent on her. A woman's strength lies in the dependence on her of the man she loves."

Rayanne turned sideways, tucking her feet under

her. "I don't understand. You mean a woman has to boss a man before she can feel secure?"

He smiled. "Definitely. Take my mother. She delights in ordering me around; she knows I'm dependent on her."

"You are?" Rayanne was startled. She would never have thought this great hulk of a man by her side could be a mother's boy.

He roared with laughter. "She thinks I am, bless her. Seriously, though, isn't it true? A woman likes to believe a man needs her, then she's happy."

"I don't like the way you put it," Rayanne said slowly. "You make women sound awful."

The Land Rover bumped suddenly and she slid down the seat against Cary.

"I'm sorry," she gasped.

"I'm the one to say that. Afraid the road is bad. Elephants don't help. Look!"

Rayanne obeyed. Straight ahead, crossing their road, if such it could be called, a herd of elephants walked, swinging their long trunks, placing each foot with deliberate rhythm, ignoring the Land Rover that had slowed up.

"Do they ever attack?" she asked.

"Never. Except when one of them is injured and in pain. Then you reverse like mad and don't stop to argue!"

The last one of the elephants crossed the road, swinging his trunk, flapping his ears, turning his head slowly to stare at them and then, as if totally uninterested, followed the herd.

Cary started the engine. "Where were we? Oh, yes. Talking about women and men. Obviously I see the way women love men in a different way from you. How would you define a woman's love?"

The Fire of Life

Her cheeks felt hot. "I... well, I don't really know." Didn't she, she found herself wondering. She went on, speaking her thoughts aloud. "I'd want to make the man I love happy. I'd study his work so that we could talk about it, so that I could share his problems and understand things better. I'd only want him to be happy. That to me is love."

There was a strange silence, only broken by the sudden shrill sound of the cicadas.

"I think that's rather wonderful," Cary said softly, and his hands gripped the steering wheel. "Have you ever been in love? You said no, but I think you have."

She tensed, afraid he might guess the truth. "I think... I think I have," she confessed.

He turned to look at her. "I hope the man will be worthy of your love," he said gently. "Ah, there's young Hardwick."

A Land Rover came bouncing to meet them with a young shirtless man in it, whom Cary introduced and who grinned cheerfully at Rayanne.

"Nice to see a girl's face. I'm getting awfully tired of hippos and lions," he joked, winking at his boss.

Their quiet talking time was over. Cary Jefferson ceased to be the relaxed man and became instead the authoritative, rather pompous boss.

IT WAS A FASCINATING DAY, Rayanne thought, as it came near its close. She had met several of the wardens and in some cases where they were married, their wives. One or two seemed happy enough, but several were like Samantha.

"See what I mean?" Cary Jefferson said once as they drove away from a nice little well-furnished house. "They kept asking you questions about your wonderful life in England. Is it so wonderful?"

She had hesitated. "I wouldn't like to generalize. I may be unlucky, but mine wasn't wonderful."

He looked sympathetic. "Why ever not?"

"Five brothers, all older and brighter than yourself, didn't make life easy. Dad is disappointed in me and mother... well, she just doesn't do anything at all. She just accepts the situation."

"You can hardly blame that on England, then." Cary had sounded amused.

"Quite definitely not. Life... don't you think this is a purely personal thing? I mean, some people can be happy anywhere—"

"And others unhappy anywhere. I agree. Would you say you are a happy person?" His eyes had been twinkling as he looked down at her.

"Not... not so far."

"Tell me, why have you got this chip on your shoulder? I mean, surely your five brothers can't be the monsters you make them out to be. I'd have thought they'd have spoiled their kid sister."

"Not my brothers," she said bitterly.

"Know something, Ray?" He had been driving past some emus as he talked and one had decided to chase them, so now Cary was driving fast, glancing over his shoulder and laughing as he spoke, watching the emu follow them with her funny bouncing run. "I think it's all your fault."

"My fault?" Rayanne had felt the anger rising in her. Just another example of a man's bias. Everything was the woman's fault—never, oh, but never, the man's!

The emu got tired and gave up the chase, so Cary drove more slowly, pointing out the monkeys on the trees, swinging from branch to branch, and the impala racing across the flat background as they heard the sound of the Land Rover's engine.

"Yes, yours," he went on. "You've so convinced yourself that you're no good that you're almost scared to open your mouth. Look, Ray, your problem is really simple. You're sensitive and you rise to bait. You're a sitting duck, if I may be corny. You ask to be teased and you rise at once. Anyone told you how much prettier you are when you lose your temper? Maybe that's why we all tease you!"

She had felt her cheeks burning and anger growing. "I...I..." she had begun, and then he slowed up.

They were close to a small dam and seven giraffes stood by it, calmly surveying the brown, welcoming water. They turned their heads gracefully and looked at the Land Rover.

"Their faces are like poker faces, aren't they?" Cary was saying. He had slid along the seat close to her. She could feel his breath on her cheek. She wanted to yet dared not turn her face, for his mouth would be near hers and....

She shivered. It couldn't be true. You didn't fall in love like this. It must be the change of climate, the altitude—there must be a reason, she thought unhappily. Stiffening, she stared at the giraffes and Cary went on talking softly in her ear.

"Amazing how bored and blasé they look, as if the arrogant creatures can find nothing of amusement or interest. Look, ever seen a giraffe drink water? It's a wonderful exhibition of adapting oneself despite handicaps. Just see the way he widens his legs and finally can get his mouth into the water."

They watched in silence as the giraffe slowly and with great dignity moved his legs apart. He drank without haste while the other giraffes looked at him thoughtfully. A group of zebras had come to join them and they were drinking fast.

"The zebras feel safe," Cary whispered, his breath even more warm on Rayanne's cheek. "You'll usually find them drinking water near the tall, quick-running giraffes. Can you see those guinea fowl over there? Look up at that baobab tree just above the dam. See it? Well, that tree could be called a game reserve in itself.

"Up in the crown of its foliage you'll find everything—birds, snakes, monkeys, baboons and bats. Most important of all, the guinea fowl. They're like deer. They know when danger is near and their metallic cackling warns everyone. Isn't nature interesting with its protective measures?"

"Very," Rayanne had whispered. Oh, was this love? This ache to be in someone's arms? This longing to touch his cheek, to look in his eyes? Yet it was so absurd. Why, she didn't really know him.

Later they had driven past a pair of proud ostriches. Mother and father walked along with stately pride while racing ahead of them, like small children, were twelve baby ostriches.

"We're pleased with that lot," Cary said as they watched the adult ostriches look at the Land Rover anxiously and obviously accept it as not dangerous. "Ostriches are excellent parents. That reminds me, Ray. I know you haven't had time yet to work out what you'll write for your thesis, but might I suggest you consider concentrating on a certain phase of animal life? Gestation and parenthood, for instance. Of course you know that a kangaroo's baby is only an inch long? Hard to believe, isn't it? Maybe you should have gone

The Fire of Life

to Australia—you could not only have studied kangaroos, but found yourself a rich husband."

The anger had stirred inside her, but she controlled it. He was teasing. So she smiled sweetly at him. "Maybe I should have," she said, and saw by the twinkle in his eyes that he had watched with amusement her battle with her temper. One win to her, she had thought. "Actually, thanks for the suggestion. If I remember rightly, elephants don't reach puberty for ten years, and gestation is twenty-two months. It's an awful long time for the poor cow to be pregnant."

"They seem to accept it. The calf is dependent on the cow for two years, and when he's weaned he goes off with the bull. Rather interesting, that. Pity mankind doesn't follow the elephant's example."

They had both laughed. It had been a lovely moment of togetherness, Rayanne remembered later that day.

"I wonder what the mother would have to say," she had said.

"In this day and age, talking about liberation and all that tripe, they might welcome it."

"All that tripe?" Rayanne had repeated slowly, as she felt angry. What right had he to dismiss...? "Look, why shouldn't a woman be treated as an equal with a man?"

"Because she isn't." He chuckled. "All right, all right! She's as tough as a man, as intelligent as a man, but can't you stupid idiots see that as you are, you have far more control of us unfortunate males than you ever would if you were equal? What an idiotic word that is! Tell me, what do you want in this equality business?"

"The same wages, the same opportunities, the same respect...."

"Hey, look! That should interest you," Cary had

said, abruptly changing his voice, grabbing her arm as he slowed up the Land Rover and pointed at two warthogs who were running down the road ahead of them, having just dived out from under the bushes. They kept turning their heads anxiously, but never seemed to think of leaving the road. "Look at their stiff little tails," Cary said, laughing. "Aren't they amusing?"

The interruption seemed to have closed their conversation, much to Rayanne's relief, and after a sandwich lunch with one of the bachelor wardens they went for an even longer drive around the reserve, during which she saw the lions sleeping while the lionesses prowled around, and she saw the hippos in deep water, and the blue wildebeests gathering at the drinking places.

"See what a pattern of protective orderliness there is," Cary had said. "Look how the young animals place themselves between the older ones. See... some of them drink while others keep watch and the way they sniff the air. They can smell danger."

Finally he drove her back to the Crisps' house.

"I hope you're not too tired," he said politely as he walked around to her side of the Land Rover. He had to help her out, much to her annoyance, but, sitting on her feet, she had got caught up with a slit in the seat cover.

His voice had changed again. Gone was the relaxed, friendly voice. Now he was Mr. Jefferson, owner and boss of the reserve.

"No, I'm fine. Thanks," she said, embarrassed as he half lifted her down. "Thanks for showing me everything. It was most interesting."

"Good. I'll send you round a Land Rover in the morning and a ranger. Then you can go and look for yourself. You brought your camera, of course?" He saw the hesitation in her face, for, though she had brought a camera, it was only a small one. "Let me know if you need one. We have plenty available. Goodbye." He shook her hand solemnly, lifted his hand in greeting to Samantha Crisp, who was standing on the *stoep*, and drove away.

Samantha smiled. "Well?" she asked. "Bored to tears?"

"Actually," Rayanne admitted, "it was much more interesting than I expected it to be."

"That's only because *he* told you about it all," Samantha said, and laughed, clapping her hands as she watched Rayanne blush. "Don't tell me you've fallen for him, too. Oh, me, oh, my... we poor women! Don't dream, Rayanne... there isn't a hope."

"I'm not dreaming," Rayanne said stiffly, but knew her red cheeks might have given away her secret. "Actually it's simply that he's very good-looking, attractive and interesting to talk to. I've never met a man like him before."

"And never will again," Samantha prophesied. "Better have a bath, if you can bear that ghastly brown water, and then come up for a drink. You must be caked with dust."

"I must look a sight," Rayanne admitted, laughing ruefully. "By the way, I met Nurse Macintyre and Miss Horlock."

Samantha whistled softly. "And how did you get on?"

Rayanne laughed. "We didn't. Obviously Nurse Macintyre didn't like the look of me, but Miss Horlock was a little more friendly. They're both very...."

"Dishy? You bet they are. Deliberately dishy. Silly clots! They ought to know that Cary will never marry.

He's married to his work and that's all that counts... but they go on hoping, go on trying. It's pathetic, that's what it is. Pathetic. Now hurry and get washed up. I've cooked a good dinner for us all."

Rayanne obeyed, shuddering as she slid into the muddy water but enjoying it all the same, grateful for the drinking water with which she washed her face and cleaned her teeth. She put on a green trouser suit and made her way to the house. Mike had promised to replace the batteries in her torch, apologizing profusely for not having checked the night before.

It was so peaceful sitting on the mosquito-screened *stoep*. Samantha seemed delighted to have an audience and talked most of the time. She did ask a lot of questions, though, about England, and Rayanne remembered what Cary had said.

"I think I could be happy here," Rayanne said slowly. "It's so quiet, so relaxed...."

"And so unutterably dull," Samantha added.

Mike Crisp joined them and asked Rayanne how she had enjoyed the day. They talked of animals and soil conservation and the importance of water, and poor Samantha looked bored to tears.

It was after dinner as they were sitting on the *stoep*, a starry-skied black night outside with an occasional howl or bark to break the quietness, when the car arrived. It was not a Land Rover but a huge Jaguar.

"Oh, no!" Samantha half groaned. "It can only be...."

Mike had already gone down to meet the visitors. Rayanne stared at the small plump little woman with snow-white hair who came up the pathway, leaning on Cary's arm. She smiled at Rayanne as they reached the house.

The Fire of Life

"My dear child!" she said, holding out her hands. "I'm so delighted to meet you. Any relation of my darling Joe is welcome."

"I'm not really a relation," Rayanne said quickly. "His goddaughter."

"What's the difference?" Mrs. Jefferson laughed happily. "He never married for years, you know. That was because of me." She turned to the silent Cary and tapped him on the shoulder. "I chose your father, Cary, darling. He wasn't as rich, but he was a darling. Like you," she added, and smiled, then turned to Samantha. "You'll forgive me if I take your guest away, won't you, Samantha? I can't bear to think of Joe's goddaughter in one of those ghastly rondavels. I told Cary so, didn't I, darling?" She smiled at him lovingly. "As soon as he came home, I was really cross, wasn't I? Rayanne must come and stay with us, I said, and your bedroom is all ready for you, dear child. I am so happy to see you... it is wonderful...."

"It might be an idea if Miss Briscoe were to go to her rondavel and pack her things, then come back here. I'm sure Samantha will make us a cup of coffee," Cary Jefferson said quietly.

His mother beamed. "A wonderful idea, darling. I always enjoy Samantha's coffee."

"I'll go with Miss Briscoe," said Cary, taking a torch from his pocket. "Come along."

They walked down the narrow path, Cary striding ahead, Rayanne not sure if she was pleased or not. Living in the same house with Cary? Sitting at the same table at meals? Seeing him so much? Would she be able to hide her secret? Or wake up from the idiotic idea that she was in love with him? How could you love a man you've only known one and a quarter days, she asked herself.

At the rondavel, Cary waited patiently while she packed. As she straightened, he smiled at her.

"I must warn you of two things, Ray. Mother has always wanted a daughter, so you'll be smothered, or rather mother-smothered, with love. I hope it won't be a nuisance, because it'll make her happy. Secondly, don't be embarrassed if she matchmakes. Mother is convinced it's time I got married and had at least four children, if not more. She's a frustrated grandmother, you see. Mind, she's very choosy. She may take a little while to decide if you're good enough for me."

"Well!" Rayanne felt about to explode. Of all the nerve...! Then Cary laughed.

"Don't let it embarrass you. I'm certain she'll find you ideal for me and do her best to throw us together in romantic situations." He chuckled. "You know, soft lights and sweet music that her generation used to go in for so much. So don't let it worry you. You're quite safe as far as I'm concerned."

Rayanne stared at him. She couldn't speak. How dared he talk to her like that! If he knew the truth... but he must never know it, that was for sure!

She managed a light laugh. "What a joke! I certainly wouldn't want to marry you if you were the last man on earth."

"Is that so?" he asked, and the amusement had left his voice. "Very interesting," he added sarcastically. "We'd better get going or poor Samantha will begin to scream. She and mother don't get on."

He led the way and she watched his back and hated him one moment and knew the next that she could never really hate him. But why did he have to be so nice and then so beastly? Saying she was safe as far as he was concerned! Indeed, the arrogance of it. And then the sarcastic way he had said, "Is that so? Very interesting." What did he mean? Didn't he believe her? Did he, like Samantha, think she had come there for one reason? And one reason only, she asked herself. Him!

Maybe if she had known him before... if they had been old friends... but how could you chase a man you had never met? A man you had no desire to meet. But now... but now?

Mrs. Jefferson was waiting for them and soon all were in the car, Cary driving. Back at the house, it was ablaze with lights. Mrs. Jefferson fussed happily as she led Rayanne to her bedroom.

"You have your own bathroom and loo, dear child, and plenty of hot water. Do you like a big or a light breakfast? In bed?"

It was a beautiful room, Rayanne thought when she was finally alone and could look around her. She stared out of the picture window at the black night with a dark sky brightened by a beautiful new moon and stars all sparkling. The trees were silhouetted against the sky. Everything was quiet. They were high above the crocodiles and the electric light wouldn't go out....

Lying in bed, Rayanne relived the day, going over her conversations with Cary, wishing the talks were still to be said, for she had enjoyed the day so much. But would he ever be like that again, she wondered.

Sleepily she lay with just a sheet on her. The room had air conditioning, so the intense humid heat of the rondavel no longer roasted her. The quick bath she had had been lovely, too, the water clear and free of mud. She wondered how they had managed it. She had said she would get up for breakfast, but now she regretted it. She was afraid to see too much of Cary, afraid he might see in her eyes the love she could not understand. For how could you love a man you've only just met, she asked herself, and yawned. She yawned again and then fell asleep.

RAYANNE NEED NOT HAVE WORRIED, for after she was called with a cup of tea, had showered, and then went to join her hostess for breakfast, Cary was not there. Mrs. Jefferson beamed at her.

"So nice to have a companion for meals, my dear. I get tired of sitting alone. That's why I'm always trotting off to stay with friends."

"Doesn't...?" Rayanne paused. She had not yet called Cary Jefferson "Cary," yet she could hardly call him "Mr. Jefferson" to his mother. "Your son...?"

"He rarely eats meals with me. He has his own flat at the other end of the house. You see, he's always out somewhere. We used to fight because he never came in at the right time for meals and I got tired of waiting for him, and he didn't like it because I had waited, so I suggested he have his own little flat, his own cook and so on." She paused, breathless. "When I know he's going to be in the house at a reasonable time, I invite him to dinner and we enjoy each other's company. The trouble with poor Cary," Mrs. Jefferson added sadly as she helped Rayanne to kidneys and bacon, "is that he's allowed his work to get control of him. He eats, sleeps and drinks conservation. He used to be so different, gay and social-minded, but that was when he was a stockbroker. He did very well. His father and I were proud of him." She sat down opposite Rayanne and smiled. "Am I boring you, my dear?"

The Fire of Life

"Of course not," Rayanne said instantly. "Please go on."

"Well, my husband died and Cary told me that he had always wanted to have his own wildlife reserve. You can imagine how amazed I was. He had never said anything of the sort to his father or to me. I knew he enjoyed coming to the reserves—he spent all his holidays there if we let him—but for a future! Not that I was worried about money. His father left us both very comfortably off and I knew Cary had been earning good money and had saved a lot of it. But it was the thought of living so far from civilization—in the midst of wild animals." She laughed and passed the marmalade to Rayanne. "You're sure you wouldn't like some more kidneys and bacon."

"Quite sure, thank you. You don't mind living here?"

"Mind?" Mrs. Jefferson chuckled. "I hated it at first, but I saw what it meant to Cary, so I put up with it. He's often away for weeks at a time and then I do miss him, so I usually go and stay with friends or invite them here. They find it very exciting. Frankly, it all rather bores me. It seems an awful waste of money to me to bother to keep wild animals when there are so many human beings who are starving to death." She sighed. "But there it is, my dear. When you love someone, you accept the fact that their beliefs are almost certain to be different from your own. All I want is for Cary to be happy."

"It's a very lovely house," Rayanne said slowly, looking round the lofty room with its walnut furniture and beautiful silver.

"It is, isn't it, my dear? Cary is so though knew how important a beautiful home is to had it built specially for me. He knows I like entertaining, so there are several guest rooms. It's quite a lonely life, sometimes, though, for when the courses start I hardly see him at all."

"The courses?"

"Yes, my dear. We have groups of students who come here for several months to have lectures and see for themselves. Cary feels strongly about this, because he wants more young people to be interested in conservation of wildlife. Next week, our next course starts. It can be quite noisy. Young people of today do like such loud music, don't they?" She laughed. "My dear child, I forgot you were one of the young people."

"I don't like loud music, either," Rayanne said with a smile.

A tall African in an immaculately cut khaki safari suit came in and spoke to Mrs. Jefferson.

"Thank you, Kwido," she said, and turned to Rayanne. "Your Land Rover is at the door and Kwido will escort you. He's a well-trained mechanic and a good shot, so you'll be in safe hands. I made sure of that. I talked to Cary last night after you went to bed. I said any relation of Joe's must be treated as a VIP. He was a darling. I've so much to talk to you about, but of course your work must come first." She stood up. "Kwido will bring you back for lunch and then we can have a long talk. See you later!" Mrs. Jefferson gave her a smile and left the room.

Rayanne went back to her own bedroom and hunted out a notebook and pencil, also her camera. She put on her blue jeans and dark shirt, remembering what Cary had said about "publicity" attracting the monkeys. What was she going to look for, she wondered. Where should she go?

Kwido was standing by the Land Rover. He lifted his hand in greeting and she lifted hers.

"You wish to drive, madam?" he asked politely.

Rayanne shook her head quickly. She had never dared to try to learn how to drive a car. What a gorgeous source for teasing that would have made! She could just hear her brothers joking about it, and if, by sheer bad luck, she had scraped the car or had an accident, they would never have let her forget it!

"I can't drive," she said simply.

Kwido opened the door of the Land Rover on her side. He waited while she got in, took his rifle from the back of the truck and put it by his side in front. He smiled, his teeth bright in his dark face.

"We will not need it," he said, and it sounded like a promise. "Shall I just take you everywhere? Or is it one kind you want?"

"Everywhere, please, Kwido." She moistened her dry mouth. If only she knew what she was looking for! Coming out here, though it seemed a bright idea at the time when Uncle Joe had suggested it, had not helped. "I just want to look around."

Kwido seemed to understand. He drove carefully and took her to the different water dams and parked the Land Rover behind huge shrubs so that they could watch the animals unseen. He showed her chameleons. Kwido seemed to know a lot. He told her how when the chameleon grows old and gray it climbs onto a green twig and is young again.

"It is sad we cannot do that," Kwido said politely, but with a smile.

Rayanne had to laugh. She made a note of what he had said. Then he showed her how the chameleon moves slowly, about an inch at a time. Its long sticky tongue shoots out to take its prey and of course it changes color according to where it is.

There were many amusing little things Kwido told her to add to her notes. That the lioness is very vicious when she has a cub. Rayanne saw large herds of buffalo, which, Kwido told her, prefer to graze in large herds, but he also showed her how the blue wildebeests and zebras can mix with impalas and also baboons quite happily.

Baboons fascinated her. She made a note to ask Kwido another time to find her some place where she could watch them, for he had already told her they have their own beauty salons, "As in big cities," Kwido had said, "where they clean their young."

Kwido took her back in good time for lunch. It had been a hot close morning with small insects flying in her face and about two pages of notes! Rayanne showered and changed into a white cotton frock. Uncle Joe had warned her it could be very hot, so she had made several very thin frocks, finding it impossible to buy really thin ones in wintry England.

"Well, my dear, learned a lot?" Mrs. Jefferson greeted her happily. "Cary is coming to lunch. He wants to know how you got on."

Rayanne knew dismay instantly. Suppose he asked to see her notes? Somehow or other she must decide what she was going to write about. Perhaps his suggestion of gestation and parenthood was the best. If he realized she had no real idea what she wanted to study, he might imagine she was here to chase him!

She was welcomed warmly by Mrs. Jefferson, who insisted that they sit on the *stoep* and have a refreshingly cold drink before they ate.

"Well, my dear?" she asked eagerly. "How did you get on?"

Rayanne stretched herself luxuriously on the long low chair. "It was most interesting."

"And Kwido?"

"Very helpful. It was most amusing about the chameleon...." Rayanne told her hostess what Kwido had said. They both laughed.

"My dear child, how delectable! The perfect joke for a dinner party. I must remember it. Did you know your Uncle Joe well? I mean, do you? What is he like now? Of course he's much older...." Mrs. Jefferson's voice was wistful.

"He's very handsome still," Rayanne could say, and saw the beam on Mrs. Jefferson's face. "He mentioned you."

"He did?" The old lady leaned forward, her eyes bright. "He really did?"

Rayanne was glad she could tell the truth, for Cary had told her she was a bad liar. "I remember he said that Cary's mother had been the most beautiful girl he had ever known."

"He really said that?" Mrs. Jefferson's day was certainly made. She leaned back in her chair, waving a little fan before her flushed face. "He was a darling. His wife?" Her voice changed. "I gather she is an invalid."

"I'm afraid so. She never leaves her house. They live in Gloucester, but he often comes down to see dad."

"You like him? Uncle Joe, I mean?" Mrs. Jefferson asked.

Rayanne hesitated. "Yes, I've always liked him very

much, but... well, it isn't awfully easy to talk to him. He's reserved."

"Shy! He always was, poor darling."

"Also I always saw him with dad and my brothers, and that...." Rayanne paused, remembering Cary's accusation that she was being ultra-sensitive about her brothers. But he was wrong and she was right, she was sure of that! "They always teased me, called me Little Girl, and wondered what had happened to my brains, as they said I had none."

Mrs. Jefferson, to Rayanne's surprise, burst into laughter, dropping her fan, clapping her hands excitedly.

"My dear, he hasn't changed at all. That's exactly what he used to say to me, and I would get very angry and then I'd see the twinkle in his eyes and I'd know he was teasing me."

"You mean he said you had no brains?" Rayanne said slowly.

"My dear child, men are all the same. They have to boost their own unsteady egos and they do that by teasing us. You must never let them see you mind. That's fatal, because it'll get worse and worse."

"It has," said Rayanne, her voice sad.

Mrs. Jefferson leaned forward. "Then don't let it, dear child. Remember that as women we are far superior to men, bless their dear hearts, and they know it and resent it. If they tease you, smile sarcastically and say something like, 'Look who's talking!' or even more corny, 'People in glass houses...' and then laugh and walk away as if no longer interested in them."

"And it works?"

"Certainly it works. Or it did more than fifty years ago. Don't let them see you mind, whatever happens."

"I lose my temper."

Mrs. Jefferson laughed. "I used to, but in the end I felt sorry for them. I knew I was superior really; if it made them happier to think they were, well, why not? I lost nothing and they gained a lot."

"I'll try..." Rayanne said slowly, leaning forward to watch something move on the sandbanks that lined the turgid brown river. "You don't mind having crocodiles at the bottom of your garden?"

Mrs. Jefferson chuckled. "Of course I don't. They're hideously frightening things, but I never go close to the water. It isn't their fault they look like that, is it? So I can't see that it's really fair to hate them, because they can't help acting that way. Besides, it's a lovely conversation starter. People just stare at me as if I'm mad."

"It's a beautiful garden...."

"Yes, I love it."

A shadow crossed them. Rayanne looked up. It was Cary.

"Gossiping as usual," he said, sitting down. "You sound like a couple of mynah birds."

"We were talk—" Rayanne began indignantly, caught Mrs. Jefferson's eyes and smiled. "Is that a compliment or an insult, Cary?"

He looked startled. Was it because this was the first time she had called him Cary, she wondered. Or because she had smiled when he teased her?

"A compliment, of course. I brought Cary up to be polite to young ladies," said Mrs. Jefferson. She looked at her son. "Cary, I told you I wanted the hedge between us and Jefferson Hall tidied up. You've done nothing about it, and it looks awful."

"You're right, it does. I'm afraid I forgot," Cary said meekly. "I'm sorry. I'll arrange it this afternoon. How did you get on this morning, Ray?"

"Fine, just fine."

"She found it most interesting," Mrs. Jefferson joined in eagerly. "She liked Kwido, too, found him very helpful."

"Yes, he's good. I'm thinking of sending him over to the U.S.A. to do a course on conservation of soil and water. They're doing some interesting experiments there that might help us."

"He seems to know an awful lot already," Rayanne began, and stopped abruptly, for Cary was smiling.

"How right you are, Ray, but there's much more for him to learn. Later I hope to start another reserve of a different nature, and one day Kwido might be head warden. I believe in training men to take responsible positions. That's a sign of genius, you know."

His mother chuckled. "Inherited from me, of course. Isn't lunch ready?"

At that moment a bell tinkled.

"Lunching with us, Cary?" Mrs. Jefferson asked.

He smiled. "But of course. Uncle Joe's goddaughter must be given VIP treatment."

Rayanne felt the anger surge up inside her. Did he have to be so beastly? She clutched the back of the chair and fought her anger, finally smiling.

"How lucky I am that Uncle Joe *is* my godfather," she said sweetly.

CHAPTER THREE

LIFE WAS CERTAINLY DIFFERENT for Rayanne now that she was living with Mrs. Jefferson. It wasn't only the large, beautifully furnished bedroom with the pale pink silk curtains and bedspread to match, the polished floor with large, soft white rugs; nor was it the clean water in which she could shower or bathe several times a day; nor the excellent food; not even the beautiful garden where they so often sat watching the hideous crocodiles slowly submerge in the muddy water or move with their slow crawl—a frightening, almost relentless crawl—across the mud. No, it was Mrs. Jefferson. She was the one who made all the difference.

When Rayanne came home, driven by Kwido after trying to make notes, to work out what she wanted to write, there would be the plump, white-haired little woman waiting eagerly. It was a warm, delighted welcome, such a welcome as Rayanne had never known before. Mrs. Jefferson liked her... no, even more than that, she loved her. And Rayanne was beginning to love the talkative little woman who was always laying down the law to her big son and bullying him—literally bullying him into doing what she wanted done. And there was Cary, standing so quietly, saying meekly that his mother was quite right and he shouldn't have forgotten what she had asked him to do. A different Cary, an inconsistent Cary in many ways.

It was pleasant, Rayanne found, to have someone interested in what you had been doing; someone who would ask questions eagerly and listen to your answers; someone who fussed over you, made sure you had the kind of food you liked, that you were not too tired.

One day Rayanne found herself alone in the garden with Cary. Mrs. Jefferson had murmured something and gone indoors. The amused smirk on Cary's face annoyed Rayanne.

"Your mother is a darling," she said, and wished she hadn't, because it sounded so childishly defiant.

"I'm aware of that," he said coolly.

"Then why don't you do what she asks you to do?" Rayanne sat up in her chair and glared at him. "It's four days she's been asking you to have that high hedge cut and—"

"Asking me?" Cary sounded amused. "You mean ordering me to have it done."

"Is that why you haven't? Because you can't take orders?" Rayanne felt her control of her anger slipping away. It was such a stupid thing to get angry about, but she hated that smug, supercilious smile he was giving. "You meekly tell her you'll do a thing, but you've no intention of doing it, have you?"

"None at all," he agreed, and offered her a cigarette, which she refused, then lit one for himself. "Why should I?"

"She is your mother."

"That wasn't my fault...."

Rayanne slid along the seat as she tensed with fury. "How dare you say such a horrible thing! If you knew how lucky you are to have such a wonderful mother! Why do you meekly say you'll do it when you have no intention of doing what she wants done?"

The Fire of Life

He smiled. "She knows very well I have no intention of doing what I—to quote you—meekly agree to doing. She doesn't expect me to do it."

"Then why does she?"

He lifted his hand to silence her. "It's a game we play." His voice changed, losing its amusement, becoming grave. "I think the saddest thing about you, my little Ray, is the fact that you have no conception whatsoever of a true parent-and-child relationship. Mother and I understand one another. You see, my father was a strong, authoritative man who laid down the law. Mother was always meek and biddable; she knew dad wasn't well and mustn't be upset, so she gave way about everything, even against, as she often said, her principles. When he died and we lived together, we came to an undiscussed arrangement. We didn't need words. We understood one another. For the first time in years, mother could throw her weight around, could boss me, order me about. So she did it, knowing full well that I would do what I thought best and certainly wouldn't do what she said if I didn't agree with her—but I always pretend to agree meekly and she knows I'm pretending, so she can say the most outrageous things... you haven't heard anything yet... and we understand perfectly what we're both doing. Do you see?"

Rayanne stared at him. She did see, yet it was hard to believe. On the other hand, if his mother expected him to do what she said, would she still love him so much when he deliberately did the opposite? *Surely,* Rayanne thought, *then it makes sense?*

"You're very lucky," she said, moving to stand up and sliding with a bump onto the grass. She must have caught her sandal in something.

"Clumsy!" he teased as he stood up quickly, bending to take her hands in his and pull her to her feet.

Her cheeks red, she thanked him.

"My pleasure," he told her, his eyes amused.

"Well..." she began, then stopped, for he was still holding both her hands tightly, looking down at her, his eyes thoughtful. "Well...."

"Ray," he said slowly, "have you no understanding like that with your mother?"

She shook her head. "I'm afraid we don't... well, in a way we do, but you see, she's so busy running around looking after dad and—"

"Your five brothers. How it irks you, doesn't it? It seems sad. Most girls would be delighted to have five older brothers."

"I'm not most girls." She heard the defiant note creeping back in her voice. If only he would let go of her hands, she thought, and then knew that that was not what she really wanted, for she loved the touch of his fingers as they curled around hers.

"That," he said dryly, "is obvious. I wonder what started you feeling this animosity toward your brothers. Can you remember when it began?"

Rayanne stared up at him. It was absurd, she knew, and she kept telling herself that though it had no effect on her feelings, but just to feel his hands around hers, just to be so near, made it hard to think.

"I'm ten years younger than my youngest brother... when I was little I always wanted to play with him, but he'd have nothing to do with me. Then I hated it when he had his first girl friend, because he was *my* brother... and suddenly he wasn't. Then at school— well, I wasn't very bright and...." She paused as his dark tufty eyebrows lifted.

The Fire of Life

"You must have been pretty bright," he said, "to get where you are."

Again her cheeks burned. "I had to work hard and just scraped through my exams. All my brothers got honors and hardly had to work. They were just naturals, like dad."

"You're like your mother?"

Rayanne nodded. "Yes, except that she's lovely. She's tall and slender with high cheekbones and gorgeous red hair. She looks absurdly young and never seems to grow old."

"But she has no brains?"

"That's what my father says, but I think he's wrong. Mother helped me a lot with my studies."

"Your father didn't?"

"He was always too busy with the boys. He's a lawyer, you see, and so are my brothers and—"

"Your father wanted you to be one?"

Rayanne shrugged. "I don't think he thought for a moment that I could be one, but definitely he'd have liked it. He wanted to be proud of me, as he is of the others, but I let him down."

"Ray, you're so wrong," Cary began, then dropped his hands quickly, as if they had burned him or even stung him. Mrs. Jefferson came out to join them, but if Cary had let go of Rayanne's hands because of that, then he had left it too late, for his mother had a happy, almost triumphant look on her face as she beamed on them both.

"You'll be home the day after tomorrow, Cary," said Mrs. Jefferson. She didn't ask. "I'm giving a little dinner party for Rayanne. I thought we'd ask those two nice vets—what are their names? Leslie Van der Mer and Loftus Jones? And Nurse Macintyre and Christine

Horlock. I haven't asked them over for some time and they must think it very rude of me."

Cary nodded. "That's fine, mother." He looked at Rayanne and his eyes were twinkling. "This time I won't forget." Then he left them.

Rayanne sat down and Mrs. Jefferson followed suit. They sat in silence, Rayanne knowing that her companion was bursting with things that mustn't be said, questions that shouldn't be asked.

"It's a lovely day," Rayanne said to overcome the awkward silence.

"Is it?" Mrs. Jefferson looked vague and then smiled. "Yes, dear child, I can see it is." She positively beamed and Rayanne felt herself blushing, for she saw that Cary's mother had completely misinterpreted her words. Mrs. Jefferson thought it was a *lovely day* for Rayanne because Cary, her wonderful son, had been holding Rayanne's hands!

And wasn't it, that mocking little voice that so often hides inside us asked. Wasn't it a lovely day?

"You have met Daphne and Christine?" Mrs. Jefferson asked. "Both of them are crazy about poor Cary and chase him to death. They must be mad."

"They're both very attractive." As usual, Rayanne found herself leaping to the defense of anyone criticized.

"Good looks!" Mrs. Jefferson said scornfully. "Comes out of pots. But they're most unsuitable for Cary. Daphne is so bossy and she just can't talk about anything, anything at all. As for Christine... all she thinks about is her microscope. She isn't a bit interested in the animals, you know, and Cary thinks the world of them." There was a little silence and then Mrs. Jefferson turned to smile at Rayanne. "I'm so glad, dear child, that you and Cary get on so well together. You're perfectly matched."

Rayanne was looking at the little old lady and saw beyond her Cary standing in the open doorway, a huge grin splitting his handsome face. He must have heard every word his mother had just said. Rayanne couldn't resist it.

"I certainly found him very attractive, but... but actually we're very different, Mrs. Jefferson. I find him far too arrogant."

"Arrogant?" Mrs. Jefferson sounded shocked. "He doesn't mean to be, I'm sure. It's just that he has such a responsible job and has to give orders."

"I'm not accustomed to obeying them."

Mrs. Jefferson chuckled. "That's the whole point, dear child. Just pretend to and go your own sweet way. I always do. It works well and makes life more fun."

Rayanne, staring over Mrs. Jefferson's shoulder, saw Cary lift his hand as if in final salute and then he walked away. She felt her tense body relax.

"You're being very kind to me," Rayanne said, deliberately changing the subject. "I'm so grateful."

Mrs. Jefferson leaned forward and patted Rayanne's knee.

"Don't thank me, dear child. I love having you here. I've always wanted a daughter—someone like you. I don't think I've ever felt so optimistic about the future before."

Again Rayanne felt her cheeks go hot. If only Cary's mother would stop planning the impossible. Rayanne was certain that Cary didn't see her as a *woman*... a woman he could love. Indeed, she wondered if he saw any women as people he could love; most of them seemed to be "headaches."

"Do you dress up when you give dinner parties?" she asked, more as a ruse to guide Mrs. Jefferson's thoughts away from her son's possible marriage. "I don't think I expected anything like that. I thought this would be purely a working holiday."

"Let's have a look at your wardrobe." Mrs. Jefferson stood up and then paused. "Is that impertinent? I mean, I didn't mean...."

Rayanne smiled. "Of course I know you didn't, and I don't mind in the least showing you."

They walked down the *stoep* to Rayanne's door, which was never locked. Inside, Rayanne showed Mrs. Jefferson the few cocktail party dresses she had.

"Do the others dress up?" she asked.

The plump little woman chuckled. "And how! It's a positive battle, Rayanne, dear. It's very funny, but also very sad. I wonder." She stood back, looking at Rayanne's figure. "I wonder.... Just wait a moment. I'll be back."

Rayanne nodded and hung up her black trouser suit, which was far too hot for this climate. Her green sparkling dress—that was also too hot. The evenings were so humid that anything but the thinnest dresses clung to your damp skin.

Mrs. Jefferson came hurrying back; hanging over her arm was a pale blue satin dress. She shook it out and held it up before her. It came to the ground and had frills on the short sleeves and a high waistline, embroidered and smocked.

"It's beautiful!" Rayanne exclaimed.

"Try it on, try it on," Mrs. Jefferson told her excitedly. "I can't wait to see it on you."

Rayanne slipped out of her yellow cotton frock and

carefully put on the soft satin one. It fitted her perfectly. She looked in the glass.

"It's absolutely fabulous!" she said slowly. "But how did you know my size?"

She saw Mrs. Jefferson's reflection in the mirror. The little old lady was shaking with laughter, unable to speak. Rayanne swung around. "What's the joke?"

"Oh, dear...oh, dear me...I'm sorry, Rayanne, dear, but I can't stop laughing." Slowly she gained control, then wiped her tearful eyes and smiled.

"It was my nightie, Rayanne—my trousseau nightie. My mother gave it to me. She said the color was romantic. I never wore it—Cary's father loathed pale blue. He had a passion for white underclothes, as we called them in those days." She chuckled. "You look beautiful in it. Of course, I was much thinner in those days. I couldn't get into it now."

"I can borrow it?" Rayanne was looking in the mirror again. The color certainly did something to her. It was just too beautiful for words and absolutely *fashionable*.

Mrs. Jefferson laughed. "No, you may not borrow it, dear child, but I'm giving it to you. It's lain all these years in a drawer; it must be bored to tears, poor thing. It's far too beautiful to be hidden away, so please let me make it a gift."

Rayanne caught her breath and stared at the happy, beaming little woman. "It's wonderful of you!" Impulsively she hugged the older woman, kissing her. "You're such a darling!"

"I'm...I'm glad you think...think so," Mrs. Jefferson almost stammered, her eyes suddenly filled with tears. She turned and hurried out of the room, leaving

Rayanne puzzled, but she soon forgot the generous little old lady, as she gently stroked the satin and turned around, gazing in the mirror. It really did things to her.

AS THE TIME for the dinner party grew near, Rayanne's self-confidence diminished. The beautiful pale blue satin dress delighted her, of course, but she wasn't happy with her hair. She had washed it—as she did every few days, for the dust from her Land Rover trips with Kwido was dreadful—but today it seemed limp and without life. Carefully she made up. If only she was beautiful, she thought, leaning forward, gazing in the mirror as she carefully applied her eyelashes. If only she was tall and slim, with long lovely legs, and high cheekbones and her mother's red hair! If only....

What good would it do, she asked herself cynically. As if it would help matters! Cary, the only person who really mattered in her life, wouldn't notice any difference if she suddenly became beautiful, that was for sure. Cary wouldn't notice anything about her, she thought miserably.

Yet, later that evening, it seemed that she was wrong. She had been waiting with Mrs. Jefferson for the visitors. The little old lady wore a scintillating pale pink voile gown, decorated with sparkling beads. Her white hair was piled high, her cheeks slightly flushed, her eyes shining.

"We'll show them, Rayanne, my dear," she said, holding Rayanne's hand for a moment. "We'll show them," she repeated triumphantly.

Rayanne wondered what she meant, but at that moment the visitors arrived.

Christine Horlock was first. The tall blonde with her lovely face and blue eyes was wearing a long black

The Fire of Life

dress, slit on either side to show her beautiful legs. She wore a long necklace of sparkling gems, twisted three times around her throat.

"Mrs. Jefferson, how well you're looking. This is very kind of you," she said in her attractive voice. She glanced at Rayanne. "Hullo," she said casually. "You're looking very smart today," she added, her voice amused.

Rayanne blushed, remembering what she must have looked like when they met before.

"She looks beautiful, doesn't she?" Mrs. Jefferson said quickly. "I think that is her color, don't you?"

"It's very beautiful," Christine agreed.

Then came Nurse Daphne Macintyre, equally lovely in a different way: tall, slim, with dark hair, lovely dark eyes and that magically attractive husky voice.

"Mrs. Jefferson, I can see your holiday did you the world of good. You look so well!"

"You have met Rayanne?" Mrs. Jefferson said with a smile.

It was strange, but Daphne Macintyre's face seemed to change, Rayanne noticed. It hardened, yet she smiled, a smile that didn't reach her eyes. "Yes, I have met Miss Briscoe. How is your work going?" she asked. "Or isn't it?" she added.

"Very well indeed," said Mrs. Jefferson, giving Rayanne no time to speak. "Too fast for my liking, because I would like Rayanne to stay forever."

Then the two vets came with Cary. Rayanne hardly noticed the two men—Leslie Someone-or-other, a tall, broad-shouldered man with dark hair and a short pointed beard, and Loftus Jones, a little man with sandy hair and freckles all over his face—for she was looking at Cary.

And then Rayanne's face flamed with embarrassment as Mrs. Jefferson said, "Doesn't Rayanne look beautiful, Cary, dear? I really think this dress was made for her."

Cary looked grave. "I agree, mother. The color is perfect and the style very fashionable. You look very beautiful, Ray," he said almost solemnly.

Rayanne wanted to run and hide, or the floor to open and swallow her. Never in all her life had she felt so embarrassed. She could see the quick amused glance Christine and Daphne had exchanged and the way the two vets were staring at her.

"Your mother gave me the frock," Rayanne said, then wished she hadn't, for perhaps Cary had seen it before, perhaps he knew it was his mother's "wedding nightie"; he might even, with his strange sense of humor, make a joke about it.

Fortunately Mrs. Jefferson took charge of the situation.

"What about a nice cold drink for us all, Cary, dear? You're the host. Your poor old mother shouldn't have to remind you...."

He smiled, bent and kissed her. "My poor old mother enjoys doing so. What'll you all have?" He led the way to the small but beautiful little bar, made of woven straw.

They followed him, Loftus and Leslie walking with Daphne and Christine, Rayanne with her hostess.

As they sat on the *stoep*, drinking and talking, Mrs. Jefferson constantly drew Cary's attention to Rayanne. Not that he seemed to mind. He sat next to her and began talking about a baby giraffe that had been born that morning.

"I had meant to tell you so that you could come and

witness it, but the giraffe fooled us all, for we hadn't expected the little one for another week. Tell Kwido to take you there in the morning," he said.

"Thank you. I'd love to see it," said Rayanne, very conscious that though Christine and Daphne were joking and laughing with the two men, who were including Mrs. Jefferson in the conversation, both Christine and Daphne kept looking her way, both had eyes that were watching her, suspiciously. Did they think she was playing up to Cary's mother in the hope of getting Cary, Rayanne wondered. If so, they must be mad. Absolutely mad!

At dinner, Rayanne sat next to Cary. This, of course, was his mother's doing! In fact, it was embarrassing all through the meal, for Mrs. Jefferson constantly said things that implied that something exciting and wonderful might soon be announced.

Later when the ladies went out to the *stoep* and the men stayed behind for their port, Daphne Macintyre sat down next to Rayanne.

"How are things going?" she asked bluntly. "You seem to have won over the old girl."

"I don't understand..." Rayanne began, hastily standing up, not telling the truth.

Daphne laughed. An ugly laugh, very different from her usual attractively husky voice. "Oh, don't be so dumb. You know very well what I mean. Is Sir Joe Letherington really your godfather?"

Rayanne's quick temper flared. "Of course he is," she said angrily. "I'm not a liar, nor," she added, "am I interested in Cary Jefferson. You can have him if you want him... that is, of course, if you can get him." She turned away and bumped into someone.

Startled as she felt warm firm hands on her arms

steadying her, she looked up, and found herself gazing closely into Cary's face. How quietly he must have come up! How much had he heard?

Now he took her arm. "I want to show you something, Ray. We won't be a moment, mother," he apologized as they passed the plump little old lady, holding court with Loftus Jones, who was laughing at something she said.

Mrs. Jefferson beamed, "That's all right, darling. Take your time."

Rayanne almost ran out of the room, but Cary's hand held her back. He took her to a room she had never been in before, obviously his study—a small high-ceilinged room lined with books with a desk close to the window. He closed the door behind him and leaned against it, releasing her arm.

She turned to stare at him. "You have something to show me?"

He smiled. "Only myself."

Rayanne frowned, puzzled. Was he joking? If so....

He moved toward her so that they stood close together, but he did not touch her. He looked down at her.

"First I want to apologize."

"Apologize?" she echoed.

"Yes, for my mother's behavior. She's so frightened I'll fall for the wrong kind of person that she'll go to any lengths. She has decided that you would make me a suitable wife, so...."

"So?" Rayanne lifted her chin. "So what?"

"So she's determined to show Christine and Daphne that you're the chosen one."

"Chosen?" Rayanne asked bitterly. "By whom?"

Cary smiled. "By her, of course."

There was a pause that seemed never-ending. Then Rayanne found her voice.

The Fire of Life 251

"Of course," she said. "If that's all...."

"It isn't." Even as she moved, he moved, too, standing between her and the door. "There is something else."

"Something else?" she repeated.

"Yes. Why do you hate men? Or are you afraid of them?"

She stared at him, bewildered. "Who ever said I hated or feared men?"

"No one. It stands out a mile. Every time a man enters the room, your whole body stiffens, your face goes hard, your eyes are full of—either fear or animosity. I can't make it out."

"But I don't hate men...." Rayanne's voice rose slightly, and at that moment the door opened.

It was Christine. She looked at the two standing there and she looked amused.

"It's taken you a long time to show Miss Briscoe whatever it is you had to show her, Cary. Maybe she doesn't understand. Perhaps I could help."

Cary laughed. "No one can help, thanks. We'll finish this discussion another time, Ray. Okay?"

"Okay," she said stiffly, and followed them back to the large beautiful drawing room where the others were talking.

What had it all been about, she asked herself as she sat by Mrs. Jefferson's side, laughing at her jokes, listening and trying to hear what was being said, for all the time her mind felt confused, muddled, because nothing made sense. Why had Cary taken her out on her own simply to apologize? Or was it to annoy Christine and Daphne? Or perhaps to delight his mother? But was that fair to his mother? Rayanne found herself thinking. If his mother really wanted Cary to marry this English girl and there was no hope of his wanting to do so, then was it fair to let Mrs. Jefferson think there was hope? It was all such a muddle, and it was hateful to have Christine look at her like that and Daphne's voice change when she spoke to whom she obviously saw as her *rival*. If only she could slip away quietly to bed, Rayanne thought miserably. She wasn't enjoying this at all....

But there was to be no escape. Mrs. Jefferson said proudly, "Rayanne tells me she's quite a good pianist."

Her face bright red, Rayanne denied it. "I didn't! I said I played by ear. I can't read a note."

"Then you can hardly be called a pianist," Daphne Macintyre said dryly.

"Let's hear you, Ray," Cary said quickly, going to the small spinet that stood by the wall facing the window. "Mother sometimes plays on this, so we regularly have it tuned."

"No, I..." Rayanne began, suddenly terrified, aware of critical eyes.

"But, Miss Briscoe, you must play for us," Christine said sweetly. "I'm longing to hear you. It fascinates me so to meet someone who plays by ear."

Rayanne stood up reluctantly, well aware that Christine was convinced it was all a lie, that Rayanne couldn't play a note, that she had lied in boasting about it and that this would betray her! How pleased Christine and Daphne would be.

Sitting at the spinet, Rayanne stretched her fingers, looked around. "What shall I play?" she asked.

"Whatever you can," said Christine, a sarcastic tinge in her voice.

"Anything you like, Ray," Cary said. "We're waiting."

Rayanne half closed her eyes, trying to shut out the

The Fire of Life

picture of those in the room. This had always been her escape—when she had felt most forlorn, most despairing of ever being "someone," of winning her father's approval and love, then she had fled to the piano. Just dreaming her way through the sound, letting her fingers take control, had always comforted her. Not that her family appreciated it; indeed she never played when any of them were around if she could help it, for she would only have got rude comments, teasing because she couldn't "learn to play properly."

Shutting out the rest of the world, Rayanne imagined herself and Cary alone on an enormous empty beach, holding hands, running, dancing along the wet sand, feeling the warm caressing touch of the incoming tide...her fingers touched the keys and she could see Cary laughing at her, could hear herself laughing, too. She could feel the happiness she had always dreamed of, the security his warm hand gave hers, the wonder of the knowledge that he loved her, that she was his.... Vaguely, she heard a haunting tune as her fingers explored sound.

Suddenly she stopped, opened her eyes and shook herself. It was strange. She looked around, stung by the silence. Had she made a fool of herself, she wondered.

"Ray, that was beautiful," Cary said slowly, his voice amazed. "Wasn't it, mother?"

"Lovely, really lovely, Rayanne, dear," Mrs. Jefferson said, her voice husky, a few tears running down her soft cheeks. "Could you play it again?"

Rayanne shook her head. "I'm afraid not. I never can."

"But you must have learned it from somewhere," Daphne said impatiently. "You couldn't have composed it."

"I...hardly heard it myself. What did I play?" Rayanne asked.

Christine laughed. "Honestly, you must have heard it! It was loud enough. Triumphant...."

"I don't agree," said Cary, his quiet voice sounding more impressive to Rayanne than if he had shouted. "I thought it was beautiful—a happy tune. The melody of a dream." He looked at Rayanne. "Am I right?"

Her cheeks flamed with embarrassment. "Quite right, Cary," she said with equal quietness.

CHAPTER FOUR

NEXT MORNING, Rayanne asked Kwido to take her to see the small giraffe. It was fascinating to watch the little animal with his unsteady legs. Mike Crisp was there and he told her a lot about giraffes that she had not realized.

"You can learn from a book," Mike said scornfully, "and know nothing. It's when you live with them that you know."

Rayanne's notes were at last growing longer. But she still had no idea what sort of thesis she would finally write.

Kwido drove her back to the house and as she walked in on her way to her bedroom, for her usual shower and change of clothes, Rayanne paused, for Mrs. Jefferson's voice was clearly audible through the half-open drawing-room door.

"Honestly, Cary, you could have spared me this. You know how I hate that girl!"

"It isn't my fault, mother. I didn't ask her to come."

"Then...."

Rayanne stood still. It was wrong to eavesdrop, she knew, and yet.... Who were they talking about, she wondered. Could it be herself?

"You must have given her your address, Cary," Mrs. Jefferson said crossly.

"I did not, mother," Cary said in that maddening,

exasperated, patient voice he often used. "Without being boastful, you must admit that everyone south of the equator—and many north of it, too—know where the Jefferson Wildlife Reserve is. I met Aileen in London at one of the conferences and have thought nothing of her since. Is it my fault if she chose to honor us with a visit? After all, Aileen Hampton is a veterinary surgeon, interested in wildlife conservation, doing a tour of the world's reserves, and she does mix with the world's elite."

"But why wait until the last moment to send you a cable? She'll be arriving this afternoon!" Mrs. Jefferson almost wailed. "I'll have to put her up here—I can't let her go into one of those ghastly rondavels."

"Perhaps she's coming to visit you, mother," Cary said, again with that amused sarcastic voice Rayanne hated so much. "After all, she met you first. That's how she introduced herself to me. She came up and said, 'Cary Jefferson, I believe?' and when I confessed she was right, she went on, 'I met your charming mother in Paris and she told me all about your wonderful reserve.' You see, mother, it was all your fault. If you didn't blow the trumpet of praise for your only son, she might never have heard of me."

Mrs. Jefferson sighed. "Well, it's too late to do anything about it."

Cary chuckled. "You have to admire her for bright thinking," he laughed as Rayanne hurried away, and added, "That's why she sent the cable."

In her own bedroom, Rayanne hastily showered; the cool water refreshed her hot dusty skin, and she brushed her hair vigorously. How conceited Cary was! Yet could you blame him, she asked herself, when girls so blatantly chased him? It was all a joke to him, some-

The Fire of Life

thing to laugh at. But was it as funny for the unfortunate girls who fell for his charm? On the other hand, was that *his* fault?

There was a simple solution, of course, she told her reflection in the mirror sternly as she carefully made up. She could run away! Run away as fast as she could before she got hurt still more! It was as simple as that. So why didn't she, she asked herself. She knew the answer, therefore it was a waste of time to put it into words. She loved the wretched man... she loved him!

She stood very still, staring at herself in the mirror, pressing her hand hard against her trembling mouth. So she would stay on as long as she could, being a fool, a stupid fool? Was that what love did to you? What would happen next? This Aileen person was almost certain to be tall and slim, with beautiful long legs and a lovely face....

Rayanne found it difficult to join Mrs. Jefferson for lunch, but it had to be done. She was surprised when Mrs. Jefferson said nothing about the new visitor; indeed, Mrs. Jefferson seemed to be in a strange mood. It could hardly be called "depressed," perhaps a more accurate word would be "thoughtful."

So the meal passed with very little said and afterward Rayanne pleaded an imaginary task of writing, for she had a strong feeling that Mrs. Jefferson would like to be alone, that she had something important to think about.

After typing out the notes she had made—Cary had lent her a portable typewriter, scolding her for her lack of thought in not bringing one out with her—Rayanne walked in the garden. It was so hot that as she walked the perspiration trickled down her face; the glare made her eyes ache, yet she felt too restless to stay in her room. If only she had a car of her own, Rayanne thought, and added: and could drive it! It would be nice to go and see Samantha Crisp and have a chat. In Africa it was essential to have a car of your own, particularly in a backwater like this.

A backwater like this... she repeated the words slowly. Where had she heard them? Samantha, of course, in one of her usual moans about the loneliness. Samantha had no car, nor could she drive, either. Both Daphne Macintyre and Christine Horlock had their own cars and Rayanne gathered that they frequently drove to the small town thirty-four miles away. Out here that distance was nothing, you got there in about half an hour. Now, Rayanne was thinking, if only she had a car she could see something of Africa and its beauty... but what was the good, for she wouldn't be here much longer. How long could she stay, she wondered. Mrs. Jefferson had begged her to stay as long as she could. That was what Rayanne wanted too, but how would Cary react?

The garden was very beautiful. She walked right down to the water's edge and shuddered as she watched a crocodile moving with his slow crawl over the sandbank, then pausing, yawning, opening his huge mouth. He looked so absorbed in what he was doing, so determined to get what he wanted. It was funny how scared she was of crocodiles, she told herself. The other animals didn't frighten her at all—except that she thought hippos and rhinos were so hideous she preferred not to look at them! Was she really so interested in wildlife conservation, she asked herself. Or was it all because of Cary?

She walked back slowly toward the house. How lovely were the trees with the bougainvilleas, a lovely purple, climbing up their trunks, and those with their small white scented blossoms. This was a beautiful place. She could live here so happily.

Rayanne's mind seemed to skid to a standstill. Surely she hadn't been stupid enough to get as far as dreaming that maybe one day...?

"Ray!" a familiar deep voice startled her.

She turned and saw Cary striding toward her. He was wearing a safari suit and had bare legs and feet. As he came closer she saw his hair was rumpled and he looked tired. This was so unusual that she found herself saying, "What's happened?"

He smiled ruefully. "Nearly a tragedy. Down the river three children were playing in the water—they said at the edge, but even that's dangerous. Anyhow, a croc grabbed the leg of one and tried to drag the child in... one boy hung on to his friend's arm, but the croc was winning, so the other one grabbed a stick and stuck it in the croc's eye... that made him let go."

"He's all right?"

"Taken to hospital, and he may lose his leg. The one that saved him raced up to one of the wardens and shouted for help. I was there, so we went down. A bright boy to think of it. His father works here."

"Then shouldn't he know not to paddle in the water?"

Cary looked amused. "Isn't it a temptation for anyone to swim on a day as hot as this?"

"Then you find it hot, too? I thought it was just me."

Cary laughed. "The *rooinek* sensitive touch, eh? No, it's unusually hot. By the way, we're having a visitor."

"We are?" Rayanne tried to sound surprised. She felt uncomfortably guilty because of what she had overheard that morning.

"Yes—a bit of a bind. She thinks she knows everything, and I can't stand that kind of woman."

"Really?" Rayanne, remembering what his mother had said, smiled. "Can you stand any type of woman?"

Cary put his hand under her elbow. "Let's get some shade," he said. "That is a provocative question."

There were several chairs and a round white table under an enormous tree, through whose branches, covered closely with dark green leaves, the sun could hardly find its way.

Cary gave her a gentle push so that she had to sit down, then he pulled up a chair and sat down opposite, narrowing his eyes as he looked at her.

"What makes you think I hate women?"

"I didn't say hate." Rayanne lifted her hand and touched each finger as she spoke. "I said can you stand any type of woman. First I hear you say women are a headache, then a nuisance and now a bind. Doesn't that rather imply that you would prefer to be without us?"

"Heaven forbid!" said Cary, smiling at her. "How miserable and boring life would be if we were all men."

"I wonder if you'd really mind. With your dedication to work, surely."

"You've been listening to my mother! Actually, I spend a lot of time enjoying my leisure. I'd say I like women very much—but in their proper place."

"And where is that?" Rayanne paused, then smiled. "In England it would be by the kitchen sink, of course, but as you're lucky enough to have a good staff, I suppose it's behind the coffee table."

"In a way, yes," Cary said slowly, as if thinking. "On the other hand, wouldn't she be a bit of a bore? I mean, Daphne is rather like that. She never reads anything, she just isn't interested in the world or its inhabitants. She's an excellent nurse... but let's face it, she admitted it to us once, she only became a nurse because she was told it was a good way of finding a husband."

"But she's very beautiful. I'm sure she...."

"Beauty isn't everything a man wants, you know." He offered her a cigarette and when she refused asked if she'd mind if he had one.

"Of course not. I just don't care for smoking."

"Sensible girl." He blew out a great puff of smoke. She felt the urge to tell him how bad it was for his lungs, but she held her tongue, because it was no business of hers! "Well, to return... what sort of woman, you asked me?"

"I did not. You twist everything. I asked where is woman's proper place?"

He smiled. "I accept the correction meekly. Now, where is woman's proper place? Perhaps I should say in a man's arms."

There was a silence, a silence Rayanne could almost hear as she stared at him. She shivered. Had he guessed the truth? Had he seen in her eyes that that was just where she wanted to be? In his arms.

Then Cary laughed and broke the moment up. "I know you're not thinking that way, Ray. I think I'd like a woman to have an interest in life: perhaps voluntary work, perhaps a career—something that makes her use her brains and mix with people. I like extraverts, rather than introverts—I don't like women who throw their weight around and think they know everything. Aileen Hampton is one of those. I daresay she's a good vet, but she needn't keep telling me so." He looked up toward the house. "Ah, she's come. Good. I'm glad I found you out here."

"You are?" Rayanne was startled. "But why?"

"I want her to see that I'm already bespoken." He chuckled. "That is, if you don't mind my using you as the dummy. I guess you're used to it by now with all mother's ramblings. She'll bring Aileen out. Try to look at me as if you like me, Ray, and not your usual haughty look."

"I look at you...." Rayanne paused. It was all happening so fast. Cary was making use of her as he believed this Aileen was chasing him! He thought it meant nothing, then... then he had no idea, Rayanne comforted herself, that she loved him?

He smiled and put his hand lightly around her shoulders after he pulled her to her feet. "We'd better go and meet them."

As they walked across the lawn, she was only really conscious of the touch of his hand on her warm arm, and then she saw the group coming out onto the *stoep* and down the few steps to the grass.

Mrs. Jefferson led the way, her plump little body in a pale yellow frock, her hands clasped in front of her waist, her face worried as she was followed by a girl and a man.

"Ah, Cary, there you are. I couldn't find you. Your guests have arrived," she called, her voice clear in the quiet hot air.

Behind her followed the tall girl, with long slender legs, a beautiful face and red hair!

Rayanne caught her breath. Why, that was how her mother must have looked when she was young. That lovely cloud of red hair, the high cheekbones, the rather full mouth, the warm smile....

"Miss Hampton. I hope the drive here from the airport wasn't too exhausting," Cary said, shaking hands. "I want you to meet Rayanne Briscoe."

Aileen Hampton smiled at Rayanne. A warm smile; genuine, surely, Rayanne thought.

"Cary—" Aileen turned to him, ignoring the formality in his voice "—I do hope you'll forgive me, but I brought a friend along, Burt West." She turned to the man by her side.

Rayanne stared at him and he stared back. There was nothing striking about him except that he was very short—about her height, she noticed. He gave her a friendly smile. His blond hair was untidy; he looked tired.

"I hope you'll forgive me, Mr. Jefferson, but it was a chance in a thousand. I'm a professional photographer and would be most grateful if you'd let me take photographs of what goes on here. I'm planning an article on this wildlife conservation," he said. "It's not easy to break the barrier of Jefferson Hall," he added, with a rather sweet shy smile, "and when I met Aileen and she told me she was coming here and suggested I escort her ... well—" he gave a little nervous laugh "—I took the chance. I'd show you the article and the photographs before I submitted them to the magazine, of course. I really am interested," he added, a pleading note in his voice.

"How funny," Rayanne said quickly, feeling sorry for him and wondering why Cary was so silent. "I'm writing a thesis on wildlife conservation."

Burt West smiled at her almost gratefully. "Then we're looking for the same thing." He turned to silent Cary and smiled. "Let's face it, I admit I've never had much time for wildlife conservation and I thought if I could see it for myself and how it works out, I might understand how you chaps feel about it."

Cary's stern face relaxed. "How right you are! We shall try to convert you. Of course you can stay with us. I don't know if we have room in the house, but there are—"

Mrs. Jefferson stepped forward. "Most certainly not, Cary. No guest of mine is going into one of those rondavels. We'll be delighted to have you stay awhile, Mr. West."

He smiled at her. "Burt, please, Mrs. Jefferson. This is awfully good of you."

"You've come at a good time," Cary said. "The next course starts in a few days, and you might be interested in the lectures and tours we take the students on."

"Oh, I will be. This is marvelous." Burt pressed his hands together and smiled at them all. "A chance in a lifetime!"

"And how are you, Cary?" Aileen Hampton asked, moving to his side. "You look a bit harassed."

"Well, we've just had a kid nearly caught by a croc, and it's always rather shattering."

"He's all right?"

Mrs. Jefferson was pale. "He wasn't...?"

"No." Cary quickly told them what he had already told Rayanne.

"I hope the crocodile's eye wasn't hurt," said Aileen. "Is he still there?"

"No, he slid off in the water when he saw us running down. I felt like shooting him," said Cary.

"It really does happen?" Burt said eagerly. "I mean...."

"Only—" Cary's voice was curt "—if you're fool enough to walk in the river, or near the edge."

Burt got the message, for he grinned. "Don't worry, I'm not a fool."

"I think we'd better show our visitors to their rooms," Mrs. Jefferson said. "And you, Cary, must go and wash your face. I've never seen you looking like that. And no socks or shoes—tch, tch! Come along, my dear." She took Aileen's arm. "I hope you'll enjoy your visit here."

"I'm sure I shall." Aileen Hampton smiled at Cary. "I've been looking forward to it for a long time."

Rayanne found herself walking by Burt West's side. He yawned and grinned, "Sorry about that. I find this heat rather exhausting. Where are you from?"

"England. And you?" Rayanne found it easy to talk to him. Maybe because she didn't have to tilt her head and look up at him, she wondered.

"London. I've known Aileen for years. A real beaut, isn't she?"

"She certainly is," Rayanne said warmly, and knew the pangs of jealousy, for Cary was talking to the girl, laughing, his hand under her elbow as he helped her up the few steps to the *stoep*.

THE NEXT FEW DAYS were strange ones for Rayanne. Sometimes she wondered if they could really be happening or if there was something wrong with her, for nothing made sense.

In the first place, Mrs. Jefferson practically ignored her. Normally this wouldn't be strange, but after the fuss she had made of Rayanne, and the real love she had shown, her sudden chilliness, her ignoring Rayanne while spending all her time talking eagerly to Aileen Hampton was so completely different that Rayanne could not help feeling hurt. Had she done something wrong, she wondered. Said something unintentionally that annoyed Mrs. Jefferson? Or was it just that Cary's mother had decided Aileen Hampton would be the perfect wife for Cary?

Maybe she would, for no one could deny that Aileen was one of the nicest people Rayanne had ever known. Very friendly, always paying little compliments about "that color matches your eyes perfectly" or "you should wear long dresses more often; they give you a glamorous look." Not silly, obviously false compliments, but words said with sincerity. Aileen and Rayanne spent many an hour late at night talking together, feeling the heat and sitting on the screened *stoep*, looking at the beauty of the starlit sky. They learned to know one another well. Aileen was an only child, smothered with love, while Rayanne felt that no one in her family cared for her. They discussed their problems, gave one another advice. It was impossible, Rayanne knew, no matter how envious and jealous she felt, it was impossible not to like Aileen very much.

The only person who didn't was Cary! This was the oddest thing to Rayanne, for she just could not understand why he was so cool and impersonal to Aileen, often formal, almost rude. He rarely talked to her alone, far more often seeking out Rayanne and sitting with her.

Right from the beginning, they seemed to have divided up into strange groups. That first evening Cary had turned to Rayanne.

"Ray, would you mind taking Burt around with you and Kwido? I'm rather short of Land Rovers at the moment. Seeing you're both interested in the same phase of wildlife conservation, it might help."

"Of course I don't mind," Ray had agreed instantly.

The Fire of Life

And so, during the mornings, sometimes in the afternoons, Rayanne and Burt would go off with Kwido. It was in many ways much more interesting, Rayanne found. She liked Burt; they were both relaxed together. Kwido showed them everything and Burt never stopped asking questions. He carried with him a small tape recorder so that later in the afternoon he and Rayanne could listen to Kwido's descriptions and make notes of what they felt was important.

Meanwhile Cary would take Aileen Hampton and leave her with Leslie and Loftus, saying that he was busy preparing for the next lot of students. It was true that the staff was already arriving and that no doubt Cary was busy, Rayanne thought, but she didn't feel this really excused his behavior, for he was little short of rude to Aileen. Not that Aileen worried about it. If she and Rayanne ever discussed Cary, Aileen was full of admiration. She thought he was a wonderful man, unselfish, dedicated, a devoted son—in fact, super! That he would make some lucky woman a wonderful husband. It was obvious she was hoping to be the "lucky woman." Rayanne learned how to agree laughingly, to talk lightly of Christine and Daphne's attempts to "hook him," and Aileen, having met them both during her introduction to everyone and everything, agreed that they "hadn't a hope."

"Cary is different. He wants someone with more than a pretty face," Aileen said. "He needs someone who understands his fanatic love not only for animals but for everything to do with them."

In the evenings Rayanne would feel sorry for Aileen, though, oddly enough, Aileen didn't seem to notice anything strange, for every night Cary chose to sit by Rayanne, making it obvious that he liked her company, doing many little thoughtful things that surprised Rayanne and hurt her as well, for she knew he was doing it for one reason only. Not because he loved her—but because he wanted to make Aileen realize there was "no hope." Yet Aileen seemed happy enough, chatting with Mrs. Jefferson and Burt, or with Leslie and Loftus, whom Mrs. Jefferson frequently invited, sometimes with and sometimes without Christine and Daphne.

Then the students arrived. Most of them were in their late teens, great husky lads full of noise and laughter that would sometimes drift across the garden to the house. There were quite a few girls, all dressed in crazy-looking clothes but obviously enjoying their stay. The lectures were in the afternoons, so Rayanne and Burt were able to attend. Burt would sit, looking entranced, as he listened to Cary's lectures.

There was no doubt, Rayanne thought, that Cary was a wonderful lecturer. He could make the dullest facts interesting. He could show them the importance of conservation, the difficulties, the plans for the future. He could even prove the importance of preserving the wildlife of the country.

Burt admitted he was converted. "Somehow I hadn't thought of it that way," he told Rayanne.

"I know, that was how I felt at first. It seemed such a waste of money to keep all these wild animals in safe comfort when so many millions of people were starving and homeless," she agreed. "Yet now...."

The students seemed really interested and there were a number of small buses that took them around the reserve every day. Of course the skill of the game catchers was demonstrated and the students saw how the animals were drugged for examination or trans-

The Fire of Life

ported to a different reserve. Naturally, the students were fascinated by the crossbow and dart that looked like an ordinary hypodermic syringe with a tail added and that when it sank into the animal's hide or skin, soon drugged him and sent him to sleep. After the examination, treatment or removal, an antidote to the drug was given and the animal recovered within seconds and without any harm having been done. In fact, wounds had frequently been treated or even operations successfully performed.

Rayanne, Burt and Kwido followed some of the demonstrations, but Cary said to them that later he would let them take part in a real one.

"I've promised to transport a dozen white hippos to England. It's going to be quite a performance."

Rayanne said nothing, but she wondered just how long Aileen and Burt planned to stay! Which rather applied to her, too, she thought worriedly. How long could you pretend it took to write a thesis? And what was she going to write? She always had the fear that one day Cary would ask to see it. How could she refuse when he had been so generous as to let her stay for so long?

Burt was producing some amazingly good photos. He even said that maybe he would write a book about it all. He smiled as he spoke.

"Aiming high, but why not? I'm a journalist."

"But are people sufficiently interested?" Rayanne asked.

"We should make them," said Burt, his freckles showing bright in the sunshine.

One evening Rayanne was late joining the "family group," as Mrs. Jefferson called it with a quick smile at Aileen, and Cary was sitting next to Aileen, listening to what she was saying, nodding his head. He looked up as Rayanne entered the room, left Aileen immediately, though she was in the middle of a sentence, and went to Rayanne, to lead her to a chair, get her a drink and sit down by her side.

Rayanne looked at him, keeping her voice very quiet. "Is it necessary to be so rude?" she asked.

Cary smiled. "Was it so obvious? Then it was successful. The best remedy is to behave so badly that the hunter loses interest," he said with equal quietness, bending close to her.

Rayanne was looking at Aileen. Surely it must have hurt her? Or was she so sure of success that things like this seemed trivial to her, Rayanne wondered. Aileen was talking to Mrs. Jefferson, who looked rather upset, glancing across the room toward her son. Rayanne sighed. Had Mrs. Jefferson decided that Aileen would be the perfect wife and was she upset because things were not going the right way?

After dinner, following the others back to the drawing room, Rayanne felt Cary's hand on her arm and he led her outside to the garden.

"Listen," he said, "the hyenas are out again."

She listened. The strange eerie howls made her shiver. They reminded her of that first terrifying night in the rondavel. Impulsively she turned to him.

"Did you put me in that awful rondavel in order to frighten me?" she asked abruptly. "Were you trying to make me change my mind about staying?"

It was too dark to see his expression, but his fingers tightened around her arm. "On the contrary, I was merely protecting you from the malicious gossip that might have ensued had I had you stay here with no chaperon...." He sounded amused as he spoke. "Can you imagine what Daphne and Christine would have said? I wonder if you have any idea just how malicious a frustrated female can be."

Rayanne turned to him quickly. "Why do you always say such nasty things about women? We're not all malicious. I think you're being absolutely hateful to poor Aileen, the way you ignore her. After all, she is your friend."

"My friend?" He sounded amused. "That's interesting. I met her once. How can you call her my friend? That reminds me—you never answered my question: why do you hate men so much? You always stiffen, look defiant, or on the defensive as if expecting an attack. Surely you can't judge all men by your brothers' behavior? No, I forgot." His voice changed and became cold. "You're not afraid of Burt West, that's obvious. What is it that Burt has that the rest of men lack? How come you're so relaxed with him, so at ease?"

"Am I?" Rayanne was startled. "Yes, I am, I suppose," she said thoughtfully.

"Why?" he asked again.

"I think because he treats me as an equal. He's never condescending, never corrects me, never patronizing. He gives me the credit of having some brains."

Cary groaned. "Must we always have this, Ray? Who said you had no brains? I told you that you had. You've got a real chip on your shoulder about it, and you'll never be the real you until we've got rid of it."

"I doubt if that's possible. Twenty-two years of being made to feel inferior, of being laughed at and even despised...."

"Ray!" His hands caught her by the shoulders and he shook her. "Stop it, do you hear me? No one considers you inferior, despicable, nor do they laugh at you."

"They do!" Suddenly Rayanne felt desperate. "Even your mother has stopped loving me. It was so wonderful when she fussed. I've never been treated like that before. She seemed to enjoy being with me, but she's changed. It's Aileen, now. Aileen, the perfect wife for her wonderful son," Rayanne added bitterly.

His fingers dug into her flesh for a moment and then he released her, almost pushing her away.

"Just how stupid can you be!" he said angrily. "Can't you see why mother is doing that?"

"Doing what?"

"Oh, for crying out loud!" He gave a dramatic-sounding groan, took her arm and walked her down the lawn, into the utter darkness. In the distance the hyenas howled, an owl hooted and somewhere a lion growled. "Look, Ray. Mother thinks she's being very clever. She forgets it's a method she's used as far back as I can remember. She has a theory that children, particularly sons, will always want what they can't have, so she believes that if she praises someone, I shall take an immediate dislike to that person. She has now decided that she's pushed you down my throat too much, having apparently forgotten this method, and that by doing so she has made me have doubts about you. Now she dislikes Aileen very much. Why, I don't know. As I know, you think Aileen is a nice girl. She'll be a good wife to someone. That someone is not me. But mother, bless her foolish little heart, thinks that if she now pushes Aileen at me, I shall revolt.... Get it?" His fingers tightened around her arm. "You do see what I mean?"

Rayanne drew a long deep breath. It didn't make sense... yet it did make sense, in a way. Just like everything else that happened in this hot, wonderful place, nothing really made sense, yet always did!

"I do see what you mean, but... but is it fair to Aileen?"

"Fair? I don't get it."

"Well, she loves you...."

Cary roared with laughter. "Ray, sometimes you slay me," he said, trying to control his mirth. "Can anyone else be so naive, so...? Look, Aileen has been in and out of love with famous, wealthy men. She's always in the news. Why she's looked at me, I honestly don't know. But love.... No, she doesn't love me."

Rayanne hesitated. "She... we talk quite a lot and... well...."

"Well?"

"Well, I think she does."

"You're wrong." Cary turned around, leading her. "We'd better get back or mother will send a search party, fearing we've fallen into the crocs. No, Aileen doesn't love me at all. Not any more than you do. You've got quite a thing for Burt, haven't you?" he asked, his voice changing again.

"I like him."

"Like? How does one define the difference between like and love?"

"There's a very big difference," Rayanne said quickly.

"And what is it, if I may ask?" Cary was being his pompous self again. He must be angry about something, Rayanne thought.

"Liking... well, you enjoy being with the person because you're relaxed, you share interests, you make each other laugh."

"That sounds to me more like an interpretation of love."

"Oh, no," she said earnestly. "You can love someone and still feel uncomfortable when you're with him. When you love someone, you want to please him and you're often afraid of saying the wrong thing and hurting him. When you love someone, you worry about that person being happy. You don't think of your own happiness, which is what you do when you *like* someone."

"I see. I hadn't looked at it that way." Cary led the way up the stairs to the *stoep*. "Would you play for us tonight, Ray?" he asked. "Mother and I did enjoy your music so much. Or are you nervous? I can't see why, when you play so well...."

Now she could see his face. He was staring at her in a strange way, a way she had never noticed before.

"You really want me to?" she asked.

"Yes, I do," he told her.

"All right," she said, "I will."

She went and sat at the spinet and lifted her hands, half closing her eyes. What should she think about?

Liking and loving... the difference between them. It was funny, because you could be so happy when you liked someone, and so miserable when you loved them.

Her fingers touched the keys, moving as if of their own accord. She liked Burt. How happy she was with him. But she loved Cary... she loved him so much, so very much, and yet there were times when life no longer had any reason, when she wondered why love had to be like that....

The sounds came wistful, puzzled, but with happy moments followed again by hesitation as if the pianist was trying to put her problems into the sound of music.

The others listened silently, and when she had finished they clapped their praise.

"It's a shame you can't remember a tune," Burt said. "That would make a good record."

CHAPTER FIVE

IT WAS A STRANGE SITUATION, Rayanne thought. The days were full and the evenings pleasant. Sometimes she was happy, sometimes sad.

Cary might be right in saying his mother was trying to push poor Aileen at him, but Rayanne undoubtedly missed Mrs. Jefferson's affection and fussiness. Now it was Aileen who apparently mattered, no longer Rayanne! Then there was Burt, still friendly, yet sometimes the way he spoke made Rayanne wonder if he was getting serious. This worried her, for their friendship would have to end if he wanted it to be more than just a pleasant friendship!

One afternoon, sitting quietly at the back of the lecture hall, looking at Cary as he stood on the dais, obviously at ease, joking as he told them about the time they had a baby elephant... she thought, *how handsome he is in a rugged way*. A man of strength, determination. It didn't seem to make sense—this being chased by girls and letting his mother think she was matchmaking. Or was he right when he'd said she, Rayanne, had no idea of a real mother-and-child relationship?

She watched him tug at the lobe of his left ear as he described feeding the baby elephant with a bottle. Cary always tugged at his ear when he was searching for words. Not that he often had to seek, for he knew just what to say and when. How smooth his dark hair always

The Fire of Life

looked; he never seemed to need a shave: this was something she liked in any man. That and good manners. These were important to her.

Yet suppose Cary did the impossible and loved her, Rayanne asked herself. Could she be happy living here? Could she? Unconsciously Rayanne shook her head. What a stupid question to ask herself. Of course she could!

Burt nudged her. "What did he say? I didn't get it," he whispered.

Rayanne stared, hardly seeing him, for her thoughts were far away. "What did he say? Well, I'm afraid I didn't hear, either," she admitted.

Burt shrugged and looked back at the dais. Rayanne looked, too. Now Cary was talking about baboons....

Was that why she came to these lectures? Not to learn or listen, but to look at Cary. She relaxed, knowing no one was looking at her, not even Cary, who might be watching with that amused supercilious smile she loathed. Did she loathe it, she asked herself. Of course she did!

After the lecture, Burt looked at her oddly. "What were you dreaming about?" he asked.

They were caught up in the crowd of chattering, laughing students and swept along past the hostels to the big playing field where the students divided up to have some "exercise." Burt and Rayanne walked down the narrow hedge-lined lane that was a shortcut to the house. Rayanne noticed that the hedge had been cut. So for once Cary had done what his mother wanted!

Later, lying in the deliciously refreshing bathwater, Rayanne tried to think sensibly, even logically. What should she do? Finish her thesis, basing it on what she had learned here, and return to England?

She shivered. She could imagine her father's eyebrows going sky-high. "You're soon back," he'd say. "Can't you settle down at anything?" and then he'd sigh as if exasperated.

And her mother? She, too, would be disappointed. She had never said so in as many words, but Rayanne knew her mother would be relieved when her only daughter got married and was safely out of the way. With Rayanne at home, there were invariably scenes with her brothers. "Why must you always quarrel with everyone?" her mother had once asked, in an exhausted voice.

"Because I won't let them get away with it," Rayanne had said angrily. "Just because I'm a girl...."

Her brothers, she asked herself. How they would laugh!

"Were you scared of the lions?" they'd ask, and probably pretend to bet that she'd run a mile the first time she saw a snake.

If only they would stop treating her like a... a nincompoop; that was a good word for it. If only they would let her be a person, if they would respect her.

Respect. Maybe if she could find a way to make them *respect* her, they would stop their infuriating teasing. Well, wasn't that what she had come for? Six thousand miles in search of "respect" and how far had she got? She hadn't even begun her thesis... all she had done was to fall crazily in love with a man who found women a *nuisance*.

She heard a hammering on her door and called out that she was in the bath. It was Aileen's voice that replied.

"No hurry, Rayanne. I'll see you later. I've got some news."

The Fire of Life

"Okay," Rayanne called.

The warm refreshing bath had suddenly turned cold. She scrambled out, rubbing herself dry, choosing a soft lilac-colored cotton frock. What good news could Aileen have, Rayanne wondered as she peered anxiously in the mirror. Not that it really mattered what she looked like. She had long ago given up any attempt to equal Aileen's loveliness, or Christine's and Daphne's for that matter.

She went to the big picture window and looked out at the garden with its gradual slope to the river, the trees crowded close to the water with their bright flowers, and the distant mountains. It was so beaut—

She stopped seeing the view as she saw Aileen and Cary talking together. He was nodding, his face amused, and Aileen was talking excitedly, waving her hands about as she spoke. Was she telling him her "good" news, Rayanne wondered. For although Aileen had only said the word "news," her excited voice had added the word "good," though it was not spoken.

Now Cary and Aileen were walking up the garden, Cary nodding his head as if in agreement. But it was Aileen who was so excited, putting her hand on his arm, pausing to stand in front of him as she talked.

Suddenly Rayanne was sure she knew what was going to happen next. The way Aileen looked up at him, the way Cary smiled. In a moment, he would take her in his arms and kiss her.

Rayanne turned away quickly, hurrying to the door, going to the drawing room. Was Cary lying about Aileen? Were they really planning for their future? Had they allowed Mrs. Jefferson to believe that she had organized the marriage, for that would give her a great deal of pleasure?

But if so, Cary had lied. Lied when he said he was not going to marry Aileen. Somehow it was hard to believe Cary to be a liar....

Burt was sitting opposite Mrs. Jefferson. He looked up with a grin.

"Our hostess is trying to teach me to play chess. She's brilliant at it."

Mrs. Jefferson hardly glanced at Rayanne. "I don't think Rayanne would enjoy it. It requires so much concentration," she said as she studied the little figures on the board. "I'm not sure you're going to be good at it, either, Burt. Your mind wanders. Not like Aileen.... She can concentrate and forget everything else," Mrs. Jefferson said proudly, almost as if Aileen was already her daughter.

Perhaps it was all settled, Rayanne thought, as she picked up a magazine lying on the long walnut coffee table and sat down. Perhaps it would be announced at dinner.

But it wasn't. Aileen and Cary came into the drawing room together and Cary handed out drinks. There was a general conversation over dinner, which was, as usual, beautifully cooked and served. But Rayanne didn't enjoy it. She was waiting... and the longer she waited, the harder it got.

Aileen's eyes were shining and her voice kept rising excitedly even when she was talking about trivial matters. She kept looking at Cary and he would give her a little smile of understanding.

Perhaps it was that smile that hurt the most, for Rayanne, after dinner, pleaded a shocking migraine and an early night if they would excuse her.

Mrs. Jefferson didn't even look up from the crochet

she was doing. "Of course. I hope you'll feel better in the morning."

Cary was talking to Aileen, who was laughing, and neither looked up. Rayanne doubted if they had even heard what she had said. It was Burt who walked down the corridor with her, looking concerned.

"Is it very bad, Rayanne? Do you often get migraines? There's some very good drugs now for it. Is there anything you'd like?" he asked anxiously, as he saw her to her bedroom door.

She shook her head. "No, thanks, Burt. It's sweet of you, but all I really want is a dark room and sleep."

The sleep was denied her, for she lay in bed, turning over, pummeling her pillows a dozen times. But she could not still her thoughts that seemed to be hurtling around her brain in circles.

Why was Aileen so excited, almost triumphant? Why was Cary suddenly devoting himself to Aileen, something he had never done before? Why did his mother look so complacent, so pleased with herself?

It could only mean one thing.... Yet did it?

Round about twelve o'clock, there was a tap on Rayanne's door.

"Are you awake?" Aileen called gently, slightly opening the door.

Rayanne sat up, switched on the bedside light. "Yes. Come in," she said, her voice husky. Somehow she must act as if it meant nothing to her. Nothing at all.

Aileen came to sit on the edge of the bed. She was glowing with happiness.

"I just can't believe it's true," she told Rayanne.

Rayanne tried to smile. "What is true?"

"About Cary. I mean, for all his funny little ways, he

really is terrific. Such a darling. I thought I'd have a hard battle, but it was amazingly easy. I just asked him and—"

"Asked him?" Rayanne almost gasped. Was it all right in these days of the so-called permissive society for the girl to make the proposal, she wondered.

Aileen nodded excitedly, her red hair swinging. "Yes. You see there's this famous man, Alto Georgius. He's absolutely fabulous, right at the top, and knowing him would probably mean I'd get a job in South America at their research station, but it's terribly hard to get in. Someone told me Cary knew Alto quite well... that's why I came out here. It was sheer luck meeting his mother in Paris. Then I saw that in England he was talking at the conference, so I went along and introduced myself, and the rest—" she waved her hands about "—easy as can be. I was frank with Cary, told him what I wanted, and he said he'd do what he could for me but would make no promise. Now he's been in touch with Alto and I'm to meet him in Cape Town. He's on tour around here and I may get the chance to go with him. Cary's coming, too, so it will be really great."

Rayanne could only blink as she tried to grasp what she had been told. Aileen had come not to "hook" Cary, as Daphne would have described it, but in search of an important introduction. There had never been any question of Aileen's being in love with him; she just wanted to *use* him.

Yet she obviously thought Cary wonderful, and if he went on this tour, too.... Both such dedicated people, both sharing the same interests?

"I'm so glad for you," Rayanne said, and thought how weak it sounded. "I really am."

"I know." Aileen smiled at her. "It's been nice knowing you and having someone intelligent to talk to, at least. Maybe we'll meet again."

"You're going?"

"Tomorrow. Burt's staying on, of course, because he and I are just friends. We have little in common." Aileen stood up. "This means so much to me, Rayanne. I just can't believe it's coming true!"

After Aileen had gone, Rayanne snuggled down in her bed. She felt dazed. She had wasted all that time feeling jealous of Aileen, envious, wondering when the wedding would be, when Aileen merely wanted something....

But why couldn't Cary have told her, Rayanne asked herself. Why had he let her believe Aileen was chasing him? Was it a sign that he knew Rayanne was in love with him and it amused him to see her hurt and anxious? No, surely not, she told herself. Cary wasn't cruel. He couldn't be deliberately cruel, of that she was sure.

However, next day after Aileen had said farewell and Mike Crisp had driven her to the airport, Rayanne wondered if Cary could be deliberately cruel, after all. Burt had vanished, saying he wanted to develop some films. Mrs. Jefferson was busy talking to the gardeners about their work for the day. So Rayanne found herself temporarily alone with Cary in the garden, drinking ice-cold drinks under the trees.

"Well?" Cary asked, his voice amused. "She wasn't after me, after all, as you thought. At least, not in the same sense!"

Inside Rayanne, anger stirred slightly. "You gave me the impression that she was."

He laughed. "What a joke! If I really thought every girl was after me, I'd end up an egoist."

"You're one now, I think."

"I thought you probably did. A proper monster, that's how you see me, isn't it?" He laughed again. "Well, at least Aileen knows where she's heading. Ambitious, hardworking, determined to succeed—what a horrible mixture for a woman!"

Rayanne sat up stiffly. "And why shouldn't she be ambitious, hardworking and determined to succeed? Can you give me any reason why that makes her a horrible mixture? Aileen is not only most attractive but a very nice person!" She paused, for she saw he was trying not to laugh, his eyes amused. "So..." she began, and stopped.

"So what? Maybe I'm an exception, but I like my women feminine and helpless," Cary said. "A successful woman is usually a pathetic creature."

"And why should she be pathetic and a man not?" Rayanne asked, indignantly again.

Cary chuckled. "I didn't say that a man wasn't. You're quoting my words before they're spoken."

"The way you spoke implied that you meant women only."

"Well—" Cary spoke thoughtfully "—let's face it, Ray. Women mean well but usually fail by trying too hard to succeed."

A cold finger seemed to slide down her back. "Now that's a nasty thing to say!"

He looked astonished, even perhaps a little hurt. "It wasn't meant to be." He spoke almost accusingly. "Now you're looking at my words out of context. What I meant was that because women are idealists, they often tackle more than they can finish."

"Isn't that better than tackling nothing?"

Cary tugged thoughtfully at the lobe of his left ear.

"You could be right...." Rayanne felt a warm flush of triumph, for he had admitted it. "I suppose," he added, spoiling it with his skepticism.

"Do you succeed in doing everything you tackle?" she demanded.

He smiled. "Of course not."

"Then why..." she began, then stopped. Sighing, she looked at him. What was the good of arguing? They could talk all night and get nowhere. He was too clever. You could never hope to win and he knew it, and let you know he knew it, too.

She was surprised when he suddenly leaned forward and took hold of her hand. "Don't look so stricken, little Ray. I think women are wonderful."

Jerking her hand free, she glared at him. "You don't, you know you don't. You like to make fun of us, make us look fools. That's what you like doing. You men are all the same. You make use of us, but you don't respect us or... or...." She had to stop, for her voice was frighteningly unsteady.

He moved with a swiftness that startled her, kneeling in front of her, his hands on the arms of her chair so that she could not escape.

"We do love you," he said, supplying the word she had been unable to say. "Otherwise we wouldn't marry you. What you women don't seem to understand is that the average man suffers from an inferiority complex. We're fully aware that you women are not only highly intelligent but much stronger than we are, and we're so terrified that you're going to dominate us, we have to try to make you feel small and insignificant. Can you really blame us? It's a battle for survival."

His face was frighteningly close to hers. For once, she could see herself in his eyes. She felt herself trembling and his eyes began to twinkle. As usual, he was teasing her.

This arrogant, hateful... she began to think, but her thoughts slid to a standstill. Arrogant, perhaps, but hateful, no, quite definitely no.

"Ray," he said. "Oh, Ray, why do you rise to the bait so quickly?"

And suddenly she was laughing.

"You are the end," she told him. "The positive end!"

He chuckled. "Play it cool, baby," he joked. "This is just a beginning."

He leaned forward and lightly kissed her cheek.

"See you," he said, rising to his feet with incredible speed, and she found herself alone, sitting back, still shaking a little, and watched him go with his long rapid strides toward the house.

What had he meant, she wondered. *Just a beginning...?*

SLOWLY RAYANNE FOLLOWED CARY into the house, meeting his mother when she reached it.

"Dear child," Mrs. Jefferson said warmly as she took Rayanne's hands in hers. "I'm so glad that girl has gone. She was such a bore."

Rayanne stared. "I thought you liked her."

"Liked her?" Mrs. Jefferson laughed. "I couldn't bear her, but she was Cary's friend, after all, and I had to be polite. I'm glad we're on our own again."

Later Burt said much the same. "I can't stand that type of career woman. She can talk of nothing but her work. Anyone would think my work was utterly unimportant."

"I thought you were a friend of hers," Rayanne said.

He laughed. "So we are, but even friends know the truth about one another. She uses me. I can be useful at times because I know the right people. Apart from that, she has no time for me. I bore her."

"But, Burt, you've never bored me," Rayanne said impulsively, then regretted it, for she saw the light in his eyes as he turned to her.

"I don't?"

They were walking along the lawn, just above the edge of the river. Several crocodiles were asleep on the hot sand and Burt was taking photographs of them. He had a movie camera and wanted the crocs to move, but they stubbornly refused, their eyes tightly closed.

"Well, we seem able to talk about anything," said Rayanne. "We argue about everything, and it's fun."

He laughed. "That's the difference between you and Aileen. In Aileen's eyes, only one person can possibly be right—Aileen Hampton. *You're* always ready to admit that the other fellow could be right. Then one can argue. Oh, Aileen's not bad. Actually I'm quite fond of her, but she does rather send me around the bend with her know-all. These dedicated women drive me mad!"

"Cary said much the same," Rayanne told him, pausing to toss a pebble into the still water, which hardly rippled in response.

"He did?" Burt laughed. "He made it pretty plain that he had no time for her. She only wanted that introduction, you know. You thought she was after him— Cary, I mean, didn't you?" He laughed again. "You and those two birds, Daphne and Christine. What do you see in Cary that makes him so special?"

Rayanne caught her breath. Had Burt discovered the truth? She breathed again as he went on casually, "I can see that most girls would find him attractive; that rather arrogant superman sort of behavior of his has a strange charm. But he's so dedicated to his work. I doubt if he'll ever marry."

"I doubt it, too," Rayanne said, unaware of just how wistful her voice was; nor did she see the quick look Burt gave her and the cloud that seemed to come over his face.

"Whoever he does marry will have a tough life," he said, his voice almost sulky.

"Yes, I guess so." Rayanne sighed. "But it would be worth it." Even as she spoke, she realized what she had said. Feeling her cheeks growing hot, she managed a laugh and added, "If she really loves him."

Burt put away his camera. "Hopeless waiting here," he said curtly. "Let's go back. We'll try another day."

Walking over the lawn, he looked at her. "What is this thing called love?" he asked.

"I sometimes wonder," sighed Rayanne, walking slowly, her eyes watchful as she stared at the house, wondering where Cary was. "It seems to me you can be very happy with someone and like him very much and yet not love him, while you can love someone and be unhappy with him because...." She paused.

Burt looked at her. "Because?"

"Because he doesn't love you." She laughed. "*C'est la vie,* as Harold would say. He's my eldest brother and he's always being philosophical. It drives you mad. No matter how bad things are he always grins and says *c'est la vie*. I suppose it is *life*, but that's no comfort."

"You've got five brothers?" Burt asked. "I'm an only child."

"I wish I was," Rayanne said quickly.

Burt shook his head. "You wouldn't if you were. It's

lonely. Besides, they expect too much of you when you're the only one."

"They do when there are five of them. Imagine my life—with a father and five brothers all waiting for me to do something dramatically important, important enough for them to say proudly, 'My sister is a...' or better still, 'Just think what my daughter has done!' That's what they're waiting for, and what on earth can I do to satisfy them?"

Burt looked at her. "This is the chip on your shoulder, is it?" he asked.

Startled, she turned. "Has Cary been talking to you about me?"

"Sure. Why not? We've both noticed your moods."

"I do not have moods," she said indignantly.

"Oh, no?" Burt laughed. "I'd say you have more silent moods than any girl I know. An aura of anger surrounds you and sometimes the way you glare at poor Cary makes me wonder he doesn't go up in smoke."

"I do not glare at Cary!"

"Oh, no? Maybe I should have a candid camera around sometime. Might shock you, rather. Why do you hate him so?"

"I do not hate him!" she said angrily.

"Don't you? Yet you get mad at the slightest thing he says."

"It's because he will tease me, and I hate—"

"Being teased?" Burt laughed. "Yet you let me tease you."

"Well...." Rayanne hesitated. "You tease differently."

"Is that a compliment or the reverse?"

It was a question Rayanne couldn't answer, or, at least, she couldn't tell *him*, though she knew the answer all right. It didn't matter when Burt teased her because it didn't matter to her *what* he thought!

"A compliment, of course," she said, uncomfortably aware of a keen look in his eyes as he stared at her. Whatever happened, he mustn't know the truth. Suppose he told Cary...?

"Actually, according to Cary," Burt went on, so Rayanne began to walk again, wishing she could end the conversation, "you hate all men. I didn't think you hated me."

"Of course I don't hate you, and I certainly don't hate *all* men. Only just a few."

"And Cary is one of them?"

"Oh, look!" Rayanne turned to him again angrily. "Leave me alone. How do I know if I hate him or not? What is hate, anyhow? I admire him very much, I like him... sometimes. He maddens me, makes me angry and then laughs at me. Naturally that makes me furious, yet he has a gift of making me laugh with him. Not *at* him, but with him against myself. No, I don't think I could say I hate him, but—"

"Rayanne, dear child, I'm going shopping tomorrow. I wondered if you'd like to come with me?" Mrs. Jefferson, coming carefully down the few steps from the *stoep* to meet them, called.

"I'd love to," answered Rayanne. "I haven't seen any of the countryside yet."

"There isn't much to see—except bushes and trees and mountains," Burt told her.

"Now, Burt," Mrs. Jefferson said with a smile, "that's not really fair. There's a lot of beauty around here."

The Fire of Life

RAYANNE AGREED next day when they left the house. Rather to her mixed dismay and pleasure, she found herself sitting next to Cary. Mrs. Jefferson had insisted on sitting in the back. It was more comfortable, she said, but Rayanne, glancing at Cary, saw the smile playing around his mouth and knew that Mrs. Jefferson had made it up; that normally she preferred the front, but she wanted to put Cary and Rayanne together! Oh, these matchmaking mothers, Rayanne thought. If only they would leave you alone!

The day was intensely hot. Her dress was wet before she even left the house. There wasn't the slightest wind and she wondered how the old lady could bear it. But Mrs. Jefferson seemed content and looking forward to her shopping.

"Luckily Cary has business to do, so we can enjoy ourselves, Rayanne," Mrs. Jefferson said, propped up in the corner of the car with various cushions Cary had found for her. "Some of the shops are quite good."

The earth road continued a long way, running alongside the high wire fence. They saw few wild animals, only a dozen giraffes galloping off with their funny movements away from the sound of the car.

At last the car was on the main road. This was also earth, but much more level, so the violent jerks and shakes that had been their lot up to then no longer happened.

Perlee was a small town, but as Mrs. Jefferson had said, there were several very good dress shops with the latest fashions. Mrs. Jefferson needed some new clothes, she said; would Rayanne help her decide what to wear?

"I like crazy clothes, but Cary, dear boy, is very conservative about what his mother should wear. However," she laughed, "I lay no store by what he says. I do what I like, and I tell him so. Don't you think I'm right?"

"Absolutely," Rayanne agreed. She sat on a chair in the little fitting room while Mrs. Jefferson struggled to get into a pale orange trouser suit.

"What do you think?" Mrs. Jefferson twisted and turned to try to see her back view in the mirror.

"It does something for you," said Rayanne, and it did. Besides, why shouldn't Cary's mother wear what she liked? After all, when you get old, Rayanne thought, there can be very few pleasures to enjoy, so why not let her enjoy this?

"Good!" Mrs. Jefferson beamed. "What about you?" She turned to the assistant. "Have you any really thin clothes? My young friend feels the heat very much."

Rayanne hesitated. Did she really need any more *thin* clothes? After all, she couldn't stay there forever, and they'd be far too thin to wear in an English summer.

The assistant brought two dresses, one leaf green and one snow white.

"They look just you, Rayanne, my dear," Mrs. Jefferson said eagerly. "Do try them on."

So Rayanne did, and Mrs. Jefferson was right. They were perfect—light, beautifully thin and comfortable. But were they really necessary?

"Do have them, Rayanne," a deep voice said.

Rayanne swung around, startled. Cary stood in the doorway, smiling at them. She was wearing the leaf green dress.

"You like it?" she asked.

He shrugged. "Does that matter? The important thing is that *you* like them, so why not have them?"

The Fire of Life

"Why not, indeed?" his mother chimed in. "It's going to get hotter in the days ahead, Rayanne, dear child. You're going to need them."

Rayanne stared at Cary. Should she ask him how long she could stay? His eyes met hers and there was a moment of silence. Rayanne had the strangest of feelings—that he could read her thoughts.

"Yes, Ray," he said gravely, "take them. You're going to need them."

CHAPTER SIX

THAT EVENING WAS STRANGE, Rayanne thought, but they all seemed to miss Aileen. Dinner was a quiet meal despite the excellently cooked food Mrs. Jefferson's cook, Matilda, had prepared for them. There were sudden silences that seemed to last forever.

Afterward, as they drank coffee in the drawing room, Mrs. Jefferson sighed.

"I think I'll go to bed," she told them. "I have what feels like a migraine on its way."

Rayanne walked with the old lady. "You'll be all right?" she asked anxiously.

Mrs. Jefferson smiled. "Quite all right. It's been a trying time for us all," she said, and closed the door.

Puzzled, Rayanne stood for a moment in the corridor. She could hear the cicadas humming away and an occasional howl of some wild animal coming from the distance. What had Mrs. Jefferson meant, she wondered. "It's been a trying time for us all." Mrs. Jefferson seemed to be rather confused; one moment she was saying she found Aileen both boring and tiring, the next she obviously missed her. One moment she had almost ignored Rayanne, making a fuss of Aileen, the next being glad Aileen had gone, and fussing over Rayanne! And now?

Back in the drawing room, the two men were silent as Rayanne joined them. She poured them all a second

The Fire of Life

cup of coffee and the silence remained. Suddenly she laughed, "You know, it's odd, but we all miss Aileen."

Cary looked up, his face creased with a frown. "And why should it be odd?" he asked. "Aileen is intelligent and interesting to talk to. Very dedicated to her work."

Rayanne felt the color in her cheeks. "Oh, I wasn't suggesting that she wasn't interesting. We used to talk for hours in my room at night. It's just that... well, I understand she hopes to go on this lecture tour with... I can't remember his name."

Cary stared at her, his face grave. "Yes, Alto Georgius. I hope to join her. It should not only be an interesting tour but may really help us make people see how important conservation is."

"You're joining her?" Burt sounded surprised.

"Yes, I am," Cary said quietly.

Burt whistled softly. "Look, Christine's giving a party to the visiting staff. She asked me, but I thought I'd be playing chess with your ma, Cary, so I said no. But there's nothing much to do, so let's go." He smiled at Rayanne. "Coming?"

She hesitated. "I wasn't asked." She and Christine had hardly exchanged more than a dozen words, and those only when Christine had no choice, for Cary was there.

Surprisingly, Cary laughed. "Neither was I. Somehow I don't think they're the sort of parties Ray enjoys, Burt."

Burt looked annoyed. "Well, we must do something. We can't just sit here." He looked at Rayanne. "Let's go and see Samantha and Mike. I met him earlier today and he said something about fixing it for me to go and film that new baboon family. You can talk to Samantha; she'll be glad to see us. She's pretty fed up, and I can't say I blame her. It's like being married to a football fan. Mike thinks of nothing but his work. Tough on the wife."

"No more tough than being married to a doctor, a merchant seaman... or practically any marriage, for a wife has to accept her husband's involvement with his work," Cary said quietly—a quietness that made Rayanne shiver for a moment. She knew he was angry about something. But what was it, she wondered. She was even more frightened when he suddenly turned to her and snapped, "How often do you see Samantha?"

She blinked for a moment. "Not as often as I should, I suppose," she told him. "We do sometimes pop in for coffee, don't we, Burt? Also, if Burt isn't with me, I get Kwido to take me there on my way back."

"I see." Cary's dark tufty eyebrows seemed about to meet as he frowned. "You say you don't see her as often as you should. I wonder if you're not seeing her too much."

"Too much?" Rayanne's voice rose with surprise.

Cary nodded. "Yes, too much." His voice was cold. "Nurse Macintyre has been talking to me about Samantha. She says that Samantha's condition has gradually grown worse since you came here."

"Condition?"

He nodded. "Daphne Macintyre reckons she's on the verge of a nervous breakdown—Samantha is, I mean." He frowned again. "She's become steadily more depressed, resentful and full of ailments that don't really exist. Daphne reckons that Samantha is like a child, trying to gain attention."

"She needs it," said Burt, almost growling.

Cary glanced at him, but ignored the remark as he went on, "As I told you when you first came, Ray, I'm

The Fire of Life

not happy about the wardens' wives meeting girls like you. It makes them discontented, resenting their isolation. After all, surely a wife's duty is to share her husband's interests. I seem to remember you telling me that once.''

Rayanne caught her breath as her cheeks grew hot. She could remember it, too, so plainly. Also the soft gentle way he had answered her, saying, "I think that's rather wonderful."

"Mike's a good chap. I'd hate to see his marriage threatened," Cary finished.

It was Burt now who was angry, so angry that his voice trembled. "Look, Cary, if you want to see someone who is threatening the Crisps' marriage, it's that Daphne Macintyre. She hasn't an ounce of brains in her head nor a soft spot in that hard heart of hers. Every time Samantha goes to the clinic, Daphne starts talking about the essential ingredients of a contented marriage, which is to share interests and have children...."

"And what's wrong with that?" Cary snapped.

Burt scowled. "Daphne hasn't a clue what marriage requires. Children are not essential—they may even harm a marriage. In this case, though, I think it's the answer, but it isn't exactly tactful of Daphne to harp on it when Samantha and Mike have been trying to have a child for the past five years. It's like twisting a knife in a wound. Samantha always comes back in tears."

"You seem to know a lot about Samantha," Cary said gruffly.

Burt smiled. "Sure I do. Mike and I are real buddies, but Samantha weeps on my shoulder." Then he frowned. "Look, let's get this straight. If Samantha has got worse since Rayanne came, it's not her fault—

Rayanne's, I mean. It's Daphne's. As for Rayanne, if anything, she's tried to interest Samantha in her husband's work. All Rayanne talks about these days is the importance of conservation." He smiled across the room at Rayanne, who was sitting very still, her hands tightly clutched together. "She's getting even worse than you, Cary, and never stops talking about it."

"Daphne Macintyre has been in charge of the clinic for several years," Cary said in the rather pompous way he sometimes used and which Rayanne hated. "I have no record of Daphne's making a wrong diagnosis. She's seriously concerned for Samantha and that a nervous breakdown might occur."

Rayanne found her voice. "That's absolute rubbish, Cary! Samantha isn't like that. She's just bored and lonely. Mike is out all day and most nights he's studying or making notes. He has a lot of paperwork, as you know." She sighed. "Burt is right, you know, Cary. The Crisps want a baby—so badly. If only...."

Burt suddenly clapped his hands. "I've got it! What fools we were not to think about it before." He smiled as he turned to Rayanne. "Look, if they can't have one, they could adopt one. Lots of people adopt children and then have some of their own. They say it's because the mother stops worrying about it, and...."

Cary stood up. His face might have been carved out of stone, it was so cold and lifeless.

"I would prefer you to refrain from interfering with the private lives of my employees, Burt. It's their affair, not yours. There are some people who find it impossible to accept other men's children. It's possible Mike feels that way."

"Then Mike would be plain selfish," Rayanne said indignantly.

Cary looked at her. "Would he? Or would it be Samantha who was being selfish?" He glanced at his watch. "I've some letters to write, so if you'll excuse me...." He left hurriedly.

Burt whistled softly as he looked across the room. "He's really mad tonight. I wonder what's rattled him. I didn't think he was that partial to Aileen Hampton's charm, but seems like he's missing her." He stood up. "Come along, Rayanne, let's go and see the Crisps. I can take the Land Rover I usually have."

He pulled Rayanne to her feet and went on holding her hands, smiling down at her, swinging her hands gently.

"Or shall we stay here, alone?" he asked, his eyes twinkling. "A romantic setting. I could put on some music, turn low the lights...."

Of course he was joking, Rayanne told herself, but a shiver went down her back. Was he? Sometimes there was a look in his eyes that frightened her. Not that she was *afraid* of Burt—but she liked him too much to want to hurt him. Perhaps it was just her imagination, but....

She managed a laugh. "Let's go and see Samantha and Mike, Burt. I wonder if they've ever discussed adopting a child. It might really be the answer."

They went outside into the perfumed, dark night with the sky's blackness broken by the beauty of the new moon. Rayanne loked up.

"It's unbelievable that man has been up there...."

Burt's hand was under her elbow as he guided her across the drive to the Land Rover. "Many things are unbelievable today." He paused and for one moment Rayanne thought he was going to take her in his arms. What should she do, she wondered wildly. He was too nice to hurt. She couldn't slap his face, or turn hers away... nor could she let him kiss her and believe that she loved him.

At that moment, a light flooded out from the house and a door of the *stoep* opened. Cary's voice carried clearly through the quiet air.

"Ask Mike to ring me first thing in the morning and I'll give him the answer he needs," Cary called.

"Okay, boss!" Burt called back, and helped Rayanne into the Rover. Sitting by her side, switching on the ignition, he chuckled. "I wonder how long he'd been watching us."

"Watching us?" Rayanne was startled. "Why should he watch us?"

"Because he's that kind of guy," Burt said, the engine roaring into life. "He sees us all as his puppets and he dislikes our playing unless he's pulling the strings."

"I don't think that's quite fair!"

"Fair it may not be, but it's true. Cary knew from the first time he met Aileen in London just what she wanted of him, but he had a good inner laugh at the way he made her behave. Rushing out here suddenly so that he couldn't get out of it, being so biddable, which Cary adores. He loves to crack the whip and watch his women obey."

"His women?" Rayanne echoed.

"Yes, aren't you all smitten by his charm? If you're not, you ought to be. Leastways, that's how Cary sees it. He just laps it all up. I doubt if Christine and Daphne would have been here so long if they didn't make out they were fighting to hook him." Burt gave a funny laugh. "Now he's trying to catch you. Then he'll make you dance, regardless of whether you'll get hurt or not."

The Fire of Life

"I don't believe it!" Rayanne turned in her seat to stare at Burt angrily. "It's not true."

Burt chuckled. "Isn't it? You only say that because you don't want to believe it. You hate believing things that are nasty, don't you? You like life to be smooth and perfect, everyone an angel. Unfortunately none of us are angels—that's why you're so hurt when you learn the truth about us. You see life through rose-colored glasses... at least you'd like to, and when people behave normally, you get upset. Take your reaction just now. You were shocked, horrified and hurt because I dared say anything against the one and only Cary Jefferson. He has to be perfect. Just as I have to be perfect, too."

"You?" Rayanne was really startled.

His hand closed over hers for a moment. "Yes, and you know darned well why. You hate being disillusioned, because it breaks down something inside you. You have such high expectations. We've all got to be as perfect as your father."

"My father?" Rayanne began to laugh, but stopped. "My father?" she repeated.

"Yes, you've got a real complex there. You're always talking about your wretched brothers who seem to spend their life deliberately hurting you by teasing. The plain truth is this: you hate their teasing you because it makes you look small in front of your father. You want your father's love. You need it." The Rover had stopped and they were parked outside the Crisps' house.

"You need it very much," Burt went on, his voice low and earnest. "You want his respect, his praise and for him to be proud of you. You'll never be the real you until that happens." He leaned across and opened the

Rover's door. "We'd better go in or Samantha will think we're necking." He chuckled. "What a hope!"

Silently Rayanne followed him up the few steps to the door. Samantha flung it open and called out in delight.

"Come in, come in. The answer to a lonely girl's prayer! Lovely to see you, Burt... and you, too, Rayanne. Why this unexpected visit?"

"The evening was dead," Burt said bluntly. "Looks like we all miss Miss Hampton." His voice was sarcastic. "Mrs. J. has retired with a sprouting migraine, Cary has gone to write some letters and we... well, we thought we'd like to see you."

"You know I'm delighted. I'll make us some coffee. Dorcas has gone home, of course. Come in the kitchen with me, Rayanne. Mike's in his office, Burt."

Samantha, in a long lush-looking housecoat of peacock colors, led the way to the kitchen, talking over her shoulder.

"It's so nice to see you, Rayanne." Then she smiled and lifted her hand, wagging one finger warningly. "Watch out, though. You were a long time sitting out there with Burt." She laughed. "Don't look so shocked. Why don't you marry him? He's crazy about you."

Crazy about me, Rayanne thought. Was he really? But she... was crazy about someone else.

CHAPTER SEVEN

IN THE MORNING at breakfast, Cary seemed to have become his usual self. He greeted Rayanne cheerfully, looked at Burt and asked them, "We're catching some hippos today to send to England. Like to come along?"

"I would," Rayanne said eagerly.

"Is it kind to take animals who are used to the lovely African sunshine to cold England?" Mrs. Jefferson asked, carefully eating her grapefruit.

Cary shrugged. "They soon seem to adjust in a land where the sun never shines."

"It does shine," Rayanne said quickly. "Sometimes we have beautifully hot summers."

"Sometimes?" Cary looked at her, a smile playing around his mouth, and her cheeks went bright red.

Once again, she had risen to the bait!

"I think most foreigners are surprised just how often the English sun does shine," Burt joined in quickly. "Most of them think it always rains."

"It can be very cold in Africa," Mrs. Jefferson agreed. "In Johannesburg, now—" she shivered "—it can be very cold indeed."

"How do you manage—I mean, it can't be easy to get a huge hippo into a crate," said Rayanne, wanting to change the conversation.

"We keep them in paddocks for some time," Cary explained. "Their food is put in the traveling box so they get used to walking into it and there's no difficulty. It's been done so often these days that there are no real problems."

"I think you're very clever, dear," Mrs. Jefferson said, helping herself from the sideboard where the deliciously cooked kidneys and bacon were.

"It's not me, mother. I just organize things and leave the rest to the staff. Nowadays we use a new anesthetic that's very successful. It's a synthetic morphinous one and it affects the brain and central nervous system. It's much more powerful than morphia and releases the animal from its inhibitions. This means that an animal is subdued. There is also a sleeping draught mixed with it, so the animal moves like a sleepwalker."

"You've gone a long way," Burt commented, "from the old days when you caught them with lassos."

Cary laughed. "We certainly have! Those were the days—the battles we had! You should try to handle a giraffe with his long legs. This is infinitely easier and kinder to the animals as they rarely get hurt."

"But how do you give them the injection?" Mrs. Jefferson asked. "A bow and arrow, I suppose."

"We use a crossbow and dart now. We also used to use a gas gun, but the crossbow goes off quietly so the animals aren't frightened. Also, the dart can be shot accurately a very long way. It can be a hundred and twenty yards, though the dart can be affected by the wind changes, so it's better to use it in the wooded regions, otherwise the wind makes it difficult."

"Does it hurt the poor creature?"

Cary smiled patiently at his mother. "I doubt it, because it happens so swiftly. The dart looks like an ordinary hypodermic syringe with a tail added. After we've finished with the animal, he's given an antidote and speedily regains his usual senses. Meanwhile all that has happened is a small wound that we will have treated with disinfectant. Nothing to worry about."

"So long as you're not catching elephants, Cary."

"Actually they're not difficult. Once they're sleepy they move so slowly and seem to behave as we want them to. The difficulty, of course, is in choosing which animals we want to catch. We have Bilkington who does most of the shooting. He's a fine biologist. You've probably heard of him, Ray?" Cary turned to her.

She shook her head. "Afraid I haven't."

"How long does it take for the drug to work?" Burt asked.

"About ten minutes. Gradually their running slows down and finally we catch up with them. Bit rough, for they charge through bushes and trees. Ray won't be allowed to leave the Rover," Cary added with a smile.

"Why..." Rayanne began to ask, but Mrs. Jefferson got in first.

"I should hope not indeed! Now, Cary, you're to take great care of Rayanne. What would her Uncle Joe say if anything happened to her? How could I write and tell him? He'd never forgive me...." Mrs. Jefferson began to sound quite hysterical.

"I won't let her run any risks, mother," Cary said gravely. "My main problem is the fact that she resents being protected and is quite capable of jumping out of the Rover and being eaten by a lion—out of sheer defiance." He smiled at Rayanne.

"Rayanne, you wouldn't?" Mrs. Jefferson was shocked.

Rayanne blushed. He was so right! "I won't, Mrs. Jefferson."

"You promise? Please, Rayanne, I shan't be able to

stand it unless you promise you won't do anything foolish and that you'll... well, do what Cary says. He does know, you know."

"I promise," Rayanne said with a smile. "Please don't worry about me. I know I'm in good hands."

"We all know that," Cary said dryly. His voice had changed again. "By the way, how is the thesis coming along, Ray?" he asked.

She was so startled that for a moment she couldn't answer. Now why had he suddenly asked her that? And what could she tell him? Not even the first page had been written yet, nor did it seem likely that it would ever be. There was a strange silence and she suddenly became aware that three pairs of eyes were staring at her, that three people were waiting expectantly for her answer.

It was a great effort, but she managed a somewhat uncertain laugh. "Not too badly, thanks. Copious notes, of course, but I'm still not quite sure from which angle...."

Cary stood up, rattling his chair on the highly polished floor.

"Today may give you inspiration. See you in half an hour. Burt, you bring her along and we'll all meet at Jock Tilling's house. See you," he added curtly, and left the room.

Rayanne buttered her piece of toast slowly, grateful that Burt was talking to Mrs. Jefferson. What had Cary meant, she wondered. Was it a gentle hint that he thought it time she left the Jefferson Wildlife Reserve?

"Is it very hard to write a thesis, Rayanne, dear child?" Mrs. Jefferson asked anxiously.

"Well, not really..." Rayanne began, and saw the look in Burt's eyes. He didn't believe she was writing one, she realized. He thought it was all an excuse...just as Christine and Daphne had done. "The trouble is—" she went on, but Burt interrupted.

"To know what you're writing about," Burt said dryly, "and why. However, I imagine she'll have to do it."

"Why are you so sure?" Mrs. Jefferson asked. "I mean, is it so important? Couldn't she change her mind?"

Burt looked across the table at Rayanne. "I very much doubt it. What do you say, Rayanne?" he asked, looking at her. It was a strange feeling, she thought. It was almost mesmeric, the way his eyes held hers so that she couldn't look away. Then he smiled, moving his head, releasing her from that strange moment. "No, she'll write that thesis all right, make no mistake."

Rayanne got up quickly. "If you'll excuse me, Mrs. Jefferson, I think I'd better change into my working gear."

She saw the amusement in Burt's eyes. He knew she was running away, unable to answer the question. He was right and yet he was wrong. She had not come here because she wanted to meet Cary, that was for sure. She had honestly come in the hope that she would find out what she really wanted to do...but was that the truth, she asked herself as she hurried to her room. She had come out to, as Burt had said, prove herself. Prove that she could do something to make her father proud of her; prove that she wasn't a moron!

It didn't take her long to change into the khaki trews and thin matching shirt she had recently bought in the town, which was not really so far away, once you had accepted Africa's standards where you thought nothing of driving ninety miles to meet someone. Then she went out on to the screened *stoep*.

She stood very still, looking at the beautiful view before her. The distant mountains, now a strange grayish green as the sun shone on them. The trees were so straight, reminding her of soldiers on parade. How beautiful it all was, she thought. How could she bear to leave it? To go back to city life, to the noise and the mad rushing of cars that seemed determined to be lethal in their behavior. Here it was so peaceful, so lovely. Just look at the fascinating colors! Lines of freshly red land where it had been plowed. And closer to the house, the slow, reluctantly moving river. Odd, but she never thought of crocodiles these days. Somehow she had unconsciously adapted herself to this new life.

A tiny lizard scuttled across the floor and up the wall. She watched it, fascinated by its movements. How wonderful to be able to run up a straight wall like that! She looked back at the garden with the great bushes, heavily laden with bright red and yellow flowers while the little birds with their long curving beaks hovered over them, seeking pollen, moving like miniature helicopters. It was all so lovely... how could she bear to leave it?

Her eyes stung warningly and she pressed her hand against her mouth as she fought the tears she mustn't shed. She would have to go, she knew that. Beyond shadow of doubt, she would have to go eventually. Eventually? And what did that mean? Was Cary's question about her thesis a gentle hint that he wanted her to go?

But how could she go?

And the thesis? Did Cary believe it was all made up

as Burt so obviously did, and Christine and Daphne, too?

The thesis must be written. It had to be written, Rayanne told herself sternly. It was time she pulled herself together. That very night she would do a skeleton draft of what it was to be about. Maybe Cary was right and the day ahead of them would help her know *what* to concentrate on. There was so much....

Someone banged on the door and Burt shouted, "Aren't you ready yet? We don't want our heads chopped off because we're late."

"I'm coming," Rayanne called. "Coming right now!" Hastily she grabbed her powder compact and studied her eyes anxiously. No, thanks be, there was no evidence of the tears she had so nearly shed.

She hurried out to join him, and Mrs. Jefferson was hovering.

"You did promise, Rayanne," she said anxiously. "You will be careful?"

Impulsively Rayanne kissed her. "Of course I will," she promised. How lovely it was to have someone who cared, she thought.

Bumping along the earth road in the Land Rover, she glanced at Burt. "I do wish I could drive."

He smiled. "I'll teach you."

"You would?" she said eagerly.

"Why not? We'll get out of the reserve as we can't risk stalling the engine if a huge angry elephant came chasing us." He chuckled. "You want to learn?"

"Oh, so badly!" Her voice was earnest. "I couldn't learn from everyone."

"You feel you could learn from me?" He glanced at her and she looked back at his kind face, his thoughtful eyes.

"Yes," she told him, "I could. You'd be patient and understanding."

"What about Cary?" Burt's voice was suddenly harsh. "Could you learn from him?"

Rayanne hesitated, twisting her fingers together, glancing at them to avoid looking at the man by her side.

"I don't know," she said slowly. "I never feel quite at ease with Cary. He changes his mood so suddenly. One moment I'm relaxed and we're getting on well, the next moment he's quite different—pompous, even cold." She gave a little laugh. "How disloyal of me when he's been so kind and generous. All the same—" she gave Burt a quick smile and then wished she hadn't, for she saw the hope in his eyes "—I'd rather learn from you."

"Good enough!" Burt sounded almost triumphant. "Look...." He pointed to a group of wildebeests that was standing staring at them. "How long... how much longer will you be here?" he asked suddenly.

As this was a question she had been asking herself, Rayanne should have known the answer, she thought, but she didn't.

"I haven't a clue," she said honestly.

She turned away, looking at the veld with its strange umbrella-shaped trees, the groups of bushes and the glimpses of wild animals that she saw now as quite normal, no longer getting wildly excited when she saw a cheetah or a wildebeest.

"How long were you invited for?" Burt asked, deftly driving around a rut in the earth road.

"No time was mentioned. I was asked to come and stay to give me the chance to study wildlife conserva-

The Fire of Life

tion. I imagine I can stay as long as I like," she said, her voice worried. "So Mrs. Jefferson says."

"But Mrs. Jefferson isn't the real boss," Burt pointed out.

He swerved as a warthog ran across the road and slowed up as the family followed, a wife and several small ones, all with their little tails pointed skyward.

"How long are *you* staying?" Rayanne asked.

He shrugged. "Any moment now I must go. I've several jobs waiting for me and I can't postpone them forever. I've got my notes and photographs, and when I've put the lot together I'll send it to Cary to see if he'll write a foreword for it."

"I'll miss you," Rayanne said impulsively, and again wished she hadn't, for Burt turned and gave her such a sweet smile that she felt absolutely mean. It was cruel to let him think she felt more for him than just affection.

Ahead of them was the game warden's fenced-in house. There were several Rovers and big trucks with crates on them waiting. Burt parked his Rover and they went into the house. Cary was standing drinking coffee. He looked at them and gave a casual nod.

Rayanne stared at him. How handsome he was, so tall and straight, so lean and strong. Somehow his khaki shirt and trousers made him look even more handsome, as did the big hat he had perched on the back of his head. As if he could read her thoughts, he lifted it off, gave her a grin and tossed the hat on the table.

"Come and meet everyone, Ray... and Burt, too, of course," he said. His arm lightly around Rayanne's shoulders, he took her around the room, introducing her.

There were so many names it was useless to try to

remember them all, Rayanne decided. The biologist who would do the shooting was a tall, big man with graying hair and sunburned skin. His son, Keith Bilkington, was with him. Then there were several vets and game catchers, who apparently went from reserve to reserve when needed. There was a lot of noise, as the room was not large and there were many of them, but Cary seemed to go out of his way to look after her, getting her coffee and even a chair. Then he looked down at her.

"You're coming with me. Okay?"

She nodded. "Okay."

"I thought it would be best," Cary said, "as my mother is so anxious about you."

Rayanne's mouth twisted a little wryly. "Very thoughtful of you, I'm sure."

"You'll excuse me if I mix a bit? I want to talk to Dr. Bilkington."

"Of course." Sipping the hot strong coffee, Rayanne looked around. Burt was making notes of something the biologist, Paul Bilkington, was telling him. Then Keith, the son, came and squatted on the ground by Rayanne's side.

"How come a dolly like you is here?" he asked with a grin. A friendly, pleasant boy, she thought at once, about her own age.

"I'm supposed to be writing a thesis on wildlife conservation."

He whistled softly. "So with good looks, brains do go, too, sometimes. How is the thesis going?"

"Not very well," Rayanne admitted. "You see, I came as a skeptic, feeling the money spent on all this should be spent on starving people. I'm still not sure

The Fire of Life

how I really feel about it, but I'm beginning to realize the importance of conservation."

Keith, with his short blond hair and suntanned skin, chuckled.

"Well, I bet you have it all stuffed down your throat. I reckon Jefferson never talks of anything else."

"Oh, he does," she said quickly, and saw the grin on Keith's face. "Sometimes," she added.

"Well, he'd have to be a bit of a fool never to talk of anything else to someone dishy as you. Who are you driving with? I'm afraid I can't ask you, as I'm going with dad. We're doing the shooting, you see. The others do the manual work." He laughed. "Sooner them than me! One thing, the hippos are so dopey you can make them do almost anything. Oh, dad's waving at me, so we've to get going." He smiled at Rayanne. "Nice to have met you. Didn't expect such a dolly in the bush. Maybe we'll meet again?"

"Maybe," said Rayanne, suddenly realizing just what a boy he was! Funny how much more mature girls in their early twenties were than men. She much preferred older men, men in their thirties, like Cary....

Cary! If only she had never met Cary.... The heartbreak that she knew lay ahead of her was really frightening. Wasn't she being a fool, she asked herself, to stay on? Surely the longer she was near him, the harder it would be to go? Yet she dreaded the thought of leaving.

"Ray!" Cary called. "Ready?"

"Ready!" she called back, and hurried to his side. Walking to the Rover, he told her briefly what was going to happen.

"We round up the herds and seek out the ones we

want. Dr. Bilkington is our adviser as well as shooter. He'll go ahead. Then we race after the sleepy animals, and when they really collapse, the Africans can handle them, with our aid, of course. The vets will give each animal a quick examination, because we don't want to cart off sick ones."

"Why are they being shipped to England?"

"Because there's always the danger that some disease will come along or something happen so that they all die or get killed and no longer exist. We're sending animals to zoos all over the world to ensure that they're not wiped out."

In the Rover both were silent as they drove out of the fenced-in garden and were in the reserve. There was one Rover ahead... that must be Dr. Bilkington and Keith, his son.

"What did you think of young Bilkington?" Cary asked. "I saw him talking to you."

She laughed. "He was paying me idiotic compliments. He must be mad to think I believed them even for a moment."

"What sort of compliments?"

"Well...." She hesitated. "Rather immature. Kept calling me a *dolly*...oh, and he told me I was dishy and...I remember now, he said, 'So with good looks, brains do go, too, sometimes.' Cheeky, that's what he was," she said scornfully.

"Would you have preferred it had he told you that he found you a real old bag? Hideous, dumb and dull?" Cary asked gravely.

Bumping about in the Rover, Rayanne looked at him. She saw he was trying not to laugh. Suddenly she was laughing, and he turned to look at her, obviously glad he could laugh now.

"Of course I wouldn't," she managed to say.

Cary shrugged. "Let's face it, Ray, you're a difficult person. One hesitates to approach you in case one says the wrong thing."

"*I'm* difficult? Why, it's..." Rayanne began, and stopped, for Cary was laughing again.

"Never," he said, "never in my life have I known a girl like you. One only has to open one's mouth and you're on the offensive, or perhaps I should say the defensive."

"I am..." she began indignantly and again stopped, frowning as she looked at him. "Am I?"

"Are you? That's no lie," he said, and swung off the earth road, the Rover bumping over the veld, brushing by the large bushes that seemed determined to mass together and stop them from moving.

Now the Rovers had separated as if searching for something. There was a two-way radio that occasionally produced a voice, saying the hippos had not yet been found.

"It's ridiculous," Cary said impatiently. "I sent guides out at dawn to trace them and they said there were several herds here."

Ahead of them a herd of enormous elephants was making its slow way to a small dam. Cary slowed up and then one of the elephants turned his head in their direction, slowly swinging his trunk, his eyes thoughtful or — so they seemed to Rayanne — rather ominously thoughtful, she decided, his great ears went back. He stood still, staring at the Rover that had come to a halt, and suddenly the elephant let out a dreadful scream.

Cary got into reverse and the Rover leaped backward as he twisted and turned the steering wheel, guiding them through the mass of bushes.

The elephant began to move as if to follow them, swinging his trunk, then seemed to change his mind, almost shrugging his shoulders and following the other elephants, who had taken no notice of what he was doing.

Rayanne felt her whole body relaxing. Cary went on reversing, his body turned around as he deftly guided the Rover through the bushes. Finally he slowed up and stopped. Then he spoke into the two-way radio, advising the other drivers of the enraged elephant.

"May be injured," he said. "Reckon young Wallace could cope. He's got a crossbow with him, only it might mess things up if the elephant goes berserk."

An answer came back from Dick Wallace and Cary turned finally to Rayanne.

"Well?" he asked cheerfully. "Hope you weren't too scared."

"Scared?" She tried to laugh, but even her voice was unsteady. Never had she been so terrified in her life— that great huge creature screaming his hatred of them, moving threateningly toward them. He could have smashed the Rover and everything in it almost in seconds.

"You'll get used to it," Cary said cheerfully, maneuvering the Rover around. "So long as the car doesn't stall, you're okay. Ah!"

A message came over the radio. The hippos had been traced. Directions were given as to how to get to them.

Cary nodded happily. "Now we go slowly until we see them...."

"Why?"

"We don't want them racing off before we're there. You wouldn't like to back out, Ray?" he asked suddenly. "You're very white."

The Fire of Life

She turned quickly to look at him. "I bet you were the first time an elephant screamed at you. Of course I don't want to back out. I'm enjoying this...it's... it's...well, it's different," she finished lamely.

"I'll say! Very different from your safe little life in London."

"Safe? With all that traffic?" Rayanne laughed. "It's not different in that way."

"Sure you feel safe with me?" Cary asked suddenly. "You wouldn't have preferred to go with Burt?"

"Of course I feel safe with you." Puzzled, Rayanne stared at him. How he liked to throw unexpected questions at her, she thought. "Why should I prefer to be with Burt?"

"I just wondered. You seem to rather fancy him," Cary said casually, looking at his watch and frowning. "You've quite got my poor mother worried about it."

"Why should she worry?"

Cary chuckled. "Well, as you know, she's decided that you're to be my bride."

"What absolute nonsense!" Rayanne's cheeks burned, her eyes flashed, her hands clenched. Just how much more of this could she stand, she asked herself. "As if I'd marry you if you asked me!" she said angrily, for attack was the best defense, her father had once said.

Cary laughed. "Wouldn't you?" he asked, and suddenly the Rover shot forward, causing Rayanne to slide down the seat, bumping into him. "Steady on," he warned. "No time for battles, now...there are the hippos!"

THE REST OF THE DAY was too exciting for Rayanne to have time to feel furious with Cary for what he had said. They had rounded the hippos and Dr. Bilkington had doped those he advised. The hippo had raced away, but slowly his or her running had slowed until finally it was a sort of drunken walk, with frequent stumbles and a final collapse. Then the veterinary surgeons had got to work, examining the animal quickly, passing him or her or saying they did not advise it. The little wound was treated with a disinfectant and those allowed to go back to freedom were given another injection that, with amazing speed, brought them back to normal. Meanwhile, the staff were driving, slowly and with patience, the huge, ungainly chosen animals into the trucks.

Later Cary drove Rayanne to see the elephant that had taken a dislike to them. He was lying on his side, still unconscious, with Dick Wallace working on him. The elephant was obviously badly injured.

"Not to worry," Dick Wallace said, seeing Rayanne's look of dismay. "It's fortunate you saw him and we found him. He must have been in terrible pain; no wonder he hated everyone he saw."

"Will you be able to cure him?" Rayanne asked.

Dick Wallace shrugged. "I reckon so. These are tough creatures, but I'm taking him back with me and keeping him under sedation to make sure the wounds heal."

It was a long tiring day, and as Cary drove her home Rayanne yawned. Cary, who had been rather silent, looked at her.

"Well, was it worthwhile?"

She smiled in the middle of another yawn. "It was absolutely marvelous." She yawned. "I'm sorry about this, but I am sleepy, I'm afraid."

"A hot bath and an early night," Cary suggested. "By the way, I hope this will have helped your work on your thesis. You don't seem to be getting on with it."

The Fire of Life

Rayanne caught her breath. Was this another hint that she was not wanted?

"I'm getting on with it all right," she said quickly, though she knew it was a lie. "I've got copious notes. It's just a matter—"

"Of knowing from which angle to write," Cary mimicked her voice. "You've told me that before. Well, has today given you that angle?"

Rayanne clasped her hands together tightly and stared ahead. It was lovely countryside, yet she was giving it so little attention.

"I'm not sure," she said slowly. Had it? Was it perhaps the importance of having found the elephant who was in pain and therefore a menace to all living creatures? Was it watching the vets as they handled the animals? They all seemed to believe their jobs were worth doing.

"Is it because you're not interested," Cary asked, "or just that you feel inarticulate?"

Rayanne frowned. She recognized some of the landmarks around her—a huge rock, carved out by generations of rain and wind into looking like a lion's head; a cluster of cypress trees that seemed out of place here in the bush, but a few clumps of bricks piled up told the sad story of the house that had once been there and probably burned in a fire. These meant they were nearly home and the questions would cease.

"I honestly don't know," she admitted. "I'm interested, very interested. I was a bit skeptical at first, but now I'm beginning to understand how important it is. I just can't seem to find...." She paused, her cheeks hot. "You must be bored stiff hearing me say that."

They were going through the last gate, Cary shouting

to the African who opened it and who replied with a big grin and a salute.

"At least," Cary said as he drove surprisingly fast down the drive, "you're honest."

Then they were there and Mrs. Jefferson came to meet them. "My dear child, you do look tired! Was it very frightening? You wouldn't get me going out like that. Why, those elephants...."

Finally Cary left them and Rayanne had her bath, a little sleep, and woke refreshed. She shuffled through the notes she had made. What should she write about? Perhaps if she made a skeleton draft... what did conservation teach the civilized world? Did the understanding, or partial understanding, of the migratory habits of certain animals really teach the civilized world anything worth knowing, she wondered. Was it important to keep the wild animals alive? Was it really necessary?

Perhaps if she answered those questions, it would get her started, she thought.

Later that evening, she excused herself and went to bed early. But not to sleep. Instead she sat by the small table and sorted out her notes. Somehow or other the thesis must be written.

During the next few days she worked on her notes, trying different angles, unable to write anything that she thought was worth even reading. She began to feel even more depressed, for it showed that her brothers might be right. Perhaps she had no brains, after all?

Cary had gone away, suddenly called by an urgent phone message. He didn't say where he had gone, but Burt made a guess that it was to help Aileen.

"He likes to play the cool, indifferent, dedicated man, but I think he really fell for Aileen," Burt said with a chuckle.

The Fire of Life

The course was nearing its end. Soon the noisy students would be returning to their hometowns and a few weeks of quietness would follow, Mrs. Jefferson said.

"Not that I mind having them around. They keep to their own quarters, but I do get a bit tired of the noise their transistors make. Do they really have to have such loud music?" she asked Rayanne.

It was Burt who answered. "Sure they do, Mrs. Jefferson. That's the only way to be part of the music." He grinned as he spoke. "At least, that's what they say. They have to be a *part* so the noise must screech through the brain, leaving you stunned."

"A funny way to enjoy music," Mrs. Jefferson commented.

He lifted a finger. "I agree, but... ah, we're not young, Mrs. Jefferson." He turned to Rayanne, who was standing by the window, watching the movements on the sand as the crocodiles came slowly out of the water. How she would miss the crocodiles....

She swung around. "What? Sorry, I didn't hear you."

"You're young, my dear," Mrs. Jefferson said gently. "D'you like loud music?"

"Loud music?" Rayanne's face wrinkled as she frowned. "Well, I don't know, but I do like to *hear* it. I mean, there's no point in listening to it if it's too soft, is there?"

She wondered why they both laughed. "I can't see the joke."

"Ah, my dear child," Mrs. Jefferson said with a smile, "there isn't a joke—it's just that the different generations see everything so differently." She looked up at Burt. "How old are you? I'd have thought you were one of the young ones."

He bowed. "Thank you, *madame*. Thank you very much. I'll never see thirty-five again. I'm going on fast toward forty so I can't be called young."

"That's not old, Burt. Cary is just thirty-five," Mrs. Jefferson said.

"I think men in their mid-thirties are the most interesting of all," said Rayanne. "I met Keith that day we got the hippos and I found him awfully boring, and he's about my age."

Burt bowed toward her. "You've made my day, if I may be so corny. What a comforting thought to a man as the years race by! Do you honestly think we grow more attractive the older we grow?"

Rayanne laughed. "Depends on how much older you do grow."

Later that day, as Burt patiently taught her to drive the Land Rover, he asked her, "Did you really find Keith a bore?"

Rayanne was concentrating on what had to be done. They were driving outside the game reserve on a rather bad road but with little traffic. "He was terribly immature."

"You prefer mature men?"

"Who doesn't?" she said as she deftly turned a corner.

"How's it going? Feeling happier?"

"Much," Rayanne smiled. "Thanks to your patience."

"Does Cary know I'm teaching you?"

"I... well, I suppose he doesn't. I didn't tell him. Did you?"

"Of course not. I was afraid he'd insist on teaching you himself and I knew it would be an absolute flop. The things you need most, Rayanne, are praise, encouragement and—"

The Fire of Life

"Patience," Rayanne finished. "Thanks to you, I've had all three."

"My pleasure," he said, and laughed. "Why do you want to drive, Rayanne?"

"So that when I get home I can buy a car and show my brothers that I can drive."

"So you are going home?" he asked, his voice becoming grave.

"Of course." She turned to stare at him and Burt grabbed at the wheel, just managing to save them from going off sideways into the deep ditch.

"Hey, watch it, young woman!" he said gruffly.

"Then don't talk to me," she told him in return.

Back at the house, they found Mrs. Jefferson in great distress.

"If only Cary were here! He'd cope with it. He can manage anything and anyone...."

"What's the trouble?" Burt asked. "Maybe I can help."

"I've just heard. Samantha has left Mike!"

"I don't believe it," Rayanne said quickly. "She wouldn't do a thing like that, I'm sure."

"Well, Nurse Macintyre was here earlier. She wanted to speak to you, Rayanne. She seems to think it's all your fault." Mrs. Jefferson, sitting down in her deep armchair, pressed her hands together, her face unhappy. "I told her I was sure it wasn't, but she wouldn't believe me. I don't think she likes you."

"How could it be my fault?"

"She says you've made Samantha restless and discontented and...."

"She was like that before I got here. Samantha knows I can't really understand why she's so miserable. Yet I can, in a way. If only Mike could interest her in his work!"

"Or give her a baby," said Burt. "That's the real trouble, I think."

Rayanne pressed her hands to her mouth, her eyes widening as she thought of something. But perhaps, she thought, it was better to say nothing at this stage.

"What's Mike doing?" she asked.

"What can he do? She went off...."

"She can't drive," Rayanne said.

"I gather she got Kwido. You weren't using him, so he took her to Perlee and she told him she was staying with some friends, so when he came back, he concluded that Mike would know and said nothing."

"Then where does Daphne Macintyre come into this?" Burt asked.

"It seems she went to see Samantha because she was worried about her. Samantha's had a bad cold for some time and... well, she was out. Daphne waited and Mike came in and knew nothing about it. Then he sent for Kwido, and... well, she's just gone."

"I'm sure she hasn't. Perhaps Mike has forgotten she was going away. He's so lost in his work that he could forget anything."

"I hope you're right, Rayanne. I do feel so upset about it. Cary won't be at all pleased...."

"Well," said Burt, "we can't do anything to help, I'm afraid. I think I'll go have a shower. You, too, Rayanne?"

"Yes, I am rather sticky with dust," Rayanne said.

Should she phone Mike, she wondered. Where was he? Had he driven to Perlee looking for her? Samantha wouldn't run away. She just wasn't that sort. She might have a terrific quarrel, but it would all be open.

Suddenly, Rayanne had an idea.... Very quietly she made her way outside, knowing Burt must still be having his shower and that Mrs. Jefferson would think nothing of the sound of a car starting up. Luckily, the key was left in it as it always was, since there were no burglars to fear.

A little nervous, because she had only had a few lessons from Burt, Rayanne started up the engine. All went well, for with no traffic around, one could take a corner badly and yet be quite safe. The African at the gate looked a bit surprised but let her through, and she drove toward the Crisps' gate. There she paused and asked Lobitha if he knew where Mike was.

"He has gone to the clinic and will then go to Perlee," Lobitha told her.

"Oh, dear!" Rayanne said, and thought quickly. Well, she had better go to the clinic, though she had no desire for a scene with Daphne Macintyre, but if Mike could be seen before he left for Perlee....

It wasn't easy and she wondered if Lobitha was amused by her antics, but she finally managed to reverse and turn around, making along the road for the clinic. Suddenly she saw a deep furrow in the road and swung sideways to avoid it, jamming on the brakes. The engine stopped.

She tried to start it again. It refused. She tried and tried, for the night was beginning to come down and she was on a lonely back road, one rarely used, she knew. Somewhere an owl hooted... she heard the chattering of the monkeys, which usually went to bed early because they feared the dark. She tried the engine again and again and it refused to start....

Should she get out and look at the engine, she wondered. What good would that do? She knew nothing about engines. Should she press on the horn, perhaps doing a S.O.S. sound? If Burt heard and found the

Rover gone, he would come to look for her. But could he hear? The road was some way from the house. But surely he would miss her soon... well, at least within the next hour, and come and look for her.

Suddenly she caught her breath. Coming through the bushes toward her were several elephants, pulling down branches, eating as if famished. She sat very still, hoping that the sight of a Rover was so familiar that they would take no notice. As long as there wasn't one that had been hurt, she thought, and felt the sweat of fear break out on her face and down her back.

They came very slowly and walked around the Rover. She closed her eyes tightly and said a little prayer. She could hear the sound of their slow heavy steps, the crash of branches of leaves torn down, and then it seemed to recede....

Opening her eyes, she saw that they had gone past her. They had ignored the Rover! She could feel the tension leave her body and she flopped in her seat. Glancing in the mirror, she saw the elephants had vanished. Instead a car was driving toward her....

Cary!

He drew up behind her and walked to her side. She looked up at him. How angry he would be! She had done the very thing he had forbidden.

"Those elephants pass here?" he asked curtly.

"Yes," she nodded, her throat seeming to close up so that speech was impossible.

"You must have been frightened."

"I...I was." She swallowed. He had every right to be angry with her. She had been stupid to come out alone.

"What's wrong?" he asked.

"She stalled, and I can't start the engine."

"Well, come back with me and I'll send one of the mechanics down." He opened the door and helped her out. As they walked back to his car, he spoke again. "What were you doing?"

She looked up anxiously. "I wanted to catch Mike before he left for Perlee. Lobitha told me Mike had gone to the clinic and then was going on to the town. I wanted to stop him."

"Why?" he asked as he started the engine and carefully reversed the car until he could find a flat part of the earth road that allowed him to turn.

"Because I'm sure Samantha will phone him tonight."

"You know why Samantha went? You knew she was going?"

"No, I most certainly didn't." Rayanne twisted on the seat to look at him. "I had no idea at all. In fact, I'm sure she must have left a note for him. She wouldn't do such a thing."

"Why didn't she tell him? Why leave a note?"

"Because they've been arguing about it and I think she was afraid of a big row...."

"How come you know so much about it all? Nurse Macintyre...."

Rayanne's cheeks were hot. "If you prefer to believe Daphne Macintyre, I can't stop you. She just wants to make trouble for me. I only know about it because Samantha discussed it with me. She wants to adopt a child, but Mike doesn't. But she thought if she could have a baby on trial... you know, just for a few months, he might change his mind."

"Baby on trial?" Cary echoed. "Sounds odd."

"It isn't odd at all. I think it's very sensible. Lots of people want babies, but when they get them and find they cry and have to be fed every four hours and so on, they no longer want them. The reverse can also occur. Mike might find what fun it was to have a baby to love and look after, so Samantha was going to try to be a foster mother. She thought that way Mike might change his mind—also, if they're successful foster parents, it might help them if they applied for a child they could adopt."

"I see. So Samantha went in to collect the baby?"

"Oh, no, you can't do things as fast as that. She couldn't phone them, because Mike might walk in at any moment and she didn't want a big row, so she thought she'd go and stay there for a night or two and see what could be arranged. I'm sure she must have left a note for Mike."

"Well, he says she didn't."

"But Daphne Macintyre was at the house before him," said Rayanne.

Cary frowned. "Are you suggesting Nurse Macintyre would hide the note?"

"She's capable of anything as far as I'm concerned," Rayanne said bitterly. "She and Christine both hate me. They snub me, ignore me, do everything they can to make life unpleasant for me."

"I think you're being rather melodramatic," Cary said coldly.

"I am not," she began angrily, and paused. "How did you come to find me?"

"I'd just arrived home and mother was getting worried because you weren't in your room. Then Burt found the Rover had gone. He went off to look for you, but I decided to see Mike first."

"Of course, he has priority," said Rayanne. "It didn't matter what happened to me!"

The Fire of Life

He looked sideways at her. "You had asked for it, you know. It was a stupid thing to do."

"I know, but... well, I'd only expected to go to Mike's. That would have been quite safe."

"Not really. No more safe than here."

Rayanne was silent, twisting her fingers together, wondering when he would really get angry with her for what she had done. Perhaps he would seize it as a good reason for telling her it was time she left Jefferson Hall. That she had outstayed her welcome—if welcome she had ever been as far as he was concerned.

Back at the house, Mrs. Jefferson was nearly in tears, but Cary said they had phone calls to make.

"Come with me, Rayanne," he told her, leading the way to his library. He put the call through to the clinic. Mike had gone! "Nurse Macintyre," he said, his voice cold, "you're sure there was no message left in the Crisps' house? No letter? What... oh, I see. Naturally you didn't look. But you didn't see one that might have been there and perhaps blown on the floor because of a draft through an open window? What... oh, I see. The windows were open, so it might have happened. I understand. I quite realize that had you seen such a letter, you would have told Mike about it. Naturally. Thank you, Nurse Macintyre." He put down the receiver and looked at Rayanne.

"Well, she says she didn't see a letter or note."

"She says!" Rayanne said, her voice bitter. "Well, it all boils down to this: either you believe her or you believe me. We'll see what Samantha says. Have you quite finished with me? I feel like a hot bath."

"Yes, quite. I expect you do."

At the door, Rayanne hesitated, then she turned. "Cary—" she began.

He looked up from some papers he was sorting out.

"Yes?" It was a cold *yes*, an uninviting one that made it even harder to do what she felt she ought.

"I'm sorry," she said. "I shouldn't have taken the Rover out alone. It was just that I was upset. I...I was surprised that you weren't angry with me. I...I...."

"Thought I'd be a monster as I usually am, like all men?" His words were clipped sharp and short as if he were angry. "I said nothing to you because I knew you'd been punished enough when those elephants went by you. It must have been a bad moment, but look, Ray, it's time we cleared up something." He put down the papers and walked toward her slowly. "Let's get this straight. Why have you this hatred of men? You hate me, I know that. Do you hate Burt? Did you hate Keith? What is it that upsets you? I've an idea that you're afraid of us. Every time a man speaks to you, you clench your hands, stiffen your body. Surely it can't just be your brothers who have given you this complex?"

She looked up at him. "I...I don't know. I've always felt like this. I think it was my brothers always teasing me, treating me as a little girl even when I was nineteen...even now," she added bitterly. "They just won't accept me as I am. Then...then nothing I ever did was right in dad's eyes. I wanted him to be proud of me. He's terribly proud of...of the others. I...began to feel it was all so hopeless, that nothing I could ever do would please him, yet it was the most important thing in the world to me: to make him proud of his only daughter." She turned away. "I suppose...I suppose I see all men as my enemies as a result. I feel every time that I'm about to do battle with them, that they're against me before I even open my mouth."

"I see." Cary's voice was thoughtful. "I wonder how we can cure you."

"I don't... don't think there's any cure. I'll never be famous, and... and...." She jerked open the door and ran down the corridor, but not before Cary had seen the tears running down her cheeks.

CHAPTER EIGHT

AFTER A SLEEPLESS, UNHAPPY NIGHT, Rayanne woke very early. She showered and dressed, suddenly feeling the walls of the room closing in on her threateningly, like those of a prison. Cary's refusal to believe her hurt her more than anything that had ever happened. If he preferred to believe Daphne Macintyre....

It had been a strange evening. After Cary had driven her back to the house, Mrs. Jefferson had burst into tears as she took Rayanne in her arms.

"My dear child, I was so frightened for you...."

And then Burt had phoned to find out if there was any news of Rayanne and when told she was safely there, had slammed down the receiver—according to Cary, who told Rayanne, a slightly sarcastic smile playing around his mouth.

Then Mrs. Jefferson had startled them by announcing that she had invited a few people to dinner but that no one need go if they desired not to. She had stood there, this little loving woman who had made Rayanne feel, for once, that someone cared about her.

"But I hope you'll feel well enough to come, Rayanne," Mrs. Jefferson had said wistfully.

Cary had strode across the room, tugging at the lobe of his left ear. "Who have you asked?"

Mrs. Jefferson held up her hand and ticked off each guest on her fingers. "Christine, Daphne...."

Cary had swung around, looking across the room at Rayanne, his eyes mocking as if in challenge.

"Of course I'll come."

"And I will, too," Rayanne said at once, stiffening, feeling that shiver slide down her back.

Mrs. Jefferson beamed, "I'm so glad. Then there is...." She had named two of the vets, and added, "Oh, and Keith Bilkington. He phoned up to speak to you, Rayanne, dear, and when I said you were out, he sounded so disappointed I asked him to dinner. I hope you don't mind?" She looked anxious.

"Of course she doesn't," Cary had interrupted, giving Rayanne no chance to speak. "Keith fell for her heavily." He sounded amused, moving with his long effortless strides toward the door.

"He didn't. It's just his way..." Rayanne had begun, when Burt came almost pounding in, hardly seeing Cary, as he brushed past him and made straight for Rayanne.

His hands on her shoulders, he shook her. "I thought...well, I didn't dare think." His voice was harsh. "I.... What happened?"

Cary stood still in the doorway, looking amused.

"She was looking for Mike and the engine stalled. Apparently you didn't teach her how to cope with such a problem."

"The car stalled?" Burt's fingers were digging into Rayanne's skin. She saw the shock that showed so plainly on his face.

"Yes—and little Ray had some elephants walk past her. Punishment enough for her foolishness, so stop being so melodramatic, Burt. It won't get you anywhere," Cary said curtly, and left the room.

Burt's hands had fallen to his sides. "Were you scared?"

Rayanne managed a poor imitation of a laugh. "It was rather terrifying. Luckily they were in good tempers."

"Why were you looking for Mike?"

So she had told him what had happened, aware that Mrs. Jefferson had quietly left the room as if not wanting to disturb them.

"And Cary won't believe me. I'm sure Samantha would have left a note. I wanted to tell Mike that I thought Samantha had gone to find out about foster mothering a baby. I didn't want him to be worried about her," Rayanne had finished.

"Was it that important?"

Rayanne nodded. "To me it was. Besides, I only meant to go to the clinic, and that's not very far."

"Nevertheless, the road goes through the reserve and it's wisest not to go alone. Was Cary furious when he found you?"

Rayanne laughed, a real laugh this time—at herself.

"I thought he would be—in fact, I was quite scared, for he was right and I was in the wrong, but it didn't seem to have worried him at all. He said my fear was punishment enough...he meant fear of the elephants."

"It was fear of him?" Burt had asked, his voice changing, becoming a little aggressive. "You're not really afraid of him, are you?"

"Well...." Rayanne had hesitated. "Not really afraid, but I am here on...well, he let me come because of Uncle Joe and the least I can do really is to...well, to conform with his regulations. And now we've got this party tonight."

"What party?" Burt had asked, so she had told him. He had looked annoyed.

The Fire of Life

"Still, it might be best for you, or else you may dream of elephants." Then his hands had taken hold of her shoulders, this time more gently. "Rayanne, there's something I must tell you..." he began, and Rayanne had known the moment she feared was there.

Burt loved her and was going to tell her—which meant that she would have to hurt him with the truth. She had felt her body stiffen as she waited.

It was that moment when the door had opened and Cary stood there. He stared at them, looking puzzled.

"Sorry if I interrupted something," he said curtly, giving Rayanne an odd look and quickly closing the door so that they were alone. But Rayanne had moved and Burt's hands dropped. He was scowling, "Never get a moment to ourselves in this house!"

Rayanne had seized her chance of escape. "I must go and change," she had said, and almost ran down the corridor to her room.

She had been careful not to join the others until the guests had come. She wore a white sheath dress with a green belt and a green ribbon around her head. As she quietly joined the guests, Keith made for her.

"Hi...I told you we'd meet again," he said almost triumphantly.

It had been a difficult evening, Rayanne was thinking this next day as she walked down the well-cared-for lawn toward the muddy river. Daphne Macintyre at the party had looked like a cat with a saucer of cream—a corny expression, yet it was true. She had not spoken to Rayanne but had obviously ignored her, almost to a point of rudeness. So had Christine, for that matter, but with Christine it had been even worse. For Cary had never left Christine's side, while Rayanne had been unable to throw off Keith, who followed her around like a lost sheep, and Burt, who kept asking her to dance, whisking her away from Keith.

It had been a relief, or so Rayanne had thought at the time, when she was able to slip away to bed. But then the real troubles had begun.

Just how much longer could she stay in this, to her at least, paradise, she had asked herself. How long would she be welcome? By Cary, that was. She was sure he had been angry because she had gone off on her own in the Rover; also, he had obviously preferred to believe Daphne Macintyre rather than Rayanne Briscoe! Then he had seen Burt upset and angry—and must have realized he had interrupted them at an important moment, and then finally his total avoidance of her during the whole evening. Not once, not even once, had he danced with her! Wouldn't it be better, she had asked herself, tossing and turning restlessly in bed, if she left? More dignified? More...more.... She couldn't find the right word and then the tears had come. Foolish, no-good tears because she loved him so much and if she went might never see him again. How could she do it?

Now, as she turned away from the river she had strolled down to, she saw little Dorcas, the African maid who looked after her, come running, holding a note.

"I could not find you...you were not in bed," she said almost accusingly. "He is waiting."

"Thanks." Rayanne took the note in her hands and, recognizing Cary's handwriting, felt fear slide down her back. Cary had something important to tell her? It could only be...it must be....

"The equivalent of dismissal" was an expression her father often used, and somehow it seemed to fit this perfectly. After a good night's sleep, Cary must have decided that Rayanne's disobedience of his regulations could only mean one thing: that she was "unsuitable for the environment," another of her father's favorite expressions. She wondered why she was thinking of her father... was it because this would disappoint him still more? That if she were packed off from here, he would have to admit again that he had a strange daughter?

"The runt of the litter," she had heard him say once. She had been much younger and had fled to her bedroom in tears. Later her mother had tried to explain that it hadn't been said seriously, that it was a joke.... But it hadn't been a joke in Rayanne's eyes, nor would it ever be.

Now she turned the envelope over several times. She was afraid to open it. It was like receiving a death warrant—for if she left here, life would no longer have any reason. Life without Cary would be... nothing. Yet that was what life was bound to be, she knew.

Opening the envelope, she was shocked to see her hands trembling. Was she showing her emotion so plainly? Would it be a tactful brush-off, she wondered. Somthing like "I feel sure you have collected enough notes and may find it easier to write the thesis in your own home." A polite way of saying, "Get out!"

She read the note. It was brief and to the point.

Please come immediately to my study, as I have something important to tell you.

Come immediately—and Dorcas had been looking for her, Rayanne realized, so goodness only knew how long Cary had been waiting. This would only add to his displeasure, his certainty that "the headache girl" must go.

She hurried indoors, not bothering to look in the mirror, for there was no sense in that since he never really saw her, and tapped on his door.

"Come in," he said impatiently.

Rayanne obeyed, closing the door and leaning against it as she stared at the man behind the desk. Cary was standing, not looking up as he sorted out some papers with a frown on his face.

"It took you a long time," he commented.

"I'm sorry. Dorcas couldn't find me. I was in the garden."

Cary looked up, his dark tufty eyebrows moving. "You had a rendezvous?" he asked sarcastically.

She colored, knowing he was thinking of Burt. "No. Just thinking that perhaps I...." She drew a deep breath. This was the right moment, the moment to tell him she knew she should go home.

"Sit down, then, and don't look scared to death. I'm not going to eat you," Cary said irritably, going on sorting out the papers. "What were you thinking of, looking at the crocs?"

"Just... well...." This was something she couldn't tell him, for it was the truth. She had been thinking of him and how desolate her life would be when he walked out of it. "I wondered what you wanted to see me about. What have I done wrong this time?" she asked almost defiantly.

He stood up, putting the papers on one side, and stared at her. "Rayanne Briscoe, isn't it time you grew up? Stop harping on that martyr line. You haven't done anything wrong. In any case, that's not why I sent for you." He looked at his watch. "There isn't time for

The Fire of Life

this ridiculous.... Look, in ten minutes I have to be on my way to New York."

"New York?" Rayanne was startled.

"Yes, and I need your help."

"My...my help?" Rayanne's eyes widened as she stared at him. Cary was asking for *her* help! She found it hard to believe.

But it was true, and he sounded really worried as he went on, "Yes. You see, this has come quite by surprise, just as my trip to Cape Town was. I can usually avoid these journeys during the courses here, but this time I've failed. As you know, there have been far fewer lectures than there should have been because of my Cape Town visit, and I had planned to wind up everything this afternoon." He patted the pile of papers by his side. "These are notes on previous talks I've given and a rough draft of how to tie up all the bits, but—and this is the important part, Ray—most of the lecture must be ad lib. The students are uninterested as soon as you start reading and it's important for them to leave here understanding why we support wildlife conservation and what this reserve is for." He paused, then smiled. "I want you to give the lecture."

Had he slapped her face, she could hardly have been more shocked. "Me?" she almost howled with surprise. "But...."

He stood up, glancing at his watch again. "There are the notes, Ray. Mike will give you any information you need. I expect you have plenty yourself that you've collected for your thesis. Use the personal touch. Tell the students you came here as a skeptic. You were, weren't you? Perhaps you still are, but tell them what you've learned, what has caught your interest. But why tell you? I know you'll manage all right."

Striding to the door, Cary smiled at her. Somehow Rayanne jerked herself into action. She had felt, for a moment, stunned.

"But wouldn't Christine be better? I mean, she's been here longer than me and..." she began.

Cary's hand was on the doorknob. "Christine's bright in the laboratory but hopeless when it comes to facts about conservation." He opened the door, then turned and said casually, "By the way, you were quite right. Mike phoned me and said Samantha told him she had left a note for him." Cary closed the door and was gone.

Clutching the papers, Rayanne made her way to her bedroom. She put them on the table, all her movements slow as if the slightest effort were exhausting. She could not believe it. Cary had asked her to take his place before his soon leaving students.

Somehow she moved to join the others at breakfast. Mrs. Jefferson leaped to her feet.

"Dear child, what has happened? You look so white," she said anxiously.

Rayanne managed a weak smile. "Cary has asked me to lecture the students this afternoon."

"So what?" Burt asked irritably. "If he can do it, so can you."

"But, Burt," Rayanne almost wailed, "I know hardly anything about it."

"Neither do they. You must have lectured before."

"I have—but not here." Rayanne sounded desperate. "I just...."

"And what's so different about here?" Burt asked, his voice suddenly cold. "It's only one of many wildlife reserves—anyone would think it was the Albert Hall or the Royal Command Performance!" he grinned.

The Fire of Life

Mrs. Jefferson stiffened herself and looked shocked.

"The Jefferson Reserve is unique, Burt. There is none other so respected or quoted. It's a very responsible job Cary has given Rayanne, but my dear girl—" Mrs. Jefferson turned to Rayanne again "—don't worry. Cary wouldn't ask you unless he were sure you're capable of doing it. You see, we're always getting requests from quite famous people who want to come and stay here to see the reserve and our experiments and also lecture. Cary always says no... he'll do the lecturing."

"I doubt if he'd have asked me today if he hadn't to rush off to New York," Rayanne said slowly. "He must have been desperate to find someone at the last moment."

"That's absurd, dear child," Mrs. Jefferson said slowly. "Cary knew for several weeks that he was going to New York."

Rayanne's legs suddenly felt weak, so she sank into a chair.

"You mean... you mean Cary knew all along that he would be away?"

"Yes, dear, he did. He was annoyed because he had to go before the end of the course, but they refused to postpone the meeting. It's extremely important—something to do with a big reserve in South America."

"So he could have arranged for anyone to lecture," Rayanne said slowly.

"Of course, dear. He could have phoned anyone and they could have flown up. No trouble at all. But he wanted you."

"What do you mean, he wanted me?" Rayanne asked. She was suddenly afraid. Was it because it meant even more decisively that he didn't like her? That he wanted her to look a fool, to make her realize just how dumb and stupid she was? That would mean he was like all men—like her father and her five brothers!

"He told me ages ago that he thought you would make a good... what was his expression? A somewhat funny one, dear girl. I've got it: *channel*. He said you would make a good channel between the students and him, that they would find you more interesting and more sincere because of your age. You're very young, you know, Rayanne, dear," Mrs. Jefferson added tenderly as she took her place at the table again and began eating.

"I suppose I am..." Rayanne said thoughtfully. Young to a man of thirty-five! "I'm no good at talking, though. I'm always scared stiff I shall start saying 'mmm... ugh... hmm... er....'"

"Nonsense," Burt sounded annoyed. "You talk very well. You must have been given plenty of notes by Cary. He's so methodical."

Rayanne glanced at him. Was he being sarcastic? Why had he suddenly taken a dislike to Cary, she wondered.

"Yes, he has, but I'm only to use them as a tie-up of the other lectures. He wants me to tell them of my own experiences here, my own feelings."

"Well, what's wrong with that? Make a good beginning for your much discussed thesis," said Burt, even more sarcastically.

Rayanne looked at him worriedly. It was so unlike Burt. Was he upset about something?

"I'm going over to young Warrender's house this morning," Burt said curtly. "Coming, or do you want to prepare for this afternoon?"

Hesitating, Rayanne thought fast. She wanted to go

with Burt, because she hated him to be hurt in any way; on the other hand, she had a lot of thinking to do.

That afternoon! How it hovered above her head, coming closer every moment.

"I think she should study her notes, Burt," Mrs. Jefferson interrupted quietly. "After all, there's always tomorrow."

He stood up, a strange smile twisting his lips. "Of course there is—but how many tomorrows will there be?" he asked, and left them.

Alone, Mrs. Jefferson smiled at Rayanne. "Don't look so worried, dear girl. Cary wouldn't have asked you to give that lecture if he hadn't complete faith in you."

Later, alone in her room, standing before the mirror and trying to start her talk, Rayanne wished she had faith in herself. If Mrs. Jefferson was right, Cary not only trusted her but had had this in mind for some time. That meant he believed she could do it.

She stood in front of the mirror and glared at herself.

"I'm here this afternoon to take the place of Cary Jefferson. I'm sure, like me, you're sorry about this, but he has been called away on an important visit to New York. He has given me some notes to tie up his previous lectures, but...."

She stopped and buried her face in her hands. How ghastly it sounded! Her voice all hoarse and croaky like a frog's. And pompous! That was the only word to describe it—smug and pompous. How on earth was she going to face all those critical faces of students waiting to see what she was like?

It was even worse that afternoon as Hubert Ellingham, in charge of the students, led the way onto the dais, introducing her to the students as they sat, notebooks open on their laps, looking up at her. Rayanne caught her breath with dismay, for in the back row she could see not only Burt, but Christine Horlock talking to him.

After being introduced, Rayanne stood up. She looked at the faces before her.

"I'm sorry Cary Jefferson couldn't be here," she began, and meant every word of it. "He has asked me to tie up the lectures he has already given you, but first I'm to talk about my own experiences here. I hope you won't be bored." She leaned on the tall lectern on the dais, her hair falling forward over her face, so she swept it back with an impatient gesture. She watched the ripple among the heads before her as they looked at one another and grinned. "Please try not to fall asleep," she added, and was rewarded with a chuckle that also seemed to ripple around the room. She took a deep breath.

"I came here," she said, beginning to walk up and down the dais, using her hands as she spoke, demonstrating with her movements, "as a skeptic. I'm afraid I had little interest in the conservation of wildlife. I felt the money would be better spent on the feeding of the many millions of starving children and people in the world...."

Another ripple of approval from her audience filled the hall and some even clapped and one shouted, "Hear, hear!"

"But since I've been here...." Suddenly she knew she had to make them understand—that it was necessary, not only to Cary but to the whole world, to make them realize the good these reserves were doing, the knowledge that they were given by experiment in water and soil conservation and that could be used....

The Fire of Life

She began to talk earnestly, seeing the faces before her as blurs, yet knowing she held their interest. She walked up and down the dais, moving her hands, pausing as she waited to let them accept something she told them.

It came as a surprise when Mr. Ellingham touched her gently.

"Time's up," he said.

"Don't stop!" someone shouted from the audience, and there was a sudden roar as everyone clapped. Rayanne stood, silent for a moment, looking at them.

"Thank you," she said. "Thank you very much indeed. I'm afraid I got carried away. I forgot about time."

"Go on forgetting!" someone shouted.

But Mr. Ellingham was standing up, pointing to his watch. Teatime!

"Can I quickly read what Mr. Jefferson wanted tied up?" Rayanne asked.

Hubert Ellingham nodded and Rayanne quickly read aloud Cary's notes. *How much better than my words,* she thought, and then it was over, the students crowding out of the hall, some coming up to shake Rayanne's hand and to say she had given them a new slant on it.

Burt joined her and they walked back in silence to the house, Burt carrying the dispatch case that rarely left his side. Mrs. Jefferson was waiting eagerly.

"I didn't come, dear, in case I made you nervous," she said. "How did it go?"

"I got carried away," Rayanne admitted, sitting down and taking the cup of tea passed to her. "I must admit I enjoyed it, but I... well, I just don't know how it went."

Burt was opening his case, taking out a tape recorder.

"I've got it all here," he said. "Like to hear it?"

"Of course, of course." Mrs. Jefferson clapped her hands excitedly. "How clever of you to think of this, Burt."

He looked up, his face almost surly. "Cary asked me to."

"Cary did?" Rayanne's hand flew to her mouth. So he hadn't really trusted her, then, she thought. He wanted to hear just what sort of fool she had made of herself. And why was Burt still in such a difficult mood? Hardly talking to her, almost grunting, and looking as if the end of the world was coming.

"He certainly did," Burt said crossly. "Now listen."

He switched on. They listened to the introduction and then Rayanne's voice came.

"I'm sorry Cary Jefferson couldn't be here," she began. Her voice was filled with emotion. Rayanne caught her breath with dismay. She had betrayed herself—anyone listening must have known she loved Cary. She looked quickly at Burt and saw him staring at her, eyebrows almost touching, mouth a thin line, eyes full of despair.

Then Rayanne forgot him as she listened to her own voice. Why, she thought with amazement, it was quite good. Clear, warm, full of emotion... she wasn't nearly as bad as she had thought....

They listened in silence until the end. Then Mrs. Jefferson clapped her hands.

"That was very good, Rayanne, very good indeed. You almost convinced me!" she laughed. "Cary will be pleased, won't he, Burt?"

"No doubt about that," Burt said gruffly, closing the tape recorder and putting it away; then he stood up, murmuring something about seeing them later, and left the room.

"What's the matter with Burt?" Rayanne asked. "I've never known him to behave like this."

Mrs. Jefferson had also stood up. "I have some phone calls to make," she said with a smile.

They walked together to the door. "Doesn't Burt seem to be behaving strangely to you?" Rayanne asked anxiously. "I'm quite worried about him."

Mrs. Jefferson gave her a strange look. "Well, my dear, if you don't know what's upsetting poor Burt, it's time you grew up. Or perhaps you should look in the mirror. Ah!" she said, her voice becoming gay as she opened the door. "We'll be entertaining tonight, Rayanne, dear. Several reporters are staying on, so I invited them over."

"Reporters?" Rayanne echoed. "What are they doing here?"

"Cary invited them. He doesn't usually, but this time they were needed," Mrs. Jefferson said, and hurried down the corridor toward her room, bouncing like a litle pouter pigeon, her eyes shining happily.

Rayanne watched her go, puzzled at Mrs. Jefferson's happiness. She had been almost triumphant. *Why,* Rayanne wondered. *Why?*

CHAPTER NINE

THE PARTY THAT EVENING was something of a nightmare to Rayanne. It was true the reporters were all friendly men, but they asked her question after question—where was she born, about her education, what had made her interested in wildlife conservation, until her head seemed fuddled with the questions.

The group of men stood around where Rayanne sat while Christine and Daphne were at the other end of the room, alone with Burt and Mrs. Jefferson. As they left, Christine said sourly, "A lot of fuss about nothing! Anyone can give a lecture."

Daphne had added, giving Rayanne a strange look, "Just as well you're not in the medical profession or they'd create like mad about all the publicity. Aren't you rather overdoing it?"

"I had nothing to do with it!" Rayanne said indignantly.

"Is that so?" drawled Daphne. "Now who'd 'a' thought it!"

As they left, Burt by her side told her softly to ignore them. "Both jealous as can be. They want to know why Cary has given you so much publicity when he hates it himself."

Rayanne turned to him, her hands imploring. "Please, Burt, what does it all mean? It makes no sense to me.

The Fire of Life 349

Cary lying about having to go to New York at the last moment...."

"That's easy to answer. He wanted you to talk spontaneously—not after weeks of worried thinking. He was right, too. You spoke naturally and I reckon you're very articulate."

"Why, thank you, Burt." Rayanne was grateful and also relieved because he seemed in a happier mood.

Now he chuckled. "Man, how they hate you! Those two dames, I mean. You've done more in a short while than they have done in months. You're the boss's pet—that's the way they see it. Spoiled, cherished and used." He walked past her quickly, leaving her to stare after him, puzzled.

Mrs. Jefferson kissed her good-night. "I think it was a very good evening, my dear. I do hope you enjoyed it."

"It seemed to me... well...." Rayanne sought for the right words as she walked with Mrs. Jefferson to her bedroom. "Well, didn't I get a lot of publicity for a very small thing?"

"Small thing?" Mrs. Jefferson sounded indignant. "Nothing to do with Jefferson Wildlife Reserve is small!"

Alone in her bedroom, Rayanne went over the day thoughtfully. Now what was Cary planning? Why had he done all that? Surely he could have given her more time to plan the talk? Was it kind of him? Or was Burt right when he said Cary was wise, that he wanted the talk to come spontaneously? It was hard not to feel thrilled, she thought, as she lay in bed. Her voice had been infinitely nicer than she had thought—and to have all those reporters interested in her!

She laughed. What a child she must be still to allow such a thing to excite and please her!

Next morning, when she and Burt went to call on the Crisps, Burt was almost silent, back into the difficult mood Rayanne had noticed. She wondered if she should ask him what was wrong, but decided to leave it to him to choose his time.

Samantha welcomed them with open arms. "I've got coffee all ready. Burt, Mike is in the office," she said, quickly getting rid of him and tucking her hand through Rayanne's arm to lead her into the sitting room. "Everything's going to be great. There's nothing definite about it yet, but they were most sympathetic and understanding. Mike realized how much it meant to me and I think he's quite keen to see how we... well, what it's like to have a baby. I just can't wait... we can make that part of the garden a play part. Sand and a tiny pool. It mustn't be deep, of course, and I'll have a net over it except when I'm with her...."

"You want a daughter?"

"Yes, to start with... we're going to repaint the guest room and... oh—" Samantha suddenly hugged Rayanne "—thanks for suggesting it."

"Actually I think it was Burt's idea."

"Burt's a darling. Why not marry him? He's obviously in love with you and he'll make a good husband."

Rayanne smiled weakly. "But I don't love him."

"You probably could, in time. Oh, that reminds me. We found the note."

"So Cary told me. Where was it?"

"In the rubbish heap. My girl found it under the sofa. It must have been blown down."

Rayanne looked at the windows. It would have to be

The Fire of Life

a strange draft or wind that could have blown the note under the sofa.

"Where did you leave it?"

"On the mantelpiece. Here." Samantha jumped up in her white trews and shirt and touched the clock. She frowned, looked at the window and the sofa. "Seems rather odd to me that it could have blown there."

"Seems very odd to me, too," Rayanne agreed.

Samantha looked at her thoughtfully. "Still, my girl might have made a mistake. Maybe she found it in the grate."

"Maybe," said Rayanne. It didn't really matter. The main thing was that Cary knew now that she had been right. "I was certain you'd never rush off without telling Mike."

"Of course not. He'd have been worried sick," said Samantha. "I'm surprised Cary even believed I would." She smiled. "Look, Rayanne, may I poke my nose in where it has no right to go? Watch out. You're waving the flag for Cary Jefferson, aren't you?"

Rayanne's bright red cheeks were answer enough. Samantha sighed. "Not that I blame you, though. He's really the ... well, how can words describe it? Just one of those things, isn't it? But you haven't a hope. You do know that? Cary just isn't the marrying kind. Or perhaps I'd say, *shouldn't* marry. All they think about is their work."

But if I could help him, Rayanne was thinking, *if we could make a team*. She had to smile. What a crazy thought! As if Cary would ever accept a woman to work with him. What was it he had called them? A nuisance, a headache, and even a pain in the neck.

It was three days later that Rayanne went to the lab to get some information for her thesis. She had begun to write, much on the same lines that she had spoken to the students, but there were a few facts to be checked. As she walked into the lab Christine looked up, her face bright with anger. She was reading a newspaper and came to meet Rayanne, thrusting the paper into her face.

"I wonder you have the nerve to come in here! What's the idea? You had no right to tell the press such a lie. Cary will be furious...."

"I don't know what you're talking about." Rayanne, wishing she had never come to the lab, looked around a little wildly at the modern equipment. Cary was certainly not cheap about such things.

"It's a lie. An absolute, outrageous lie!" Christine fumed on.

"Look, let me read it," said Rayanne. She leaned against one of the tables and read the printed news:

Cary Jefferson, one of the well-known leaders of wildlife conservation, hopes that the young biologist, Miss Rayanne Briscoe, whose lecture at the Jefferson Reserve was welcomed and admired by everyone, may work for him in future as he finds it difficult to fit in the lectures required by the courses with his necessary travels around the world. This is most unusual in many ways, for until now Mr. Jefferson has rather shied away from women biologists, for no admitted reason. Miss Briscoe must have made an impression on him, one that she proved by her first lecture, which was so successful.

"But it's not true!" Rayanne gasped, lowering the paper.

The Fire of Life

Christine looked triumphant. "Exactly. I told you so. But why did you tell such a lie? Cary will be furious."

"But I knew nothing about it. The press must be making it up. Unless Cary did...."

Christine laughed, an ugly contemptuous sound. "Oh, yes! Then if so, what did you do to Cary? Twist his arm, or burst into tears and beg for the job?"

Rayanne clenched her hand that was holding the paper. "Neither, and you know it. I'll let you have the paper back, but I must show it to Mrs. Jefferson."

"She'll be delighted. This is what she's been fighting for all the time. A sweet, biddable little English girl to marry her wonderful son!" Christine laughed bitterly. "How long will you last before he's bored to tears with you? Why, you're nothing but a...."

Rayanne turned and walked out of the lab. She was shaking a little. Who could have told such a lie? How would Cary react? Would he believe that she had nothing to do with it?

Mrs. Jefferson looked anxious when Rayanne joined her on the *stoep*. "Now what's happened, Rayanne? You look so upset."

"Read this," Rayanne said curtly, then blushed. "I'm sorry—would you please read this, Mrs. Jefferson? I can't understand it."

Mrs. Jefferson's glasses were hanging around her neck on a thin silver chain. Finally she got them on and slowly read the newspaper. Rayanne stood while she waited, staring blindly out of the window.

"I didn't tell the press...it's just a lie," said Rayanne, and heard the rustle as Mrs. Jefferson put down the paper.

"But it's quite true, dear girl," Mrs. Jefferson said gently.

Rayanne swung around, her face startled. "I don't understand."

"Actually, I don't think it should be in the papers yet. Cary would have asked you when he returned. He wanted you to give the lecture first as he said you had no confidence in yourself and it had to be proved—to yourself—that you could do the job. Of course you'll take it, dear. I'm so happy about it and it will be a great help for Cary. He's always getting tangled up with appointments overseas and his lectures. Now he'll be able to relax."

Walking slowly to an armchair, Rayanne lowered herself into it. "You mean, he really is going to offer me the job?"

Mrs. Jefferson nodded. "Yes. Of course you'll take it and it will be lovely to have you about all the year round. I shan't have to travel so much, because I won't be lonely anymore."

Rayanne tucked her feet under her. "I can't...I mean.... Well, it just doesn't make sense."

"Why not, dear girl? You're clever, Cary says. Articulate, according to Burt West. You're interested in the work. I think you've been happy here. Or do you find it too lonely?" Mrs. Jefferson's voice was wistful.

"I've been very happy here, but...I don't know...." Rayanne brushed back her hair. "I just can't believe it!"

Mrs. Jefferson laughed softly. "Neither can I, my dear. You'll be like the daughter I've always wanted."

Rayanne had been thinking fast. "But Cary hadn't heard me lecture. How can he know I'd be all right?"

"He never doubted it for one moment. He said you had an ideal voice and showed emotion when you talked. He can't stand speakers who stand stiffly and talk like robots. Is that the right way to pronounce it, dear girl? I always get so muddled with these new words. Now I must go and see Jacob. He will plant the flowers just where I don't want them...." She stood up with some difficulty, leaning on the chair's arms, and smiled at Rayanne. "I'm so happy, dear girl, so very happy," she said softly, and left the room.

Alone, Rayanne couldn't sit still. She got up and began to pace up and down. She would have gone outside, but the heat was at its height and she needed to feel cool in order to think.

Was it all a hoax? A funny kind of joke, she asked herself. Yet how could Mrs. Jefferson know about it unless it was the truth? Would Cary tell his mother if he didn't mean it?

The door opened and Burt stood there.

"Well?" he asked, his voice strange. "So you know."

"I know?" Rayanne looked at the newspaper she was still clutching. "Oh, yes, I see you've read it."

"Seeing that I gave the information, I didn't need to read it," Burt told her. He walked slowly toward her.

"You told them?" Rayanne caught her breath. "Then it's all a joke? A funny kind of joke," she added bitterly. "A lie. Christine accused me of lying about it."

"It isn't a lie," Burt said, his voice lifeless. "Cary asked me to tell the press."

"But...but...." Rayanne stared at him. "I just don't understand."

A thin smile moved Burt's lips. "Apparently—according to Cary—you don't exactly hit it off. He said you were always either aggressive or on the defensive. You seemed to see him as an enemy and you were on guard. Some tripe about women's equality. Is that right?"

Rayanne could feel the color burning in her cheeks. "In a way, yes."

"Well, Cary said that if *he* offered you the job, you'd jump down his throat, accuse him of patronage or cruelly teasing you, and probably refuse the job without even considering it. He said he failed to get through to the real you, that you wouldn't let him. He even thinks you hate him... simply because he's a man."

"I... hate him?"

Burt nodded. "Absurd, isn't it? Well, Cary wanted you to know he was going to offer you this job for a few days before he came back. So I told the press you were going to be offered it. You'll notice that I didn't say you would take the job." He paused. "But of course you will."

Rayanne put out her hand vaguely and was absurdly glad to feel the back of an armchair. She felt dazed, unable to think properly.

"I see no 'of course' about it," she managed to say at last.

Then Burt moved—fast, surprising her, taking her in his arms, kissing her, his mouth hard against hers.

She struggled for a moment and then lay still in his arms, passive but not returning the kiss. He let her go abruptly and just caught her from falling. He gave her a strange look.

"Don't say you're sorry. I know it's not your fault." He gave a funny little laugh. "I was a fool not to have seen it from the beginning. You'll take the job all right." He turned and left her standing there, silently staring at the closed door.

Somehow she got to her room, took a straw hat because of the sun and went out into the garden. She walked right down to the water's edge and found a stone on which to sit.

The Fire of Life

A huge crocodile lay there, sleeping peacefully, but then, almost as if he had sensed her presence, he began to move. Slowly but with a frightening strength of purpose as he made his way into the water. Rayanne shivered but still stayed where she was. It was very hot, the perspiration sliding down her face, her thin yellow dress clinging damply to her back. She had to think — she had to think!

It was a dream come true. Working with Cary. Seeing him every day — or nearly every day, for he was obviously away a lot. Living in this lovely quiet place, having work she enjoyed. Maybe she could even write a book about it. She had always dreamed of one day being a writer.... There was so much to tempt her.

But — and it was a very big but — wasn't she asking for heartache if she stayed? Suppose Cary met a girl he could respect and love, and brought her back as his bride?

If she stayed, Rayanne told herself, every day would increase the danger of heartache. Even if he didn't marry, the mere fact that he didn't *see* her would hurt her. Each day, she knew, she would love him more, and each day would make the final ending more painful.

On the other hand, had she the strength and courage to break away? To return to England, to get some miserable unrewarding job and let the family tease and laugh at her again?

What a difficult question it was! She wanted to stay; with all her heart she wanted to stay. But if she did stay, what would it do to her heart? Break it?

CHAPTER TEN

SOMEHOW RAYANNE WASN'T SURPRISED, when she joined Mrs. Jefferson for tea, to learn that Burt had gone.

"He asked me to apologize for not saying goodbye to you, dear girl," Mrs. Jefferson said as she lifted the Queen Anne silver teapot and carefully poured out the tea. "He says he thought it was better this way. I imagine you understand."

"Yes, I understand," Rayanne said, her voice sad. Poor dear Burt, suffering as much as she was. If only she could have loved him! He was such a dear, so kind....

As the days passed, what was most embarrassing was the fact that Mrs. Jefferson took it for granted that Rayanne would accept the job. So did the others. Samantha was thrilled, but she also said she felt Rayanne had made a mistake.

"This is dangerous driving," she said, her eyes narrowed worriedly. "You do know that? If you don't watch out...I mean, let's face it, he's married to his work."

"I know," Rayanne answered. "I'm still not sure I'll take the job."

Samantha laughed. "You will," she prophesied.

Alone one night Rayanne tried to come to a decision. She got out a piece of paper and put "FOR" and "AGAINST" at the top of the page. Then she carefully thought out and typed neatly.

She read the result, and then burst into tears. The list read:

FOR	AGAINST
I love him	He can only break my heart, as he doesn't even see me.
I love his mother	
I love the country	I hate his sarcasm and stuffiness.
I love the work	Would he ever treat me as an equal?
	The antagonism of Christine and Daphne.

There was no answer. No answer at all. She felt tempted to pack her clothes and get away, right away, six thousand miles away where perhaps she could get a job that so enthralled her there'd be no time to think of Cary.... Wasn't that the most sensible thing to do? Wouldn't that be less painful in the long run? Yet how could she run away and leave Mrs. Jefferson alone? And the job? How could she turn down the job?

Three days later, a letter came from England. Surprised, because her family, including herself, were all very bad letter writers, she saw it was from her mother. The contents startled her even more.

My dear Rayanne,
 Your father and I are delighted at the news that you have at last found what you have been looking for all this time. You can imagine how thrilled dear Uncle Joe is. He also talks of coming out to see you and to meet his old love, Mrs. Jefferson, whom he can remember very well. I enclose the newspaper cuttings, as obviously this is your first step on a career that could make your name

known all over the world, so you may want to keep them. You can't think how proud we are of you, Rayanne. I always knew that one day you would prove yourself. Your brothers all send their love and say "Bully for you." Not a very gracious remark, but you know it means a lot for them to say that.

With love from us all,

Mother

Rayanne's eyes were smarting with unshed tears as she carefully folded up the letter before she looked at the many newspaper cuttings. The news seemed to have been in every newspaper in England. There was even a photograph of her. One she recognized immediately as taken by Burt.

Was Burt still in this? Had he sent the news around, knowing her father's name was well-known, as were the names of her brothers? Yet the papers merely quoted what had been written in the South African newspapers, though all expressed amazement at a girl being offered the post! Apparently Cary Jefferson was well-known as a permanent woman despiser, or perhaps woman avoider!

"Good news, dear?" Mrs. Jefferson asked.

Rayanne looked at her, seeing a blurred figure. "Yes, wonderful. The nicest letter I've ever had in my life." Suddenly she was dancing around the room, singing happily. "Just think!" she said, stopping in front of Mrs. Jefferson, leaning down, one hand on each arm of the chair. "Just think—they're proud of me! They're proud of me for the first time in my life." Her voice rose excitedly. Then she remembered something and stood up. "Oh, and mother says Uncle Joe wishes to be remembered to you and he hopes to come out and visit us."

"Your Uncle Joe?" Mrs. Jefferson looked excited. Her hand went to her hair. "I wonder when he's coming. I must go to the hairdresser. Oh, my dear girl, isn't life exciting these days?"

But was it, Rayanne wondered that night as she went to bed. This had merely added another problem to the one she couldn't solve. Her family was proud of her. What would they say if she turned down the job?

The next day after she had been to see Samantha, Kwido drove her back. It was rather early for lunch and there was no sign of anyone in the house. Rayanne hesitated in the lounge, looking around, wondering where Mrs. Jefferson could be. The sound of a door opening made her swing around. It was Cary.

"Why, Cary!" she exclaimed, and moved instinctively toward him with a betraying eagerness. Now as she colored, she added, "We didn't expect you yet."

"I'm aware of that." He closed the door and leaned against it. "I've just been listening to your lecture." His voice had no warmth, no approval in it.

"What did you, er, did you . . . ? Is it all right?" Rayanne stammered.

He frowned, those great, tufty eyebrows moving. "Of course it's all right," he said, almost crossly. "Why shouldn't it be? I knew you'd make a good speaker. Very articulate. The kind of voice one can listen to indefinitely."

She blushed with pleasure. "I'm glad you liked it. Cary, about this job...."

"What job?" he asked, staring at her.

"Well, the job of... of lecturing for you when you're away," Rayanne said, suddenly nervous. Had it all been a joke of Burt's? A strange unfunny joke, but the result of knowing she didn't love him?

"Oh, that." He moved forward, coming nearer to her with surprising quickness. "I'm afraid that's off."

"It's... off?" Rayanne went white; she could almost feel the blood leaving her face. "You mean, you don't want me?"

It was like a slap in the face. All this time she had been trying to make up her mind, trying to decide whether it was better to grab at what happiness she could, even if the price was high to pay. And it was all off. The job was not to be hers. She would have to go away....

Her nose seemed to prickle—a frightening sensation, since it was usually a warning she was about to cry and crying was the very last thing she must do.

"Yes, I've been thinking about it. I'm often away for several weeks."

"And you couldn't trust me?" Anger was sweeping away her dismay. They were back at square one. "Just because I'm a woman!"

His hands gripped her arms. "Look, for crying out loud, will you stop this liberation nonsense? It has nothing to do with your sex at all."

"Then why...?" She felt breathless and trembling, angry yet excited, a strange combination of emotions.

"Because I intend to take you with me," he said.

"Go with you?"

He smiled. She caught her breath. If only....

"Of course. It's usual for a wife to accompany her husband."

"A *wife*?" Rayanne could hardly speak.

"You are going to marry me, aren't you? I thought it was all arranged."

"Arranged? You mean by your mother?"

The Fire of Life

He smiled. "If it makes her happy to think so, why not let her? I knew as soon as I saw you, that day at the Crisps'. You looked so tired and frightened, I wanted to gather you up in my arms and kiss you, but I knew you weren't in the right mood. You were the girl I'd spent my life looking for. And you?"

"Why, Cary, I knew... I knew it was you then, too. Oh, Cary, it can't be true. It just can't!" she gasped, her voice bewildered. "This must be a dream and I'll wake up...."

His arms were linked now behind her back as he pulled her closer.

"Not a dream, Ray. It's real. Right from the first moment I loved you, but it seemed absurd. How could you love someone you didn't even know?"

"That's how I felt, too. It was absurd, but...."

"It was true. My mother said at once that you loved me, but I didn't believe it. You were so aggressive at times, I often thought you hated me. Then there was Burt West. You were always together."

"Burt's a darling. I like him, but...."

He frowned, his tufty eyebrows drawing together. This time she could do what she had always longed to do, lift her hand and gently stroke the thick hard brows. Then she traced her finger down his nose and either side of his mouth.

"There's just one thing, Ray," he said. "You know what you're tackling? A lonely life."

"Lonely?" She laughed and put both her arms around his neck. "Oh, Cary, if you knew how happy I am! How could I ever be lonely married to you?"

THE IMPOSSIBLE DREAM

The Impossible Dream

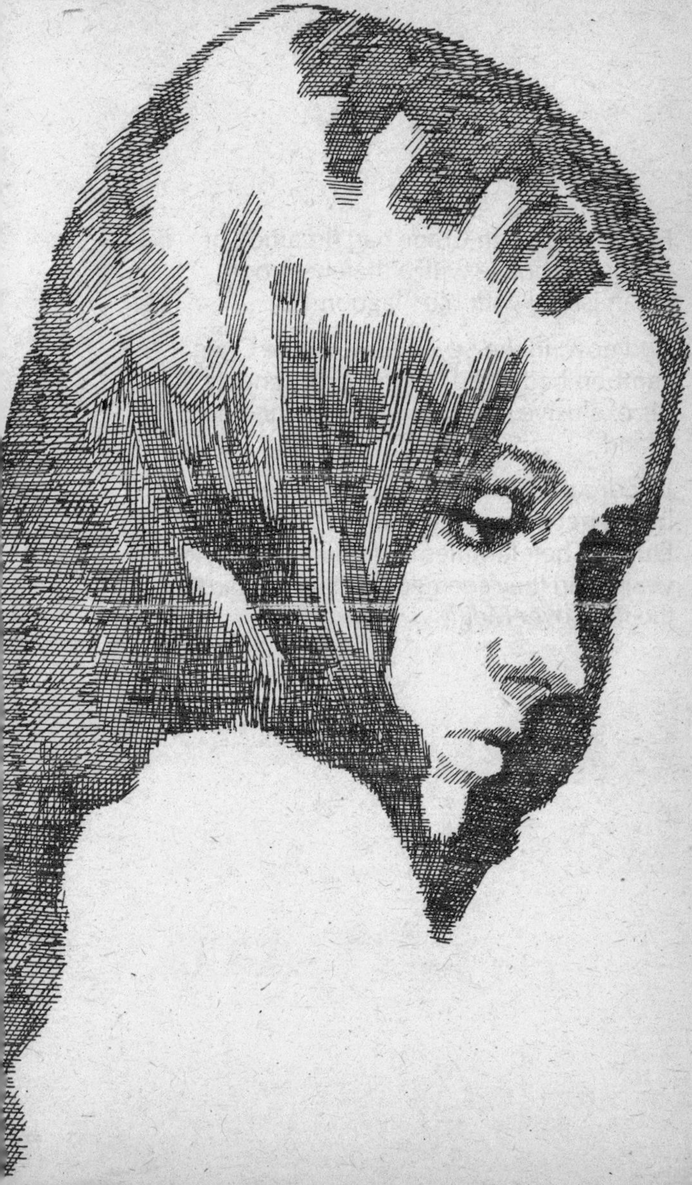

For years Megan Crane had dreamed of living in a house with a thatched roof on an island with blue lagoons.

And now, in the Seychelles, where Craig Lambert had hired her to teach dancing at his exclusive school, Meg had found her island.

Her dream was flawed, however, by the bad blood between Craig and his rival, Gaston Duval. Their families had been fighting for years, and they seemed destined to carry on the feud over Meg.

CHAPTER ONE

As THE SCHOONER slowly approached the opening in the coral reef, Megan Crane could see the jetty, crowded with people. The water was the wonderful deep blue of the Indian Ocean, the sky cloudless; even the wind was warm against her cheeks. The town looked small, with the little houses huddled together as if seeking the sanctuary offered by the tall mountains towering above them.

"Well," Miss Wilmot by her side said, "here we are. I wonder if Mr. Lambert himself will come and meet us. I doubt it, as we're not the VIPs he honors."

Megan Crane turned to look at the tall, slim woman with her elaborately dressed hair. "You don't like Craig Lambert?" Megan asked.

The words were impulsive and Megan regretted saying them. Her hands tightened around the rail of the ship. Nor did she like Craig Lambert, she thought angrily, for he was ruining her brother Patrick—deliberately, too.

Then why was she here, she asked herself, on the way out to this island near the Seychelles, to work for Mr. Lambert?

She smiled wryly. What choice had she? She looked at the white-flecked waves. She'd had no choice. Her father had thrown her out, so she needed the job badly. In addition, though she and Patrick had shared little love with each other, at least he was her brother, and if she could find a way to help him....

Miss Wilmot, Mr. Lambert's personal assistant who looked after his affairs in England when he was away, smiled. "What a question," she said. "I work for him. Surely that's answer enough?"

"I wonder," Megan replied.

The schooner was rolling gently as it waited outside the reef opening. The lagoon they could see was not large and a schooner was already anchored by the jetty.

Suddenly Megan's fears had to be put into words. "Miss Wilmot," she asked, her hair, honey colored and long, swinging as she turned her head, "how will I get on? What is Mr. Lambert like to work for? As I've told you, I had no real training as a dancer, even less as a dance teacher." She tried to laugh. "I'm really worried. Why did I get the job?"

Clara Wilmot looked at the anxious girl by her side and gave an odd smile. "Your Mrs. Arbuthnot gave you a good reference. She's known you for years, I gather. Also—" her mouth twisted into an even more cynical smile "—you appear to have made a good impression on Mr. Lambert."

"Did I?" Megan found herself laughing. "If you'd known how I felt at that time! My whole life had been turned upside down. I'd been looking after my father for four years, thinking he needed me and what a good daughter I was being, then—quite suddenly—he told me I was a burden, that if I could find a job and a bed-sitter, it would solve his problem. I didn't know what to do for...well, I wasn't trained for anything, going straight from school to look after dad...." She paused, watching the small launch that was skimming over the lagoon, leaving a wake of white beauty behind it.

The Impossible Dream

"Then Mrs. Arbuthnot said a *gentleman* had been making inquiries for a dance teacher for an exclusive school and she thought I would be suitable. I couldn't believe it. Anyhow, he came one day. Luckily I didn't know he was there, because he watched me give several lessons." Megan laughed again. "If I'd known he was there, I'd have made an awful mess of it, for I'd have been petrified. Then I met him and he asked me the strangest questions. They seemed to have nothing to do with the job."

"Mr. Lambert is like that," Clara Wilmot said slowly. "He's more interested in his employees' characters than their credentials. After all, he has to be careful because this is an exclusive school. We often get children from abdicated or thrown-out European royal families as well as the very rich. We have to protect the children from unwanted publicity... or I should say we have, but it's not been so easy since Gaston Duval took over."

"Gaston Duval?" Megan repeated slowly. She had read Patrick's desperate letter to his father asking for financial help, mentioning a friend who was away or there would have been no need for this appeal. Could Gaston be the friend, Megan wondered.

The launch was coming fast toward them, she saw. Would Mr. Lambert be in it, she wondered. No, she decided, it could be the pilot. Perhaps the opening in the coral reef was tricky.

"Gaston Duval and Craig Lambert are enemies," Clara Wilmot was saying slowly. "Like their fathers were, and their grandfathers. It's a family feud. Gaston wants the island to become a world-famous holiday place."

"Yes," Megan agreed. "I remember when Patrick and Georgina came out—"

"Patrick Crane..." Miss Wilmot said slowly, her voice rising, her face changing as she turned to look at the girl by her side. "Is he a relation of yours?"

"My brother." A faintly defiant note crept into Megan's voice. Though she didn't love Patrick, she was allowing no one to run him down!

"Why on earth didn't I...? The name—I should have thought...." Miss Wilmot sounded agitated, unusual, for normally she was not only efficient but impersonal. Now she began to look angry. "Did you tell Mr. Lambert?" she asked.

"Of course." Megan was puzzled. "As soon as I knew where the Lambert School was, I told Mr. Lambert my brother lived on the island."

"And what, if I may ask, was his reaction?"

Megan frowned. She had a fey look in many ways, with the cloud of hair that kept falling over her face, the unhappy eyes, the wistful smile.

"Well, in a way, he wasn't very pleased."

"I'm not surprised," Miss Wilmot almost snapped.

Megan's hands clenched. "And why not?" she demanded.

"Your brother and his wife are part of the island's lesser-liked population. They're friends of Gaston Duval. That alone is damning."

Megan nodded silently—so Gaston Duval *was* Patrick's friend.

"What did Mr. Lambert say when you told him?" Clara Wilmot asked, her voice crisp.

"Nothing, really. It was the way his eyes narrowed as he stared at me. He asked me if that was why I had applied for the post, but when I said I hadn't even known where the school was and that Mrs. Arbuthnot

The Impossible Dream

had arranged everything, Mr. Lambert seemed to relax."

"He believed you?" Clara Wilmot gave a strange laugh and Megan blushed.

"Well, it was the truth."

"Maybe, but he doesn't usually. Still, maybe he has a reason. Craig Lambert does nothing without a reason. By the way, in case you meet Gaston Duval, watch out. He's said to be most charming, but knowing him could cost you your job. Gaston is said to be very handsome and Craig Lambert—"

"Is the ugliest man I know," Megan said angrily. What right had Craig Lambert to lay down laws about whom she could know? It was true, as well, that Craig *was* ugly—a strange ugliness that attracted you against your will. Would she ever forget the first time she met him, introduced by Mrs. Arbuthnot? A tall man with incredibly broad shoulders, sun-tanned skin, square chin, high forehead, dark hair cut too short by modern standards and a grave unsmiling face. He had stared at her thoughtfully, narrowing his eyes in that skeptical way, and she had seen the mole on his cheek. His voice had impressed her: a deep vibrant voice, full of life and strength. And impatience.

"Is that so? I had no idea," a deep, vibrant but amused voice asked. It was Craig Lambert himself.

Megan swung around. She had forgotten about the launch, but as she looked about her wildly, seeking the right words to say, which in any case would be quite inadequate for she had been unforgivably rude, she saw there was no sign of the launch. So Craig Lambert *had* come to meet her.

"I...I..." she began nervously, looking up at the

grave-faced man staring at her. He was wearing a thin white suit.

Miss Wilmot, always tactful, came to her rescue.

"I didn't expect you to meet us, Mr. Lambert," she said. "It's nice of you."

"You won't think so in a minute," he said dourly. "Someone had to meet Miss Crane, because you're going back immediately. The schooner is waiting, so...."

"But I thought...." The elegantly dressed, so composed Miss Wilmot, in her pale pink shantung suit, looked as if she was going to cry, Megan thought.

"So did I. Sorry," Craig Lambert said quickly but not as if he really meant it. "Things have changed. That merger with Cox is important and something has come up, so I need you on the spot. You know as much about it as I do, perhaps more. You can come out another time." He moved his hand impatiently, as if brushing away her disappointment. "We're going ashore in the launch as I have to get Miss Wilmot on the schooner that's waiting for her," he said with equal curtness to the silent Megan, whose red cheeks had returned to their usual color but who still felt horrified at what she had said and he had heard. It was hardly, she was thinking, a good start to a job she was afraid she didn't qualify for.

He led the way to the waiting launch. Only Miss Wilmot's luggage was to be taken.

"Miss Crane's will come later," Craig said curtly.

The launch bounced about in the rough waves that came roaring to break up on the coral reef, but once through the narrow opening, the water was as smooth as any village pond. Craig Lambert was talking briskly to Miss Wilmot, who looked slightly green but was dutifully making notes of what he told her. No one looked

The Impossible Dream

at Megan, so she sat very still, grateful because she wanted the chance to look at the land that was going to be her new home... for as long as she could keep the job!

As they came closer to the island, she could see how beautiful it was. So much color. Trees with huge red flowers, arches covered with purple blossoms. The dark-skinned men crowded on the jetty wore white trousers and sleeveless shirts as well as straw hats, but the women, crowding with them, seemed all to be wearing bright crimson or vivid yellow dresses.

Palm trees were standing along the quayside, their slender trunks bent as if the wind had pushed them down for so many years that they had given up the fight. To Megan, palm trees meant so much. They were part of her impossible dream.

The impossible dream, she said silently, staring at the island before her. The dream she had so often had in her life—oddly enough, usually after an unhappy day. Looking back she realized just what a lot of unhappy days she had had in her twenty years of life. Always there had been this impossible dream—that one day she would live on an island where palm trees were silhouetted against the mountains, where the ocean came racing in, tossing fountains of sun-kissed water in the air as it hit the coral reefs, then coves of white soft sand that caressed your skin while the sun browned it, the exciting deep blue sea where strange fish lived and trees full of chattering monkeys and tiny brightly colored birds hovering over flowers....

She had seen the island so often, getting brochures from travel agents and keeping the chosen picture hidden from Patrick's curious eyes. Sometimes she had decided on Barbados or Jamaica or the Canaries, but never, somehow, had she thought of the Seychelles. Yet here she was.

It had been Mrs. Arbuthnot who reminded her of her dream on that terrible day when the rain poured down and a gale blew along Hastings's front and her father had just told her Patrick, her brother, was in trouble. Patrick always was in trouble, she had thought rebelliously. Patrick could do no wrong. But this, it seemed, was serious. He needed the money urgently.

How worried her father had looked! "If only you had a good job, Meg, and could live on your own, in a bedsitter perhaps, then I could sell this house," her father had said.

She had felt frozen with shock. "But what about you?"

He had nodded. Apparently it had all been arranged and nothing said to her, yet her father must have known this would happen, for he had gone on, "Your Aunt Lily wants me to live with her. She's bought this cottage in Dorset, but she says it's very isolated and she would like a man around."

"But you and Aunt Lily..." Megan had begun, pausing again as her father looked at her. He was doing this for Patrick, she knew—Patrick, who could do no wrong. Yet dad had never got on with deaf Aunt Lily, who rarely stopped grumbling.

"Perhaps Mrs. Arbuthnot could help you find a job, Meg?" her father had suggested. "One with a better salary, full-time."

Now, as the launch approached the jetty, Megan could remember the frozen desolation she had felt that day as she hurried to Mrs. Arbuthnot's College of Dancing, running through the rain, stumbling through puddles, bent as she went along the front, battling

The Impossible Dream

with the high winds racing across the channel. Mrs. Arbuthnot had been sympathetic. It was then she had told Megan about the *gentleman* who had been to see her, having heard high praise of her dancing college.

"You might just do, Megan," Mrs. Arbuthnot had said excitedly. "One door closes and another opens. Perhaps this is your impossible dream? I just can't understand your father—after all you've done for him, given up your dancing, your schooling, just to look after him, and yet he can treat you like this."

"He's never loved me," Megan had told her. "Aunt Lily said it was because I killed my mother."

How angry Mrs. Arbuthnot had been! Her cheeks were bright red, her eyes flashing. "Your Aunt Lily! Look, your mother was told to have no more children after Patrick was born. She should never have had you. But you didn't *ask* to be born. I blame them. They should have been more careful."

"Are you all right, Miss Crane?" Craig Lambert's harsh voice penetrated Megan's dreams. "You're very quiet."

She jerked back to the present, to the launch that had drawn up by the jetty, with Miss Wilmot being helped out and Mr. Lambert scowling.

"I'm sorry, Mr. Lambert. I was thinking...."

"I'm not surprised," he said. "You must have a lot to think about. Come along, I haven't all day," he added.

He helped her climb the ladder, and then she was surrounded by the chattering, laughing Creoles who had crowded the jetty, many laden with handmade goods they hoped to sell. Mr. Lambert spoke to them curtly in a strange kind of French that Megan found hard to translate, then he turned to her.

"Wait here while I get Miss Wilmot settled."

The tall, elegantly dressed woman shook hands with Megan formally, but Miss Wilmot had a shocked look as if her surprise and disappointment were still upsetting her.

"Goodbye." Miss Wilmot looked around and saw that Craig Lambert was striding down the jetty, the people moving out of his way, much as waves seem to do as a launch moves through them. "Good luck," Clara Wilmot said quietly. "You'll need it."

Feeling dismayed, Megan stood very still, staring at Miss Wilmot's straight back as she hurried away.

Why was she going to need good luck? And why had Mr. Lambert given her the job if he disliked Patrick? Was he going to use her as a weapon against Patrick? That was another question, but it was absurd. How could he hurt Patrick through the sister Patrick had never loved? Yet perhaps—indeed, of course—Mr. Lambert couldn't know that.

What sort of man was she going to work for, anyhow? Curt, dominant, impatient, arrogant and apparently ruthless, according to Patrick.

She could no longer see Miss Wilmot, who had not turned for a final wave, so Megan looked at the island. The islanders, obviously respecting whatever it was Mr. Lambert had said to them, kept away from her, talking to one another excitedly, with laughter filling the air.

How lovely it could be living here, Megan thought, relaxing as she leaned against the railing of the jetty. It was hot but not too humid, and the slight breeze caressed her cheeks with a pleasant warmth. She looked at the small town. How crowded and small were the stone-made houses. They all seemed huddled around a center square where there was a large white cross. Then the road seemed to vanish in a mass of trees and start to climb the mountains that sheltered the valley. On the mountainside she could see tiny houses clinging to the soil, some cattle grazing and several waterfalls so far away that the water looked like a silver pencil line down the green grass.

"Well?" The deep vibrant voice made her jump as Craig Lambert joined her. "What do you think of it?"

Megan's hair swung as she turned her head. Her cheeks were flushed from the heat, her eyes shining with excitement.

"It's very beautiful."

"Good. Not that you'll come here often. Of course, you'll want to visit your brother. That can be arranged. Are you very close to each other?" he asked curtly, starting to walk away.

She almost had to run to keep up with him, for his strides were long, quick and apparently effortless. She had always prided herself on being a good fast walker, but this was no joke. Nor could she hear all he was saying as he spoke over his shoulder.

"Not... very," she managed to say.

"I see. Not a close brother-sister relationship. Just as well, perhaps. We prefer to keep the girls out of certain parts of the island. Lately so much has deteriorated. Unfortunately there has been little I could do about it, but now—" his voice sounded triumphant "—things are going to change."

She wondered what he meant. Was the destruction of poor Patrick part of Craig Lambert's plans?

A huge white Rolls was waiting for them. The chauffeur, dark skinned, wearing a smart green uniform, opened the car doors. This had never been part of the dream, she thought, a Rolls-Royce! White, too!

The chauffeur drove slowly. He had little choice, for the narrow main street was crowded with cars, cyclists and a kind of chair on wheels drawn by a Creole running in the shafts and which carried two people. Everywhere there was color. The shop windows sparkled with scintillating swinging toys or the bright green or purple materials draped around dummies. The sidewalks were crowded, too, and no one seemed to be in a hurry. Nor did any of them look alike, for she saw Chinese faces, Indian and Creole as well as white skins.

It was as if Craig Lambert read her mind. "We have a real international mixture here. These islands were invaded so often in the past, leaving behind these souvenirs." He gave a strange smile that seemed to relax his stern face.

They drove past the white cross, which had wreaths of flowers leaning against it, and then, as they left the town behind, the road became emptier and their passage faster. It was fascinating, Megan thought as she looked eagerly on every side. All these colors: all the trees and bushes seemed ablaze with brightly colored blossoms. As the road twisted and turned to take the steep mountain gradually, she looked at the funny little houses and the small children waving and she waved back; sometimes there were groups of women, their skirts tucked around their waists as they walked into the narrow streams to wash their clothes.

As the car took a slow turn on a miniature plateau, Megan caught her breath. She could now see the other side of the town and stretching up in the middle of this small group of buildings was what looked like a thick finger reaching up toward the sky. It was so hideous, so out of keeping with the quiet beauty of the island that it shocked her.

"What's that?" she asked impulsively.

"Hotel Anglais. Run by Gaston Duval," Craig Lambert said sharply. "You've heard of him?"

She hesitated for a moment, but there was no point in lying.

"Yes, I...."

"Met him?" Craig Lambert snapped.

"Of course not." She was annoyed by his way of throwing questions sharply at her. "How could I? I've never been here before."

"That may be, but Gaston Duval gets around the world quite a bit. Your brother's dancing school, by the way, is quite near the hotel."

"Is it?" She wondered what was best to say and decided to say as little as possible.

"Your brother and you are not good friends?" Craig Lambert asked abruptly.

Megan felt the surge of loyalty rising inside her.

"I didn't say that. I said... well, we are friends, but that's all."

"Why don't you get on better?" Perhaps he saw the look on Megan's face, for he lifted a phone from his side of the car and gave instructions in the strange French he had used on the jetty. The chauffeur, sitting very upright as he drove, nodded and at the next plateau, always placed where a severely sharp turn came, drove off onto a narrow side road that the trees lined, their leaves meeting overhead so that it was like a cathedral, and there was a green light as the sun was shut out. Then, as they turned a corner, Megan saw the most beautiful view. The trees had gone, save for a few palm trees on a lawn, underneath which were some tables. The small square house was half-hidden by purple flowers.

"I'm having coffee, or would you prefer a cold drink?" he asked curtly as he led the way to one of the tables, settling Megan in a chair. "My favorite view."

"It's beautiful. Coffee, please."

"Black or white?" he asked.

"White, please." Megan, leaning on the table, rested her face on her hands as she stared at the view before her, the blue ocean spreading away. There were no quiet coves below here, just the ocean speeding in, rushing madly toward the rocks, tossing as if furious with the world. It was so...so....

"Why don't you like your brother?" Craig Lambert's curt voice jerked her back to the present.

"I didn't say I didn't *like* him," Megan said, giving him a quick glance, for she wondered why he had suggested stopping here. Surely they could have had coffee at the school?

"No, but you implied it. Look, there are some questions I want to ask you. It's simpler here than at the school because I'm always busy there."

Megan looked away quickly. What sort of questions, she wondered. She must be careful what she said—in case it affected Patrick.

"Excuse me a moment," she said. "I just want to look at this lovely view."

She walked across the lawn to where a wall had been built of rocks. Leaning against it, she found she could look down on the small town they had recently left. How tiny it looked, she thought. Why, the houses were more like a group of children's dollhouses and the yachts so still in the smooth lagoon looked like little paper toys.

"Are you jealous of your brother?" The words, close to her ears, made her jump. She turned quickly and found Craig Lambert by her side, leaning on the wall.

"Jealous?" She was really startled. Never had she thought of herself as being jealous, but....

She looked up and found Craig Lambert's eyes were narrowed thoughtfully. He was not smiling, so it was not a joke.

"I...well..." she began, then nodded. "I suppose I am," she said. "My mother died when I was born and my father never forgave me. He adored Patrick. He'd do anything—" She stopped abruptly. Perhaps it would be unwise to let Craig Lambert know about Patrick's recent desperate cry for financial help.

"That's unusual. Usually the father adores his daughters, and it's the son who gets neglected." He paused and again, suddenly, his question seemed to jump at her: "Why did you want a new job so badly?"

"Be—because..." Megan began, then paused. Had she to answer these questions, she asked herself. Had he the right to expect her to do so? Had he the right even to ask them? Maybe he had, for—as Miss Wilmot had said—his responsibilities at the school were terrific and that was why he was more interested in his employees' characters than their abilities.

"Why?" she repeated slowly. "Well, it all came as rather a shock to me. My father wanted to go and live with my aunt in Dorset. She lives in a lonely part and said she needed a man about the house. She's very deaf and nervous and I suppose she thought a man would keep vandals away. Not that I can see poor dad doing much," Megan went on, her voice wistful. "He has this wretched arthritis and is always losing his balance. He's so afraid of falling that he hardly dares to walk anywhere."

"So you had to find a job? You like your aunt?"

Again Megan hesitated. "Yes and no. She's deaf and rather difficult. She looked after us for all my life and nothing anyone did was ever right. Then when... when...."

"You were sixteen when she left you," Craig Lambert finished for her. "I understand you had to leave school, though you had a promising future, and also had to give up dancing. You like dancing?"

A little puzzled, wondering how he could know so much, Megan nodded. "We were all dancers, you see. Mother and dad danced a lot and often won international competitions. They were really good. Then she died and he began to get this wretched arthritis. So did—" Megan paused, not sure if it was wise or not to mention her brother. Yet Patrick's name could not be left out without it seeming strange. "Patrick and Georgina danced a lot and won prizes. I also had a partner."

"What was his name?"

The question startled her because she hadn't thought of her onetime partner for ages. "Reggie... Reggie Blake."

"You still meet him?"

"No." She was even more puzzled, since she couldn't see what connection it had with her job. "He was furious when I said I couldn't go on dancing. You see, you have to practice all the time and be free to travel about, and I just couldn't leave dad alone. He had this dreadful fear of falling down and breaking a hip."

"So you gave up dancing, too," Craig Lambert said thoughtfully, then turned to look at her. "Willingly?" he asked.

"Willingly?" Puzzled, Megan had repeated the word.

"Yes. I mean was it your idea or did your father have to ask you to give up dancing?"

"He didn't know why I stopped. Of course I didn't tell him. He wouldn't have liked it at all. He's very independent in many ways. I had no choice as far as I could see it. Dad needed me—and that was all."

"I see. Oh, the coffee's come. We'd better go and drink it," Craig Lambert said, leading the way back to the table. "I can't help wondering what made your father suddenly decide to live with your aunt. Did they get on well together? Would she be a good nurse?"

Megan hesitated again. Whatever happened, she wasn't going to tell Mr. Lambert that the house had been sold in order to help Patrick—and that was why she had been practically thrown out of the house that had been her home all her life.

"She's not very patient. She thinks he's seeking attention and has no sympathy. I can't see how they...."

"Maybe he felt you were leading too narrow a life and that it would do you good to go out into the world."

"I doubt if he ever thought about me," Megan said bitterly, then wished she hadn't been so honest as she saw Mr. Lambert open his eyes wider as he stared at her.

"You could be wrong, of course," Craig Lambert said slowly. "Well, you had to find a job. I take it you told Mrs. Arbuthnot and she told you I had already been there, asking if she could recommend someone. I know it seems strange, with a school like ours having to look for a dance teacher, but I've set a very high standard for the staff and I wouldn't take just anyone. Often the girls have what used to be called 'crushes' on the staff and I want to be certain that the staff concerned will be a good influence on them. What I can't understand is why Mrs. Arbuthnot, who obviously valued you highly and had no desire to lose you—why did she tell me about you? You've known her for some time?"

"All my life. She taught me all I know about dancing. She was a great dancer once but broke her hip and it never healed properly. I think she wanted me to get a job far away because she was afraid Aunt Lily would rope me in to look after them both...."

"And of course you'd have gone."

Megan looked at him. "I'd have had no choice, would I?" She laughed. "Mrs. Arbuthnot is a darling. She said that would be the end for me and my whole life would be ruined."

"And you'd have had no chance to find a nice husband," he said.

"I...." Megan looked at him again. "I never thought of marriage. You see, I couldn't... well, I just couldn't leave dad. He isn't so old, though his arthritis made him retire much earlier than he should have done and he could live for another thirty or forty years. The doctor says he's in fine health—"

"Apart from his arthritis." There was a slightly sarcastic note in Craig Lambert's voice that annoyed Megan at once.

"It can be terribly painful," she said quickly.

"I'm aware of that, Miss Crane," he said. "You seem to lay great stress on doing your duty. Unusual in this day and age. Do you feel the same sense of duty as regards your brother?"

There was a long pause as she stared at him. What did he mean? What was he trying to trick her into saying?

The Impossible Dream

"In a...in a way I suppose so, but I can't imagine Patrick's ever needing me."

Craig Lambert stood up. "That's what you think," he said. "We'd better get going. I'll tell you more about the school on our way."

Back in the spacious, luxurious car, Megan found it hard to concentrate on what Craig Lambert was saying, for she couldn't forget the way he had said, *that's what you think*. What had he meant? Was he planning to play some mean trick on Patrick and include her in it?

The car crawled along the winding narrow roads that wound up and down the mountains, into the deep valleys, then up far above them again. Megan sat meekly, trying to listen to what Craig Lambert was saying. She had her hands folded, but she had to dig her nails into the palms as she tried to force herself to concentrate.

"My grandfather had one son and three daughters. It was the girls he adored; he had no time for his son. Perhaps that was why my father...." Craig Lambert paused and then went on, "My grandfather searched the world for a school good enough for the girls. He couldn't find one, so he built this one. Soon it became famous, selective, and it had a long waiting list. When he died, my father took over." His voice changed. "Unfortunately he hadn't been properly trained to handle the responsibility of the job and soon it began to deteriorate and lose prestige. When he died, I came back from South America and had to repair the damage caused to the school and its name. I succeeded until a new problem arose. This island was far from the madding crowd, but suddenly it became a holiday center. A number of people have come to live here whom we consider completely undesirable." He looked at the girl sitting silently by his side and paused, as if giving her a chance to speak.

Megan said nothing. She felt it was wiser to hold her tongue, for she could feel the anger again. Why did he so condemn poor Patrick? All Patrick was doing was to earn a living, a living that wasn't made any easier by the extravagant girl he had married.

"Gradually, however," Craig Lambert went on slowly, "we're gradually erasing them."

Megan had to cling her fingers together as anger swept through her. *Erase?* Could there be a more callous expression? In other words, wipe them out, force them to become bankrupt and lose everything just so that he could get rid of those he disliked?

"We have to have strict rules at the school," Craig Lambert continued. "There's always the danger of kidnapping to be faced, of course, also of the wrong type of friends being made. These are not children we have at the school. Many of them are old enough to have been married several years, but their parents refuse to let them leave school because they feel they're safer here until a suitable husband can be found. This, as you can imagine, can cause some friction. No girl is allowed to move about the island alone. This is plainly understood."

Poor things, Megan thought quickly. "And the staff?" she asked, unable to resist saying it.

He showed no surprise or annoyance. "That's quite different, of course. We employ only those we can trust, but we do ask them to always leave notice of where they go. This is to ensure that we can contact them immediately if they're needed."

"What about transport?" Megan asked. "The school seems an awfully long way from the town."

The Impossible Dream

Actually it isn't far. Perhaps I should say *unfortunately*, because I'd prefer us to be farther away. However, we came this long way so that you could see something of the island and its beauty. Most of the staff have cars of their own. There are also buses on Wednesday and Sunday, going both ways. Naturally, when you want to visit your brother we can arrange a lift."

"Thank you..." Megan began, not sure if she liked the sound of that. Was Mr. Lambert planning to keep her under observation when she visited Patrick, she wondered. "Oh, look, isn't it gorgeous!" she cried impulsively, leaning forward as they passed a huge, aged tree whose trunk and branches were twined with the long clinging tendrils of a purple-flowered bougainvillea. "What a marvelous color!"

"What? Oh, yes, the bougainvillea. You know the name of the island we prefer? It has many names—ours is the Isle of Purple Flowers. Quite suitable."

"It's all so beautiful." Megan's voice was awed. Now they had left the mountains and were driving through what seemed like the avenues of trees they had passed earlier, then coming into the sunshine, passing by waterfalls that had looked like silver lines from the schooner but now were amazingly wide as the water frantically pushed its way through the rocks.

"We'll be there soon. Just around that cluster of trees. I hope you will find Miss Tucker congenial—our headmistress, a fine woman but rather out-of-date in her views. Comes of a military family, hence very keen on discipline. As you can imagine, very few today can accept that, but here they must."

Megan shivered. There had been something ominous in the way he had said, *they must*. She could almost imagine him with a horsewhip in one hand... then she had to laugh. What an imagination she had! He couldn't be such a monster or he wouldn't have been so friendly that day, going to the trouble of meeting her and bringing her this long way around....

She caught her breath. Or was it because he had wanted to question her? Had she unwittingly said something that could hurt Patrick, she wondered.

What would life at the school be like, she asked herself. It was beginning to sound like a prison. What he was implying was that you had to conform or get out! No wonder the salary was so generously high and once a year return fares were paid to the staff so that they could go home for the long holiday. In addition Miss Wilmot had told her there was an efficiency apartment for each member of the staff, who could cook for herself or go to the communal dining room as she preferred. Megan wondered which she would do. It rather depended on the other staff, she thought.

"Here we are," Craig Lambert said, his voice proud, as the car left the trees and slowed up along the road leading up to the Lambert School.

Megan gasped. She didn't know what she had expected to see, but it was certainly not this massive mansion built in the shape of an *L*, with courtyards, and two sides facing the sea. The chimneys were Elizabethan, long and decorated. The windows on the ground floor were large picture ones, on the two floors above, the windows were smaller, but each room had a balcony. The garden in front was gay with flowers, everything symmetrically arranged so that nothing was out of place. On either side of the doorway stood a huge white-blossomed gardenia. On the other side of the

The Impossible Dream

building stretched tennis courts, hockey fields—she could even make out a distant golf course.

"Well?" Craig Lambert asked impatiently. "You look surprised."

She turned to stare at him. "I didn't expect this. It's so English!"

"You sound disappointed. What's wrong with looking English?"

"Nothing, oh, nothing at all. It is beautiful, really marvelous," she said quickly, and meant it.

It was just that it was the opposite of what she had expected, which was absurd anyhow. What had her foolish impossible dream to do with a school of this size? Yet she still felt disappointed. Had she come nearly seven thousand miles from England just to live in an English house?

"What a lovely lot of..." she began enthusiastically.

"Facilities for games? Yes, we watch our students' health carefully and always make sure they can play their part in a social world. Here we expect the staff to help and play *their* part. Now, Miss Crane—" Craig Lambert's voice changed, becoming grave and almost stern "—I'm not always here. You must appreciate that Miss Tucker is always in charge and conform to her wishes. Is that clear? The staff you may find difficult at first. It's inevitable in such a small confined community that adults of different nationalities will not always see eye to eye, but I must ask you to remain neutral as far as possible, since we have enough temperamental females here as it is."

Megan colored. Was that what he thought she was? A temperamental female?

"Not to worry," he went on. "I feel I know you well

enough to trust you to soon adjust yourself, taking your part in the social life of the school as well as passing on your very excellent talent as a dancer. One final point." His voice hardened. "Please remember that you are on the staff. Do you understand? No nonsense about sympathizing with the students. You're on the staff's side. Understand?"

A little puzzled, she nodded. The car was drawing nearer the huge house that seemed to tower above them almost ominously. Was she going to be happy here, she wondered. She glanced quickly at Craig Lambert. But he was staring proudly up at the school, no doubt delighting in the fact that he had made it become what his grandfather would have liked.

His school. Craig Lambert's school... that he was afraid some people were trying to destroy.

He turned to her. "When we arrive, I must leave you at once. The servants will show you your flat. I'll send for you in about two hours' time—that'll give you time to wash and change before you meet Miss Tucker." Even as he spoke, the car stopped. He was out of the car immediately, striding up the wide white steps into the door that had been opened.

Megan sat alone. Never had she felt so alone before.

A tall slender dark-skinned girl came to the car.

"Would you this way please come?" she said politely, leading the way into the tall hall with its curving staircase and huge oil paintings on the walls.

Megan followed her up the stairs, down a long corridor, then the girl opened the door, stepped back and gave what might resemble a very mild curtsy.

"I hope it is all well," the girl said. "I am Odette. This is your flat."

Slowly Megan walked in. First there was a not-so-

The Impossible Dream

large (but nor was it small) squarish room, brightly decorated with pale yellow walls, deep sea-green curtains that showed a wide-open French door that led to a balcony. Megan was drawn immediately to the window and then stood there, hardly able to breathe, it was so beautiful.

She could look straight out over the garden to the Indian Ocean. How far away seemed the horizon, not a sign of a ship or even a fishing boat. When she turned, Odette had left her, so Megan explored on her own. The sitting room had two armchairs, a desk, a small table and two chairs. Everything was very tidy and polished vigorously. The bedroom led out of the sitting room and was narrow with a built-in wardrobe and a divan bed. Here again, the walls were pale yellow, the curtains and bedspread green. Out of the bedroom was a small bathroom with a shower and alongside it a tiny kitchen annex with a small electric cooker, refrigerator and dresser.

It was far nicer than she had dared to hope, Megan thought as she wandered around. Her luggage was waiting for her. The air was hot but not too humid.

She began to unpack, frowning a little as she shook out the well-cut dresses of drip-dry material, some pale blue, others green or white. Miss Wilmot had taken her shopping. Part of the contract was that the school would supply what Craig Lambert called a "uniform." Megan thought he had evidently been shocked by her drab clothes, and she had felt furious with him for suggesting that she couldn't buy her own clothes or even choose them—but talking to Miss Wilmot had made Megan see it in a different light.

"The staff must set an example of perfect taste and good dressing," Miss Wilmot had said gravely. "They must be up to date but definitely not avant-garde."

"How does the staff react? Or is it only me who's being treated like this?" Megan had asked, trying to hide her indignation.

Miss Wilmot's horrified expression had been answer enough.

"Of course not. I always advise the staff when they're first engaged. Certainly a few are difficult, but most of them will accept the common sense of it. They are allowed to wear what they like when they go off duty, but not if they are still in the school. Only if they go into the town, for instance. Even then, there are limits."

"It sounds like a convent or a prison," Megan had found herself saying. "Does the staff really accept it?"

Miss Wilmot smiled coldly. "They don't have to take the jobs, do they? It's up to them. The salaries are high, the perks even greater. The school has a name to keep up, and we can't risk damaging it."

Not that she should complain at all, Megan told herself as she carefully hung up the clothes. Never in her life had she had such lovely well-cut dresses. There were even several evening dresses, for apparently the social life of the school was considered important. Miss Wilmot had shopped carefully, occasionally asking Megan if she liked the dress but more often consulting the assistants and proving difficult to please.

Now, as Megan hastily showered and brushed her hair, twisting it around her head, leaving her slender neck exposed, she tried on a pale green dress. As she stared in the mirror at herself, she thought how grateful she should be. Never in her life had she dreamed of wearing a dress like this....

With her eyes watching the clock because she mustn't be late on this first day, Megan tried to work out to whom

The Impossible Dream

she should be grateful. Miss Wilmot for choosing such attractive clothes? Craig Lambert for footing the bill? Mrs. Arbuthnot for finding her the job? Perhaps her father for turning her out, Megan thought sadly, for it still hurt... or should the thanks go back still farther? To Patrick for needing money so urgently that it had triggered off the whole... whole incident, if it could be so called?

A gentle tap on the door made Megan jump. It was Odette.

"If *mademoiselle* will follow me," she said politely.

A little nervous, Megan obeyed. Craig Lambert's comments about the headmistress had not been exactly comforting: *a fine woman but rather out-of-date,* also Miss Tucker had come *of a military family,* hence *very keen on discipline.* He had even said he hoped she would be *congenial*—so it sounded as if he wasn't too sure they would be....

Odette led the way back downstairs, down the lofty cool hall to where it seemed to divide into various tributaries of corridors, leading away. She stopped outside a closed door, knocked, opened it and stood back.

"Mademoiselle Crane," Odette said, then quietly left Megan and closed the door.

Megan stood just inside the room. She couldn't believe her eyes, for there was an almost monastic simplicity about the room that was in complete reverse to what she had seen, so far, of the rest of the school. Severely white walls, white curtains, a broad walnut desk with a chair behind it and an armchair. A shadow of someone standing by the window moved.

He turned. It was Craig Lambert.

Looking her up and down, he nodded. "Miss Wilmot has superb taste," he said.

Flushing, Megan nodded. She couldn't speak, she was so angry. In other words, *she* didn't have superb taste? He was comparing her old-fashioned drab dress with this...this one that had cost probably twenty times as much as the dress Megan had worn and all she could afford.

"Miss Tucker won't be a moment. Sit down," Craig Lambert said curtly.

The coziest, most comfortable-looking item in the room was the armchair that Megan sank into, facing the desk.

"Well, how do you like your flat?" There was a note of impatience in Craig Lambert's voice. Was it because she hadn't said a word so far, Megan wondered. Somehow she found her voice.

"It's lovely. It's really lovely," she said.

He smiled. He smiled so rarely that it always startled her, for it completely altered his face. Normally it was so stern, almost as if carved in stone, but when he smiled it was as if the skin, drawn taut over the bones, relaxed.

"I'm glad you like it. No regrets?" he asked, and then added, "So far?"

"No, of course not," Megan said quickly. Why was he always hinting that she was going to regret it, that it wouldn't all be roses and honey?

The door opened, Craig Lambert turned around promptly and Megan scrambled ungracefully to her feet.

Miss Tucker.

Megan saw a tall, thin woman dressed in a severely plain white jersey dress. She wore a crimson stone on a thin gold chain around her neck. She was not beautiful, yet in a way she had a fascinating face, for she had high

The Impossible Dream

cheekbones and red hair. Really *red* hair, naturally red, Megan thought quickly, comparing it in her mind with Miss Wilmot's, which was obviously dyed.

"Welcome, Miss Crane." Miss Tucker came forward, holding out her hand, shaking Megan's firmly, then releasing it. "I'm sorry you had to wait. Do sit down," she said, going behind the desk, then looking up at Craig Lambert.

"There's no need for you to be detained, Mr. Lambert," Miss Tucker said coldly. "I think it would be wiser if we talked alone."

He stood, feet apart, hands on his hips, his eyes narrowed a little.

"I agree entirely, Miss Tucker, but first I want to make a few things clear, if you have no objection."

"Naturally I can have none," Miss Tucker said even more coldly. "Would you care to sit down? I can get a chair." Her hand was on the bell on the desk, but Craig Lambert put up his hand.

"Please don't bother, Miss Tucker. I shall be here only a few moments."

"I see," Miss Tucker replied, quite obviously showing by her tone of voice that she didn't, and had no intention of trying to see.

Megan, sitting silently, her hands moist with nervousness, was puzzled. Why this hostility between the headmistress and the owner of the school?

"Well?" Miss Tucker asked, the fingers of one hand drumming lightly on the desk.

Craig Lambert was not disturbed at all. He half smiled before he began talking. "In the first place, Miss Tucker, I must warn you that Miss Crane suffers from an outsize inferiority complex...."

Megan caught her breath, feeling the color surge

through her cheeks. If they looked as red as they felt hot, she hated to think what she must look like. A boiled lobster, perhaps! How dared he! How could he be so cruel?

"She will, of course, deny this," Craig Lambert continued, still looking with half-closed eyes at Megan. "She's a fine dancer, one of the most natural I've ever seen. Unfortunately through her father's inability to move without help, Miss Crane had to leave school early after her O-levels and also give up her dancing, which was, I consider, a great loss to the world.

"You may wonder, as she obviously does, why I went to a comparatively unknown school in Hastings to find a new dance teacher. Actually I had been told by several people that the school had a good reputation. I must confess I'm rather tired of having entirely classical ballet dancing. I think dancing should interpret what the music means to you. Mrs. Arbuthnot, who had instructed and then employed Miss Crane, allowed me to watch Miss Crane at work without her knowing it. As I think I've said, I was impressed. I liked the way she handled her pupils, too, and the way she behaved herself. I felt she would be an asset to the school.

"It's time we moved with the times." He smiled again as if at himself. "I think Miss Crane will satisfy us in every respect." He stood straight, glancing down at his hands for a moment. "I'm telling you this, Miss Tucker, because Miss Crane may come up against some hostility; it may be asserted that she's not fully qualified because she had not taken the usual examinations. I say it's time this was no longer considered necessary. I employed Miss Crane because I believe her to be an excellent dancer and teacher. I know that having

The Impossible Dream

asked you to support me in this, I can rely on you to give Miss Crane all the assistance required. That's all. Thank you." He walked to the door and smiled at Megan. "Don't look like a terrified rabbit, Miss Crane. I'm sure you'll be happy here and I know Miss Tucker will help you. I can rely on her," he added, and left the room.

There was an uncomfortable silence as Megan stared at Miss Tucker. What had that all been about, she wondered unhappily. It was as if he had been cracking a whip, subtly threatening Miss Tucker... or, even worse, warning he would not tolerate any hostility shown toward Megan. Would there be hostility, Megan wondered anxiously.

"Mr. Lambert is right, Miss Crane," Miss Tucker said, her voice suddenly friendly. "Don't look so frightened. I won't eat you."

"I'm sorry." Megan felt the bright color again, which made it all worse. "I'm rather tired and... and Mr. Lambert is right, I can't help wondering if I'm capable of doing... I mean, I wasn't trained as a teacher and...."

"If Mr. Lambert has seen you dance and listened to your methods of teaching, you can rest assured, Miss Crane, that you *are* capable of coping." Miss Tucker's face creased into a smile. "Mr. Lambert knows what he's talking about and is a good judge of character."

"But why... what did he mean about... well...." Megan hesitated, looking for the right words. "The hostility he talked of...."

"Well, that *is* rather difficult." Miss Tucker stood up, moved to the window, drawing back the curtain a little so that both could look out of the window at the girls playing tennis. Miss Tucker turned around. "Unfortunately Mr. Lambert dismissed our last dance teacher for no apparent reason. Quite abruptly, too. I'm aware that he made it worth her while to go, but there was no doubt about it, she didn't want to go. I'm afraid there's a feeling here that she was... well...."

"Erased?" Megan found herself saying, then wished she hadn't.

"Erased?" Miss Tucker repeated, a smile warming her face. "A good word, and appropriate. I'm afraid the staff resent this—they feel Miss Pointer was sacked in order to give you the job."

"But that's absurd! He didn't even know me." Impulsively Megan was on her feet, going to join Miss Tucker at the window. "When did he... when did Miss Pointer leave?"

"Six weeks ago."

"Well, I wasn't looking for a job then," Megan said. "Please believe me, Miss Tucker. It all happened so quickly about three weeks ago...."

"Three weeks? Is that all? Suppose we sit down and you tell me just why you applied for the position, how you came to hear of it and so on." Miss Tucker's voice was kind so Megan went back to her chair quite happily.

"It all began when—" Megan stopped in time. She had been about to say, *when Patrick wrote, saying he needed money urgently,* but instead she told Miss Tucker about the startling announcement made at the breakfast table.

"When my father said he wanted to sell the house and go and live with Aunt Lily, I felt awful," Megan confessed. "I had thought dad needed me and suddenly I was a burden, a nuisance, in his way. I was very upset, and when Mrs. Arbuthnot—I worked for her—

saw me she made me tell her. I said I didn't know how I'd ever get a full-time job as I wasn't trained for anything, and then...."

"Then...?" Miss Tucker leaned forward over the desk, her face thoughtful.

"Then Mrs. Arbuthnot told me that someone had visited her, asking if she could recommend anyone suitable for...for this job. Of course, believing I was tied down with dad, she never thought of me and she had no one suitable and told him so, but this man—she didn't even mention his name—gave her a phone number in case she ever should have someone suitable."

"So your Mrs. Arbuthnot phoned him and he came to watch you, unseen by yourself? And then, I imagine, interviewed you?"

"Yes. I was amazed, but—" Megan smiled "—it was the answer to my prayer, because I was feeling desperate."

"It hasn't taken long for you to get here."

"No. That was one of the conditions—that I had to come out at once. I couldn't leave dad, so we sorted out everything, sold our furniture, though dad took quite a lot down to Dorset—that's where Aunt Lily lives—and the house is up for sale. Dad went straight down to Dorset as soon as he could and Miss Wilmot...."

"Supervised the purchase of your wardrobe," Miss Tucker said dryly. "Did you mind?"

Megan bit her lip. "In a way, yes. In another way, no. I've never been able to afford such clothes. I was angry at first, I thought it was...well, suggesting I couldn't afford to buy good clothes or had any good sense, but Miss Wilmot made everything plain."

"She would," Miss Tucker said dryly. That was another surprise to Megan. So Miss Tucker didn't like

Miss Wilmot, either? "It must have been chaotic—with the house to clear up, clothes to buy, a passport to get, for I imagine you hadn't one, the necessary injections."

"It was," Megan agreed with a smile. "I still don't seem to know quite where I am. It's all happened so fast."

"And it wasn't, then, until three weeks ago that you knew you needed a job?"

"Yes. It was quite a few days before I met Mr. Lambert. I was so surprised when he engaged me. I mean, I've not been trained."

"Miss Crane—" Miss Tucker's voice had become cold and stern "—I don't wish to hear you say those words again. Mrs. Arbuthnot obviously trained you satisfactorily or she would neither be employing you nor have recommended you to Mr. Lambert. That point is settled. You may not have passed the usual examinations, but you are suitably trained. Is that understood?"

"Yes, Miss Tucker," Megan said meekly, startled by the change in the headmistress's voice.

"Second, you must not allow any malicious gossip or even teasing to affect you in any way. Some of our staff have a peculiar sense of humor and you may find yourself called the teacher's pet."

"The teacher's pet?" Megan echoed, shocked.

Miss Tucker let herself smile. "They can be very childish, the staff, and also easily jealous. We must make it plain to them that your being employed here has nothing to do with the dismissal of Miss Pointer. There must be some reason for doing that. I think Mr. Lambert should have consulted the board before doing anything so drastic. But there is, of course, another side

The Impossible Dream

to it. Miss Pointer was always rather a rebel, not willing to conform happily with our way of living, so it's quite possible that she did something that we couldn't tolerate. Mr. Lambert would keep it quiet to save her being hurt. He has such a soft heart," Miss Tucker added a little contemptuously.

A soft heart, Megan thought, unable to believe it. How could Craig Lambert have a soft heart and be doing his best to ruin poor Patrick?

"Well, now." Miss Tucker drew out some sheets of typed notes from the drawer of the desk. "I'll give you these to read. It's a list of the classes you will teach, the rooms they will be in, the names of those who will play the piano for you. You will see it's a pretty heavy program, but I feel certain you can cope. As your hours are long, you will be left out of intracurricular tasks, but I would like you to join in our social life. Certain nights of the week we play bridge, for instance. You can play?"

"I'm afraid I can't."

"How tiresome. Well, you can join the evening classes with the girls. Mr. Parr will teach you. Mr. Parr...." Miss Tucker added, frowning thoughtfully. "Not always an easy man to work with, unfortunately. He's an artist, certain he's no good." Miss Tucker smiled. "How hard it is to convince people who lack self-confidence! I often wonder why they don't trust themselves to be able to do anything they tackle."

"Perhaps... perhaps no one has told them they can," Megan began.

Miss Tucker nodded. "You could be right, I suppose. When one is young, one needs a certain amount of praise. You got none?"

"No."

"There are many of you in the family?"

"Just two of us. Patrick—" Megan stopped dead. Now why, she asked herself miserably, had she to bring in Patrick? She saw the way Miss Tucker's face had changed.

"Not *the* Patrick Crane?" Miss Tucker sounded shocked.

Megan's cheeks flamed. "He lives on the island," she said defiantly.

"Does Mr. Lambert know?" Miss Tucker literally demanded.

"Of course," Megan told her. "Naturally I told him I had a brother living here. It seemed such a coincidence."

"It certainly does...." Miss Tucker seemed to relax in her chair, folding her fingers together, not looking at Megan. "A most strange coincidence. Now, where was I? Oh, yes, Miss Weston will be able to advise you as to where the different rooms are. She's in the flat next to you. You are used to dealing with children?"

"Yes, and... and adults," said Megan.

Miss Tucker smiled, an oddly cynical smile. "Adults! I'm afraid you'll find some very strange girls here. Now, tonight is our social night. Please wear an evening dress. We all mix together and dance. Dinner is served at eight o'clock, but I'll tell Miss Weston to take you down. That's all, thank you."

Megan stood up. "Thank you, Miss Tucker." She glanced at her watch. It was four hours to dinner time. "Is there anything I should do?"

"No, Miss Crane. You start work tomorrow. Why not wander around? Get to know the school. Most of the classes are over by now and the girls will be outside, playing games. There's plenty to watch."

"Yes, I'm sure, thank you, Miss Tucker." Megan almost ran to the door, eager to be outside. Miss Tucker, despite her superficial friendliness, was rather terrifying in many ways. Now Megan could understand Craig Lambert's remarks about Miss Tucker's military family. Megan could almost hear Miss Tucker's huge, furious voice shouting out commands.

As she closed the door, she jumped. Craig Lambert was waiting in the hall. He came to meet her.

"She took a long time! Come along, I'm going to show you around," he said.

But should he, Megan was wondering. If she was already being called *teacher's pet*, wouldn't it make things worse if she was seen being shown around by him?

"Perhaps we... I mean, it might be..." she began, stumbling over the words.

Maybe Craig Lambert understood what she was trying to say. He took her arm firmly in his hand.

"Of course we should," he said. "It was not a request I made, but a command I gave."

Looking up at him, startled, she saw the impatient anger in his eyes and she shivered. What had she let herself in for, she was asking herself as they walked down the endless corridors, pausing by the empty rooms, which were huge in many cases.

It was a very fine school, Megan thought, and yet somehow so different from an ordinary school. She could hear the shouts and laughter from outside where the girls of all ages were playing games. From behind some closed doors came the sound of music or the chatter of girls arguing but they met no one at all. It was as if the school had been deserted. She listened as Craig Lambert talked; he was interesting, his views on education fascinated her, there was no doubt he was determined the school should be a good one in every respect.

But equally obvious, she thought with a shiver, that he was determined to keep it that way. No matter what it cost.

CHAPTER TWO

THAT FIRST EVENING was rather a nightmare for Megan for she felt absolutely exhausted, and everything, even a smile, was an effort. She couldn't explain her feelings; she wasn't actually tired, yet the ability to do anything, to say anything or even to think sensibly seemed to have left her and she felt as if all the life had been squeezed out of her.

Craig Lambert escorted her all over the huge building, and this alone was tiring, for he strode ahead, talking over his shoulder, making it hard for her to hear what he said and to give intelligent answers. He showed her the laboratories, the gymnasium, the girls' sleeping quarters, their playrooms, the senior girls' own sitting rooms, the staff's common room. It was impressive, but Megan was too tired to appreciate it.

Later, when she escaped from him, she took refuge in a deep, warm bath, trying to relax, but her brain refused to slow down as inside her head it whirled her anxious thoughts.

Could it all have happened by chance, she asked herself, or was it far too much of a coincidence? Had Craig Lambert employed the sister of a man he was determined to wipe out? Financially, not physically, she thought hastily, though it was physically in a way, for Mr. Lambert would obviously like Patrick to leave the island!

Was it purely by chance that the sister of the man Mr. Lambert wanted to *erase* had been given this job?

After all, it could so easily not have happened, though, she thought as she turned on the hot-water tap again, loving the feel of the water against her skin, feeling for the moment safe, for she did not have to keep tense, watching her every word, waiting for one of Mr. Lambert's suddenly-thrown-at-her questions that always found her off guard.

Now look at it sensibly, she told herself. Nothing could have happened if Patrick hadn't written that desperate letter asking for money. Nor could it have happened had her father not already discussed with Aunt Lily the sharing of her cottage in Dorset. In addition to this, Miss Pointer had been teaching here, so how could Mr. Lambert have known she was going to leave?

Megan caught her breath. But it was Mr. Lambert who had sacked Miss Pointer. How could he have known Miss Pointer would do something that deserved dismissal? Perhaps she hadn't. Perhaps he had just got rid of her in order to give Patrick's sister the job. But there again, Megan thought, she came up against a lot of contradictions. The time element, for one thing. How could Mr. Lambert have known *when* Patrick was writing to his father? How could Mr. Lambert have known Megan would ask for Mrs. Arbuthnot's help? Indeed, how could Mr. Lambert have even known that Patrick's sister lived in Hastings and worked for Mrs. Arbuthnot? None of that made sense, Megan told herself as she stood up, dripping with water, and wrapped the towel around her body.

Of course, she went on thinking, there were other things that didn't make sense. For one, how was it Mr. Lambert knew so much about her? Small things, yet

The Impossible Dream

things she felt sure she hadn't told him herself? Of course it might have been Mrs. Arbuthnot, for she was fond of talking.

She looked at her watch. Comfortably off for time, she saw. She went to the window. How dark it was! A thin slice of the moon shone bravely in the sky. She could hear the roar of the ocean as it pounded against the rocks.

She dressed carefully, choosing a pale green dress, long, high necked but sleeveless. Her hair she had swept up from her face, pinning it carefully, allowing only two curls to fall on her cheeks. She looked at her reflection in the long mirror carefully. She wanted to make a good impression this first night particularly. She was twenty, but she was always being told how much younger she looked. Carefully she made up, using the false eyelashes that Miss Wilmot had shown her so patiently how to use.

"It is essential," Miss Tucker said, "that you take care not only of your deportment and behavior but your appearance. It is so easy for a rebellious teenage girl to make herself look a mess as part of her defiance. This we will not tolerate."

Megan had wondered how they kept the girls at school, for how many today would tolerate such treatment? She thought how interesting in many ways it would be to meet the girls and find out what kind they were.

There was a knock on her door and even as she spoke it opened. A tall girl stood there. One of the staff, Megan wondered. She looked young, too.

"Miss Crane? I'm Petronella Weston. I think Miss Tucker told you about me."

"Of course. Please come in," Megan said eagerly.

Petronella Weston was tall and slender and had very dark hair and matching eyes. Her voice was husky and friendly in an impersonal way.

"Well, what do you think of the convent?" she asked with a smile.

"It's very impressive."

Miss Weston gave a little snort. "It's supposed to be."

"It seems very strict. I mean for this day and age."

Laughing a little, Miss Weston sat down. "But we get paid well. Isn't that right? We don't have to stay."

Megan nodded. "Very right."

"How do you get on with Miss Tucker?"

Hesitating a little, Megan said, "Not too badly, but she was a bit... well...."

Miss Weston laughed. "How right you are! A very good description. *A bit... well....* She can be quite a dragon, but she does a good job. Trouble is that she and Craig Lambert rarely see eye to eye. By the way, what do you think of him?"

"Think of him?" Megan's mouth was dry. She must be careful what she said. "Well, I hardly know him. I'd only met him once before today."

"Once?" Miss Weston sounded startled. "He engaged you after meeting you once?"

Megan, perched on the edge of a chair, smiled. "Well, he saw me twice before, but I didn't know he was there."

"I don't get it."

"I know, but... well, it sounds funny, but... but Mrs. Arbuthnot—I taught at her dancing college—knew I was nervous, so maybe it was her idea."

"Sounds more like his," Petronella Weston said dryly. "Go on."

"Well, there's not much to say. Apparently he watched me take two classes without my knowing he was there. Mrs. Arbuthnot has always had...."

"I know, one of those windows." Miss Weston sounded impatient. "Then you met him and he asked questions. Right?"

"Right." Megan laughed. "Did he do it to you?"

"He does it to us all. I think he must have a sadistic streak in him because he seems to delight in cutting one down to size. Has he done that to you yet?" Petronella Weston's dark eyes were narrowed as she looked at Megan's face.

Megan was thinking fast. Had Mr. Lambert ever made her feel small? "No, actually he hasn't...oh, yes, he did, but then I found it happened to everyone."

"What happened to everyone?"

"Miss Wilmot's choosing my clothes. I felt... well, I thought Mr. Lambert was implying that I couldn't afford to buy decent clothes... which, actually, I couldn't!" Megan laughed. "And also implying my lack of taste, but I gather Miss Wilmot is always given the task?"

Petronella Weston laughed. "Usually she has fights with us. I imagine you were more biddable. We'd better go down—mustn't make you late on your first night. Miss Tucker is a maniac about punctuality—so is Craig Lambert, for that matter."

Outside the flat there seemed a lot of people. Men, older women and girls, all swirling around, going down the curving staircase, laughter and voices filling the air. Megan found herself being introduced to so many people that she gave up the vain attempt to remember faces and link them with names. At dinner she sat next to a silent man with dark hair and a thin mouth. His name was Paul Taft. On the other side was a girl whose long black hair fell almost to her waist. She had a rebellious, sulky mouth. Her name, she said, was Anarita.

"You're going to teach us to dance?"

Megan smiled. "Yes."

"Why did Miss Pointer go?" Anarita asked.

Megan's heart seemed to sink. Oh no! Were the pupils also involved in it? The silent man on Megan's other side looked coldly at the girl.

"She broke one of the school's rules so she had to go," he said sternly, and then looked away.

"Rules!" Anarita almost snarled the words. She looked at Megan. "How old are you?"

The man turned around again. "That is a question ladies do not ask, Anarita."

"But I'm not a lady," Anarita said, tossing back her hair.

"Obviously not," he said dryly. "Though we're trying to make you one." He turned away again.

Megan felt uncomfortable. A sort of fight was going on across her.

"You liked Miss Pointer?" she asked.

Anarita shrugged. "She was all right, I suppose. A bit of a bore. I hope *your* teaching methods are more interesting."

At last the dinner, which had been very good, was over and everyone was supposed to mix. The hall where dancing was held seemed crowded and might have been any ordinary party, Megan thought, but for the main difference, which was too few men! Megan found herself dancing with all the male staff in turn. Some she liked, some made her feel uncomfortable as they kept asking her how she had heard of the job. Obviously they all felt strongly about Miss Pointer's dismissal and it was not helping Megan to feel wel-

The Impossible Dream

comed. Finally, feeling tired and bewildered, she found somewhere to sit out of sight, on a stone bench, half-hidden under the stairs by curtains. But as she sat down, she found she wasn't alone, for a man sat there. He scrambled to his feet with some difficulty.

"Miss Crane, I imagine?" he said, holding out his hand.

Megan shook his, grateful for the friendly gesture. She couldn't see him very plainly, but there wasn't much to see. He was the type of man no one could describe with his pale brown hair, a pale skin and freckles on his nose.

"I'm Frank Parr," he said. "Won't you sit down?"

Megan obeyed. "Thanks. I've heard of you. You've got to teach me bridge."

He pretended to groan. "Heaven help us both, because I'm an appalling teacher!"

"And I shall be an appalling pupil?" Megan laughed again. She suddenly felt relaxed, no longer afraid.

"I'll soon see to that," Frank Parr smiled. "You're much younger than we expected."

"I'm twenty."

He grinned. "I'm twenty-eight, so you seem quite a kid. Think you're going to be happy here? By the way, is it true you're Patrick Crane's sister?"

Taken aback, for it was a question she hadn't expected, Megan stared at him.

"Well, yes, I am," she said defiantly, her body stiffening.

"No business of ours," he said as if reading her thoughts. "It just makes it all rather surprising."

"It does?" Megan drew a deep breath. "What makes what surprising?" she asked.

Frank Parr turned to look at her. "If you don't know, maybe I'd better not tell you."

Megan twisted her fingers together, gazing down at them. "Well, I rather gather Mr. Lambert doesn't approve of my brother."

"Understatement of the year. That's why it's so odd that he should have engaged a member of the Crane family. Did he know you were Patrick's sister?"

"I don't think so. When I told him, he seemed surprised and rather...."

"Shocked?" Frank Parr chuckled. "If he didn't know, I bet he was. How do you get on with your brother?"

"I haven't seen him for three years. Not since he got married and came out here."

"What does he think of your coming out here?"

"I don't know."

Frank Parr chuckled. "It must have been a shock to him. His sister on the other side of the river! The acceptable side, of course. Have you met Gaston Duval?"

"No, I haven't. You're the second one who's asked me that." Megan was getting a bit annoyed with all the questions.

"I bet I know who was the first. Craig Lambert. Right?"

Her cheeks were red, much to her annoyance. "Yes, he did. So what?"

Frank Parr chuckled. "So what? Nothing. Just my cheeky inquisitiveness. Sorry, Miss Crane. Now seriously, how come you're here sitting talking to me when you should be dancing?"

"I was dancing, but...."

"No one very enticing, eh?" Frank Parr chuckled.

The Impossible Dream

"Wouldn't do to have handsome men on the staff. Bad enough the girls' crushes as it is. Just think, they have crushes on me!" He laughed.

"And why not?" Megan asked, her eyes demure.

He chuckled. "You don't fool me, girl. I know I'm one of those men who might just as well not exist."

Megan remembered what Miss Tucker had said: that Frank Parr had an outsize inferiority complex.

"And what's wrong with you?" Megan asked. "I've enjoyed talking to you."

"*Mademoiselle*, you are so sweet..." Frank Parr said dramatically, lifting Megan's hand and kissing it.

At the same moment the curtain was jerked back and Craig Lambert stood there.

"I've been looking for you, Miss Crane," he said accusingly.

Megan and Frank Parr both stood, Frank obviously having a little trouble getting up.

"I was tired," Megan began.

"Can you blame her?" Frank Parr joined in. "The miles she's flown, the new life, leaving her father... I bet you miss him, Miss Crane...."

Megan felt her eyes fill with tears. Perhaps that was why she felt so alone. All her life her father had been there, needing her, yet being someone she could turn to at any time. And now there was no one. No one she could trust.

"Yes, she must be tired," Craig Lambert said curtly. "Just one dance with me, Miss Crane, and then off to bed."

Megan hesitated. She had no desire to dance with this man she couldn't trust, yet like all the things he said to her, it hadn't been a request but a command.

"Thank you, Mr. Lambert," she said demurely, but as she said good-night to Frank Parr, he winked at her.

On the floor, in Craig Lambert's arms, Megan felt everyone must be staring at her—and talking about her, she thought unhappily. Was Mr. Lambert making the situation any easier for her by insisting on dancing with her?

All the same he danced well and in a few moments she lost the tension she felt and relaxed, delighted without realizing it at the way he led her, his long legs covering the ground with surprising speed. As the music came to an end he smiled at her—one of his rare smiles, which made them more noticeable.

"You're a good dancer," he said.

She was so relaxed she could be honest. "I was just going to say the same to you. I enjoyed it."

"I'm glad," he told her, and led her off the dance floor. "Now, time for bed."

"Should I say good-night to Miss Tucker?" Megan, conscious of the eyes on them, asked nervously.

"I'll explain," he said, and led the way to the central hall with the beautiful curving staircase.

They were silent as he escorted her to the door of her flat. Megan felt ill at ease, wondering if she should talk; wondering, too, if he always escorted the staff to their flats.

He waited as she fumbled in her small diamanté handbag; he waited until she had opened the door and turned to say good-night. Then he frowned.

"It's not very wise, Miss Crane, on your first night here to sit alone with one of the staff. Already the girls are talking about you because you're the youngest and most attractive member of the staff, but surely for your first night...."

"I didn't know he was there. I was tired and found the seat...."

"I see," Craig Lambert said, but she knew he didn't. Nor did he believe her. "Frank Parr has been with us for some time. He's a brilliant artist, gifted with the art of passing it on to others. Hitherto he has been without any blemish on his character."

Megan's cheeks were flaming red; she was so angry she felt herself shaking. "Are you suggesting I was trying to seduce...?"

Craig Lambert chuckled. "Hardly, Miss Crane. You're not the type. Unfortunately Frank Parr has a sentimental heart and you might... well, I'm just warning you, Miss Crane, we do not tolerate affairs among the staff. I would advise you to avoid being seen alone with Mr. Parr in future."

"But that's absurd," Megan said angrily. "He was the only really friendly one. I'm not going to snub him simply because—"

"You aren't?" Craig Lambert's voice rose slightly.

She stared at him and struggled to regain control of her temper.

"Please believe me, Mr. Lambert," she said, her voice still uneven. "Mr. Parr was not making passes at me, nor is he the sort of man to do so."

"Why was he kissing your hand?" Craig Lambert demanded.

Megan could laugh. "It was a joke. Miss Tucker told me he had an outsize inferiority complex." She paused for a moment, wondering if she should tackle him about saying *she* had such a complex, but decided not to at the time. It could wait. "Then he said some of the girls had crushes on him and he said he couldn't understand it as he was the sort of man who might just as well not exist. I remembered what Miss Tucker had said, so I treated it as a joke and asked him what was wrong with him and said that I'd enjoyed our talk. Which was true," she added defiantly, "because he was the most friendly one of all I've met tonight. So he said something like, *mademoiselle, you are so sweet,* and kissed my hand. It was just... well, one of those things. It didn't mean anything to either of us."

"I see," Craig Lambert said slowly, but she knew he didn't believe a word she had said. "So long as you're both aware that it meant nothing. You are, however, very young and Parr is a romantic. We can't afford to lose our dance teacher as soon as she arrives." He turned away, but she acted without thought, clutching him by the arm.

"Mr. Lambert, why did you sack Miss Pointer?" she asked.

He turned back and looked at her. His face changed; it was just as she had seen it before, as if it was made of stone.

"That," he said, "is my business. Good night."

CHAPTER THREE

MEGAN'S FIRST FEW DAYS at the Lambert School were not too happy, but her real shock was to come on the fourth day.

When she awoke the morning after the social evening she went and stood by the window, drinking in the beauties of the deep blue sea and the foam-tossed waves, and then she shivered. How was the job going to turn out? She felt she had so many enemies, which was perhaps rather absurd, but Frank Parr had been the only really friendly one.

She washed and dressed quickly, choosing a rather demure pale blue dress, and went down to the dining room. The girls were all sitting at their tables and the roar of voices hit her as she walked in. She stood still for a moment, looking around, then she heard a soft whistle. Looking in that direction she saw Frank Parr beckoning to her from where he sat at what was obviously the staff table.

Sitting by him, as he talked and joked she found some of her nervousness going. Several other members smiled and spoke to her, but it was Frank who seemed to have taken her under his wing.

"Did the old devil tick you off for sitting alone with me?" Frank Parr asked Megan suddenly.

Her red cheeks made it impossible for her to deny it. "In a sense, yes, but when I explained...."

"He said he understood. Right? I suppose he warned you to keep away from me." Frank Parr's eyes were amused as he watched her telltale cheeks. "I know. I'm the Don Juan of the college." He made a dramatic movement of his hand going across his heart, and Paul Taft, sitting opposite, frowned.

"It's hardly fair to Miss Crane to attract attention, Parr," he said curtly.

Megan remembered Paul Taft from the dinner the night before. He had been so quiet until he scolded the girl.

Frank Parr laughed. "How can she avoid attracting interest, Taft, old boy, when she's such a choice dish?"

"Really, Parr!" Paul Taft looked disgusted and then turned to Megan. "Please forgive my friend for his brashness. I trust that you will be happy with us." He spoke with almost pedantic politeness, yet Megan found herself liking him.

"I understand, Mr. Taft," she said with a smile. "Don't worry, I won't take Mr. Parr seriously."

"Oh, woe is me, alack, alas!" Frank Parr pretended to groan. "She's seen through me already. I have no hopes!"

It was the same all through the meal, with Frank joking and making Megan laugh, and even dour-faced Mr. Taft's mouth kept quivering as if he was trying not to smile.

After that, Megan consulted her rota lists and made her way in search of the right room and her pupils. It turned out to be far easier than she had expected. Indeed, the actual teaching was the easiest part of her life those first days. The pianists, generally elderly men, were charming and really gallant, playing well and with

The Impossible Dream

feeling. The girls, chatting away until she stopped them, seemed to be eager to try her new ideas on dancing.

Perhaps it was the meals that were the biggest trial. Megan would go and join the staff at their table, hoping she might find an empty seat by Frank Parr. Usually she did, and then it was all right, but if she sat next to another member, a "stranger" really even though they had been introduced, it was rather an ordeal, for the questions came pounding at her like the waves against rocks.

"Weren't you lucky to get this job?" "I imagine you have some relative who knows the Lamberts?" "What made you come out here—wouldn't life in London be more fun?" "How long have you known Craig Lambert?"

The last question was the one most used and Megan began to get tired of constantly saying she had met him only once and that was three weeks before. She often wondered how much Miss Tucker had told them, but no one mentioned Miss Pointer, the dance teacher who had been sacked for some unknown reason before Megan Crane swiftly moved in to take her place.

All the same it worried Megan, though she couldn't see that any of it was her fault. Perhaps Craig Lambert had been displeased with Miss Pointer for some time and had therefore made inquiries for her replacement? That would explain a lot of things.

That evening she had her first bridge lesson. There were quite a few other pupils, mostly girls over fifteen, and with Frank Parr's jokes it was rather hilarious. There was probably more laughter than learning, Megan thought once when she glanced up thinking she had seen Craig Lambert glancing in the doorway, but did that really matter? They would all learn bridge more easily if they enjoyed doing it.

Oddly enough, apart from that quick glimpse that might, she thought, have been her imagination, Megan didn't see Craig Lambert until the fourth day. By then she had begun to settle down and make several friends among the staff, and of course there was always Frank.

She had just finished a class and was wearing her leotard, as they had been doing modern dancing and she had demonstrated the way it should be done, when Mr. Anstruther, the elderly pianist, clapped impulsively, so the girls joined in. Afterward Mr. Anstruther, his white hair slightly ruffled, for he had a knack of running his hands through it when he came to the end of whatever he was playing, said, "You are too good a dancer to be teaching, Miss Crane." He spoke gravely as he collected his music.

Megan flushed happily. "Thank you," she said.

"It was a pity you had to stop training, but blood is thicker than water, isn't it?" Mr. Anstruther said, then sighed. "What a lucky man your father was to have a daughter like you!"

The girls had streamed out of the room and Megan gave it one quick look around, for things were apt to be left behind and it was easier to trace their owners if the class concerned was known. So it came about that she left the room alone and was startled to find Craig Lambert waiting in the corridor.

"Miss Crane," he asked in that authoritative, snapping manner, "could I have a word with you?"

"Of course," she said. Wondering what she had done wrong this time, Megan followed him to a small room lined with books. Just inside the door Craig Lambert stood on one side, letting her go through ahead, then closing the door.

"I'm going into town this afternoon and I see you are free, so I wondered if I could give you a lift, Miss Crane. I'm sure you're eager to see your brother. You've heard from him?"

The sun was making the sea glitter like a million diamonds, Megan saw as she stared out the window, taking a deep breath for she must be on her guard now and careful of what she said.

"No," she answered with equal curtness, for it was no business of Craig Lambert's.

"You mean to say he hasn't written or telephoned? Surely a brother...." There was the amused sarcastic note she hated in Craig Lambert's voice.

"I don't think he knows I'm here," she said. "Unless my father wrote and told him."

"But surely you want to see him? Your own brother?" The sarcasm was growing more intense and Megan's nails dug deeper into the palms of her hands as she controlled her temper. "Or Georgina, his very beautiful wife. Aren't you good friends with her, either?"

Megan could feel the color in her cheeks. "Georgina and I were never friends. I hardly knew her when she married Patrick and they went abroad almost immediately."

"I see. A very strange relationship. I would have thought you would be eager to meet them. Anyhow, I'll take you in this afternoon. Meet me at the front at two-fifteen," he finished quickly, turning, opening the door and waiting for her to go out.

It was a ruthless brush-off, Megan thought as she hesitated. What should she do, she asked herself. Tell him the truth, that she had no desire to see either Patrick or Georgina? Or would he immediately think she was involved with them? She just didn't know what to do. Or if she went, would he go with her? Using her as an instrument to *erase* Patrick? Yet how could she be used in such a way? Surely she was exaggerating the whole thing.

So she nodded. "Thank you, Mr. Lambert," she said politely, and left the room.

As the door closed behind her, she sighed. If she had had any idea there were to be so many complications she would have refused the job. She had no desire to hurt Patrick—after all, he was her brother, and as nice old Mr. Anstruther had said, blood was thicker than water!

She dressed carefully after lunch, choosing a leaf-green silk suit, carefully making up, wondering if Patrick would recognize her. Three years ago she had been little more than a schoolgirl. Now.... She frowned at her reflection: if only she didn't look so young, she thought.

The white Rolls was waiting for her. Craig Lambert walked out the front door just behind her.

"Full marks," he said. "Punctual to the second."

She glanced at him quickly but could see no smile. So he wasn't joking. Who did he think he was, anyhow, she asked herself. A sergeant major?

The road went along the coast, the palm trees bending against the wind and the little sandy coves most inviting on this hot day. It was a much shorter way than the one they had driven when she arrived and she remembered that Craig Lambert had said he wanted to show her the beauties of the island. Very thoughtful of him and, considering his behavior over other things, rather surprising.

The Impossible Dream

They drove through the small town, along the wharf, past the jetty. No schooner was in, so there were few people on it, but still people crowded the sidewalks by the shops, and the cars and cycles seemed to be having a perpetual fight. Past the town everything changed. It lost the tropical old-world look that had delighted Megan and suddenly became almost American in its modernization.

The tall pencillike hotel soared up into the sky, the grass before it scattered with brightly colored sunshades tilted over tables. Along the front were all sorts of enticements for the tourists' children: donkey rides; a pool with self-piloted small boats; small zoos with monkeys and snakes apparently their main attraction.

"It seems so unlike the other side of the island," Megan said, so surprised she forgot to watch what she said, as she had warned herself to do earlier.

"Naturally," Craig Lambert said, his voice bitter. "This is not my land."

She turned to look at him. "The rest is?"

"Yes. Seven-tenths of this island is mine, but the rest is not. Surely you've heard of the Lambert Folly?" When she shook her head, he went on, "As you know, my grandfather bought the island and built the school. Unfortunately my father was a different kind of man. A gambler...." He paused, then repeated the word as if it left a nasty taste in his mouth. "A gambler. He gambled with the land as his money. Always there have been people after the island, seeing it as a good tourist center. I bought back most of what my father had sold...but I haven't got it all back," he said almost sadly, Megan noticed, and then he added, "yet."

There was a strange disturbing threat about the way he said *yet*, a vicious ruthlessness, she thought. In other words, no holds barred, but he was going to get back the whole island!

Now the car was pulling up before a single-storied building with large curtained windows and above the door, the notice Crane Dancing Studio.

On the other side was a very modern single-storied house with an enormous picture window and a garden, bright with vividly red, yellow and blue flowers and two palm trees moving gently in the wind.

The chauffeur opened the door of the car and Megan got out. Her hands felt damp. How was Patrick going to take this, she wondered worriedly. Maybe—and this thought had not struck her before—maybe he would see her as Craig Lambert's accomplice... or he might even think she had come out to see if he was telling the truth and really needed the money he asked for. It seemed to her that no matter what she did, she would always be suspected.

To her dismay she found Craig Lambert walking with her to the front door. She rang a heavy bell whose carved handle jangled as she pulled it.

"I'll fetch you at five o'clock," Craig Lambert was saying, turning away as he spoke, just as the door opened.

Megan stared at the man standing there. Three years since she had last seen him, now he looked taller, much thinner, his blond hair cut in a modern style, huge circles of sunglasses hiding his expression.

He frowned, looking puzzled. "Can I...?"

Megan's eyes stung suddenly. He didn't even know her!

"Patrick, it's me, Megan. Don't you remember me?"

His surprise was evident. It was as if seeing her had

The Impossible Dream

jolted him, because for a moment his mouth sagged open and it was obvious he found it difficult to greet her normally.

"Why, Megan, this is a surprise!" he exclaimed, and the words suddenly died, as if sliced, for he saw Craig Lambert standing there looking at them both thoughtfully. "What on..." Patrick began to say, his voice harsh, but Craig Lambert lifted his hand.

"I'll fetch you at five o'clock, Miss Crane," he said, and turning walked to the waiting car.

Patrick stared at him and then turned to Megan. "What the devil are you doing out here?" he asked, sounding annoyed. "And how did you get mixed up with that... that...?" Then he seemed to realize that Craig Lambert must be able to see them, so he stepped back. "You'd better come in," he told Megan.

The hall was lofty and cool. Georgina came running out of a room. She was even more beautiful than Megan had remembered—tall and slim, dark hair piled high on her head, dark eyes, a full, rather sulky mouth.

"What's that man doing here?" Georgina asked angrily, then stopped dead. She had obviously not seen Megan, who must have been just out of sight of the window. "Megan? What on earth...?"

"That's what I want to know," Patrick said angrily. "Come in and sit down. Just why are you here?" he demanded.

It was hardly the welcome of a sister he hadn't seen for several years, Megan thought, glad that Craig Lambert was not there to make a sarcastic comment. She looked around while Georgina rang a little silver bell and told the Creole servant to bring in the ice.

"We must have a drink to welcome you here, Megan," Georgina said almost cheerfully, frowning at

Patrick, who was standing glowering down at Megan. Patrick was wearing a smart silk smoking jacket, Megan noticed, and white trousers. He didn't look desperately poor, she thought. Nor did Georgina in her lush red silk trouser suit.

"Just what are you doing with Lambert?" Patrick asked. "And why are you here?"

"I thought dad would have written to tell you," Megan said, after thanking Georgina and saying she would prefer a cold drink but no alcohol. "It's a bit early," Megan said, but Georgina laughed.

"I haven't heard from dad for... for ages," Patrick told her.

Megan wondered if he was lying. After all, that desperate, pleading letter had arrived only three weeks before and her father was sure to have written to reassure his beloved son!

"Dad's gone to live with Aunt Lily in Dorset," Megan said.

"He must be mad!" exclaimed Patrick. Megan felt furious, for her father was sacrificing his freedom for Patrick. Surely Patrick must know that? "But how does that bring you out here?" he added.

Megan sipped her ice-cold orange squash and looked around. The room was tastefully and expensively furnished. She liked the lilac shade of the walls, the deep red silk-covered armchairs, the polished floor with the beautiful rugs. It certainly didn't look like the home of a man so desperate for help that his father had to sell his own house! She stifled a sigh. Perhaps Patrick had been writing all these years for financial help when he didn't really need it and she and her father had sacrificed many things they enjoyed in order to help him.

"How did I get out here?" she said slowly. "I've just

The Impossible Dream

told you that dad has gone down to Dorset to live. That meant I had no home. I had to get a job, and—"

Georgina laughed. "I bet you were glad to be free of the old man. A real hypochondriac, that's what he was."

"He suffered a lot of pain," Megan said quickly.

"Maybe, but he made use of it," Georgina said. "He adored being made a fuss of and you and Aunt Lily completely spoiled him. There was absolutely no need for you to stop your dancing just because he was lonely when you weren't there—and when you were, was he a real companion? His nose buried in the newspaper or his eyes glued to the telly?" Georgina went on, her voice sarcastic. "You were so soft, you fell for it. He didn't need you—he just wanted to have someone around. Now he's got Aunt Lily." She laughed. "Aunt Lily is growing old—it won't be long before they send for you."

Megan twisted her fingers together. So much of what Georgina said was true, but also so much untrue. Her father did like attention, but he needed help. He didn't need *her*—that she knew now, and that was what hurt her so much. No one needed her. And to live a full life, you must be needed by someone.

"For crying out loud," Patrick said impatiently, "could we drop this cross talk? Give Megan a chance to tell us what made her come out here."

"Okay, okay, big brother." Georgina curled up on the couch. "Fire ahead, Megan. What are you doing here? Snooping on us?"

Megan colored. She had been afraid they would think that—it seemed she had been right! "Actually—and I know you won't believe me, but it's the truth—I got the job just by chance. I was teaching for Mrs. Arbuthnot and she had had inquiries from the Lambert School, which was looking for a teacher. This was quite a while ago."

"Why... well, why should they go to a miserable little school like hers?" Patrick asked.

"It isn't a miserable little school," Megan told him quickly. "It's getting a very good name because a lot of our pupils do well. Anyhow, the Lambert School did. Mrs. Arbuthnot said nothing to me because she knew I'd never walk out on dad, but when I went to her and said I simply had to find a job and I didn't see how I could for I'd had no proper training in teaching dancing, she notified the Lambert School."

"What—wrote out here?" Georgina lit a cigarette slowly.

"No. They have a representative in London—Miss Wilmot."

"And then?" Patrick was pacing the room, hands clasped behind his back, his head stuck forward, rather like a giraffe's, Megan thought, grateful for a moment of amusement, for she was not enjoying her afternoon. As she had feared, they didn't believe her.

"Then I was interviewed by Mr. Lambert. Apparently he had watched me teaching—you remember Mrs. Arbuthnot had that special kind of mirror."

"To make sure the teachers were doing their stuff properly," Georgina said nastily. She had taught in Mrs. Arbuthnot's school for a short time, Megan remembered. A very short time, and that was where she met Patrick and married him.

"Well, it was while Mr. Lambert was interviewing me that I learned where the school was."

"Mrs. Arbuthnot hadn't told you?" Georgina asked, her voice unbelieving.

The Impossible Dream

"No. I knew it was an exclusive school and that it was abroad. I'd hardly had time to think of asking where. Then when Mr. Lambert told me, I realized it was here on the same island as you."

"You told him?" Patrick snapped.

"Of course." Puzzled, Megan looked from Georgina to Patrick and back to Georgina. "Naturally I told him. It seemed such a coincidence."

"Coincidence, my foot!" Patrick spluttered. "It's all part of his plot to get rid of us. He's got you out here to use you against me, Megan. I'd have thought you'd have the sense and decency to stay away."

"I never thought of it. Why should I?" Megan asked. It was obvious that Patrick and Georgina were both being careful—they were wondering just how much her father had told her about Patrick's plea for help. After all, for all they knew, she might not have even seen the letter, much less have read it. In fact, unless they knew she had read the letter, they had no means of knowing that she had read what Patrick had said: that Craig Lambert was determined to ruin him.

She decided it was wiser to avoid involvement of any kind, so she looked at them with an innocent smile.

"I don't understand. I'd no idea you would mind my coming out. After all, I am your sister and it was a very good job, and as far as I could see, there was no reason at all why I shouldn't take the job."

Georgina leaned forward. "She's right, Patrick. After all, she'd never heard of Craig Lambert, had you?"

"Of course not. Is he famous or something?" Megan looked her sister-in-law in the eyes. "What is all this about, Georgina? Patrick's making me feel I've done something to hurt him in coming out here. After all," she added bitterly, "we needn't meet. I'm on the other side of the island."

Patrick stormed out of the room, banging the door. Georgina shrugged. "Poor Patrick! He's going through a difficult phase just now. Life here isn't being as rewarding as we had hoped, Megan. What made your father decide to sell the house so promptly?"

Sell the house, Megan thought instantly. So her father *had* written and no doubt sent them the money. She had not said anything about selling the house, only that her father had decided to live with Aunt Lily in Dorset! So they were both of them hiding the truth from her? Obviously they believed she knew nothing about Patrick's plea for help!

"I don't know," she said, deciding to pretend she hadn't noticed Georgina's slip of the tongue. "He suddenly told me that Aunt Lily had asked him to go down to Dorset with her as she found it isolated and a man about the house could be a good defense."

Georgina grunted. "Fat lot of good he'd be as a defense! I know you're loyal, Megan, but honestly you were a fool to throw away your chance to become a good dancer. Mrs. Arbuthnot had trained you well, and then...."

"Well, what else could I do when Aunt Lily walked out?"

"Couldn't your father have had a housekeeper?"

"A housekeeper!" Megan said scornfully. "How could he afford it?"

She was so angry she made herself get up and go to the window, staring out blindly. When she thought of how Patrick had got money from her father—money they needed so badly themselves, and all the time he had been living in a house like this, with a maid and goodness knew what else....

The Impossible Dream

"You like the house?" Georgina asked.

Megan forced herself to smile. "Very nice. I like your view, too. It's a bit scruffy by the hotel."

"Yes." Georgina yawned. "Bad management, there. I tore strips off Gaston for being such a fool as to leave it to the Piggots. Of course you don't know them. You never will unless you come and visit us," she added. "We live on the wrong side of the island, according to Craig Lambert. What's he like?" Georgina asked suddenly, her voice changing, becoming almost wheedling. "He's certainly not handsome."

"No, but...." As usual, the need to defend whomever was attacked rose in Megan. "Actually he can be kind, but he can also...."

"Be horrid? I'm surprised he engaged you. How did you tell him you were Patrick's sister?"

Megan returned to her chair and curled up in it. "I told him as soon as he said the Lambert School was on an island near the Seychelles. I said at once that I had a brother out there somewhere, but I wasn't sure which island."

"No." Georgina pulled a wry face. "I'm afraid we're not very good at writing letters, Megan."

Only when you need money, Megan thought, and clenched her hands tightly.

"Was he angry, Megan?"

"Angry? Oh, you mean when I told him? No, I'd say he was startled."

"You don't think he knew?" Georgina's voice had changed again; now it sounded cautious.

"I certainly don't because he didn't look at all pleased—nor was Miss Wilmot when I told her. I got the impression that Mr. Lambert didn't like your being on the island."

Georgina laughed. "He lives in the past—or else he's

crazy about money. He wants the whole island to himself. He can't open his eyes to see the possibilities here. It could become a great tourist center. All he thinks of is himself."

Here, Megan felt inclined to agree, but before she could say anything the door opened and Patrick walked in, followed by the most handsome man Megan had ever seen. He was the sort of man you saw on television and if you were that sort of person you swooned or shouted excitedly, for he was tall, lean and dark, with long sideburns and thick hair and the most charming smile.

Now he came toward her, his hand held out in greeting.

"Ah, but this is wonderful! Patrick's young sister. I am delighted to meet you." He shook her hand, his fingers curving tightly around hers as if desiring to pass on a message. His eyes shone. "I am Gaston Duval. You have, it may be, heard of me, no?"

Megan caught her breath. Now she knew why Miss Wilmot had warned her to watch out! Anyone could fall for a man as attractive as this.

Not only did his looks charm her; so did his manners. He sat by her side, twisting around so that he could stare at her, letting his eyes seem to go slowly over all of her he could see and then smiling at her with that secret look that told her that what he had seen he had liked very much.

"Gaston came along," Patrick was saying to Georgina, who was looking angry about something.

"But a coincidence," Gaston said now, and laughed. "It is too strange, is it not? A coincidence," he repeated. "That you should be offered, ah, a very good position—on the island where your brother is." He

The Impossible Dream

laughed. "A strange coincidence, is it not so? Of all the islands, and there are many, in the world, fate chose this. There must be a reason." He looked at the silent Patrick and Georgina. "There can be nothing done but with a reason. We will find it." He took Megan's hand in his, turning it to look at her palm. "I tell fortunes. I am very good. Yes?" He looked at Georgina with a smile, but she didn't return the smile. "Ah, Miss Crane—or may I call you Megan?" He said the name slowly, almost as if it was a caress. "A beautiful name for a lovely girl," he said, then looked at her hand. "I see you have a character that is strong. That you are— how is it said—loyal to those you love and even to those you do not love. Is it not?"

He smiled at her. Megan tried to concentrate on what he had said and what it had meant. *Loyal to those you love and even to those you do not love.*

She wished as she had so often wished during the afternoon that Craig Lambert had left her alone, never brought her here to Patrick. She managed to remove her hand from Gaston's grasp without doing it too obviously and then looked at her watch.

"Mr. Lambert is picking me up in ten minutes. Could I go and wash my hands, Georgina? It's very humid."

"Of course. This way." Georgina led Megan down the corridor. Through half-open doors she saw two bedrooms, a very modern kitchen, and then she was in the bathroom. "Do you like him?" Georgina asked as she showed Megan into the mirror-walled bathroom.

"Like him? Oh, you mean Mr. Duval?" Megan turned on the water so that she could talk over her shoulder without letting Georgina see her face. "He's very handsome, isn't he?"

"Yes, I suppose so. But I said did you *like* him?"

Megan turned. Now she could laugh. "I've only known him for half an hour, Georgina. How can I know if I like him?" she asked.

Which wasn't true, of course. For she did know if she liked him! She liked him a great deal too much for her own comfort; that was the trouble.

CRAIG LAMBERT SMILED as Megan joined him in the car. She didn't glance back, for she knew that neither Patrick, Georgina nor Gaston would be in sight. They had said goodbye to her and left her at the front door, closing it as soon as she had moved outside.

"Enjoy yourself?" Craig Lambert asked, and there was an amused twinge in his voice she disliked.

She looked at him defiantly. "Very much. I met Gaston Duval."

If she had expected to surprise or anger Craig Lambert, she was disappointed, for he looked amused.

"I guessed he'd turn up. I trust you didn't fall for him as most females do. A bigger rogue I've yet to meet." His voice was suddenly harsh.

"He has perfect manners," Megan said quickly.

"Of course." Craig Lambert's smile this time was cynical. "That's part of his trade. His favorite line is to make some old lady think he adores her, then she leaves him all her money when she goes. He also has a devoted mother he drains. She, at least, has sense enough to avoid scandal, so she keeps a firm hand on him."

"That doesn't sound like him." Megan turned to glare at her companion. "Are you suggesting he kills the old ladies off?"

Craig Lambert laughed. "Of course not. He's much

The Impossible Dream

too clever. He sees them as investments. He's a man who is completely amoral in every way. Your brother was a fool ever to have trusted him."

"I..." Megan began, but stopped herself in time. She wasn't sure just how much she should say, so she decided to say nothing.

There was a silence and then Craig Lambert spoke on his phone to the chauffeur, who nodded twice. No more was said for ten minutes and Megan was beginning to feel more and more uncomfortable. Craig Lambert's silences were always ominous. Was he annoyed because she had defended Gaston Duval? Would he tell her he found she was unsuitable for her position at the school?

She noticed they were going inland now, having left the coast road. That puzzled her, for that wasn't the way they had come. The road was winding and slowly rising, with trees on either side and large creepers of purple bougainvillea on every support, be it a house, fence or arch.

The car turned sharply to the right and Megan caught her breath. It couldn't be true... but it was. Her dream house was there... standing in front of them. A single-storied house with a thatched roof and a wide veranda, with flowers growing up the walls and a wide lawn stretching in front of it. Behind, the mountain grew larger, covered with trees, but here there were palm trees, upright as could be, and huge bushes of scarlet flowers.

"My house," Craig Lambert said quietly.

"Yours?" She was really surprised. Somehow she had not imagined that Craig Lambert would choose such a simple house.

"Yes." The car stopped. Megan prepared to get out,

not quite sure why she was being taken to Craig Lambert's home. It was kind of him to show her so much, but the next moment he was looking at her. "I won't be a moment," he said. "I have to collect something."

She sat back as if slapped. So he hadn't brought her here to show her his house. It was mere chance that she had seen it, for obviously the private life of Craig Lambert must never be mixed up with his public life. She looked around all the same. It was lovely—so quiet. The palm trees were just as she liked them, the flowers so lovely. How happy she could be here, she was thinking when Craig Lambert returned, spoke to the chauffeur and got in the car.

Craig Lambert ruffled through some papers he was holding, totally ignoring Megan until they got on the main road again.

"Well, what did you think of it?" he asked, looking at her.

"I thought it was lovely."

He smiled. "Aren't you being rather tactful? Most people think I'm mad to live there. I like it because it's so quiet. For once I can't hear the cackling of female laughter and their noisy chatter, nor the roar of the sea."

"You live there?"

"Yes, I drive home every night and have a few hours of bliss. By the way," he added, frowning a little, "it might be as well not to mention to any of the staff that I took you there. They're already apt to see you as teacher's pet, which is why I avoid you at school, for some of the staff are a funny lot—jealous, malicious, apt to alter the context of everything so that only the worst of it can be seen." He spoke crisply, narrowing

The Impossible Dream

his eyes as he looked at her. "I hear you're still good friends with Parr."

"Of course I am. He's the nicest on the staff."

"I thought he'd help you; that's why I was so nasty about him," Craig Lambert said.

Megan twisted around on the seat. "You... you said those things on purpose?"

Craig Lambert nodded. "Of course. You're a strange female, Miss Crane, and have to be handled tactfully. I knew you'd need a friend, but I also knew if I recommended anyone you'd run a mile to evade him. You're so convinced that I am ruthless, cruel, indifferent and your brother's enemy. Right?"

Megan didn't know what to do or say, for she knew her cheeks were betraying her as she looked at him in dismay.

Instead he smiled—his nice smile this time. "Don't look so upset, Miss Crane. I quite understand. Your brother is so dominated by Gaston Duval that he'll believe anything he's told. And I'm afraid you're the same."

The car had reached the school and when it came to a stop, Megan got out slowly. What should she say? What was there to say? Craig Lambert knew everything.

As they went into the hall, Miss Tucker was there talking to several of the staff. She looked a little surprised as she saw Megan come in with Craig Lambert by her side.

"I've been looking for you, Mr. Lambert," she said, a note of accusation in her voice.

"I had to go into town, so I gave Miss Crane a lift as she wanted to see her brother," Craig Lambert explained.

Miss Tucker looked horrified. "Her brother?" she repeated.

Megan looked at the tall ugly man by her side. "Thank you for the lift," she said politely, and escaped upstairs to the quietness of her room.

She went out on to the balcony, gazing at the beautiful blue sea, and drew a long deep breath. It had been quite an afternoon! She took out the folding chair she had found behind the bathroom door, unfolded it and sat in the late sunshine. Everything had that golden color the world assumes as the sun goes slowly down. She buried her face in her hands, feeling absolutely muddled.

Now whom was she to believe? Craig Lambert? Was he right when he said Gaston Duval was a rogue? Was it true that Gaston Duval was cheating and lying and had brainwashed Patrick into believing that Craig Lambert was his enemy?

Or was Patrick right in his belief that Craig Lambert was determined to get rid of everyone he disapproved of who lived on the island? Could Gaston Duval, with his charming manner, his ability to make you feel beautiful and admired, to feel breathless after he had held your hand even for a short time... could he be what might be called a "baddie"? She found it hard to believe.

Or was it because she still could feel the warmth of his hand, the admiration in his eyes, the knowledge that here was a man, a real man?

Had she fallen in love with Gaston Duval, she asked herself. And if she had, then what would happen?

It seemed as if nothing was going to happen, for as the days passed, Megan's life became almost routine and she didn't meet Gaston. She began to relax and enjoy

The Impossible Dream

her new life. Craig Lambert avoided her; if they met he was coolly polite, but he didn't suggest giving her another lift to see her brother. Several of the staff had given Megan lifts into the small town to shop or have coffee, but she never asked them to take her to the Crane Dancing Studio, for she had no desire to see either Patrick or Georgina. She was still so angry with both of them when she thought of the money they had got from her father and herself—money they obviously didn't need half as much as her father did.

The days passed swiftly. The weather was perfect, for it was too early for the monsoon. Every day Megan found herself in one of the small coves that were below the school and where they all swam in the lagoon—a safe lagoon, as it had no opening to the Indian Ocean and the water came in with the high tides, tossing over the reef.

Of all the pupils she taught, Megan made few friends. She was not sorry about this, yet she found herself watching the girl Anarita Marco worriedly.

Anarita was always in trouble. It was true she asked for it, for she was defiantly rude and frequently refused to do what she was told.

"But Frank, she's seventeen," Megan said one evening to him as they sat on in the big room where he taught them bridge.

"Seventeen or not, she isn't entitled to be damned rude," he said crossly.

"She's unhappy here. She's much more mature than the other girls."

"Then why does she stay here?" Frank gathered the cards together. "There are other schools with less strict rules."

"She has no choice," Megan told him. "Her parents are dead; she has a guardian who's about as out-of-date as the dodo. She can't do anything she wants until she's twenty-one and then she'll inherit—"

"A small fortune, which is why the guardian wants her to be protected," Frank told her. "He doesn't want any smart Tom, Dick or Harry to marry her and lay his hands on her wealth. Protection, Meg, not frustration—that's our motto."

That was something Megan had learned since she came to teach dancing at the Lambert School. Many of the pupils were from European countries whose parents or grandparents had once been kings and queens. Others came from the East, of wealthy families who insisted on protection and proper behavior. The strict rules of the school were part of the curriculum, not to harass the unfortunate girls but to protect them.

One day Megan had a chance to talk alone to Anarita.

"They don't mean to be unkind," she explained.

"They just don't care. Nobody cares!" Anarita said angrily.

"I care," said Megan.

Anarita gave her a strange look, her long black hair swinging. "I believe you do," she said, her voice surprised. "Why?"

"Perhaps because I'm only three years older than you. Perhaps because I've known that same kind of frustration, wanting to do something I'm unable to do. I wasn't at school, I was looking after my father." Megan told her about her life in Hastings, and after that Anarita often talked to her.

"If only we weren't shut up in here like a lot of young nuns!" Anarita said angrily. "One day we've got to meet men. How long do we have to wait?" She sighed, twisting her long black hair around one hand

The Impossible Dream

slowly. "After all, lots of girls marry when they are fifteen or sixteen. I ought to have a chance to meet men. I know what it is. My guardian, he seeks the right husband for me. He does not care in case I hate the man. Oh, no, that is not important. Look, you read the magazines, you read the papers. Everywhere people love one another, but me...oh, no, no question of love for me."

"But he can't make you marry if you refuse, if you don't love the man," Megan pointed out.

"I know, but then neither can I marry the man if he refuses permission—my guardian, I mean, of course. So...so I must wait until I am twenty-one. Four more years." Anarita sighed. "You are so lucky. In a year you will be twenty-one."

"In England now you can marry at eighteen, even if your parents disapprove."

"Ah!" Anarita smiled. "I wish my father had been English, then, for it would be only a year to wait."

"You want to marry?"

"I want to marry, yes. I suppose I want to be loved," Anarita said.

Megan found it hard to forget Anarita's pathetic words: *I want to be loved*.

IT WAS PURELY BY CHANCE that Megan found herself alone with Craig Lambert one day. She had had a very energetic class, and when it was over she had several hours before the next one, so she went outside into the sunshine, strolling down toward the golf course. Only the roar of the distant sea and the chatter of the birds broke the stillness. In many ways this was a realization of her dream, her impossible dream, Megan was thinking, if only....

If only she had the answer to a few questions. Could she trust Craig Lambert—or should she believe Patrick and... and Gaston? Why had Mr. Lambert dismissed Miss Pointer so suddenly? Had Mr. Lambert deliberately, Megan wondered, brought her out here to use her as a weapon against her brother? If so, in what way could he use her?

She was asking herself this question, leaning against the sturdy trunk of a tree, watching two honey birds hovering like minute helicopters over the vividly yellow flowers, when she was quite startled to hear a deep voice say, "Dreaming—as usual?"

Craig Lambert! She turned around quickly. "I didn't hear you."

"You were miles away. What were you dreaming about?" he asked.

Megan hesitated. She couldn't tell him the truth—suddenly she knew this was the opportunity she thought she would never get.

"I was thinking about Anarita."

"I've heard you seem to be getting on with her quite well. A pleasant change from hearing about her insolence and tantrums."

"The girl is unhappy. She talks to me."

"You are more or less the same age group, of course," Craig Lambert said. "I suppose she feels she can. What were you thinking about?"

She told him how Anarita felt that she needed to be loved. "She seems never to have had anyone to love her," she said gravely.

"And now you've turned up?" Craig Lambert asked.

Megan was surprised. "Well, I hadn't thought of it like that, but if she feels someone cares for her and wants her to be happy...."

"You think you can help her?"

"I can try."

"Okay. What do you want me to do?"

Megan hesitated. "I don't honestly know. I was wondering if I could take her into town sometimes. We could go on the bus and—"

Craig Lambert's face changed; it might have been made of stone. Megan recognized the sign at once, for she had seen it so often.

"On one condition," he began sternly.

Megan glared at him. "You don't have to tell me, Mr. Lambert. On one condition—*that you don't take her anywhere near your brother*. That's what you were going to say, isn't it?"

Craig Lambert smiled, his face relaxing. "Actually, for once you're quite wrong. I was going to say that you don't take her to the wrong side of the town. You know where I mean. This has nothing to do with your brother, but lately a rough crowd has turned up there, whether for a holiday or to seek work, I don't know, but they're highly undesirable for our girls. Most of them are artists—but typical hippies. Our girls' parents would be horrified if they thought we allowed their daughters to mix with these creatures."

"What's wrong with hippies?" Megan began, but Craig Lambert gave her no time.

"Two things: dirt and drugs. I'll run no risk of the girls being involved in such circumstances. I know what you're getting at and I agree that not all hippies are bad—but many are, and those many are the ones I will not let my girls mingle with. Understand?"

"Yes, you're right, of course," Megan agreed. "If you tell me where the border is, I promise you I won't let Anarita cross it."

He told her, giving the name of a row of shops. "Just stay on the main road and everything will be okay."

"Should I... I mean, you did tell me I took my orders from Miss Tucker."

Craig Lambert lifted his hand. "Leave it to me. All the same, let Miss Tucker know. I'll see that it's all right," he said, and strode off across the field.

Megan watched him go. He had taken that very well. It would be nice to take Anarita in, to encourage her to talk, to let her feel part of life.

So a new routine began. Whenever Megan was offered a lift into town, she asked if Anarita could go with her, too. No one refused to take her, so then Megan would go to Miss Tucker for her permission.

"Personally I think you're wasting your time, Miss Crane," Miss Tucker said the first time. "That girl needs a good spanking. However, Mr. Lambert thinks it's a good idea of his, so I must agree."

Megan had hurried away, trying to hide her smile. Mr. Lambert! Cunningly pretending it was *his* idea, for he knew very well how Miss Tucker resented accepting any of the staff's suggestions.

These trips into town were great fun, Megan found. So did Anarita, who loved going around the shops with Megan while they discussed and argued about what clothes they thought were "in." Or to stand in the market and watch the Creole women selling their goods, the tiny dark-colored babies smiling away, showing their tiny white teeth, and the small children playing in the dust.

"Thanks to you I feel part of the world," Anarita said one day.

"But you've been in to town before?" Megan asked.

The Impossible Dream

"Oh, yes, but with some dull old cow."

"Anarita!" Megan had to laugh even while she scolded. "That's not a nice word."

Anarita looked very innocent. "Isn't it? But the Aussies use it."

"Yes, but not as a compliment. And we're not Aussies."

They had their favorite café and would sit under the bright sunshades on the sidewalk outside, watching the people go by.

"You're not an old cow," Anarita said once. "Not even a young cow."

Megan had to laugh. "Thanks. What am I, then?"

"Nice," was all Anarita said, but it was enough to make Megan's cheeks glow with pleasure.

Occasionally in the crowd Megan would lose sight of Anarita, but she always saw her later, standing outside a shop waiting for her.

"Where did you get to?" Anarita would ask, her eyes amused as she saw Megan's anxious face.

"Looking for you," Megan said.

Anarita laughed. "You don't need to worry, Megan. I can look after myself."

"Mr. Lambert doesn't think so."

"Mr. Lambert!" Anarita said scornfully. "Pity he's so square, for he's terribly attractive."

"Attractive?" Megan was surprised. "I think he's very ugly." Her hand flew to her mouth. "Oh, dear, I shouldn't have said that!"

Anarita's eyes twinkled. "You shouldn't, because I shall tell my friends and the whole school will know Miss Crane thinks Mr. Lambert is very ugly."

"Anarita, please," Megan begged. "Please!"

"All right," Anarita promised reluctantly, "but it's a shame, because they're all talking about you. We thought you and Mr. Lambert were in love. I mean, it was odd your coming so soon after Miss Pointer left, wasn't it?"

"Pure chance," Megan said quickly. "I keep meaning to ask you, Anarita, why do you speak such perfect English when you are Italian?"

"But I'm really English. It's just that my father was Italian. He was never at home and I lived with my mother in Venice, but we always talked English at home. Then they both died and... they sent me here."

"How long have you been here?"

Anarita sighed. "Too long. Far too long. Ever since I was ten."

"It is a long time," Megan agreed.

Often she found herself thinking about her brother Patrick. After all, even if they didn't get on well they were brother and sister. Yet obviously he had no desire to see her even though she was so near.

Actually she had been thinking about this one day as she swam in the warm sea with Frank—or rather, Frank sat on the beach and watched her. He was, he had said, allergic to salt water. Although he had laughed, Megan wondered if it was the real reason.

Now as she floated on her back happily, she thought how wonderful it would be if Patrick and Craig Lambert could become friends, if the strange mystery she had somehow become involved in as to why she was out here could be solved.

This job was indeed her "impossible dream" for the staff seemed to have accepted her, the classes were proving most satisfactory and she was amazingly happy— but there was always this business of Patrick and Craig

The Impossible Dream

Lambert—not to forget, her conscience reminded her, Gaston Duval. She could not forget him somehow. She just could not.

Walking up to the school, talking to Frank, Megan wished she could trust him and tell him everything. Was it all her imagination? Was it simply a question of Craig Lambert's being naturally annoyed at losing part of the island he so obviously treasured?

When they got back to the school Frank walked on as she hovered around the board where the letters were stuck. She had not heard once from her father or Aunt Lily. Megan had written several times and although she knew her family were bad letter writers she couldn't help feeling worried and a little hurt. There was a letter for her this time, but it wasn't from England. It was posted in Coeur Mêlé, the small town nearby.

Puzzled, she opened it. It was a printed invitation inviting her to a champagne party at the Crane Dancing Studio on the seventeenth. In writing was added, "Bring your boyfriend, too, if you like. Patrick."

What was she to do, she wondered. Was she, as well as the pupils, barred from the wrong side of the town? Did she want to go? Gaston would surely be there.

She looked up and saw Craig Lambert walking by. She ran after him. "Mr. Lambert!" she called a little breathlessly.

He turned to stare at her. "What's the trouble this time?" he asked.

"I don't know what to do. My brother has invited me to a party and to take a friend. Would you mind...?"

"If you went?" he asked. "Of course not. You're an adult, presumably capable of protecting yourself. I only meant the pupils when I said it was banned. On the seventeenth, is it? I hope you'll enjoy it," he said.

"Time you met a few more people," he added as he walked away.

Megan stood still for a moment, gazing at the card in her hand. Whom could she take with her? What had Patrick meant when he said, *your boyfriend*?

CHAPTER FOUR

THE INVITATION CONTINUED to puzzle Megan, for surely Patrick could have written a letter or phoned her. What had Patrick meant, too, when he wrote, *boyfriend*? The only real friend she had at the Lambert School—masculine, that was, and to a party you usually took a man—was Frank. She wondered how he would react.

She chose a good moment. She had come out of the warm sea and the drops were trickling down her skin as she dried herself. Frank, his straw hat tilted over his eyes as he lay on his back on the sand, said, "What's worrying you, Meg?"

She sat down by his side, looking along the cove. Groups of the girls were swimming or sunbathing with Miss Weston in charge. Miss Weston, though she had the flat next to Megan's, had had little to do with her. Always polite, yet there was a coldness in her smile. Even now she was sitting with her back to them when she could easily enough have come to sit with them.

"I've been invited to a party at my brother's dancing school," Megan explained.

Frank was so startled he sat up. "Good grief! Lambert won't be very pleased about that."

Megan had begun to dry her hair, which was hanging down over her face, so she parted it to look at him.

"He didn't seem to mind."

"You asked him?"

"Of course." Megan tossed her hair back and smiled. "I had no choice, had I?"

"And he didn't blow his top?"

Megan laughed. "Of course he didn't. He said he hoped I'd enjoy myself, that it was a good idea for me to meet more people... and that, though that part of the island was banned to the girls here, he thought I was mature enough to protect myself."

"Golly!" Frank pretended to groan. "Just how pompous can he get? He's wrong, though, you know. You're not at all mature, you're a foolish little romantic. I wouldn't let you loose at that party with all the gigolos and whatnots."

"What do you mean *whatnots*?" Megan pulled up her legs, rested her chin on her knees and turned her head to look at him.

She could see Miss Weston staring down their way and quickly looking away again as she scolded one of the girls. They were gathered around her as if prepared to go back to the school, for it was nearly teatime.

"What do I mean by whatnots?" Frank repeated the words slowly as if making time in which to think. "I don't mean anything nasty, just that the Crane school supplies the hotel with male and female dance hosts so that all the tourists, no matter what their age, can be sure of a pleasant evening. Actually I was thinking of the biggest gigolo of them all: Gaston Duval."

"Gaston?" Megan stretched out her legs and turned angrily. "He's not a gigolo!"

"So you've met him?" Frank ran his hand through his hair. "Ye gods and little fishes—does Mr. Lambert know that?"

The Impossible Dream

"Yes. I told him so," Megan said defiantly.

"And he still lets you go to that party?" Frank shook his head. "Either he's crackers or he wants to get you into trouble."

"Frank, that's not a nice thing to say," Megan began angrily, then paused. The main thing she wanted to ask him had still not been said. "Frank, I can take a boyfriend. I wondered if you'd come with me."

"Me?" Frank gasped. "Me? Well, I...."

"I know you're not my boyfriend, Frank," Megan said quickly. "But you are my best friend and I always feel so safe when I'm with you."

He gave her a hard, long look. "Thanks for the compliment," he said dryly.

"Well, to be honest, Frank, I need your help." Megan curled up on the sand so that she was facing him and no longer staring at the calm blue lagoon. "My brother and I—my sister-in-law, too—don't really talk the same language. I'm going to feel awfully alone there."

"With Gaston Duval?" Frank asked sarcastically. "I doubt if he'd give you time to breathe."

"Oh, Frank, do please listen. There's also the problem of transport."

"Ah, now I really understand! You want me to be your chauffeur?" Frank began to laugh. "I'm only teasing, Meg. The real thing that stops me going is that I can't dance." He waggled his right foot. "I was in a car crash once and my foot was badly crushed. It's not a pretty sight."

"Is that why you don't swim?"

"Yes, I'm too proud, I'm afraid. I also hurt my hip—that's why I walk so badly. You must have noticed."

"I didn't. I noticed you limped a little, but...." Megan laughed. "Look, Frank, this is a party and not a dancing competition. If you take me, you won't have to dance. Just...."

"Keep an eye on you, eh? Drive you there and back and watch a mass of handsome young males fighting for your company."

"Frank...." Megan paused. "Look, I'm not all that keen to go so if you'd rather not, say so."

"Then you won't go?" Frank scrambled to his feet, leaning heavily on his right hand as he did so, and began to collect the towels.

"Not without you." Megan got up, too, putting on her short toweling coat.

"You win," Frank said as they turned to walk up toward the school.

"Bless you!" smiled Megan. "Think you should tell Mr. Lambert?"

Frank went bright red. "I do not think anything of the sort. There are limits to what I'll accept."

"Why are you here, Frank?" she asked as they got nearer the school. "Mr. Lambert told me you were a very fine artist."

"Sweet of him, I'm sure," Frank joked, then frowned. "I wanted to be an artist, but there comes a moment in your life when you realize it's just a dream...."

"An impossible dream?" Megan asked eagerly.

Frank nodded. "Yes. I discovered I could never be a *real* artist. The next best thing was to help youngsters have the training I had and that I failed to use."

"But why did you choose girls? I'd have thought...."

"Because I like girls, you idiot," Frank was saying as they went through the swing door into the corridor.

Several of the girls ahead turned to stare at them and

The Impossible Dream

then put their heads together, their laughter sounding as they ran away.

"Boys are so exhausting," Frank said, mimicking a singsong voice.

"And girls are such chatterboxes," said Megan, knowing that within an hour it would be all over school that Mr. Parr had called Miss Crane an idiot! Anyhow, her problem was solved. "Thanks, Frank," she said as she turned to go up the back staircase. It really led to the girls' part but it was a shortcut to her flat.

"My pleasure," he said, looking up from below and smiling.

For a moment, she felt worried. Frank couldn't possibly be falling in love with her, could he, she asked herself. They were such good friends... she needed him so badly, for in the difficulties of this school life he made all the difference in the world for her.

She showered and dressed quickly, then wrote an acceptance for the party invitation. "I'm bringing a friend with me," she wrote.

When Megan ran down to the dining room she was stopped in the hall by Craig Lambert. How ugly he was, she thought as he beckoned to her. How different from Frank, who for all his insignificant look at least had a pleasant face.

"Are you going to the party?" Craig asked curtly.

Megan showed him the letter in her hand that she was going to drop into the hall box. "Yes."

"You've got a boyfriend?"

"I've got a *friend*," she said.

A smile seemed to crack the sternness of Craig Lambert's face. "I'm glad," he said, turning away. "Now I needn't worry."

She watched him walk down the hall and then she

went to the letter box, frowning a little. Why had he said that? Had he been worried? If so, why had he consented to her going in the first place, she wondered.

Much to Megan's surprise, next day Miss Weston said she was driving into town that afternoon and would Megan like to go. They were talking just outside the building, watching the girls play tennis before lunch.

"Thanks, I'd love to go," Megan said eagerly. It always made a change. Much as she liked her pupils, there was always a noise at the school, apart from the tension caused by the unfriendliness and obvious criticism of the members of the staff who had still not completely accepted her. "Can I bring Anarita?"

"Of course. She's your shadow, isn't she? Do you think it's a good idea to let her become so dependent on you?" Miss Weston asked.

"It was Mr. Lambert's idea," Megan said meekly— which wasn't quite the truth, but as that was what he had told Miss Tucker it must be backed.

Miss Weston looked annoyed. "I can't understand why he chose a newcomer like you when most of us knew her so well and for so long."

Megan gave a quick look at Miss Weston's face. "I think it was because of the age group," she said, then realized she had made a terrible mistake for Miss Weston looked furious.

"I'm not completely senile yet, Miss Crane," Miss Weston snapped. "I'm only just thirty."

"But you're Mr. Lambert's age group, aren't you?" Megan said seriously, trying to repair the damage she had done. "I mean, I'm just twenty, and that is much nearer seventeen, isn't it?"

"I suppose so..." Miss Weston said reluctantly.

The Impossible Dream

"But I would have thought she'd feel more at ease with us when she's known us for so long."

"Perhaps too long?" Megan suggested. "I'm someone new—and someone new usually gets the interest to start with. I expect she'll soon get tired of me, too."

"Indeed? Well, don't keep me waiting, at three o'clock sharp," Miss Weston said. "I have to go to the dentist. Frightful nuisance."

"Poor you," Megan said sympathetically. "Well, I'll go and see Anarita."

She had quite a search for the girl and finally found her in the library talking to several other girls. There was a sudden silence as Megan came through the wide swinging glass doors, so she knew they had been talking about her!

"Anarita," Megan said as she walked up to them, "I'm going to town this afternoon. Like to come?"

"Who's driving us?" Anarita asked, her long black hair swinging back.

"Miss Weston."

"Whew, that's a change, isn't it?" Anarita laughed. "I think this is the first time My Lady Weston has condescended to take me in. What's happened?"

"Anarita, there's no need to be rude," Megan said quickly. "It's very good of Miss Weston. If you'd rather not come, then just say so."

"Of course I want to come—with you," said Anarita.

"Good—then two-forty-five this afternoon. Right?"

"Right," Anarita said with a smile.

Megan walked to the dining room. She was the first to sit down at the staff table. The quietness vanished as the girls came tumbling in, all talking at the top of their voices. Gradually the staff table filled up, Frank by her side.

"You're looking very thoughtful," he teased. "What's wrong this time?"

"Nothing," Megan told him. "Just something that puzzles me."

"Be my guest—I'm good at solving problems."

"I don't think you could solve this one," she said.

Later as she changed into a clean dress in her flat, Megan thought again how odd it was that Miss Weston had suddenly offered her a lift. Why—when for all these past weeks Miss Weston had barely spoken to her, and certainly not at all unless she was so obliged? Why now?

Could Mr. Lambert have asked her to check up on Megan's behavior? To watch what happened when Megan and Anarita went to town? Megan had an uncomfortable feeling that she was constantly under supervision, but perhaps it was absurd. After all, why should Craig Lambert want a report of all she did?

Unless he still distrusted her and believed she was working for her brother.

Working for him? *Just how stupid can you be,* she asked herself. In what way could she *work* for him?

As she hurried downstairs, glancing anxiously at her watch, for she had deliberately told Anarita an earlier time because the Italian-English girl seemed to delight in keeping people waiting, Megan herself wanted to be there first, as it was in some small way setting an example.

She had just reached the curve in the wide staircase when she saw Craig Lambert coming up the stairs two at a time. As he saw her he stopped.

"Ah, just the person I wanted to see," he said curtly. "I've had a letter from your Mrs. Arbuthnot. How come you've never written to her?"

The Impossible Dream

Megan's hand flew to her mouth. "I meant to, but I forgot. I'm... I'm not a very good letter writer."

"That's no excuse at all. She's anxious about you, eager to know how you've adapted yourself. How have you?"

"I'm very happy here," Megan told him.

"You get on all right with everyone? The children, pianists, staff?"

Megan moistened her lips. "In a way, very well."

He smiled, his face relaxing. "I get the message. And in a way, not. By the way, Mrs. Arbuthnot said an old friend had phoned up asking for your address. A... a Leontine Harrap."

"Leo?" Megan exclaimed. "I haven't heard from her for ages. Her parents went to Australia."

"That must have been when you were at Everglades, I suppose."

"Yes, it was." Megan paused, staring at him, puzzled. "But how do you know that? I never told Mrs. Arbuthnot about it, as she and Mrs. Harding, who ran Everglades Dancing School, were rivals. I was only there one term and I hated it—that's why I left and went to Mrs. Arbuthnot, but how could she know?"

A smile crossed his face—a smile that annoyed her, for it was not only amused but sarcastic. "Mrs. Arbuthnot didn't have to tell me. I know all about you, Miss Crane, right back to the day and place you were born. Excuse me." He walked by her and then turned. "Would you please write to Mrs. Arbuthnot and give her my best wishes? I'm rather busy. I've got to go over to the mainland tomorrow for a few days."

And then he was gone, almost flying up the stairs. Megan stayed where she was for a moment, her hand clutching the banister. He knew everything about her, he had said. Everything—right back to the time and place she was born.

But why? He had no right....

She went down the stairs slowly. In other words he had collected what she believed was called a dossier. But this was no cloak-and-dagger business, no F.B.I. or whatever it was in detective stories. Why—why did he have to know everything about her?

She was still trembling with anger as she went outside. Anarita was there first, a triumphant smile on her lovely face.

"Beat you to it, Miss Meg!" she said happily.

"Yes, you did."

"Something wrong?" Anarita asked.

Megan managed a smile. "No—not really." She looked around her at the colorful garden and the distant blue water. "It's very beautiful here, isn't it, Anarita?"

"I suppose so," Anarita shrugged. "I'm getting awfully tired of it. I often have to spend my holidays here, too, you know."

"You don't?" Megan was shocked.

Anarita laughed. "It's not as bad as it sounds. Miss Tucker goes off and Mr. Lambert takes over. He takes us for super schooner trips to the other islands, and twice we went by air to Mombasa, which was great fun."

"Mr. Lambert does that? Himself?"

Anarita laughed. "Yes. He yells at us if we don't obey, but the rest of the time he's really rather sweet. He's a lonely man, you know."

"Lonely?" Megan echoed. "How do you mean, lonely?"

Turning to stare at Megan, Anarita laughed. "You

The Impossible Dream

know what I mean all right. Any woman is lonely without a man—and any man lonely without a woman. The staff all chase poor Mr. Lambert, and I don't blame him for keeping them at a distance. Apart from you, they're a lot of real duddies."

"Indeed, how interesting!" Miss Weston's voice was sharp as she joined them. "The car is around the back."

It was a quiet journey into the small town. Megan tried to think of something to say, yet she and Miss Weston had nothing in common. Anarita in the back seat neither spoke nor moved. She seemed to be ignoring them both.

Miss Weston left them at the market.

"I'll pick you up here in an hour's time," she said as Megan and Anarita got out.

"Thank you," Megan said with a smile. "We'll be here." She turned to Anarita as the car moved away. "Now look, you're not to lose me today!"

"I don't lose you, you lose me," Anarita laughed.

They wandered around the market with the huge bowls of fruit and great bunches of sweet-smelling flowers, the crowds of people either hurrying along or milling around the goods for sale. Twice Megan lost Anarita and she was getting a bit annoyed the second time when she found her looking in an antique-shop window.

"Anarita," she said firmly, "you must not leave my side. I'm responsible for you."

"Oh, Miss Meg, do grow up," Anarita said with her sweetest smile. "Look, I'm seventeen, going on eighteen, and this is the 1970s, not the Victorian age. What harm could be done to me?"

Megan hesitated. She didn't want to suggest that

what Mr. Lambert had said was right; any of these wealthy girls could be good for kidnapping.

"Please Anarita, it is my responsibility."

The girl smiled. "I'll try, but you're so slow... you're too gentle in a crowd. You should just push your way through them, using your elbows," she said. Then she clapped her hands. "I'm dying for a cold drink. Let's sit at the café by the church. It looks rather nice."

Megan hesitated for a moment. The church was very close to what Mr. Lambert had described as the banned area—but still, it was on the *right* side!

"Okay," she said. Anything was better than losing sight of Anarita!

They had a good view of the market at the end of the road and the cars and bicycles going by as well as the strange little carts drawn by the Creoles. There always seemed so many people in the town, and as they sat under the bright-colored sunshade at the small table, Megan and Anarita talked again about her childhood. It was certainly a sad one, Megan thought. She had always been sorry for herself, but now she felt sorrier for Anarita.

Megan was glancing at her watch, for Miss Weston must not be kept waiting—or that would be reported to Mr. Lambert, no doubt, Megan thought bitterly—and soon they ought to go.

"May I join you?" a deep masculine voice said.

Megan turned and saw herself staring at a hippie, as undoubtedly Mr. Lambert would have called him. The long brown hair that came down his back was beautifully silky and he was wearing a thin crimson silk jacket and purple trousers.

"There isn't another table," he said pathetically.

The Impossible Dream

It was true. All the tables had filled. "We're going in a moment," Megan said, "so do sit down."

"I'm Tracy Thompson," he said, holding out his hand and shaking Megan's, then turning to Anarita.

"Hullo," she said coldly, hardly letting her hand touch his and turning away.

Megan sighed. Why did Anarita always have to be so rude? To try to make up for it, she chatted to the hippie. Even if he was one, he was a very nice one, and anyway, what was wrong with being a hippie, she thought. Everyone has a right to have a personality of his or her own....

"I'm an artist," he told them. "Marvelous views here. You on holiday?"

"I work here," Megan said, "and... and...."

Anarita turned her head and looked at him contemptuously.

"I'm a schoolgirl," she said, her voice bitter.

Tracy Thompson's eyebrows were lifted in surprise. "What, at the famous Lambert School? How do you like it?"

"Not much," Anarita said, and turned away. "We'd better go, Miss Meg. I'll pay this time," she said as she stood up and walked into the café.

Megan hesitated and stared after the girl. "I teach dancing at the school and...."

"What's your name?" He smiled at her.

"Megan."

"Welsh?"

"No, but my grandmother was."

They both laughed. Anarita returned, looking impatient.

Megan said goodbye and hurried after Anarita. They got to the market much too early. They talked as they waited and finally Megan said, "I thought he was rather nice."

"I thought he was pretty ghastly. So immature. I prefer older men," said Anarita.

Maybe it was just as well, Megan was thinking as Miss Weston's car came into view, for Mr. Lambert would certainly not approve of a friendship between Anarita and Tracy Thompson!

Back at the school Megan was alone in her flat when there came a knock on the door. She had just showered and was in her thin, psychedelic-colored housecoat, her hair hanging wetly around her face.

It was Craig Lambert. His eyes were narrowed, his voice low, tense with anger as he strode into the room slamming the door behind him and swinging around to stare at her.

"I thought I could trust you!"

Megan stared back. "You can."

"A fine example of it, then. Why were you and Anarita sitting with that ghastly-looking hippie?"

"We were not sitting with him. There were no seats and he asked if he could join us. As we were just leaving, I said of course. I could hardly have refused, could I?" Megan asked.

"He bought you cold drinks?"

"Of course he didn't. He... or rather, we weren't there long enough."

"He asked for your names?"

"No. He told us his... oh, and he asked me mine. Anarita went to pay the bill and—"

"Of course you told him yours," Craig Lambert said sarcastically.

"I only said, 'Megan.' I didn't give him Anarita's name at all. In any case, how do you know? Did you send Miss Weston to snoop on me?" Megan's anger was mounting fast. "I hate all this spying. Why do you do it? Either you trust me or you don't. If you don't, I'll go!" She almost shouted the words at him.

Craig Lambert turned away, his hand on the door handle.

"I doubt if your brother would want you to do that," he said dryly. "Why not ask him when you see him?" he added, and left the room.

Megan stood still, hugging herself angrily. He had no right ... no right at all. She was tired of all this stupid ....

He had no right at all. She hated him. She had a sudden impulse to get out her suitcases and pack all her things and go home....

Home?

She took a deep breath. That was something she no longer had.

WHEN THE DAY of the party came, Megan was rather worried whether or not she was doing the right thing by going. But Craig Lambert had agreed, had even thought it a good idea. She and Frank decided it was best to keep it to themselves, so no one was told, and as Megan left her flat Petronella Weston, going into hers, lifted her eyebrows.

"Going to a party?" she asked, sounding surprised. "I didn't ...."

Megan smiled. "Yes," she said, and hurried down the corridor, giving Miss Weston no time to ask with whom! She was quite capable of doing so, and Frank had suggested that if asked, Megan could say simply that she was going out with him.

"That'll give the girls something to talk about," Megan had said, and laughed.

"Do you mind?" Frank had asked, suddenly serious.

"Not really. It's not malicious chatter."

"That's true," he had agreed.

Now as she ran down the beautiful curved staircase Megan thought how different it seemed without Craig Lambert there. He had gone to the mainland, she knew, but for how long? Everything changed when he was away, she had noticed. Somehow or other he kept the peace, kept everything even, but since he had gone there were small quarrels among the staff and a considerable number of arguments with Miss Tucker.

Frank was waiting in his car outside. He leaned over and opened the door for her.

"So you made it," he grinned. "Did the old dragon see you?"

"No, but Miss Weston did." Megan snuggled down into the seat. "She obviously longed to ask me who I was going with, but I just ran."

He laughed as he started the car. "Probably tomorrow Miss Tucker will send for you and say, 'We do not allow affairs among the staff.'" He mimicked her voice well.

"So what? I shall tell her we're not having an affair, we're just good friends. Look, surely a man and a woman can be good friends without getting involved?"

Frank took a difficult corner carefully, for the night was pitch-dark with not even a slice of moon to light the sky.

"A man and woman, yes, I agree—but a girl and a man? I wonder," he said.

"Oh, let's forget them all, Frank," said Megan, sliding down the seat so that she could lean against him.

The Impossible Dream

"Let's just enjoy ourselves. I'm a bit worried about going and...."

"Because of me?"

"Goodness, no. You're my... what shall I call you? My guardian. It's just that—well, Mr. Lambert and Patrick don't get on and...."

"Mr. Lambert said you should go."

"I know. That's what worries me." Megan hesitated. As often before, she wished she could tell Frank everything, hear him sort it out in his humorous practical way and help her to see sense. Yet something always stopped her. "I expect it'll be all right," she added quickly, lying back in the seat and half closing her eyes.

She imagined she was looking at Craig Lambert's house. She wished she could tell Frank about that—wished she could describe the beauty and peacefulness of the thatched house, with the palm trees standing so gracefully and with no sign of violence in their straight trunks. She had fallen in love with the house as soon as she saw it. It had been almost uncanny, for it was just what she had always seen in her impossible dream. A strange house, she had thought, and still did, for a man like Craig Lambert. A romantic house in a way, and he had said how he loved the quiet stillness of it. Yet he was such a virile man, a man knowing just where he was going and making for it, regardless of obstacles that he swept out of his way.

"Are both Mr. Lambert's parents dead, Frank?" she asked.

"Yes. It was a good thing his father died when he did or there'd be no school today. Poor Craig. He was in South America, making a fortune on his own—I'm not sure how, but everything that man touches turns to gold. Then his father died and his mother sent for him. She was desperate because she had just discovered about her husband's gambling and wasn't sure quite how much of the island was left to them. This was about eight years ago, when he was in his early twenties. He really worked hard at it. You've got to hand it to him, Meg. He's a hard worker and expects the same of others and somehow gets it out of them. All seemed to be going well, then his mother was ill and passed on. We all wondered what Craig would do—sell the lot? Because he wasn't the type of man really to run a school. At least, you wouldn't think he was, yet he's surprisingly successful. He generates confidence, makes the anxious parents feel they can trust him—and trust him they can," Frank said.

"So he didn't sell the school?"

"No. He began bringing it up-to-date. His main pain in the neck is Miss Tucker, of course. I wonder why he doesn't get rid of her. Mind, she's been with the school for some fifteen years. She was a close friend of his parents and bitterly resents any suggestion that the success of the school is due to Craig. She likes to think it is she who has done it. Ah, this is where we get close to danger," Frank chuckled as they reached the town. "Might do Miss Tucker a bit of good to go to Paris or better still, Hamburg, if she wants to see a bit of *real* nightlife. Ever been?"

"No. This is the first time I've been out of England."

Megan was busy looking at the lighted shops and the groups of people chatting and laughing. The locals were a happy lot, she thought, so often singing and nearly always joking.

Now they were driving past the hotel that was ablaze

The Impossible Dream

with light, throwing shadows on the brightly lighted front, and then they reached the Crane studio. Frank parked his car and took Megan's arm. It was so hot that she had merely put a thin shawl over her shoulders. She was wearing a white dress, sleeveless and backless. She had been surprised when Miss Wilmot had chosen it.

"You'll be so hot out there," Miss Wilmot had said, and how right she was!

The studio was a very big hall that could be divided into different rooms with folded-back louvered doors. It seemed to be packed with people, standing and sitting, some dancing, others drinking.

Frank and Megan hesitated as they went in and then Georgina came toward them. She looked even lovelier than usual in a deep red dress.

"Megan, how nice to see you!" she smiled, holding out her hands, surprising Megan, who wasn't used to such friendliness from her sister-in-law. "And this is...?" She looked at Frank, puzzled.

"Frank Parr, an artist," Megan said. "Frank, this is my sister-in-law, Mrs. Crane."

"You must come and have something to eat," Georgina told them, and led the way toward the long tables covered with plates of food, around which the guests were standing. "I thought you were bringing Craig Lambert," she whispered to Megan.

"Craig Lambert? Why should I? You didn't invite him."

"We said 'your boyfriend.' He is, isn't he? He seems to let you do a lot he won't let the others. For instance, always bringing that Anarita Marco into town."

"You know her?" Megan was startled.

"Everyone's heard of her. She used to come in, of

course, but not as often as she does now. How do you and Craig Lambert get on?"

"He employs me," Megan said coldly.

Georgina laughed. "You haven't changed—just as prickly! Come, Frank, because I can't call you Mr. Parr, come and get us some drinks."

Later Megan was standing alone when to her surprise Patrick came up.

"Come and dance. It's many a year since we took to the floor together," he said quite cheerfully, taking her by the hand and leading her to the dance floor.

His arm went around her and they were off... from then on, it was a nightmare for Megan. She knew Patrick was doing everything in his power to make her dance badly or bungle it and look a fool.

He tried everything, every trick that luckily she knew so well how to combat and even anticipate. If only she was in Craig's arms, she found herself thinking.

That startled her, for it was the first time she had thought of him as *Craig* and not *Craig Lambert*. Now what had made her do that? Was it the memory of the wonder of the dance she had shared with him, the strength of his arm, the courtesy of his leading, the... togetherness—there was no better word for it—the togetherness of dancing? She couldn't forget it. She would never forget it.

This was the exact opposite. It was a battle—one she was determined to win.

As the music stopped, Patrick let her go. He looked thoughtful.

"You're a darned good dancer, Meg," he said, sounding surprised. "You're wasting your time teaching kids. You could make a fortune if you became a professional."

"I'm happy where I am."

They walked back toward the buffet tables. "I don't get it. How can you stand that man?" said Patrick, his voice disgusted. "It must be a nightmare to have him always prowling around."

"He doesn't prowl around!"

"That's what you think, Meg. I bet he knows every single thing about you."

Megan felt herself blush. Patrick was so right. "He may have a reason," she said stiffly. "At this sort of school you've got to be careful whom you employ."

"Too right," Patrick laughed. "So you're one of the chosen few. All the same, I wouldn't work for him. Rather starve. You just can't trust the man."

"Patrick, dad told me you said Mr. Lambert had... well, nearly ruined you. What did he do?"

She saw the shock on her brother's face. "Dad shouldn't have told you."

"He was worried about you and very upset. But I want to know what Mr. Lambert did."

Patrick lifted his hand and waved to someone. "It's too long a story to tell you now, Meg. Next time you come over, I will. Now Georgina and I have to dance. We give exhibition dancing always at the hotel on Saturday nights, you know, so this is an extra. Georgina and I are very popular. See you!"

Gradually the room was cleared, the guests standing or sitting in a big circle, leaving the center of the room for the two dancers.

Megan leaned against a wall and watched. Patrick was still as good a dancer, but this time he was dancing differently from the way he had danced with her! She could see how he guided Georgina. He was undoubtedly the stronger. But Georgina was graceful and good and they deserved the wild applause they got as they finished the different dances and then bowed to the audience.

"Megan—*ma chérie,* for you I have been looking," a deep voice said, and she turned to find Gaston Duval by her side.

Something inside her seemed to be doing a wild dance. She decided it was her heart. It wasn't fair that any man should be so handsome.

"Hullo," she said, trying to keep her voice calm.

His hand closed over her arm, sliding down it to take her hand in his and lift it to his mouth.

"I saw you dance with Patrick. Very good, you were. You are wasting your life at that school, my little Megan. You are too good a dancer."

Megan laughed. "That's what Patrick said, but I like my job."

"This is something I have no power to understand," Gaston said, leaning against her a little, his hand still holding hers tightly. "How can you work—with that pig?" he added angrily.

"Look, Mr. Lambert isn't—"

"Excuse me, Megan, it's time we went back," a voice said.

Gaston seemed to jump, dropping Megan's hand as if it burned him. "And who is this?" he asked.

"Frank Parr, my... my friend," said Megan. "Frank, this is Gaston Duval."

The two men stared at each other. They were so different that Megan found herself tempted to laugh.

Just as Frank was insignificant, so unobtrusive with his pale skin, his light brown hair, his ordinary unexciting features—so Gaston was the reverse with his lean handsome face, jet-black hair, dark warm eyes and that smile...: No one could ever overlook Gaston, she thought.

"What's the time?" Megan asked, and when Frank told her she gasped. "We *must* go! Miss Tucker doesn't like us to be out too late."

"And what right has this... this Miss Tuck... Tucker to say it is time for you to be in bed?" Gaston asked stiffly.

"The headmistress," Megan said, and laughed. "Look, say goodbye to Patrick and Georgina for us, Gaston. Come on, Frank." She took Frank's hand and smiled at Gaston. "Good night," she said.

They walked to the car in silence. Frank spoke only as he drove away.

"So you've fallen hook, line and sinker," he said with a strange sadness in his voice.

"Oh, Frank, not really, it's just..." Megan began.

"I know. Just.... I don't blame you. I've never met a woman yet who hasn't fallen for that sexy face and that smooth smile," Frank said bitterly. "Just imagine being married to him and knowing that he could get any girl he wants just by smiling at her."

"I'm not thinking of marrying him," Megan said quickly.

Or was she, she asked herself. If you let yourself love a man like Gaston, you would be jealous, possessive and determined to make him your own.... You wouldn't be able to help it, she knew.

"Look, this is only the second time I've met him," she began again as the car shot along the deserted road toward the school, the beams of light showing up the palm trees and the flowering shrubs.

"I imagine the first was enough to do the damage." Frank looked down at the shadow by his side. "Just watch out, Meg. You're too sweet a kid to get hurt, and a man like that can really harm you. I wish... oh, how I wish you'd never come here," he said with a sigh.

Megan sat up. "Frank, that isn't a very nice thing to say. I thought you liked me," she said accusingly.

His hand covered hers for a moment and then left it.

"That's the trouble, kid," he said. "I like you too much, and I'm darned afraid you're going to get hurt."

"Oh, Frank, don't worry. I'm not a child."

"Aren't you?" Frank gave an odd little laugh. "I'm just wondering what trouble we're getting into tomorrow."

"It's not as late as that," she protested. "It's only three o'clock."

But three o'clock was unforgivable in Miss Tucker's eyes, as she had no hesitation in telling Megan next day after sending for her.

"I understand you were not back until three o'clock this morning," she said, her cheeks red with anger, her eyes cold. "This is no example to set our young people."

How had Miss Tucker known, Megan wondered. It could only be Petronella Weston! Had she lain awake all night to check up on her neighbor?

"I'm sorry," she said sincerely. "The evening went so fast I had no idea what time it was."

"You enjoyed the evening?" Miss Tucker spoke as if referring to a den of lions where the Romans tossed the Christians in those distant days.

"Yes. Why...?"

"I think it was very bad taste on your part, Miss Crane, to go. You are fully aware that your brother and Gaston Duval are two of the most undesirable characters in the town."

The Impossible Dream

"Miss Tucker!" Megan stood up, so angry she could hardly speak. "Patrick Crane happens to be my brother. You have no right to say—"

Miss Tucker was on her feet, too, her cheeks an even brighter red now.

"I have every right. I'm in charge of these girls and must allow no one of dubious nature near them. Mr. Lambert engaged you, and why I cannot think. You should never have been given the job. What he'll say, though, when he hears you went to that party—"

"Miss Tucker, he told me to go." Megan managed to get a word in and Miss Tucker gaped, her mouth falling open.

"He told you to go? He...?"

"Yes, Miss Tucker. I asked his permission and he said he thought it was a good idea." With that, Megan walked out. Why should she stand there and be insulted by Miss Tucker? And what right had she to call Patrick an undesirable character?

Megan went back to her flat. In half an hour she had a lesson to give, but until then she would sit on her balcony, basking in the sun, loving the beauty of the deep blue sea, the chatter of the birds. What would happen next, she wondered. Miss Tucker was sure to have a row with Craig Lambert about it. Who would win?

And if Miss Tucker did, was that going to be the end of this life, Megan wondered. Yet how could Miss Tucker win, she thought, feeling suddenly certain. Craig would never let her!

CHAPTER FIVE

CRAIG LAMBERT DIDN'T RETURN until the end of the week and Megan was glad when she saw him in the big dining room.

Miss Tucker had said no more to Megan about her "late night out," yet Megan knew she must have told many of the staff, for quite a few of them now ignored her completely. Frank Parr, too, had been interviewed by Miss Tucker and had lost his temper, telling her she had no right to control his private life and that 3 A.M. was not such a terrible time.

"At least I brought Miss Crane back!" he had finished angrily, and stormed out of the room.

Now he, like Megan, was waiting for Craig's reaction.

"In a sense," Frank had said only the day before as they lay in the sunshine on the beach, "he has to stand up for the headmistress. On the other hand, it's rather Victorian to expect the staff to be in by midnight. After all, these precious girlies are going out into the wicked world in a few years' time, so shouldn't we break it to them gently that adults can stay out after midnight?"

Megan had laughed. "I just wonder what Mr. Lambert will say!" She had shaken her head. "I'm afraid he won't like it." This, though she had not told Frank, was what worried her most. Had she let Craig down, she wondered. He had trusted her enough to let her go

The Impossible Dream

to the party; had it, then, been up to her to see that she obeyed the school's rules?

The longer she lived on the island the more she loved it, she had thought as they walked up to the school. Tiny colored birds were hovering over the flowers whose fragrant scents drifted on the warm breeze, the palm trees moved gently and the whole atmosphere....

She had grown to know many of the girls quite well and she looked forward to her classes. Several of the staff, too, were getting more friendly. Now, if Craig decided she must go.... So the tension had been great, which made her smile perhaps more warmly than usual as she glanced down the table. He lifted his hand and smiled, as well.

Miss Weston, sitting next to her, snorted.

"You think you can talk him out of it?" she asked, helping herself to another roll.

Startled, Megan turned. "Talk whom out of what?"

Miss Weston looked amused. "Craig Lambert, of course. You seem able to twist him around your little finger."

"I don't!" Megan blushed.

"Don't you? It seems you do. You can break the school rules and get away with it."

"If you mean because Frank and I were late that once—"

"Once is enough. You should never have gone to the party."

Megan drew a deep breath. "Look, Miss Weston, let's face it. I didn't mean to be late. It was simply that the time went fast. In any case, Mr. Lambert said he thought it a good idea that I go to the party—"

"There you are!" Miss Weston said triumphantly.

"Just what I said—you can do what you like. None of us could have gone."

"Please...." Megan lowered her voice, for several of the staff were looking down the table at them and it would not be a good welcome to Craig if she was involved in a fight with Petronella Weston in the dining room! "I think you forget that Patrick Crane is my brother. That was why Mr. Lambert thought I should go."

Mr. Taft, the math teacher, who rarely spoke, leaned across the table. "I understand you are a good choreographer, Miss Crane?"

Welcoming the change of subject, Megan looked at his stern face and saw the friendliness in his eyes. "Yes, I used to do quite a lot in England," she said.

"Well, we're planning the end-of-the-year concert and I wondered if you would work out the choreography of a dance that could involve the different classes, showing their slow but steady improvement, not only in dancing but in every way."

"It sounds a marvelous idea!" Megan said eagerly. "Could we discuss it?"

"I'll be delighted to," said Paul Taft. "We've another month before the end of term. The holidays will give you time to work it all out."

Petronella Weston stood up noisily, scraping her chair back and calling attention to herself as she left the table.

"What's the matter with her?" asked Megan, startled, aware that both Miss Tucker and Mr. Lambert were looking down at them.

Paul Taft, who so rarely laughed, did laugh this time.

"Take no notice of her, Miss Crane. She's suffering from malicious jealousy," he said quietly across the

The Impossible Dream

table. "Don't let it worry you. Poor Petronella, she can't help it."

"Help what?" Everyone had begun speaking noisily, so Megan felt she could talk across the table without anyone hearing.

The elderly man smiled. "You haven't noticed? My dear girl, you are very young." He shook his head. "Some other time," he added, as the meal came to a close.

Megan had just finished her last class for the day when the message arrived: "Mr. Lambert would like to see you immediately."

So it had come, Megan thought. Soon she would know the worst. Would she and Frank be asked to leave? Or perhaps she was the one at fault?

She hurried past the girls, but Anarita stopped her for a moment.

"Miss Meg, it isn't true, is it?" she asked, her lovely face worried.

"What isn't true, Anarita? Look, Mr. Lambert wants to see me."

"Is he going to sack you?" Anarita looked even more dismayed.

Megan laughed. "I hope not. What makes you think...?"

"Everyone's talking—they're saying you and Mr. Parr are...are in love." Anarita frowned. "I don't think you are."

"We are not in love." Megan patted Anarita's arm. "Look, Mr. Parr and I are good friends—that's all. Now I really must go, Anarita. We mustn't make Mr. Lambert cross."

"He must be to have sent for you. Miss Meg, if he sacks you we'll all go on strike," Anarita promised.

Megan laughed. "Bless you, but that won't be necessary," she said, and hurried down the corridor.

As she went past a wide-open door, the warm fragrant air came in to envelop her and for a moment she paused, looking out at the blue cloudless sky, the beauty of it all. Suppose Craig was going to sack her? Suppose she had to leave this?

Craig? She thought with a shock that these days she always thought of him as *Craig*. Why? He had never told her to use his Christian name. She hardly knew him... and yet, in a way, she did know him. And what she knew didn't make sense—it didn't fit in with all Patrick and Gaston had said about Craig Lambert's selfish, brutal ruthlessness.

She knocked on his door and heard a curt "Come in!"

Suddenly unsure of herself, even almost certain that she would leave the room without a job, Megan obeyed. Craig was bent over his desk, talking on the phone. He looked up and pointed to a chair, so Megan sat down.

She looked around the room. It was so typically him, she thought. She tried to relax but could not help feeling worried as she watched his face change as he talked angrily into the phone.

"That's absurd! You had plenty of time. No, I do not agree, and I will not tolerate it. I gave you warning. No, I will not agree." He put down the receiver and looked at the slight girl looking so terrified as she sat in the chair, her hands tightly clenched.

"Well," he began with a smile, "I hear you enjoyed the party so much that you forgot the time. Parr was an equal sinner, of course."

"It wasn't so much that I enjoyed it," Megan tried to explain. "We didn't get there very early and there was food to eat and then Patrick danced with me...well, time must have flown. Then he and Georgina danced and we all watched and that took quite a while. When Frank...I mean, Mr. Parr told me the time, I was really shocked."

"So was he, I gather," Craig said with a chuckle. "I must congratulate you on persuading Frank Parr to go. He's always rather worried me. What I call a loner. You seem to get on well?"

"Oh, yes, we do. He's great fun and—well...." Megan paused.

"You don't find much friendship from the rest of the staff?"

"In a way, yes. Mr. Taft is awfully nice and so is Herta Bauer, the German teacher, and Aline Delaine. I get on all right with them, but... and the accompanists are very friendly, too."

"Mr. Taft was telling me he has asked you to choreograph the dancing for our next school concert. He said you were interested."

Megan nodded. She was feeling more relaxed. "His idea was a good one. But...." She hesitated as she looked at Craig Lambert. "I really am sorry about being late that night, Mr. Lambert. We didn't mean to be."

"I'm aware of that." Craig almost clipped the words impatiently.

"I'm afraid Miss Tucker was very angry."

"So I gather." A smile curled around his mouth. "I also gather you stormed out in a temper."

"Yes, I'm afraid I did, but she said something very nasty about Patrick and he is, after all, my brother," Megan said, leaning forward, her hands twisting together again. "I mean, no matter what you or she may think of him, I'm not going to stand by and let you . . . ."

"I quite agree. Family loyalty is a natural thing," Craig acknowledged. "Well, that's all, I think. I wanted to see you to ask you to cooperate with Mr. Taft. He always organizes our concerts and I think you'll find him very pleasant to work with." He stood up and Megan did, too.

She felt stunned a little. "That's all? You're not angry with me?"

"Should I be?" he asked, coming around the desk toward her. "What crime did you commit? You went to your brother's dance with my approval. Naturally you couldn't walk out in the middle, but I understand you left almost as soon as the exhibition dancing was over."

"Yes, we did." Bless Frank, Megan was thinking, for he obviously hadn't mentioned Gaston Duval!

They walked to the door and as he opened it Craig looked at her gravely. "Just one thing, Miss Crane. This is for your own good and has nothing to do with the school, but I would ask you to be on your guard. Gaston Duval has a way with women, particularly romantic-minded girls." He closed the door before she could answer. She stood still for a moment and then went up to her flat. Craig had been on her side, after all. He had understood and trusted her. But why must everyone warn her about Gaston? She had met him only twice and was unlikely ever to meet him again.

She stood out on her balcony and stared at the sea as she suddenly realized that everything was all right and she had not been sacked. She was so glad she wanted to dance and sing. She had known she wanted to stay at the Lambert School, but it wasn't until now, when she

The Impossible Dream

knew she *was* staying, that she realized how much it meant to her.

It was not only the beauty of the island, not only the friendliness of the girls she taught and the sweet old men who played the piano for the dancing lessons, not only Frank and his jokes and big-brother attitude, nor the German and French women who were helping her with her languages, but it was something more.

This was her home.

It sounded ridiculous. She hadn't been with them a whole term yet—and still it felt like home. This was her dreamland, the dream she had had as a child whenever she was unhappy: a land of palm trees and huge roaring waves dancing against the coral reefs, and the voices of the locals singing and laughing, the chatter of the monkeys, the sweet song of the birds...this was her home. She felt she never wanted to leave it, never to return to England and Hastings, which seemed a thousand million light-years away....

She was staying! That was all that mattered.

As THE DAYS PASSED, they slipped back into the old routines, with Megan's lessons changing as she tested each class to find what kind of dancing they enjoyed most. She had long talks with Mr. Taft about it and he agreed that that was good.

"Not what they do the best," Megan said gravely, "but what they enjoy doing most—that way they'll express themselves."

He nodded, "An excellent idea."

Some of the staff had dropped their icy disapproval, Megan's French and German lessons continued, but Miss Weston ignored Megan whenever she could. One day Megan talked to Mr. Taft as they sat on the terrace at the back, slightly above the tennis courts. He had a sheet of paper before him as they planned the number of dancers they could have for each session, for there had to be sufficient room to move them off.

"Mr. Taft, why did you say Miss Weston couldn't *help* it?" Megan asked suddenly, looking at the elderly man by her side, his dark hair slightly gray. "You wouldn't tell me at the time, but she's so very unfriendly. Did I offend her in some way?"

His grave face relaxed. "It was not your fault, my dear. You are young and attractive."

"But so is Petronella Weston. I think she's beautiful, and that husky voice...."

"I agree, but it's no competition against a twenty-year-old with an innocent, fey little frightened face."

"Is that me?" Megan was startled. "Do I look fey and frightened?"

"Sometimes." His eyes twinkled. "Not to worry, it adds to your charm. Now let's return to our work."

"No, Mr. Taft." Megan pretended to be stern, smiling at the same time as she looked at him. "You haven't told me why you were sorry for her."

"Surely," he said slowly, "you can see that she, like all the female staff, is in love with Craig Lambert."

"In love with Craig?" Megan repeated slowly. "I hadn't realized it."

"You walk as in a dream, my dear." Gently he put his hand under her chin, tilting up her head so that he could look in her eyes. "Are you sure you're not in love with him yourself?"

Megan was startled. "Of course not! Why, I've hardly known him any time."

"Love doesn't take *any time*," Paul Taft said with a smile. "Now if we could concentrate on this work...."

The Impossible Dream

"Yes, Mr. Taft," Megan said meekly, but although she listened to what he said, his voice seemed to be coming from far away, nor could she concentrate on what she had to suggest for she found his words going over and over again in her mind.

Are you sure you're not in love with him yourself?

In love—with Craig Lambert?

It was ridiculous, she told herself. Of course she wasn't. Yet she had noticed how different a room felt when Craig walked in. He had started a habit of looking in at the dancing classes, asking questions and watching the girls, and the whole atmosphere of the room seemed to change immediately. Was that love?

It couldn't possibly be, she decided. She liked him, indeed she liked him very much, for he had stood on her side, trusting her, and although there was this old family feud with the Duvals, in which Patrick seemed involved in some way, Craig had not allowed it to influence his opinion of her.

That was all it was, she decided.

But later that day, dancing with the girls on their social evening, Anarita said to her, "Is it true everyone is in love with Mr. Lambert?"

"How would I know?" Megan answered with an innocent smile.

Anarita tucked her hand through Megan's arm.

"Are you?"

Megan laughed. "Of course I'm not. I admire him, that's all."

"But you must be in love with someone," Anarita persisted. "I mean no girl can really live unless she loves someone."

"Well, I seem to be living very well. So do you, Anarita," Megan teased.

The lovely Italian-English girl looked thoughtful.

"Do I? Yet I feel unfinished. I don't feel a real me, if you know what I mean. I just can't wait to be married. It will be so... such a happening. Have you ever been in love?"

Megan thought. "No, actually I haven't. I never had a real boyfriend because of my father, and—"

"Do you mind? I mean never having had a boyfriend? Don't you feel sort of... well, as if you're not a real woman yet?"

Megan laughed. "Look, Anarita, there are millions of perfectly happy women who have never had nor ever want to have a boyfriend. That doesn't mean they're not real women. Some of us love and some of us don't."

"Well," Anarita sighed, "I don't think you're the kind who don't.... I know I'm not."

"Good grief!" exclaimed Frank Parr, slightly limping as he joined them. "I've just broken my glasses. I'll have to go in tomorrow to get new ones. Want a lift in, Meg?"

"Thanks," Megan smiled.

"Can I come, too, Mr. Parr?" Anarita asked quickly.

He looked inquiringly at Megan. Megan had been rather worried recently because every time she and Anarita went into town, Anarita got lost. Or rather, she lost Anarita, and when she found her, Anarita always accused Megan of being the one who got lost. This had been going on for some time, but lately Anarita had been "lost" for longer intervals.

"Look, Anarita," Megan said slowly, "I know you may think it's a great joke, but you are my responsibility and I don't like the way you vanish."

Anarita pouted, "I don't mean to."

The Impossible Dream

"Don't you? I sometimes wonder if you do. I don't find it funny at all."

"So if we take you, Anarita," Frank chimed in, "it's understood you don't get lost. Right?"

She looked at him. "Is it my fault if Miss Crane gets lost? I have to look for her, don't I?"

"Let's cut out that blarney stuff. You promise not to get lost?" Frank Parr demanded.

Anarita shrugged. "I promise to try not to let Miss Crane get lost."

"All right. One more chance," said Frank.

Later he talked to Megan about it.

"That girl has changed a lot in the past weeks," he said.

Megan smiled, thinking what a beautiful warm night it was, with stars sparkling in the dark sky as she and Frank stood just outside on the terrace.

"Has she?"

"Is it your influence, Meg?" he asked, looking down at her.

"I can't see what I've done to help," Megan began.

"You've made her feel that someone cares," a deep voice interrupted.

Both Megan and Frank were startled as Craig came through the open French doors.

"I apologize for overhearing what you were talking about," Craig Lambert said, "but your voices came in clear. I think it's Miss Crane who has helped Anarita, Parr. She was a difficult child from the day she came here. Do you think she's mixing better with fellow students? She's not depending on Miss Crane too much?"

"I don't think so," Frank said quickly. "She rarely has a tantrum these days—remember how she went on a hunger strike once because she failed her exams?"

he chuckled. "She was a real handful. I must say I notice a big difference in her. The deliberate cheekiness that was a form of rebellion has also vanished."

"Yes," Craig agreed. "I think we can thank Miss Crane for that," he said, and went back into the school.

Frank whistled softly. "You are in favor, Meg," he said quietly. "He's right, too. You've done Anarita a world of good."

"I'm glad if I have helped. I'm very fond of her and yet at times she puzzles me. It's as if she's laughing at me, as if... well, as if she's triumphant about something or other, somewhere she has got the better of me."

"It all sounds very complicated," Frank laughed. "We'd better go in or Miss Tucker's tongue will begin to quiver. Has she said anything more to you about our night out?"

"No. She hardly ever talks to me except about some extracurricular work."

They went inside the school. The dance hall was empty, but the record was still playing. Frank turned to Megan.

"Meg, if you don't want to then say so, but I'd like to try to dance. I've... well, maybe it was cowardice or pride on my part, but I used to love dancing. I wonder if my foot would be the handicap I thought."

"Of course I'll dance with you, Frank. Let's start the tune again." Megan ran across to the record player. "What would you like? Modern or an old-fashioned waltz?" She laughed. "The choice is yours."

"What about a nice romantic tango?"

"Okay," Megan called, putting on the record.

As the music began, Frank limped across the room, holding out his arms.

The Impossible Dream

"Oh, my love..." he chanted. "My dear and sweet love, come into my arms, my dear one...."

He put his arm around her and took her hand... and they danced. Frank's first steps were clumsy, but that, Megan knew, was from nervousness. As the music went on, his self-confidence returned and his lameness was hardly noticeable.

As the music came to an end Frank stopped, his arm still around Megan. He leaned forward and kissed her gently.

"Thank you."

"It was..." Megan began, but the words died in her mouth, for she saw over Frank's shoulder that in the doorway stood Miss Tucker, her cheeks bright red, her eyes flashing, her hand on Craig Lambert's arm. He was looking at them gravely, his eyebrows drawn together.

"You see, I told you! That's why I fetched you. When I saw how they were behaving!" Miss Tucker began. "You wouldn't believe me...."

Frank swung around, releasing Megan. He held out his hands expressively. "Just think what a fool I've been all these years, Miss Tucker. I thought I couldn't dance, but Megan has shown me I can. I feel I'm reborn." He laughed. "If you knew what it means to me to be able to dance! Well, Miss Tucker," he went on cheerfully, "at least now your girls will have another male partner to show them how it goes."

As FRANK DROVE THEM into the small town next day, Anarita chattered away happily while Megan found herself thinking of the day before and Miss Tucker's startled, almost disappointed voice as she heard what Frank had said, and Craig Lambert had walked across the floor, smiling approvingly. Poor Miss Tucker—she had looked so squashed as she almost hastened away.

"Miss Crane seems to be quite useful around here," Craig had observed with a friendly smile, and Frank had nodded.

"We needed some young blood, I think," he had said.

It was then that Craig had surprised them both as he looked grave. "I think you're right. That's been my opinion for some time, but...." He had laughed. "Well, I'm glad about the dancing, Parr. Why not practice a bit while you've got the chance?" And he had walked out, leaving them alone.

Frank had whistled softly. "He is in a good mood, Meg, my dear! Looks like you're working a miracle."

Which was absurd, of course, Megan was thinking as she sat in the back of the car because for a treat Frank had let Anarita sit in front. Despite the girl's seventeen years, Megan was thinking, Anarita was very young in some respects, and now as she sat sideways, looking at Frank, her legs curled up under her, she seemed unable to stop talking.

As the town came in sight, Frank arranged where to meet them.

"We could have a cup of coffee or something cold before we go back."

"I promise I won't let her out of my sight," Anarita said with a laugh, tucking her hand through Megan's arm. "So don't try to run away, Miss Meg."

They all laughed as they stood near the market, which was their usual meeting place. It was bright and noisy, with all the gay colors and women chattering, huge baskets of fruit and food and small children running around and playing.

The Impossible Dream

Frank walked off to see about his glasses and Megan led the way down the crowded street. It was certainly much slower with the two of them walking arm in arm, but she decided to say nothing, as Anarita must not go off on her own. Not that any harm could come to her, Megan was certain of that, but she felt responsible to Craig; he trusted her and surely that meant she should be loyal to him.

On the other side of the street she suddenly saw Tracy Thompson. He waved his hand and Anarita was pushed back a little, so Megan didn't see if she waved to the hippie artist, as they called Tracy, but Megan, who quite liked him and couldn't understand Anarita's contempt for him, lifted her hand and smiled.

Strolling past the shops, discussing clothes and what the next fashion would be, Megan caught her breath with dismay as she saw walking toward them a familiar figure. Gaston Duval!

Oh, no, she thought. Craig would never forgive her if Gaston stopped to speak to them and she had to introduce Anarita. Craig, like Miss Tucker, had a poor opinion of Gaston for some unknown reason, and it would be a wonderful weapon for Miss Tucker to use if she could say that Megan Crane was introducing the pupils to undesirable characters. Megan could almost hear Miss Tucker speaking.

Hastily she looked around. They were close to a bazaar.

"Let's go in here," she said quickly, turning to the girl by her side. "I want to look at some bracelets. I've got to get one for a present."

Anarita followed her into the shop. It was crowded and Megan went to the far end, pretending to be interested in the bracelets on display. She hated telling lies, but anything was permissible if she was to do what Craig expected of her.

"Do look at this, Anarita," she said, and wondered why her voice was so shrill.

Was she nervous, frightened of Craig's anger, she asked herself. It wasn't that, she knew very well. But she appreciated the fact that he trusted her, that he relied on her to keep her side of it. And introducing an attractive man like Gaston to a romantic-minded teenager was surely not a good idea.

The shop began to empty a little and Megan, glancing down the narrow aisle that divided the two counters, could plainly see the doorway. And Gaston Duval stood there! Waiting?

She looked around and saw that Anarita was staring at a long black-and-white beaded necklace.

"That's pretty. Are you going to buy it?" she asked, fumbling in her handbag for her wallet and hastily looking for the cheapest bracelet she could see. "It's awfully hot in here, Anarita—makes me feel I can't breathe. Would you buy that bracelet for me? I'll wait outside."

If Anarita was surprised she didn't show it. She took the money and waited patiently for the two assistants to get through their many customers and get to her.

Meanwhile, Megan had hurried outside to speak to Gaston.

"Look," she began, "I'm sorry about this, Mr. Duval, but the school is very strict about allowing the girls to come into town, and...."

He smiled. "And they mustn't meet undesirables? It is so? Ah," he laughed, "it is old-fashioned, that school, is it not? You wish me to take no notice of you? But that would be rude."

The Impossible Dream

"Hullo, Gaston... nice to see you again." Anarita's loud voice seemed to pierce Megan's head as she turned and saw the girl, so lovely, so young and so vulnerable in her white sheath dress, smiling at Gaston.

Gaston bowed. "Ah, it is Anarita Marco! But you have grown, my child. You were so young...."

Anarita laughed. "The years have gone." She turned to Megan "Why didn't you tell me Gaston Duval was visiting the island?"

"I didn't know you knew him," Megan said weakly.

"Of course I know him." Anarita laughed with some contempt. "Everyone in Europe knows Gaston Duval. Isn't that true?" she asked, tilting her head, her long black hair swinging.

He smiled at her, his eyes narrowed. "I am flattered by your remark, Anarita." He bowed. "Time has worked a miracle. You were a fat child with untidy hair, and now—" he gave another little bow, his face crinkling into a smile "—words could not describe your beauty."

Anarita laughed. "I am flattered by your remark, Gaston. I got the bracelet you wanted, Miss Crane."

Gaston lifted his hand. "Ah, but I am not right in the head. I was looking for Miss Crane as I have a message." He turned to Megan. "It is from your brother. His wife is ill—"

"Oh, no! I am sorry."

"It is not serious, so do not feel disturbed, but they would like to see you. I think Patrick needs your help. Georgina is being—how do you call it—difficult. She will not listen to him, she says she is very ill, but of course that is nonsense. She is just being...." Gaston smiled at them both, a quick intimate smile that seemed to imply that he thought the girl he looked at was the most beautiful in the world, Megan was thinking, crossing her fingers and hoping Anarita would not fall for Gaston's French charm. "Perhaps if you had a talk with her? We could go now."

"Oh, no, we couldn't," Megan said quickly. That would be the last straw in Miss Tucker's eyes, she knew. "I've got to go back to school now, but I'll come in later. I can always get a lift."

"That is good, yes? I can drive you back," Gaston promised.

"Thank you." Megan took hold of Anarita's arm. "We must go. We can't keep Mr. Parr waiting."

"Why not?" Anarita asked. "He often keeps us waiting."

Gaston laughed. "Ah, but I can see, Anarita, *chérie*, you have not changed much." He bowed to them both and walked down the street, immediately merging into the crowd.

"Anarita, where did you meet Mr. Duval?" Megan asked as they made their way down toward the market.

"Four years ago in Rome." Anarita gave a little skip. "I was thirteen then and longing to fall in love. I was staying with my father's aunt. She is the Contessa Marco and a real socialite. Of course I adored Gaston, he was so romantic. He hardly noticed me, but I didn't mind that. I knew that one day he would." She laughed happily. "Isn't he absolutely gorgeous?"

"He's very attractive," Megan agreed reluctantly, thinking that these visits to the small town might have to stop, for whatever happened, Anarita must not be encouraged to fall in love with the handsome Gaston Duval. Not even Craig would be able to forgive Megan for that, Megan was thinking as they hurried to meet Frank.

The Impossible Dream

"We met Gaston Duval!" Anarita said triumphantly as Frank came, slightly limping, toward them.

"You did what?" The shocked horror on Frank's face merely intensified Megan's dismay. "Let's have a coffee."

Sitting down under the gay red-and-yellow sunshade, they drank their coffee and Anarita told Frank excitedly how she had met Gaston four years ago.

"He didn't even see me, but today he did, didn't he, Miss Crane?" Anarita turned eagerly to the silent Megan. "You could see that from his eyes. He thought me terrific...."

"I imagine he makes every female think that," Frank said dryly.

Anarita laughed. "You're just jealous, Mr. Parr. I bet you'd like to be as handsome as that."

Megan remembered something and hastily interrupted Anarita's teasing. "Georgina, my sister-in-law, is ill, and Patrick wants me to go and see her. I wondered if you'd bring me back after we've taken Anarita back to the school."

Frank frowned. "Look, we'll drop you off after this, then I'll take Anarita back and I'll come and fetch you in, say, three hours' time. Right?"

"Frank, that would be wonderful," Megan began, but Anarita was laughing.

"You're afraid of Gaston Duval, Miss Crane? He offered to drive you back. Wouldn't you rather have him than Mr. Parr?"

Megan felt a tremor of anger go through her. "There's no need to be cheeky, Anarita. You're old enough to know better. Mr. Parr is my friend and naturally I'd prefer to come back with him."

Anarita chuckled. "I just don't believe you. I bet

Gaston's got a white sports car and never drives at less than a hundred miles an hour."

"In that case," Megan said, finishing her coffee, "I'm very glad Mr. Parr is fetching me."

Frank promised to explain why Megan would not be at the school for dinner. "I'll see Miss Tucker," he said, looking significantly at Megan, and she smiled back gratefully, knowing he would tell Miss Tucker that Anarita had met Gaston Duval at her great-aunt's castle near Rome and that it had nothing to do with Miss Crane!

But would Miss Tucker believe him, Megan worried silently. She could just hear Anarita's gay triumphant voice as she told her friends about the handsome Frenchman who had told her she was too beautiful for words to describe!

Anarita was certainly in a happy mood, Megan thought miserably, for she herself was not. Now Anarita was teasing Frank again.

"Do you honestly think I should drive back to school alone with you, Mr. Parr?" Anarita asked, her eyes dancing. "Won't Miss Tucker be shocked? Aren't you afraid you might lose your job? Don't you think it's daft, Miss Crane?" She twisted around to look at Megan in the back of the car. "I'm seventeen, yet at this miserable school I can't even have a boyfriend."

"Your misfortune, Anarita, is your money," Frank said dryly. "Your guardian is terrified you'll marry someone after your money."

"Lovely, I must say!" Anarita replied sarcastically. "Of course you're right, but it makes me mad, all the same. Anyone would think I was hideous or something if all the men think of is my money."

Frank turned and smiled at her. "Never mind, Anarita. You'll soon be twenty-one."

"Soon," she said bitterly. "Four miserable wasted years."

Frank stopped the car outside the Crane Dancing Studio.

"This is your brother's?" Anarita asked eagerly. "It looks super. Maybe you'll take me there one day?"

Megan hurriedly got out of the car. "Maybe," she said, and added silently, *maybe not!* Somehow she couldn't see Craig's agreeing to that. She only dreaded the thought of what his reaction was going to be when he heard about Gaston Duval. "Thanks a ton, Frank," she said, and he smiled at her understandingly.

"Bye!" Anarita called gaily as the car drove away.

Megan felt quite sorry for Frank, for Anarita in a gay mood could be rather irritating after a while.

Megan rang the dangling bell. A Creole girl in a flaming red dress let her in and showed her through to Patrick's small office.

He was writing a letter and looked up. "Hi! So Gaston found you?" He grinned. "Hope it didn't embarrass you too much—you had the girl with you, I hear."

Megan went to stand by his desk. "How did you know?"

Patrick laughed. "I have my spies, as well as the Lambert School. Seriously, though, I want you to tackle Georgina. She's being positively grotty. She's made up her mind she's ill, and though the doctor says she isn't, she says he doesn't know what he's talking about. I've got to get her well." His face had lost its softness as his mouth hardened. "I've simply got to, Meg."

He stood up and took her into the lounge, pouring her a cold drink and preparing one for himself.

"Do sit down," he said irritably, and straddled a

chair near her. "Look, talk some sense into Georgina's brain, Meg, or...." He sighed. "We've got to give an exhibition dance on Saturday. Now this isn't just an ordinary Saturday night. By a stroke of luck, I managed to contact one of the biggest blokes in the business and invited him for the weekend. If he likes us—our dancing, I mean—it could open up a new world for us."

He began to walk about the room impatiently, striking a fist against the palm of his other hand.

"I'm fed up to the teeth, Meg. Fed up with Gaston's wonderful ideas. He has wonderful ideas, I'll grant that, but they just seem to shrivel up. I didn't realize what we'd be up against here. That... that Craig Lambert would be too wealthy, too powerful with his influence for us to succeed in fighting. If only Gaston would accept that—but as you probably know, it's more involved because of a family feud that goes back several generations. Absolute tripe!"

Patrick went to stand by the window, his fingers restlessly pleating the white silk curtain.

"I wish I knew why Craig Lambert has this thing about us. It just isn't fair. All Gaston and I have done is to bring money into the island, get people to invest it here, even come and live here, because it's a pretty ideal life. I just can't understand Lambert, Meg. It wouldn't affect his school. All Gaston and I want is to make it a perfect holiday resort. Lambert doesn't seem to realize—or maybe I should say, doesn't *want* to realize—that it would bring more and better-paid jobs for the locals and a much better future because better schools and hospitals could be built, too. The sky's the limit. Craig Lambert is so darned greedy... he wants it all his way. I bet he's making a fortune out of that school. Apart from anything else, there's a lot of land here that no one is using. That could be built on, but he won't sell it to us."

"So you feel you want to get out of the island?" Megan asked.

Patrick swung around. "I must. It's driving me around the bend, like banging my head against a brick wall. If it wasn't for that lousy school...."

"It's a famous school, going for a long time."

"Time it was closed, it's hopelessly out-of-date. I know the millionaires like to send their little girls there, but I wonder if it's as safe as they believe." Patrick was scowling.

"I think that's why Mr. Lambert doesn't like all this... well, this publicity and tourists coming, Patrick. It used to be a quiet island on which a stranger was instantly recognized."

"Well, let him find another island where there's no one and rebuild the school. Why aren't we allowed to make money as well as he?"

Megan stood up. "Maybe I should see Georgina, though I can't think how I can help, because she... well, I don't think she's ever liked me."

"Georgina likes only one person," Patrick said bitterly as he led the way down the corridor toward the bedroom. "*Georgina Crane*, and that's the truth."

Megan went into the luxuriously furnished room rather reluctantly, for she and Georgina had never been friends, nor could Megan forget, looking at the wide double bed, the heavy rose-colored silk curtains, the beautiful dressing table, that it had all been bought with the money Patrick got from his father, money she and their father had sent him, sacrificing many things they needed.

Georgina smiled weakly. "Patrick asked you to talk sense into me?" she asked.

She was propped up by pillows, but Megan was shocked to see the difference in her face from the beautiful if hard face it normally was. Now she looked pale, her skin taut.

"What's wrong?" she asked.

"The doctor said nothing. He should have the pain I've got!" Georgina lightly touched her stomach. "Gastroenteritis, I think they call it. I think it was food poisoning. I feel like... well, ghastly, and all Pat can do is talk about Saturday night. That means more to him than I do."

"He seems unhappy here."

"Unhappy! Your brother is unhappy anywhere. If your dad hadn't spoiled him..." Georgina said bitterly. Her usually beautiful crown of dark hair was limp and lifeless, hanging around her pale tired face. "Pat expects everything to be handed to him. He can't see you have to work for it. He should have been born with a fairy's wand—or is it Dick Whittington's magic lamp? I always get confused." She laughed. "I'm sorry, Meg, but Patrick is just a spoiled brat, and as for Gaston... that man can squeeze money out of an empty turtle shell. Watch out—for your money."

"Money?" Megan said slowly, looking at the pale face before her. Now wasn't the right time, she decided, to be truthful. Money—what hope had she or her father ever had to have money when Patrick was always in need? In need.... Megan, looking around, wondered what her father's reaction would be if he could see this house and the dancing studio. "No, I've only got my salary. Look, Georgina, you may feel all right on Saturday. This sort of thing can go quite quickly sometimes."

"Sometimes," Georgina echoed. "Look, Megan, I gather you and Craig Lambert get on well. Everyone's surprised. I don't know how you do it, because from what I hear, he's absolutely the end."

"He's very nice," Megan said quickly. "Understanding and tolerant. He's... well, I just don't understand why people say such things about him."

"Maybe he's different with you. Look, Meg, I love this island and this way of living and I don't want to go. Couldn't you talk this *very nice, understanding, tolerant* Craig Lambert into seeing some sense?" she asked, sarcastically repeating Megan's own words. "All we want is to make some money. I'm fed to the teeth with debts piling up. If Craig Lambert would only be sensible."

Patrick opened the door and came in. "Visitor to meet you, Meg, so come along." He hardly looked at his wife and she was gazing thoughtfully at her fingernails, Megan noticed, as she said goodbye and followed her brother to the lounge.

He bent and whispered in her ear, "Gaston's mother. She's the one with all the money, so be nice to her."

Before Megan could reply, he was opening the door.

"Here she is," he said gaily. "Madame Duval, this is my sister, Megan."

Gaston Duval's mother, Megan was thinking as she followed him.

A small slight woman with snow-white hair stood up. She had Gaston's dark eyes and his smile.

"I have wanted to meet you," she said. "Do sit down."

Megan obeyed and they sat for a moment, just looking at each other. Mrs. Duval—or Madame Duval, for that was what Patrick had called her before he left them—was a beautiful woman, Megan thought, simply but elegantly dressed in an amber-colored silk suit.

"Yes," Madame Duval said thoughtfully. "I can see what Gaston means."

"What he means?" Megan echoed. "I...."

Madame Duval smiled. "You know, of course, that he wishes to marry you."

"Gaston?" Megan's surprise resounded in her voice as well as in the name. "I had no idea. He's... I mean, we hardly know each other."

Madame Duval smiled. "Is that so essential when you are young? You find him attractive?"

Megan blushed. "He's very...."

"'Smooth' is perhaps the best word." Madame Duval, who was obviously English, chuckled. "Ah, he can't help it. Women always collapse when he smiles at them. He has been in and out of love for many years. That's why I was so happy when he wrote and told me he wanted to marry an English girl. I came from Devonshire a very long time ago." She laughed again. "So— I thought—Gaston at last is ready to settle down. That is why I came at once."

"But... but please." Megan leaned forward. "Please, I think Gaston must have been joking. We've met only once or twice and... well...." She felt confused as well as surprised.

"I know when my son is joking." Madame Duval's voice changed a little. "He's like your brother. It's not always wise to have such wealthy parents. It spoils them. They expect to have everything on a silver platter, and when it doesn't come they're indignant, feel they've been cheated. I know it so well...."

The Impossible Dream

Madame Duval's voice seemed to be coming from far away to Megan, for she was trying to grasp one thing. Madame Duval had said, "He is like your brother," meaning Gaston was like Patrick because "it is not always wise to have such wealthy parents." What did she mean? Patrick didn't have wealthy parents. Did Madame Duval think that the Cranes were wealthy?

She realized that Madame Duval was still talking, and with an effort she concentrated on what the old lady was saying.

"I find it so amusing, you know. This family feud, I thought it was only in legends that it happened, yet it is true. When Gaston insisted on coming here, I tried to argue with him. It would be hopeless, I said. You cannot win in a battle with a man like Craig Lambert."

Megan's limbs seemed to stiffen, but Madame Duval did not notice as she went on, "I expect you know that Craig Lambert's grandfather was in love with a beautiful girl, but my father-in-law married her. I never knew her, but judging from the portraits I've seen she was very lovely indeed. Anyhow, this started a most foolish sort of feud. Everything my father-in-law did, old Mr. Lambert did his best to ruin. It was the same when we lived here, but my husband was more clever." She chuckled. "Or perhaps the luck of the Duvals had changed, for Craig Lambert's father had one great weakness. He was a gambler. My husband always won. That is how we got so much land here on the island. So when my son declared that he wanted to make this a holiday island I knew why. Gaston loved his father—they would talk for hours about the Lamberts. So—" she laughed "—I understood. But I knew it would be no good. Craig Lambert has brains and he is not a gambler. He has no weakness.

He is tough. Ruthless," she said thoughtfully, her eyes watching Megan.

"I don't think he is that," Megan said quickly. "He has the reputation of the school to consider, you know. The school means a lot to him."

"I'm not surprised—the money it must bring in."

"I don't think it's only the money..." Megan began, but stopped as she saw Madame Duval smile.

"Ah, I see that Gaston has a rival," said Madame Duval. "You *are* in love with Craig Lambert?"

Megan tried to will her cheeks from going red as she clenched her hands and made herself smile. "I admire him in many ways, but that isn't love."

"But he loves you? That's true, isn't it?" Madame Duval put her hands up to her snow-white hair and patted it. "Gaston told me so. Everyone knows that Craig Lambert is in love with you and that you can do nothing wrong."

Megan's face now was bright red, judging from the way her cheeks burned.

"That's not true! Mr. Lambert isn't..." she began, but Madame Duval laughed.

"You're so innocent—or appear so, my dear. You didn't know Gaston loved you and now you declare that Craig Lambert doesn't. It is the old feud again—a Lambert versus a Duval. I wonder who will win this time." She looked at her watch. "I must go. I have an invitation for dinner." She held out her hand and took hold of Megan's. "I am glad we have met. I think I shall like you as my daughter-in-law."

"But please...." Megan tried to speak, but Madame Duval was on her feet, opening the door, just turning with a last smile.

"That is, of course, if Gaston wins."

And then she was gone. Megan hurried to the window and saw a waiting car with a chauffeur standing ready.

She sat down on the couch, her legs suddenly weak. What did it all mean? Was Gaston in love with her or had he pretended it in the hope of pleasing his mother and perhaps getting more money? Patrick must have lied about his family and led the Duvals to believe that the Cranes were wealthy people. But what really worried Megan was who had started the rumor that Craig Lambert was in love with her? How absolutely awful if Craig got to hear of it.

It was a relief when Frank arrived and Megan gave a hasty goodbye to Patrick, then looked in on Georgina and found her asleep before hurrying out to Frank.

They had just left the town behind when Frank said, "What's wrong?"

"Just about everything," Megan admitted. "How did you get on?"

"I couldn't find Miss Tucker, so I got Lambert. I explained the situation and he quite understood."

"You mean he wasn't mad about it? Did you tell him about Gaston Duval?"

Frank chuckled. "Of course. The whole school knew within half an hour. I guessed Anarita would have a whale of a time talking, so I got in first. I told Lambert the truth, the simple truth—that you did your best to prevent Anarita from meeting Duval but that Anarita had already met him at her aunt's home in Rome, so he couldn't be mad at you about that, could he?"

Megan smiled her gratitude. "He may not want her to come in so often, though."

"That's a point." Frank jammed on the brake and then apologized. "Those damn goats! Nearly hit one of them. On the other hand, Meg, I don't think Gaston Duval is Anarita's cup of tea."

"You don't?"

Megan had not been able to hide her surprise and she saw an odd smile on Frank's lips.

"No, he's more the type girls of your age go for. Sure you're not interested?"

"No. I do find him rather... well...."

Frank chuckled. "I know."

"Frank, I'm worried about something," she confessed.

"I knew it. Weep on my shoulder, then."

"No, it's not like that, but... look, Madame Duval, Gaston's mother, was there. She's awfully nice—English, born in Devon but lived on the Continent most of her life. She said some rather odd things."

"Such as?" Frank drove carefully as they turned a blind corner. It was a dark night, the stars brightening the sky, but for once clouds had closed over the moon.

"Well, I think it sounds absolutely mad, but... but she said Gaston Duval wants to marry me."

"*What?*" The car swerved and Frank was occupied for a moment straightening it. "Sorry about that, but it was a shock. I didn't know you knew him that well."

"I don't—that's the point. I've met him only—I think three times. I'm wondering...." Megan paused. Should she be confiding in Frank, she wondered. Or was he on Craig's side? So what if he was? Wasn't she? She felt confused, her head aching. "Look, Frank, we've never been alone together. I mean, he's never...."

"Chatted you up?"

She laughed. "Of course he hasn't. I hardly know him. It seems that Madame Duval has all the money

The Impossible Dream

and she's eager for him to settle down, so I'm wondering if Gaston said it to...."

"Reassure her?"

"Yes, I suppose one could call it that. Anyhow, she came to the island on purpose to meet me and she seemed to think I would do."

"Well, that's nice, I must say. Very, very nice," Frank said dryly. "And how do you feel about it?"

"I think it's absolute...." Megan gave a little laugh. "Look, Frank, it's daft. I don't even know him."

"But you find him attractive?"

"What if I do? You don't want to marry every man you find attractive."

They could see the school in the distance.

"But, Frank," Megan said almost desperately, "that's not the end of it. She also said rumor had it that Craig wants to marry me. She said it was quite a joke, like a repetition of the reason for the old feud and she wondered who would be the winner."

Frank had slowed down as he drove into the school grounds.

"And how do you feel about that?" he asked, his voice suddenly hoarse. "Has Lambert...?"

"Of course he hasn't. That's just it, Frank. Suppose he hears the gossip?"

Frank stopped the car and turned to look at her. The light from the big house made it possible to see each other's faces.

"You haven't answered my question. How do feel about that? I mean, marrying Lambert? Supposing he did ask you?"

"Well—" Megan took a deep breath "—it isn't likely to happen. Please don't tell anyone, Frank."

"You can trust me."

"The awful part is... suppose he hears the rumor and thinks...?"

Frank laughed. "That you started it? Could be, of course. Even if he didn't, I can bet on quite a few of the staff who would accuse you of it."

He got out of the car and opened the car door for her.

"Don't worry, Meg," he said. "It'll all work out. Soon be the end of the term, anyhow. I'm just going to park the car. See you later?"

"I'm tired. I think I'll have a shower and off to bed. Thanks for everything, Frank," she called softly as he walked around the car.

The front door she found was open and Miss Tucker was walking down the hall, her back stiff with disapproval. Had she heard Megan's farewell remark, Megan wondered as she hurried up the stairs to the quietness of her flat.

CHAPTER SIX

MEGAN WAS DISCUSSING the planning of the concert with Mr. Taft when the letter came. It was delivered by hand and she recognized Patrick's handwriting. It was a few days since she had seen him and she wondered if it was to say Georgina was worse.

"Will you excuse me, Mr. Taft?" she asked.

The elderly man smiled at her. "Of course—it might be urgent. I'll take a walk outside."

He left her and went through the French windows to the terrace. What a beautiful sunny cloudless day, Megan was thinking as she opened the envelope.

As usual Patrick's writing sprawled across the page.

This is urgent, Meg. Georgina is worse and the doctor forbids her to dance. It means so much to me—better publicity, a more secure job, higher pay. Could you get Saturday off, come early so we can rehearse and you can take Georgina's place?

Megan read it twice and then folded the letter slowly, her eyes puzzled as she frowned.

"Bad news?" Mr. Taft, coming in from the terrace, asked sympathetically.

"In a way," said Megan. Saturday? That was tomorrow. Should she go? After all, Patrick was her brother. But how would Craig react? Or Miss Tucker?

"Look—" Mr. Taft folded up his notes "—suppose we postpone this for a few days? We have plenty of time and everything is going well."

"Thanks a lot, Mr. Taft. It's very good of you." Megan still had the puzzled, unhappy look on her face.

She folded her notes and went out into the garden as in a dream. Should she go and help Patrick? She knew she could dance nearly as well as Georgina. And if it meant so much to Patrick....

Deciding to ask Craig Lambert himself rather than get involved with Miss Tucker, Megan had to hunt for him, but he was nowhere to be found. No one knew where he was. Several of the staff asked her why it was so urgent. Megan had no answer for that, but she knew it was urgent, for she should ring Patrick and let him know if she could help him or not.

Suddenly she wondered if Craig was at his own house. She found Frank after tea and asked him to take her there.

Frank frowned. "Is it a good idea, Meg? Lambert doesn't like his privacy invaded."

"This is urgent," she said. "I think he'll understand."

"All right," Frank agreed.

They drove in silence, for Frank had been there once.

"Only once, mind, in all these years," he said, breaking the silence as he deftly drove over the bad road, missing the huge bushes that grew close to the gravel and sending a small group of colored parakeets screeching as they flew up out of the way. "I'll wait in the car. I hope you know what you're doing."

So do I, Megan thought, but she had a feeling Craig would understand. These past few days she had been

The Impossible Dream

expecting him to send for her, but he had seemed, she thought, rather to avoid her. Obviously Frank had convinced him of her innocence where Anarita and Gaston were concerned.

Megan stared at the lovely house as Frank stopped—the thatched roof, the huge windows, the garden bright with red and yellow roses and tall bushes that were a mass of cream flowers.

"I shan't be long," she said.

Frank gave a funny grin. "I hope I don't have to pick up the pieces."

"Craig isn't like that," she said as she got out of the car.

"That's what you think," he told her. "I wonder if you've met the real Craig Lambert yet."

Feeling far from the braveness she was posing, Megan walked down across the lawn. She paused, looking around her. There was the most lovely view...right over the bushes to the blue water. The lagoon was so quiet and still, the waves too far away to be heard. There was this quietness....

"What on earth...?" Craig's annoyed voice broke the stillness and Megan swung around to find him frowning at her.

"Could I speak to you, please?" she said. "It's urgent."

"It must be. Is that Parr out there?"

"Yes. He said he'd wait in the car. I had to see you and I was afraid you might not come back tonight and...."

"You'd better come in," Craig said. He didn't sound at all pleased and Megan followed him rather nervously.

She looked around, loving everything she saw, the

oil paintings on the walls, the cream of the rugs on the polished floors, the deep armchairs and long couch, the French windows opening onto an enclosed garden with roses climbing up the brick walls and a tiny pool in the middle.

"Sit down," Craig said curtly. "What's the trouble this time?"

Megan told him as briefly yet as completely as she could. She finished by saying, "If he satisfies this man, it might mean a whole new life for Patrick. He'd go away, and that... well, surely that would please you?" she asked.

"Why does he want to leave the island?" Craig asked.

Megan hesitated. "Well, he isn't happy here. He says there are too many frustrations, that... that things aren't working as he had hoped and...."

"His wife is too ill to dance? Can you take her place without practicing?"

"If I could go in early tomorrow morning, I can. We'll rehearse all day. I expect Patrick will use the dances I know very well."

"You did a lot in England?"

"Not so much recently. I did several years ago."

"That was before your aunt left you?"

Megan nodded. "Yes."

"Did you mind? I mean, giving up the dancing?"

"In a way, yes," she said, thinking back. "I used to enjoy the dancing because it was a sort of challenge."

"You miss it now?"

Megan was startled. "I never think of it. That's just a part of my past life."

"You'd like to do this dancing with your brother?"

She stared at the man facing her, his stern ugly face

sympathetic. How was it so many people hated him, she wondered.

"Not very much, but... but if it would help him."

Craig nodded. "I thought as much. Well, you have my permission. You can go, of course, early in the morning. I'll be going in, so I'll take you. I'll be coming over early to have breakfast at the school."

Megan hesitated. "Miss Tucker?"

"I'll settle that."

"Thank you... oh, thank you so very much," Megan said, and suddenly the words seemed to plunge out of her mouth, beyond her control. "Thank you for being so understanding," she went on. "I'm awfully grateful. But I just can't understand one thing—why are you so much against the island's coming up-to-date? I mean, it doesn't seem like you, somehow. You're so tolerant, so understanding, yet on this subject, you're...." She paused, but he said nothing, a faint smile flickering around his mouth, so she went on. "Is it fair to the islanders? I mean, wouldn't they be better off if it was a big holiday island? Better wages and things? I mean, too, it needn't affect the school, need it?" She paused, wondering if she had said too much, but he looked amused rather than angry.

"I can see you've been brainwashed," he said. "Would you really like to see this beautiful island packed with bingo halls, a casino, hotels? Don't you see that higher wages would mean that the locals would drink or gamble the money away? Do you really think I'm indifferent to the people on the island? The school means a great deal to me because I respected my grandfather and think there's a need for this kind of school, though I do feel we're out-of-date in many ways and this must be revised in the near future. As regards the locals, we have sufficient schools and hospitals already. They are my people, so I supply these. Like my grandfather, I see the locals as my children and I shall do my best to protect them from the temptations of the so-called civilized world."

"But... but shouldn't you trust them to resist temptation?" Megan asked. "I mean, you won't always be around to protect them."

"I agree up to a point, but they must first be educated enough to recognize temptation and its cost. The next generation will, I'm sure. This island was my grandfather's originally and one day it will be completely mine again," he said firmly.

Megan hesitated. He wasn't at all angry, so she felt she could talk to him frankly.

"But is it really fair to them? I mean, they mightn't all of them gamble away the money, and those that wouldn't are being... well, deprived of the money they need and would use."

He smiled. "This is, of course, the problem. But isn't it better for a very few to suffer to save the lives of a great many? While I could keep account of the visitors to the island, we were safe. Today anyone could come in. That's what worries me—drugs, thieving, drinking too much... it's changing the island already."

"But hasn't change got to come?" Megan asked earnestly. "I mean, isn't it progress?"

He stood up. "Depends what you mean by progress. Obviously we have different versions. Poor Parr, sitting out in the car—I should have asked him in. Well, is that all right? I'll take you into town after breakfast." Leading the way to the door, he spoke over his shoulder. "Just one thing. Don't tell anyone—not anyone, not even Parr—about this. That understood?"

The Impossible Dream

"Of course," Megan stood on the white paving stones outside the front door and looked up at him. "I don't know how to thank you for being so understanding."

He gave a slight rueful smile. "Sometimes I think I understand too well. See you tomorrow!"

Stepping back into the hall he watched her hurry across the lawn to the waiting car, saw Frank leap out and open the door for her and watched them drive away before closing the front door.

"Well?" Frank asked.

Megan laughed happily. "He was absolutely super. I can't think why everyone is so frightened of him or else they hate him. I find him most understanding and kind."

"You going to tell me what you wanted to ask him?" Frank inquired with a smile.

"No, I'm not. That's the condition, Frank. Craig has agreed to let me do something, but no one must know about it."

"I see." Frank whistled softly. "Very cloak-and-dagger!"

"Oh, no, it isn't." Megan laughed happily. "It's much more to protect the school. Look, is there a phone booth where I can speak without someone listening?"

Frank chuckled as he drove. "I think there's one near the hospital. You've never seen it? Good, we'll go that way. You have a phone call to make? I needn't ask to whom. Gaston Duval, I imagine."

"Then you're quite wrong..." Megan began, and her hand flew to her mouth. "Now you're trying to make me talk, and I mustn't!"

Frank chuckled. "My curiosity is aroused. I shan't be content until I know."

"I doubt if you ever will know," she told him triumphantly. "I can see no reason why you or anyone should."

One of the nicest things about Frank, she thought, was that he would accept things.

"You're dead serious?" he asked now.

She nodded. "Dead serious."

"Okay, let's forget it. Look, there's the hospital... can you see it?" He pointed to a long white building built on what looked like a plateau dug out of the side of the mountain. "One thing about this island—we don't have to go to the mainland for surgery or anything. Lambert keeps good doctors and surgeons here. There's the public call box. Lambert had a bit of a row over having it put there, but as usual he got it." Frank chuckled. "He was right, too. You go visit a friend and he's worse, so you want to stay on, you have to call someone at home. You used to be able to phone from inside the hospital but somehow it didn't work. There were complaints that people used them socially." He parked alongside the call box.

Megan soon got through to her brother. "I got your letter, Pat. I'm coming in immediately after breakfast tomorrow," she told him.

"Great!" Patrick sounded pleased. "How did you work it?"

Megan heard her voice go stiff. "Mr. Lambert consented—he realized this meant a lot to you."

"How very kind of him," Pat jeered. "You really have got him on a bit of string, Meg. I wish you could talk some sense into him."

Megan closed her eyes for a moment as she tried to keep her temper. Patrick was never satisfied. "One

The Impossible Dream

thing, Pat," she said. "No one must know it's me. That understood?"

"Not know it's you? I don't get it," said Patrick. "Why not?"

"I don't know. Perhaps it isn't considered the right thing for the dance teacher at the Lambert School to do exhibition dancing," Megan said with a laugh. "In any case, what does it matter? The main thing is that I can help you out."

"Right, Meg. I was thinking maybe we could make you look like Georgina. She's got a wig—anyhow, we'll see in the morning. Goodbye."

"How is she?" Megan began, but Patrick had hung up the receiver.

She went out to the waiting car thoughtfully. Maybe that would be a good idea—wearing a wig to make her look like Georgina.

"Okay?" Frank asked with a grin.

"Okay," she said. "Look, Frank, I think I'll have an early night as I don't want to slip up and let anyone know."

He nodded. "I bet I could...make you slip up, I mean."

Impulsively Megan turned to him. "You really are a darling, Frank. I don't know what I'd do without you."

He looked surprised and a little sad. "We are good friends, aren't we, Meg?" he asked.

"Of course we are," she told him. "You're my very best friend."

"Your best friend," he repeated quietly as the car neared the school. "I suppose I must be content with that."

CHAPTER SEVEN

THAT NIGHT, MEGAN FOUND IT hard to sleep. She couldn't forget the wistful note in Frank's strange words: *Your best friend. I suppose I must be content with that.*

What did he mean? Could he...? No, he mustn't, she thought unhappily, for he would only get hurt. She was very fond of him, in fact she loved him in a way, but it wasn't the way you loved when it meant marriage. That would be a totally different kind of love, the sort of love she felt for....

She made herself stop thinking, for she was suddenly afraid. She couldn't be in love with anyone, for there were two men in her life, and if you really loved anyone, there could be only one!

Each man meant so much to her, each man in a totally different way. When Gaston smiled, she felt wrapped in a warmth of happiness; when he talked to her, she found herself wishing he need never go. It was a strange love to her, if love it was. She found him fascinating—and yet at times she felt it must be purely a physical kind of love, not the real kind, for the real kind made you want to help him be happy, to look after him, stand up for him. Did she feel like that about Gaston?

What was the good of thinking like this, she asked herself, tossing and turning restlessly. It was a hot night and even the open screened windows brought in only more heat. Maybe she should never have come out here, she thought, for whatever she did in the future she felt was bound to hurt her.

Marry Gaston? How could she? He must have made it up to please his mother, for he had made no attempt to meet *her*, Megan thought, or to get to know her better. But if he was serious....

Marry Craig? That was completely out of the question, for he would never see her except as a rather tiresome young person with whom he had to be patient!

But if....

She jumped out of bed and swallowed two aspirin, hoping they might send her to sleep, for her mind was on dangerous ground. Craig must not be thought of in that way. He must just be thrust out of her mind.

Finally she slept, and when she awoke and saw the clock she leaped out of bed, for whatever happened she mustn't be late for breakfast! Luckily she sat next to Mr. Taft, who never asked questions, but she was startled when Craig suddenly stood up, walked across the room to her and said, "Ready, Miss Crane?"

There was a sudden silence in the usually noisy dining room and Megan knew that every member of the staff must be staring down at them, wondering why and where Mr. Lambert was taking her!

As for the girls, Megan could guess how Anarita would be talking, for she loved to appear to know everything that no one else did.

In the car they hardly talked, but as they neared the town Megan turned to the man by her side.

"I do appreciate your letting me do this, Mr. Lambert. I told my brother that no one must know it's me. I think I'll be wearing a wig as he wants me to look like Georgina."

Craig turned and looked at her, his eyebrows lifted. "That won't be easy. She has a hard face."

He left her at the Crane Dancing Studio. "Good luck," he said with one of the smiles that transformed his face. "You have more courage than most girls would have. I'll arrange for you to be collected tonight," he added as he drove off.

Megan hurried to the front door, but even as she went to ring the clanging bell, the door was opened and Patrick stood there.

"Good. I was afraid you'd chicken out. We haven't danced together in years. We'd better get to work. We've got to be good."

Where dancing was concerned, Patrick was not only a perfectionist but a hard taskmaster. She was quite exhausted when they stopped for a coffee break. Then she had the chance to ask how Georgina was and Patrick looked surprised.

"Didn't I tell you she was in hospital? The doctor doesn't seem to know what's wrong, so she's in under observation. That reminds me...." He hurried from the room and returned in a few moments with a dark wig, tossing it to Megan. "Try it on."

The wig was made in the elaborate built-up way Georgina's hair was set, but Megan couldn't even fit it on, for her own blond hair was too long and thick.

Patrick, pacing the room impatiently, was annoyed. "We'll get in Louis—he's Georgina's hairdresser—and see what he can do. I've also got a makeup girl and after lunch the dressmaker is coming to alter Georgina's dresses, because she's much bigger built that you and we can't have the dresses falling off."

"Is the man here, Patrick?" Megan asked.

"The man?" Patrick looked puzzled for a moment.

The Impossible Dream

"Oh, yes, *the* man. Yes, he is. Now let's have another go...you weren't too good...."

Back to the studio they went, and Megan danced as she hadn't danced for years. In a way she was enjoying it. Patrick was a good dancer when he was in a good mood...but she decided she wouldn't like to be his permanent partner, for he had a nasty habit of shouting at her if the slightest thing went wrong.

They had a light lunch, then the dressmaker, a tall dark-haired woman, came, pursing her lips thoughtfully as she tightened Georgina's dresses so that they fitted Megan—beautiful, expensive, pearl-decorated dresses, one white, one green. Louis, the hairdresser, worked hard, but when he had finished and they all looked at Megan's reflection in the mirror, Louis shook his head sadly.

"I could never make you look like Georgina. You are too different, but you are both beautiful."

Patrick said much the same, though not so politely.

"It can't be helped—we'll just say nothing to the man. He knows I dance with my wife and he may take it for granted that you are my wife, and if he's heard she had dark hair, we can always say it's dyed. Now...."

Back to work, and when the time came to bathe and dress ready for the evening, Megan ached all over. It was only because she was out of training, she told herself, but all the same, she was glad this was a one-night show!

Everything was different when the moment came. The excitement raced through Megan's veins like magic as Patrick led her into the huge ballroom at the hotel, bowing to the audience while Megan curtsied. There were several flashes of light and she could see some of the visitors standing near the orchestra with small cameras. Then the music began....

It was the music that had the magic in it, the rhythm, the harmony, as they began to dance. She had no feeling of nervousness, no worry at all as she simply relaxed and let the music lead her.

Afterward as they bowed again and again to the roar of applause, Megan seemed to come back to life. It had been like a dream....

"You are so good a dancer," exclaimed Gaston, coming to stand close beside her, taking her hand in his and kissing it. He looked around, but Patrick had vanished. "You are so much better than Georgina. You should be Patrick's partner. You will dance with me?"

The orchestra had begun to play again and gradually the great empty floor was getting covered with dancers. Gaston took her in his arms and they danced.

Megan felt his cheek brushing hers, his fingers curled around her hand. He turned his head to smile at her.

"My mother—she told you?" he asked.

"She told me what?" Megan hedged for time, for he had startled her.

"That we are to be wed." He smiled almost triumphantly.

"But that's absurd..." she began.

"Why is it absurd?" he asked as the music stopped and they came to a standstill. She saw that he had danced her off the main floor and they were standing in a quiet deserted corner near the bar. He kept his arm around her, turning so that they stood side by side as he bent and kissed her.

Even as he did, there was a sudden flash of light, and Megan pushed him away.

"What was that?" she asked sharply.

Gaston frowned. "What was what?"

"That light... it flashed."

"Probably a car outside. It happens as they park." He pulled her close to him again. "Tell me, Megan, why is it absurd? You will not marry me, is that what you say?"

"Look, Gaston." Suddenly Megan knew beyond a shadow of doubt that though Gaston had a strange effect on her, it was not love. "I don't know you and you don't know me."

"We could learn to know each other. It makes my mother happy," Gaston began, his face breaking into the smile that must, Megan thought, have broken the proverbial thousand hearts.

"That's why you want to marry me, isn't it?" she asked him.

He looked startled, his arm falling down. "You are suggesting...?"

"Miss Crane?" Craig's deep authoritative voice interrupted them. "There you are. I couldn't find you. I've come to fetch you." He came striding across the end of the room toward them.

Gaston moved forward. "It is far too early. The evening has not begun."

Craig looked at him with contempt. "The evening, as far as Miss Crane is concerned, is over. I agreed to her dancing with her brother."

"But not with me?" Gaston smiled. "You are her guardian?"

"No, I'm her employer. Collect your things and change, Miss Crane. My car will be outside the studio."

Megan hesitated as she looked from one man to the other. It was the first time she had seen them together and the difference in them was almost amazing. Craig, a well-built man with his square chin, high forehead, short dark hair, dark eyes and that ugly yet handsome look, made Gaston look like a university student with his long curly hair and that strangely fascinating smile. Craig was a man, but Gaston....

"Yes, Mr. Lambert," she said meekly. "I'll be as quick as I can."

She turned and hurried out of the hotel and into Patrick's house, went to the guest room where her clothes were, hastily changed, removed the makeup and brushed out the carefully curled hair.

Craig was in the car when she went outside. He didn't speak as he drove away and then abruptly, without looking at her, said, "Your dancing was superb. I wonder why Patrick didn't make you his partner."

Megan turned eagerly. "You saw us?"

"Of course. Unfortunately I came in a little late, so I missed the first dance. He's a good dancer, too, your brother."

"He's a perfectionist. I wouldn't like to work for him. Maybe that's why he and Georgina keep quarreling—he's so convinced he's always right."

A smile hovered around Craig's mouth. "Maybe he is."

Megan laughed. "Maybe, but he needn't shout about it."

"Did the man you said would be there say anything? I mean, offer him the job he wants?"

Shrugging, Megan shook her head. "I have no idea. As soon as we stopped dancing, Patrick vanished and...."

"Gaston Duval took over," Craig said dryly. "Is he serious?"

The Impossible Dream

Startled, Megan looked at him. "Serious? Oh, I see what you mean. He says he is, but I think he's only saying that to please his mother."

"His mother?" Craig's voice changed. "You've met her?"

"Yes, the other day. It seems Gaston wrote and told her he was going to marry me."

"Marry you?" Craig's voice rose. "Are you out of your mind?"

Megan laughed a little uncertainly. "Of course not. It's just what he says, that he wants to marry me, but I don't think he does."

"Then why?"

"Because, as I said, he wants to please Madame Duval. She's English."

"I know. I met her many years ago when I was a schoolboy—a beautiful woman but hard as nails. Gaston is an only child and very spoiled."

"That's what she said—" Megan stopped abruptly as she glanced at him. "She said he was like Patrick, and I think she's right. Patrick can get anything out of my father, anything he wants." She added wistfully, "Dad never loved me. He just makes use of me."

"He may be the type of man who finds it difficult to show emotion."

"He shows plenty over Patrick," Megan said bitterly.

"So when young Gaston told you he was going to marry you, what did you say?" Craig's voice had changed, was almost accusing.

"I said it was absurd, that we didn't know each other and... well, then you came along."

"And had I not come along?" They were nearing the school now as Craig asked that.

Megan looked at him. "I'd have said the same. I don't even know him."

"But you find him very attractive?"

"Well...." she hesitated. "He is rather fascinating...that smile and.... But that isn't love," she added solemnly.

"It isn't?" Craig drew up outside the school front door and turned to look at her. "Then what is love?"

"I...." She looked around her, anywhere away from his eyes, which seemed to be looking right into her mind. How could she tell him the truth, the truth she had known as Craig stood by Gaston and she could compare them, the truth that she loved Craig, loved him with every single inch of her. "Loving is wanting to make a person happy, to feel the person needs you."

"A romantic idealist!" Craig sounded amused. "You're very young," he added, getting out of the car and walking around.

But she was too fast for him, battling with the car handle but getting out as he reached her. *You're very young,* he had said. Just as she had thought and feared, that was how he saw her.

Fortunately she was so exhausted physically that her worried thoughts failed to keep her awake and she was asleep almost as soon as her head touched the pillow. In the morning, her body ached a little and her limbs felt stiff, but it was Sunday, so there wasn't much to do. She managed to avoid the rest of the staff. After lunch she slipped away to sit with her book in a shady corner sheltered by great rocks balanced perilously on one another, the shade supplied by the palm trees. But she couldn't read. She sat, her hands clasped around the book as she gazed blindly into the distance.

Now she was in real trouble, she told herself. There

The Impossible Dream

was no doubt in her mind whatsoever—it was Craig she loved.

Could there be anything more impossible than that? First of all, there had been her impossible dream of the island, and she had found it. Now there was the impossible dream of being Craig's beloved wife.... What hope had she that such a thing could ever come true?

Craig saw her as a very young person. It was not a passionate or exciting description. A young person he was sorry for and very patient with... not the sort of woman he would seek to be his wife.

What sort of woman would he love, she wondered. Someone with a husky voice and beautiful features like Petronella Weston?

It was four days before she knew. And as it was in a time of shocked surprise, the knowledge didn't help in the least.

It all began with a curt order from Miss Tucker to present herself immediately, so Megan hurried to the headmistress's room. As she entered she saw that Craig was standing by Miss Tucker's side, both silent as they watched Megan walk across the room.

Never had the room seemed so long, never had Megan felt so nervous, for never had she seen Craig look like that....

He held out a newspaper. "Look!" he said curtly.

Megan's hands were trembling as she obeyed. She caught her breath with dismay, for it was the island's newspaper and on the front page were two photographs: one of her dancing with Patrick; the other of her in Gaston's arms as he kissed her.

The headlines were Famous Lambert School's Dance Teacher finds Romance.

"I...." Megan looked up, horrified, unable to speak.

"I told you that no one was to know you were taking part in the exhibition dancing, Miss Crane." Craig's voice was cold as ice; it seemed to cut its way through her. "You knew they were taking photos?"

"I saw a few flashes. I thought it was the hotel's guests." Megan's hand flew to her mouth. "I did ask Gaston what it was, but he said a car's headlights as it parked. I had no idea. I told Patrick that no one was to know!"

"A likely story!" Miss Tucker chimed in. "The harm you've done to the school since you came! You should never have—"

"Miss Tucker, kindly leave this to me," Craig snapped.

The headmistress looked as if she was about to explode, but she moved back, sat down and waited.

"I told Patrick..." Megan said. "He told me he wanted the man to think I was Georgina...."

"Your name is there," Craig snapped. "Georgina, it seems, is in hospital. This is not the type of publicity we're seeking."

Megan was very close to tears. "I'm terribly sorry, Mr. Lambert. It was awfully good of you to let me help Patrick, but if I'd thought anything like this would happen...." She stopped speaking, pressing the back of her hand against her mouth. "I had no idea...."

"I don't know what to say," Craig told her slowly. "I trusted you."

Miss Tucker exploded. "I told you not to. We don't want girls of that caliber here. I told you from the beginning that she was most unsuitable, quite apart from her being mixed up with those dreadful people."

The Impossible Dream

"That's all, Miss Crane," Craig, ignoring the angry woman by his side, said curtly. "I would suggest that for the next few days you remain in your flat. I'll arrange for food to be sent up. It will give you a chance to complete the dancing program for Mr. Taft."

"Stay in my flat?" Megan, feeling stunned, echoed.

"Yes," he said curtly. "We may get journalists here and I don't want you to make things worse."

Megan looked at him, her eyes filling with tears. "Please believe me," she said. "I had no idea, no idea at all. If I had...."

The tears were so horribly near falling that she turned and ran, hurrying across the hall and up the stairs, going into her flat and flinging herself on the bed.

How could Patrick have been so wicked? So cruel? So selfish—for this would mean the end of her job. She wouldn't be asked back next term, that was for sure, she thought as she wept.

BUT WORSE WAS TO COME, for on the third day Miss Wilmot arrived, coming to see Megan in her flat.

"Miss Wilmot?" Megan said, delighted to see someone who would break the miserable loneliness she was suffering, and went forward eagerly to greet her but stopped dead as she saw the anger on Clara Wilmot's face.

In her hands were several English newspapers as well as a French one. "The harm you've done with these photographs—and the news," she said. "Parents are ringing me from all over the world. This isn't the sort of publicity they or we want. How could you behave so badly? It was good of Mr. Lambert to give you the job in the first place, despite your unfortunate relationship with Patrick Crane and Gaston Duval. How could you do this to him?"

Suddenly the most awful thing happened, for Clara Wilmot's composed, beautiful face seemed to crumple and she sank into a chair, her hands hiding her face.

"How could you...how could you do this...to Craig?"

Megan stood stiffly and silent. So Clara, too, was in love with Craig?

"I knew nothing about it, Miss Wilmot. I told Patrick I was allowed to help him but that no one must know and.... I don't suppose you believe me," Megan added.

Miss Wilmot lowered her hands. Streaks of mascara ran down her cheeks. "The Lambert School means so much to Craig—I know that. I know, too, that it needs to be modernized, that Miss Tucker must go, but Craig's heart is too soft about her. She's due to retire next year, so he wanted to wait until then...but this...." Clara Wilmot touched the newspapers. "Goodness only knows the harm you've done. Gaston Duval is known everywhere as a jet-set playboy, kissing every girl he meets. I'd have thought you'd have more sense. How can we trust the girls with you? As for letting them photograph you...."

"I didn't—" Megan bit her lip. No one would believe her. She knew that. No one at all, least of all Craig.

"Look—" Clara Wilmot's voice changed, became almost wheedling "—the best thing you can do is to resign and leave the island. Craig won't want to hurt you. But if you go, he'll be glad. You're nothing but a nuisance. In any case, when I come out here permanently, I wouldn't keep you. I consider you far too young. Next

The Impossible Dream

year, when Miss Tucker goes, I'm going to be headmistress. Craig and I will run the school together."

Megan began to see light—and she didn't like what she saw.

"You and Craig...?" she said slowly.

Clara Wilmot nodded. She went to the mirror and cleaned her face, speaking over her shoulder.

"Of course. We've known for years, but there was no hurry. We're still young."

"And... and you think I should resign?"

Clara Wilmot swung around, looking pleased. "It's the only solution. Write a note to Mr. Lambert and I'll arrange for your flight back to England. There, that's not too bad," she said, peering closely in the mirror. "Goodbye," she added, leaving the flat.

Megan stood very still, her hands pressed to her face. Yes, now that she came to think of it, Clara Wilmot was the sort of woman Craig would marry. Beautiful, dignified yet efficient, witty, friendly yet firmly sure of herself in every way, she would make a perfect wife.

Suddenly the tears won and Megan flung herself on the bed, hugging the pillow tightly as she cried. Why, oh, why had she ever come out here, she asked herself miserably. It could only lead to heartache. It had already led, and there was nothing she could do about it. Nothing at all.

CHAPTER EIGHT

MEGAN HAD TO FACE UP to the truth: Miss Wilmot was right. There was only one thing to be done. Megan knew she must hand in her resignation.

Craig was too kindhearted to do it himself, but as Miss Wilmot said, he would be glad to be rid of the dance teacher who had caused so much trouble!

Looking at the clock, Megan saw that soon her lunch would be brought to her on a tray. If she wrote the letter quickly, she could give it to whoever brought the tray and ask her to take it straight to Mr. Lambert.

It wasn't an easy letter to write. In fact, she crumpled up three attempts until finally she decided it was the best she could do.

> Dear Mr. Lambert, I am sorry I have caused so much trouble. I hope you will believe me when I say I didn't mean to. I can't help feeling that the best thing is for me to leave the school, so may I hand in my resignation? I am sorry, as I am very happy here, but I really do think it is the only thing I can do.
>
> Yours sincerely.

She signed it, reread it to make sure her spelling was right and then found an envelope. She had just sealed it when there came a knock on the door and Odette brought in her tray.

"Please give this immediately to Mr. Lambert," Megan asked.

Alone again, Megan had no appetite at all and she played with the food. So that was that... the end. The end of her dream, the end of everything.

Now she would have to plan what to do next. Miss Wilmot said they would fly her back to England, and once there, what sort of job could she get without proper training? What kind of reference would Craig give her? Perhaps she could go back to Mrs. Arbuthnot in Hastings.

She went out on to the balcony and breathed in the warm fragrant air. How still the lagoon was. She turned to look at the mountains that dominated the island. How she loved it all, and soon she would see it for the last time as the schooner took her to the mainland and the waiting plane.

There was a knock on the door, so thinking it was Odette again Megan called, "Come in!"

She was startled to see, as the door opened, that Craig stood there. He pushed the door to behind him and came toward her, her letter in his hand.

"What's this nonsense about?" he demanded.

"I... I thought you'd like me to go."

"It has nothing to do with my liking anything," he told her impatiently. "If I allow you to leave it will look like an admission of guilt, and I don't believe for a moment that you were to blame for what happened."

Megan clasped her hands tightly. "I'm most grateful. Please... I honestly had no idea."

"I know you hadn't. I've told you before that you're a rotten liar. Sit down." He jerked a chair out from the side of the table and straddled it.

Megan sat down slowly on the edge of the armchair, holding herself stiffly as she waited.

Craig stared at her. "Do you think your sister-in-law was really ill?" was the first question he shot.

Megan was startled. "Yes, I did... I do think so. I've never seen her look like that before. Her hair was in an awful mess and her face very white."

"Well, there is such a thing as makeup. I've just phoned the hospital and they say she's been discharged and that there's nothing wrong with her."

"I can't understand it. That's what her doctor said, but honestly... honestly, she looked dreadful. So pale and...."

"I see. As I said, there is such a thing as makeup, of course," he said dryly. "It was obviously a plot designed by someone to cause bad publicity to the Lambert School. You agree?"

Megan nodded miserably. It could only be the truth.

"Unless... unless the photographers were there because Mr.... Mr....." She paused.

"You mean the important man your brother wanted to impress? What was his name?"

"Yes." Megan hesitated, for she didn't know it.

"Was there such a man?" said Craig. "Or was your brother playing on your sympathies?"

Megan brushed her hair back with her hand.

"I don't know," she confessed. "I didn't think it at the time, but... but now that you ask me, I do remember saying to Patrick something about *the man* and he—Patrick, I mean—said something like 'The man? What man? Oh, yes, the man.' I thought then it was rather odd. As if he...."

"As if there was no man at all. That's what I believe. I must say the whole thing seems to me like a woman's scheming. What about your sister-in-law? Was she eager for you to take her place as her husband's partner?"

"We didn't talk about it. You see, when I saw her it was several days before she was taken to hospital. There was no question then of my taking her place."

"Do you think she would have minded?"

Megan sighed. "I honestly don't know. When I went there to rehearse, as I said, she had gone. I know she wasn't very keen on impressing the man."

"She mentioned him then?"

"Yes. She said Patrick was more concerned with the man's opinion than with her feeling so ill. She doesn't want to leave the island. She loves it here."

"I see." Craig looked thoughtful for a moment, gently tugging at his ear. "Was Madame Duval there at the time?"

"Gaston's mother?" Megan asked, then felt uncomfortable because of the way Craig looked at her. "Yes. I was with Georgina when Patrick came and told me I had a visitor. I went with him, and that was when I met Madame Duval."

"How did you get on with her?"

"I rather liked her. She was most friendly."

"And very bitter about me, of course."

"Not really, just resentful, because she feels it couldn't make any difference to you letting Gaston make money here."

Craig gave a little grunt. "Sometimes it's convenient to be blind to the truth. I wouldn't trust her. Like most mothers, she's completely amoral when concerned about her children. They don't want the school to stay here. They want to close it down and have the whole island to themselves. They think that if they make life impossible for the school—and they've done their best in the past with anonymous letters and malicious gossip—I might go back to my real work and sell them the island."

"Your real work?" Megan asked.

His face relaxed a little. "I'm an archaeologist by desire. I gave it up when my father died and I had to come here to take over. This is my responsibility. I respected my grandfather very much. He was good to me, understanding and stepping in where my father wouldn't bother, so I felt I owed it to my grandfather to do my best to keep his ideal of a school going. Of course, as I've said before, we must change quite a few things here. I plan to start that next year...." He frowned suddenly. "I mustn't waste time chatting like this."

He stood up and looked at her thoughtfully. "I think everything has been smoothed out now and even the irate parents have accepted Miss Wilmot's diplomatic letters." He smiled. "She's an amazing person. I often wonder what I'd do without her."

Megan thought that what Clara Wilmot had said must be the truth. Next year Miss Tucker would go, Craig would marry Clara and they would modernize the school.

Craig walked toward the door. "Only ten more days before the end of the term, so we'll return to the routine." He looked at his watch. "How time flies! Look, Frank Parr is going into town tomorrow as he's having trouble with his new glasses. I suggest you go with him and call on your brother." At the doorway he paused. "You might shock him into truthfulness for once," he added as he went out.

Megan stood up, standing very still, her hands

The Impossible Dream

pressed to her face hard. So now what? She was staying, but....

For how long? Next year, when Miss Wilmot became Mrs. Lambert and took over, the first person to be sacked would certainly be Miss Crane!

However, now she was free to return to her usual duties, so she hurriedly changed her dress and went down into the school, seeking Mr. Taft as she had been studying his notes and there were several questions. He was friendly as usual and no reference was made to her behavior. Dinnertime would have been a nightmare, but Frank took care of her, seating her between himself and Mr. Taft. No one spoke to her except them; in fact, she had a strange feeling of not being there because it was so obvious that Petronella Weston and the other staff had decided to stay far from her in case they got involved!

Afterward Anarita came up, her dark hair swinging, her lovely face happy.

"We threatened to go on strike, Miss Crane, when we heard you were housebound, but Mr. Lambert explained it was to protect you from the journalists. Miss Crane, it was such fun. There were journalists and men with cameras and it was just like war; we weren't allowed out so we waved from the windows...." She laughed happily. "Are you going to town tomorrow with Mr. Parr? I know he's going, only I'd like to go, too."

Megan hesitated, very conscious that several members of the staff were looking at her disapprovingly; they were probably afraid that some of her "wickedness" might come off on poor Anarita.

"It's rather awkward, Anarita. You see, I was going to see my brother and—"

Anarita laughed. "He's out-of-bounds as far as I'm concerned. Right? I only like going with you, Miss Crane. The other girls get lifts in, but I wanted to wait for you."

Megan smiled. "That's nice of you. Look, why not ask Mr. Lambert yourself? Say I wasn't sure if he'd agree." She looked around. "There he is. Come on, I'll go with you."

Craig was standing on the terrace talking to Petronella Weston. He turned with a frown as Megan and Anarita went up to them.

"Well? What is it this time?" he asked.

Anarita spoke first. "Could I go into town tomorrow with Miss Crane?"

"Of course you can," Craig said irritably. "You always do."

"I wondered..." Megan began.

Craig scowled. "Don't wonder, just do what I say. I told you life had returned to normal." He turned away almost rudely.

Anarita giggled as they walked away. "He's in one of his moods! Anyhow—" she gave a little skip "—that'll be nice. See you tomorrow, Miss Crane," she said, and danced away to join her friends.

Megan returned to her flat. She felt she didn't want questions, comments—or, what was even worse, to be sent to Coventry, which seemed to be what most of the staff were doing.

Tomorrow.... But how was she to see Patrick if Anarita was with her? Could she ask Frank to chaperon Anarita for an hour or so? It was all so old-fashioned, Megan thought restlessly. Yet she remembered she had been told that girls in Spain and Italy are chaperoned even today, so perhaps it was wiser, in a school where there were so many different types and nationalities, to be on the safe side.

The next day Anarita was waiting by the car when Megan joined her. Frank was sitting behind the wheel, listening to Anarita's chatter. Not that it stopped once they were in the car, for Anarita seemed thoroughly miserable.

"I've just heard, Miss Crane, that I've got to stay here for the holidays. I'm so mad! I thought I'd be going to Rome this time, but my aunt is ill and none of my other relatives will have me, so my guardian says I must stay here...."

Megan, twisted around in the front seat so that she could talk to Anarita, smiled. "Is that so terrible?"

"It certainly is. At least it will be this time. There are only eight of us and the others are kids—no one of my own age group. Are you going to stay for the holidays, Miss Crane?"

Megan was startled. Somehow she hadn't really worried about it, but it was a problem. If she didn't, or couldn't, stay, where could she go? Certainly not to Patrick's. She felt so angry with him that she knew there was going to be a really big row. She had done her best to help him and what had he done in return? Made her look an absolute heel, someone not to be trusted, someone cheap and nasty—if it *was* Patrick, of course. But the more she thought of it, the more she felt Craig was right, for who else could it have been? Patrick had talked of *the man*, had said Georgina had to go to hospital, and he must have known about the photographers and given the press her name, although she had told him that no one must know she taught at the Lambert School.

The car was approaching town as Anarita leaned over

the side, pointing toward the jetty. "Look, Mr. Parr, isn't that the schooner? I didn't know they came on Saturdays."

"They don't usually," said Frank, swerving deftly to avoid a herd of goats strolling across the road. The small pastel-painted houses were coming closer now and they could plainly see the jetty going out into the harbor. "There was a breakdown of some kind, so it didn't go yesterday." He glanced at his watch. "It'll probably go about four o'clock or a little later."

"Look, Miss Crane," Anarita said excitedly. "There's a baby monkey on his mother!"

"So there is," said Megan, a little puzzled, for they were always seeing monkeys and as a rule Anarita ignored them. "Got some shopping to do, Anarita? I want some toothpaste and some airmail-letter forms."

She should write again to her father, she knew, though he never bothered to answer her letters. But he would have seen the headlines in the papers and perhaps even her photographs and might be wondering what she was up to. If he cared, that was, she thought unhappily.

Frank dropped them as usual just below the noisy colorful market and Megan led the way to the post office, Anarita following meekly by her side.

As they left the post office they met Tracy Thompson, the artist, in his trendy gear.

"Hi!" he said in his friendly manner.

Anarita turned her back and strolled a few steps away to pretend to look in a shop. Megan frowned. Even if Anarita preferred older men, that was no excuse to be rude.

"Hullo," Megan said in a friendly way. She liked this hippie-type artist, for he had good manners, and she liked his long curly brown hair that was so clean it shone in the sunlight. "How are things?"

"Not too bad," he told her. "I'm pretty lazy. Not used to this heat. It makes me sleepy when I should be painting." He glanced at Anarita's back and looked at Megan with a wry smile. "Why is she mad at me?" he asked.

Megan laughed. "At the moment she's mad at everyone. I'm sorry she's like it."

"An adolescent temperament," Tracy said with a grin. "Be seeing you!" He walked away, merging into the crowd.

Megan joined Anarita. "There's no need to be rude," she scolded.

Anarita laughed. "You don't know that type. Give them a smile and they're after you. I don't like being pinched."

"But he's not Italian."

"It isn't only Italians who pinch," Anarita said with a sigh of exasperation that made Megan feel about sixty years old.

"Let's—" she began, and stopped, for—blocking their path—Gaston Duval and his mother stood.

"My dear child!" Madame Duval exclaimed, holding out her hands as she looked admiringly at Anarita. "You remind me of your mother. She was a beautiful woman, too."

Gaston's hand was under Megan's elbow. She shivered a little and he obviously took it as encouragement, for his fingers tightened, digging into her flesh.

"Let's have a cold drink," said Anarita. "I'm thirsty."

"But..." Megan began, then paused. Back to normal, Craig had said, so how could she refuse to let Anarita have cold drinks with people she had obviously known for years? She could see no choice, so she walked with them to the café, then they sat near the road, under a green-and-white sun umbrella.

Gaston talked to Megan. "What a tyrant that man of yours is, is he not?" he asked her. "The way he has no manners at all. We had danced but once, and...."

Megan drew a breath. If he was involved in the conspiracy he had no right.... But was he involved? That was the question.

"I heard Georgina was discharged from the hospital as being perfectly well," she said, her voice sharp.

Gaston shrugged. "The hospital, they are perhaps mad. Like her doctor. But who is the one to know the pain? I say to Patrick, this is a serious matter. Take her to the mainland. Go and find a proper doctor."

"I was told the doctors here were very good."

"'Good'!" Gaston said scornfully. "What is good on this island?"

Angry yet not wanting to make a scene there in public, Megan turned to Madame Duval and found to her amazement that Anarita and Gaston's mother were talking in Italian.

Madame Duval, who had looked a little depressed, Megan had thought, seemed to have changed completely. Her face had brightened, her eyes were sparkling. She even clapped her hands, nodding her head so that her small mountain of white hair swayed gently. Then she seemed to remember Megan and turned quickly.

"I'm sorry, my dear. How very rude of us, talking Italian when I know you can't speak it." She smiled at Anarita. "You're just like your mother, my dear—full of bright ideas. I hope it works out. And what did Mr.

Lambert say about your portrait in the paper, Miss Crane?" Madame Duval asked, her voice amused.

"He wasn't at all pleased," Megan said, her voice controlled. "Nor was I."

"Ah, but why? It was just a warning...to our friends, perhaps?" Madame Duval chuckled happily. "You're staying for the holidays, Anarita? I shall be here. Maybe you could come to me?" She looked inquiringly at Megan, who had caught her breath. "What do you think, Miss Crane?" Madame Duval continued. "You, too, for I imagine you've got nowhere to go. That would be very nice, wouldn't it, Gaston?"

"But of course," he said quickly with that special smile of his, but this time it left Megan completely cold. "We would have fun, that I am sure."

"I imagine Anarita's guardian would have to be consulted," Megan said coldly.

She saw the quick look that Gaston and his mother exchanged, so she went on, "Anarita, I have some shopping to do, so we must go. If you'll excuse us, Madame Duval."

"So soon?" Madame Duval looked disappointed and then she smiled at Anarita. "But perhaps it is not too soon."

Finally Megan managed to get Anarita away and they walked down the street toward the market.

"We're much too early, you know," said Anarita.

"I know, but...."

"Why don't you like my meeting the Duvals, Miss Crane?" Anarita asked. "They're nice people."

"I know, but...." Megan hesitated. What could she say? Then she had a bright idea. "I think Mr. Lambert is afraid you'll fall in love with Gaston."

"That layabout?" Anarita's scorn was harsh and

startled Megan. "He lives off his mother and likes to think every girl falls for him. Well, I'm one who doesn't. I like my men...."

"To be older?" Megan laughed.

Anarita paused outside one of the big bazaars.

"Let's go in here. I hear they have some super silk scarves," she said. "Down at the end." She pointed to a crowd of plump Creole women in their bright dresses, all talking at the top of their voices, laughing happily, standing around a table.

"It's a bit of a crush..." Megan began, holding back, but Anarita caught her by the hand.

"Come on, Miss Crane. We just push like they do!"

The scarves were there. They were silk, in beautiful colors. Megan picked one up in her hand to look at.

"Isn't it lovely, Anarita?" she said to the girl by her side, turning to look at her.

Her heart seemed to skip a beat, because Anarita wasn't there! Dropping the scarf, turning around, trying to push her way through the crowd of women, Megan tried not to feel frightened, for surely Anarita was only playing her favorite game again. But it was a nightmare as she forced her way through the groups, trying to find the girl, but she wasn't in the bazaar, Megan was certain finally. Outside the bazaar in the hot humid air, she shook back her hair and looked up and down the street. Anarita was just having a rather stupid joke! She would find her demurely waiting for Frank and his car.

But Anarita wasn't there. Frank was, though, and Megan told him quickly what had happened.

"Not again?" he said, and frowned. "Honestly, Meg, I'd have thought you'd have more sense!"

Megan's eyes stung. That was hard coming from Frank. What would Craig say?

"Anarita went in the bazaar and there were so many

people there, but it all happened so quickly. I spoke to her and looked around and she wasn't there...."

Frank frowned again. "That child needs a good spanking. It's not my idea of a joke."

"Nor mine."

"Look, Meg, you search down that side of the street and I'll do this side. I'll bet she's hiding somewhere just to see us looking worried. All that girl wants is attention."

"And love," Megan put in quickly.

"She doesn't deserve love when she deliberately gets you into these messes. We've asked her so many times not to get lost," snapped Frank, sounding exasperated.

"I know. Well, I'll try this side," Megan said miserably.

It was hard going: fighting to get into a shop, fighting to walk around, looking everywhere, and then another fight to get out, so when Megan met Madame Duval walking slowly along the sidewalk she almost ran to meet her.

"Have you seen Anarita, Madame Duval?" Megan asked, her face flushed and dusty, her hair hanging listlessly, her eyes tired.

"Anarita?" Madame Duval smiled. "I saw her go with you."

"I know she did. We went into a crowded bazaar and...."

"She vanished?" Madame Duval sounded amused. "Girls of that age have a weird sense of humor. Her mother was much the same. We wouldn't think it funny, but she did. How she would laugh and—"

"I'm terribly sorry," Megan said desperately, "but I'm afraid I must look for her."

"But of course," Madame said with a smile.

As she left her and pushed her way through the noisy crowds, Megan wondered why Madame Duval looked so amused. To Megan it was not funny, not funny at all. Craig had been so patient with her, so tolerant—but if she had really lost Anarita this time, what would he say?

At the end of the street she stopped. She couldn't see Frank in sight. Perhaps he had worked his way down faster than she had. She saw a public telephone booth and on an impulse hurried into it.

She got through to the Lambert School with blessed quickness, but the slightly singsong voice of the young clerk who handled the school's switchboard irritated her.

"No, I don't want Miss Tucker," Megan said again and again. "I want Mr. Lambert. It's urgent."

"Urgent? You are hurt?" the girl asked, sounding alarmed.

Megan gripped the earpiece. Whatever happened she mustn't cause a panic. "No, I just want to speak to him. It's important. Tell him it's Miss Crane."

"Oh, Miss Crane, of course! I didn't recognize your voice!" the girl said, her voice implying that only people like Miss Crane would make such a frenzied call. "I'll try to get him."

Megan waited as patiently as she could, aware that several people were queueing up outside and looking annoyed so that when at last she heard his voice she spoke impulsively.

"Oh, Craig, thank goodness it's you! I'm so worried. Anarita has vanished."

"Vanished?" he echoed, sounding annoyed. "But you told me she often does it as a joke. Why this panic?"

"Because I don't think it's a joke. I think it was planned. She chose the most crowded bazaar and we...she led the way through the crowds. Looking back, I think I...."

"Have—as usual—made a mess of things," Craig said coldly. "All right, I'll come out right away. Meet you at the market. By the way, you're not to tell anyone that the girl has vanished. Understand?"

"Yes, but..." Megan began, but heard the receiver slammed down and replaced hers slowly. She had told Madame Duval. What would Craig say when he knew that?

ACTUALLY, TO MEGAN'S SURPRISE, Craig took the news very well that she had told Madame Duval.

He had arrived at the market at the same time Frank had joined her, looking irritated as he shook his head.

"No sign of the kid, Meg," Frank had said. "When I get my hands on that girl, I'll..." he began, even as Craig's car drew up.

Craig leaned out the window. "Both get in so we can talk," he said curtly.

Megan and Frank obeyed. Craig drove a little farther away to find a parking place, then turned and looked at her.

"Start at the beginning. What happened?"

Megan drew a deep breath. "Well, we...we were walking along and...." She hesitated. Was it necessary to mention Tracy Thompson? She decided not, for it had no bearing on the subject at all. "We met Madame Duval and Gaston and they insisted on our having a cold drink. Actually it was Anarita's idea."

Frank groaned softly and Megan looked at him.

"How could I refuse without being rude?" she

asked. "After all, Anarita has known both Gaston and Madame Duval for years, ever since she was a child."

"Go on...you had cold drinks with them," said Craig. "And then?"

"Well...well, I was a bit worried as I wasn't sure how you'd feel about our being with the Duvals, so I said we must go to meet Frank, er, Mr. Parr. Anarita pointed out afterward that it was much too early and she'd heard that a certain bazaar had some wonderfully cheap things. We went in there. I tried to stop her because it was so crowded, but she just went on, so I kept close to her. I was looking at a scarf and she was by my side, and then... then I turned to speak to her and she was gone."

"Just like that?" Craig asked. "How long were you looking at the scarf?"

"Only a few minutes," Megan said desperately. "I hunted all through the bazaar and couldn't find her, and then I saw Frank and he said we'd do one side each. It was then I bumped into Madame Duval, so I asked her if she'd seen Anarita and...I'm awfully sorry," she said again, looking at Craig worriedly. "If I'd known you didn't want anyone to know I wouldn't have told her."

Much to her relief and surprise, Craig smiled.

"It was natural for you to ask if she had seen the girl, so don't worry about that. I understand Anarita often plays this trick on you?"

Frank spoke first. "She does, and I gave her a real talking-to, threatened never to bring her in again if she did it once more. I know how it upsets Meg."

"Naturally. Was Anarita her usual self today?"

"She was very depressed. It seems she'd hoped to go

The Impossible Dream

to Rome for her holiday and had just heard from her guardian that she had to stay at school," Megan said.

"Why did she mind so much? She's often stayed at school."

"She said all the other girls were little kids. Could she have run away?" Megan asked.

Craig frowned. "I doubt it. No clothes and no money—as far as I know, that is. Did you get that impression?"

"We did notice the schooner was in the harbor," Frank said. "And she was interested. That right, Meg?"

"Yes, she seemed surprised. Oh!" Megan's hand flew to her mouth. "Something else I forgot to tell you. When we were having cold drinks with the Duvals, Gaston was talking to me and then I found Anarita and Madame Duval were talking in Italian. I wondered what it was about, because Madame Duval seemed very pleased about something. When we first met her, she had been quiet and rather... well, miserable, if you know what I mean, but after talking to Anarita, Madame Duval changed completely. She even told Anarita she was like her mother, full of good ideas."

Craig sighed. "Look, I'm afraid this is a matter for the police. You'd both better come with me as you were the last to see her."

"The police?" Megan was suddenly frightened. "You think she's in danger?"

Craig shrugged. "Anything can happen. That girl is my responsibility and as such must be found. Whether she's run away of her own accord or been kidnapped is neither here nor there. She has to be found."

"Kidnapped?" Megan almost whispered the word. "Who'd kidnap her?"

Craig looked at her, his face seeming to be made of stone, it was so hard and cold.

"I wouldn't put it past your charming Madame Duval," he said. "As I told you, she'd do anything to get the island."

"You mean the ransom could be the island?" Megan said very slowly. "Do you really think they'd do that?"

"I don't know. Look, Frank, you follow us in your car. After we've seen the police, you take Megan back to the school. You're neither of you to say anything. If asked where Anarita is, say she's visiting friends and will be fetched later. However, you'd better tell Miss Tucker the truth. Understand?" Craig's voice was harsh. He looked at Megan. "That goes for you, too. Also tell Miss Tucker *no one* must know. Right?"

"Yes. I'm so awfully sorry. . . ." Megan's voice was unsteady.

"I should have known better than allow her to come in with you," Craig said as Frank hurriedly left them, running back to where his car was parked.

The police turned out to be courteous, but Megan got very tired of repeating the same story over and over again. Of course they were trying to trip her up, she thought; they had to make sure she was telling them the same each time. Well, she was. She was telling the truth.

Frank drove her back to the school and they hardly spoke. Megan had the uncomfortable feeling that for once Frank blamed her for her carelessness, so it was a relief when, nearing the school, he smiled at her.

"Don't look so frightened, Meg. That kid'll be all right. It wasn't your fault. She can take care of herself."

The Impossible Dream

"You think she ran away?"

"I think she's trying to frighten us... well, look, you know Anarita. She loves publicity, I wouldn't mind betting she's hiding somewhere in town and will let the press have some extraordinary story."

"I hope you're right," Megan said miserably. "Now we've got to look normal. What do we do about Anarita?"

"I think we'd better see Miss Tucker," Frank said with a rueful grin, "and get it over."

It was an unpleasant interview, with Miss Tucker's cheeks and nose getting redder and redder, her voice more and more unsteady.

"We should never have engaged you," she said angrily to Megan. "Never in the past have such things happened to us."

"It wasn't Miss Crane's fault," Frank said.

Miss Tucker glared at him. "How can we trust you, either? You might both of you be in this. Never—ever—have we had such a scandal. One of our girls kidnapped!"

"Miss Tucker," Frank chimed in, "Anarita may not have been kidnapped. She may have run away."

"Why should she run away from a school like this?" Miss Tucker was indignant. "She was happy here."

"She wasn't," Megan said. "She resented lots of things—especially having to spend the holidays here."

"That's absurd! The girls have a pleasant time. In any case, that's beside the mark. Anarita was in your care, Miss Crane, and you have failed to stand up to the responsibility entailed. This is the final thing. I shall speak most sternly to Mr. Lambert about you—"

"Mr. Lambert said no one must know, Miss Tucker," Frank said, looking toward Megan. "He made that very plain. No one—but no one—must know," he added, his voice hard. "We're only telling you. If anyone asks where she is, Mr. Lambert says we're to say she's visiting some friends and will be back later."

"Will she?" Miss Tucker said bitterly, twisting her hands together. "If she isn't killed. That would be the end of everything. Never has this school...."

"Come on," Frank said quietly to Megan as Miss Tucker walked toward the window, talking angrily, but as if to herself. "I'll see you at dinner," he said quietly. "Remember, we have to act as if nothing has happened. Probably they'll have found Anarita by then, so try not to worry."

"I'll try," Megan said, smiling at him but seeing his face through a blur of tears.

Alone in her flat, she saw the letter waiting on the table. It was from England, the writing faintly familiar. She opened it. The letter was from her father! She began to read it eagerly, but her pleasure became dismay as she read what he had written.

I was horrified to see your photo in the Sunday newspaper. What sort of people are you associating with out there? In any case, I think you must come back. Your Aunt Lily's health seems to be deteriorating and you know I can do nothing, so the sooner you're back the better.

Megan read the letter several times, puzzled. Somehow it didn't read like her father's normal speech. Maybe he was ill, too. Perhaps the arthritis had affected his hands, because the writing was odd, too.

Go back? Was it her duty to go back if her father

The Impossible Dream

needed her? She went out on to the balcony. The blue lagoon was still, its lovely color in the late sunshine strikingly beautiful. Go back? Go back to nurse Aunt Lily and her father, to listen to their perpetual quarrels, to know that nothing she could do would ever be right? Yet he was her father, after all.

Megan dreaded dinner but Frank as usual helped her through it, and as few of the staff had decided yet to talk to her, there were no awkward questions. There was no sign of Craig, though, and that worried Megan very much. Surely if Anarita was just trying to frighten her or perhaps tease her—for somehow she couldn't think of Anarita's wanting to hurt her—surely if that was all it was, Anarita would have been found by now?

Later, walking outside with Frank, talking quietly, Megan reminded him how once she had told him that she had the strangest feeling with Anarita that she was playing a game that Anarita was winning and that Anarita, in addition, was aching with the desire to tell Megan all about it.

"I know that sounds involved, but...."

"I understand," Frank said thoughtfully. "But why should she want to play a game with you? No point in it if you didn't know you were playing it."

Megan sighed. "I just don't know. As long as she's all right...."

"I'm sure she is," said Frank. "Quite sure."

Megan looked at him. "I wish I could feel as sure!"

She hardly slept that night and, waking with the dawn, she got up, quickly dressed and slipped down out of the school and then on down to the edge of the lagoon. There was a pathway alongside the water and she knew it could not be many miles. She *had* to do something about it all—had to face up to Patrick and Gaston and Madame Duval to make sure they were not in it.

She reached the town at last and found her way to Patrick's studio of dancing and to his house next door. Ringing the bell, she waited until the door was opened by their manservant, Victor. He looked startled.

"Mr. Crane? Tell him it's his sister," Megan said, and walked into the house and straight to the lounge.

It was quite a few moments before Patrick joined her, tying the belt around his dressing gown, blinking sleepily as he gazed at her.

"What the hell do you want at this hour?" he demanded.

"Is Anarita here?" Megan said.

"Anarita?" He looked puzzled. "Oh, Anarita." His face broke up into a big smile. "Of course she's not. Why?"

"The police are looking for her," Megan said, and watched his face but he showed no dismay or fear. Ought she to have told him, she wondered, yet surely if Madame Duval knew, then it was certain she would have told Gaston and Patrick. "They think she may have been kidnapped."

"Kidnapped? I wish we'd thought of that," said Patrick. "We could have asked for a fortune—or the island!"

"Then someone has kidnapped her!" said Megan. It was as if a hand was clutching at her throat, making it hard for her to breathe.

"What on earth...?" Georgina said sleepily as she came into the room, wearing a very elegant silk housecoat. "What are you doing here, Meg?"

Megan looked at them both. "How could you be so mean!" she said angrily. "You lied about being ill, Georgina. You lied about the man wanting to see you

The Impossible Dream

dance, Patrick. You lied about everything to get me in that mess."

Patrick grinned. "So what? It worked, but not as well as we hoped. Maybe this time we'll do better."

"What do you mean?" Megan's voice quavered a little. "You've kidnapped Anarita?"

"Of course we haven't," said Georgina. "Patrick hadn't the brains to think that out. All the same, it's nearly as good. It'll be in all the papers today." She smiled maliciously. "Headlines, I expect. 'Famous heiress, pupil of the once-renowned Lambert School, has disappeared. Kidnapping is feared. How much ransom will be demanded?' It'll be as good as if it had really happened. What do they say? 'There's never smoke without fire.'" She laughed. "Your fine Mr. Lambert will be wiped out!"

"But..." Megan began, and paused.

Patrick was laughing. "A bit of luck, that was what it was. Gaston and his mum bumping into you and the girl saying she was going to elope—"

"Elope?" Megan's mouth was dry. "With Gaston?"

Both Patrick and Georgina laughed. "Not on your life!" said Patrick. "It's that artist chap...Tracy something or other."

"Tracy Thompson?" Megan gasped, finding it hard to believe.

Georgina laughed. "Sure. That's what she told Madame Duval. They've known each other for years, it seems, and have got tired of waiting for her to be twenty-one. Anyhow, Megan, I guess you'll be looking for a job soon, because that school will crash."

"You...both of you!" Megan was so angry she couldn't speak. She looked around her wildly at the expensive furniture paid for by the money they had talked her father into giving them. She turned and rushed outside into the street, then hurried to where she knew was a taxi stand. It might cost a lot, but she had to get back to the school as soon as possible.

As she arrived, she ignored the startled gaze of several of the staff who came down to breakfast early.

"Miss Tucker!" Megan, not realizing how flushed and untidy she was, hurried to the headmistress. "Is Mr. Lambert here?"

"No. He's at his house." Miss Tucker frowned. "Why?"

"I've something to tell him. Something important."

"You can use the phone in my office then," Miss Tucker said, looking rather worriedly at the girls who were all talking loudly and laughing as they ate. "Some news?" she asked softly.

Megan nodded, her honey-colored hair swinging forward, and she pushed it back. "I think it could be good news," she said.

She soon got through to the house—the house she loved.

When she heard Craig's voice, she reminded herself that the girl on the switchboard might be listening.

"Mr. Lambert?" she asked. "I've... I've seen my brother and...."

"You have something you wish to discuss with me?" Craig Lambert's voice was crisp. "I don't want to come in just now and this is a good place to talk, so I'll send my car in to fetch you," he added curtly, and she heard the slam as he put down the receiver.

Not in a very good mood, she thought as she hurried up to her flat to brush her hair, make up her face and put on a clean dress. There were clouds piling up in the sky. She wondered if there was a storm brewing up.

The Impossible Dream

She was in the hall when she saw, through the open door, Craig's car. She hurried out before anyone could stop her or even ask her where she was going, but as the chauffeur opened the car door Megan looked up at the school and saw Miss Tucker and Petronella Weston standing at a window gazing at her. They looked pleased in a strange way. Perhaps, Megan thought, they saw this as the end of her. Even Craig's tolerant patience could not be tried too far and surely this time he must be so angry with her that she was bound to leave? Megan, sitting in the car, shivered. They would be glad to see her go. Neither had liked her right from the beginning. In fact, she had only two real friends at the school: Frank and Mr. Taft.

Craig was walking in the garden in front of his house as she reached it. He came slowly to meet her. His face seemed blank, as if he was wearing a mask. He waited for the car to drive around the back and then looked seriously at Megan, who was finding it hard not to tell him her news.

"Well? You wanted to see me?" he asked coldly.

"I think she's all right." The words now fell out of Megan's mouth. "I saw Patrick and Georgina and it was all done deliberately—the other business, I mean. You were quite right... but I wanted to know about Anarita and they told me she had eloped." She paused, breathless, staring at him as they walked slowly across the grass.

"I know," he said.

It was a shock. "You know, and you didn't..." Megan began.

Craig lifted his hand. "I was about to ring you when you rang me. I had just heard from the police that they traced Anarita and her boyfriend to the mainland but don't know where they are now. Judging from the description I imagine it's Justin Newell."

"It isn't," Megan said eagerly. "It's Tracy Thompson. He's an artist and we used to see him in town...." Hurriedly she told Craig about their occasional meetings with the hippie artist. "I liked him, but Anarita wouldn't speak to him. She said she preferred older men."

Craig's stern face creased into a smile. "How naive can you be?" he asked. "Naturally she didn't want you to guess that she and this lad were deeply in love!"

"You knew?" Megan stood still as she stared at him.

"In a sense, yes. She and Justin have been in love since she was fourteen, but naturally her guardian refused to treat it seriously. He declared it was adolescent infatuation. We argued about it, because I felt that Anarita was too mature and too eager for life to be happy at our school, but her guardian, Jerome Hardwick, was adamant. However, he agreed that if they stayed in love for several years, he might relent. It's a pity you didn't tell me about this artist."

"I... well, it didn't seem necessary, because Anarita just ignored him. I wonder...." Megan's eyes widened as she thought of something. "I wonder if they used to have secret meetings when I lost Anarita? That would explain... but yesterday when we met him she moved away and wouldn't look at him. I wonder if they decided to elope on the spur of the moment because Anarita didn't want to spend the holiday here."

"I'm not really surprised," said Craig, his mouth amused. "She'd have no chance of seeing him because there are few staff here during the holidays and I doubt if Anarita would get a lift into town at all, and that would have spoiled everything. After all, the lad only

The Impossible Dream

came to the island in the hope of meeting her occasionally, I imagine."

"The schooner was there," Megan said eagerly, then paused, her face clouding. "But I'm forgetting the worrying part. They've—" her mouth was dry "—they've—and I think Patrick meant Madame Duval—sent the news to all the papers that Anarita has been kidnapped. That'll be dreadful for you. Madame Duval thinks it will ruin you completely."

"I guessed they'd do something like that." Craig pushed open the front door and they left the humid fragrant air for the cool air of the hall. "So I got through myself to London. Pity Miss Wilmot wasn't there at the time, because I could have contacted her. However, the newspapers know it was a hoax. That there never was any question of kidnapping and the romantic story of the seventeen-year-old girl who after four years of waiting has eloped with her love will be the *real* exciting news, because Justin is heir to an even greater fortune than Anarita, so from that point of view her guardian has no reason to disapprove. I think he'll accept the fact that their love is sincere and give them his blessing."

He led the way to his book-lined study and asked her to sit down, then got them both iced drinks.

Megan could feel the tenseness leaving her body slowly as she relaxed in the chair. Everything was going to be all right. When Craig sat down on the other side of his desk she said eagerly, "Then... then they can't hurt the school?"

He smiled. "For the moment, no. Next week is end of term. Next term... well, let's hope we'll have no repetition of this term's unfortunate incidents." His voice seemed to have grown hard.

Megan fumbled in her handbag. "I think it would be best if I leave. I seem to have brought you nothing but bad luck." Her voice wavered for a moment, wishing he would deny it, but he said nothing, just went on watching her. "I... my father wrote to me and wants me to go back." She passed over the letter.

Craig read it silently and then looked up. "You want to go?"

Megan shook her head violently, then stopped. She hadn't meant to react like that! "He *is* my father. Perhaps I should."

Turning the letter over slowly in his hands, Craig said, "Were you surprised to get the letter?"

"Very. My father hasn't written to me once since I've been here."

"You've written to him?"

"Of course." Megan hesitated, but Craig seemed sympathetic, so she went on, "I was surprised when it came. It's so unlike him. I mean, he's always been impatient with people who use long words. He says short words are good enough for him, but in this he's used long words. Another thing, I really wondered if perhaps his hands are bad, because the writing isn't like his was—"

"Just a moment," Craig interrupted. He stood up and went to a tall filing cabinet in the corner of the room, pulling open a drawer and taking out a folder. He went back to his desk, turned the pages of the papers before him and brought out a letter. "I see what you mean," he said slowly. "There is a slight difference in the writing."

"When did my father write to you?" Megan asked, half-rising, but Craig gestured to her to stay where she was, so she sank back in the chair.

The Impossible Dream

"He didn't."

"Then how have you got a letter of his?"

Craig leaned back, folding his arms, looking at her with a slightly supercilious smile.

"It really began several years ago when your brother moved in on the island. Naturally I had to find out if he was a genuine dance teacher or if this was some drug-taking project. I had his background looked up in England, and this included his father and sister."

"Wasn't that... well, you ...." Megan hesitated.

"Look, I'm responsible for these girls and their lives, for their parents trust me, therefore I'm careful. I already knew all about Gaston Duval's past, his mother's determination to get the island for her beloved son, but Patrick Crane was a new personality, so I had to find out all I could about him. What I found out reassured me. He had a clean background, had always danced and taught dancing. Georgina was the same—you, too. So I did nothing to stop your brother from opening the Crane Dancing Studio. Indeed, I could see nothing wrong in it—until he became more deeply involved with the Duvals. I knew then that they would stop at nothing, that the ridiculous feud between the Duvals and Lamberts would never end. I began to distrust your brother. I see I was right."

"But if you doubted Patrick, why did you engage me?" Megan asked. "Did you think I was involved in some way and want to keep me under your eye? That reminds me... what about Frank and Miss Tucker? Shouldn't they know Anarita is all right?"

"They do. I rang up soon after you'd rung me and told them."

"Miss Tucker and Petronella watched me leave."

He smiled. "I expect they looked pleased?"

"They did," Megan said bitterly. "They've never liked me—nor has Miss Wilmot."

"No...I can understand that." Craig turned over the letter still before him. "In a way, though, I find it utterly deplorable." His smile softened the last word.

"I suppose they know you're going to sack me?" said Megan. "That's why they looked so pleased."

"I did give them that impression," Craig told her.

Megan clenched her hands together tightly. She didn't want to go. Never to see him again? And yet she knew it was the only answer.

"I...I don't seem to have been much help to the school, I'm afraid," she sighed.

"On the contrary, you've been of great assistance," Craig told her. "You've opened my eyes to many things. Also the way the Duvals have behaved has put them in my power. I shall now be able to sue them... or threaten to, and believe me, Madame Duval will be off this island and take her son with her within seconds. She can't bear the danger of her name being involved. She's a very proud woman and she loves her son and will always give him money... but it ends there. I think they'll recognize that they've lost the battle, for nothing, not even the destruction of the school, will make me leave the island."

"But I must go," Megan said slowly.

"Yes," Craig told her. "You must go."

CHAPTER NINE

MEGAN KNEW that it had to come. She had expected it, though she had steeled herself for when it came, but all the same it hurt her terribly. Fortunately for her, giving her time to overcome the shock, the phone bell shrilled at that moment and Craig answered it.

As she sat, dazed, yet knowing it had to be accepted, for she could see no other solution, she realized suddenly that Craig was talking to Anarita.

"Yes, it *was* naughty of you. Poor Miss Crane was very upset.... I understand. I know, it wasn't her fault. Thank you for telling me, Anarita. You phoned him? Good girl... very sensible!" Craig was nodding, smiling as he spoke. "He agreed? I'm glad. Yes, I'm sure she'd love to. What was that?" he asked, and nodded. "Yes, you can speak to her. She's here with me now." He held out the phone to Megan. "Anarita would like to speak to you," he said.

Megan stood up, moved nearer the desk and took the phone in her hand. "Anarita?" she said.

Anarita's excited voice drummed in her ears as she listened to her apology.

"I hadn't planned to go. Justin was willing to wait, but knowing I'd be there all the holiday and hardly see him was just the end, Miss Crane. Then seeing the schooner in seemed that fate was playing with us, so when I skipped out of the bazaar and met Justin... I bet you've guessed that I always met him when I got lost?" Anarita laughed happily. "I said to him, let's get out of here, and he agreed. We just caught the schooner at the last moment. Luckily I had my passport with me. I always carried it as I knew one day we'd get tired of waiting. You can imagine how we felt! Anyhow, I phoned my guardian and he says we can get married. Isn't that super?"

"Wonderful, Anarita," Megan said warmly. "I'm so glad for you. I wish I'd known."

"How could I tell you?" Anarita asked. "You'd have had to tell Mr. Lambert and he'd have had to stop it, wouldn't he? Anyhow, Uncle Jerome is planning a big wedding for us in about a month's time. He insists on that, and I was wondering, Miss Crane, if you'd be one of my bridesmaids?"

"Me, a bridesmaid?" Megan was startled. "I'd love to, but... well, I don't know where I shall be."

She was even more startled, for Craig had moved, come around the desk to stand by her side and put his arm around her, leaning down to speak into the receiver.

"Don't worry, Anarita, she'll be there. I'll see to that," he promised.

"Thanks, Mr. Lambert." Anarita's laugh was gay.

Megan handed the phone to Craig and tried to move away, but his arm tightened around her. She stood very still, willing herself not to tremble, fighting hard to hide her misery.

You must go, he had said earlier on. *You must go,* and though she had known it had to happen, it was still too terrible to accept. But how did that fit in with her being a bridesmaid?

He was talking. "Don't worry, Anarita. Yes, I know

The Impossible Dream

it's in all the papers, but I've sent news of your elopement. They knew, though...? You what? You told the press? I see. You wanted it all to be aboveboard." He chuckled. "You certainly twisted poor old Hardwick's arm. He was only concerned for your good, you know. Yes, we are old squares, I agree, but I don't agree with your statement that we don't understand. Believe me, we do. And it's just as painful for us. Right, Anarita. Thank you for phoning, and I'm glad everything is working out so well."

He put down the phone and looked at the girl standing so still in his arms, her face drawn and miserable, her cheeks very white. He moved away and saw how slowly she walked to her chair and sat down. He went behind his desk.

"This letter," he said, lifting it in his hand. "Forget it, Megan. Your father didn't write it."

Megan's face came to life. "You don't think he did?"

"I'm sure he didn't. As I said, comparing it with this other letter of his, I'm sure he didn't. In any case, last week my man in England went down to Dorset. I wanted him to check. It was a bit of luck—" Craig smiled "—but he got lost just outside your Aunt Lily's cottage. Your father was working in the garden—"

"But he always said he couldn't," Megan began.

Craig smiled. "I can imagine. Anyhow, he and my man had quite a talk. Your father is very happy, it seems. Your Aunt Lily, too, is well and putting on weight."

"So I needn't..." Megan began, and stopped. Her father didn't need her. No one did.

Suddenly she realized something. "But if my father didn't write the letter, who did?"

"Miss Wilmot."

"Miss Wilmot?" Megan gasped. "But you and she...."

Craig smiled. "She may think so, but I've never given her cause. So many women indulge in wishful thinking... as you know," he added.

Her cheeks were hot. Had she indulged in it, she wondered, and did he know? Was this a not-so-gentle hint?

"But Miss Wilmot said..." she began.

"Ignore what Miss Wilmot said. She has always, unfortunately, been jealous and possessive, and this is the last straw. I find it hard to understand how she could be so foolish—she's stuck one stamp from another envelope. This letter was written *here*." He frowned. "There are going to be big changes. I've decided to make them at once. Miss Tucker must go. I'm arranging for her to retire a year earlier than normal, but I shall make this financially better for her. Quite a few of the staff will go, including Petronella Weston, who has extremely annoyed me with her behavior."

"Miss Wilmot said *she* was to be headmistress."

"Miss Wilmot?" Craig threw back his head as he laughed. "That really is absurd! She hasn't a clue about children. No, I'm offering the job to Frank Parr."

"Frank?" Megan was startled. "Headmaster of a girls' school?"

"Yes. It happened at Roedean, didn't it? I can trust Frank, he has a good sense of humor, tolerance, he gets on well with both staff and the girls and he isn't handsome enough for them to have crushes on him."

"Frank is..." Megan began quickly.

Craig chuckled. "Standing up for someone, as usual, Megan? I know Frank has *something*... that's why I'm

The Impossible Dream

offering him the job. I hope he'll take it. Think he will?"

Megan leaned back in her chair, half-closing her eyes, remembering the long talks she had had with Frank, how often he had told her he was against too much discipline. "It should be *self*-discipline," he had said. "I trust children and then they are to be trusted. It's laying down ridiculous rules that causes rebellion and friction."

Megan nodded slowly as she looked at Craig. "I should think so. He'd be a wonderful headmaster."

"Are you in love with him?"

The unexpected question was a shock. "No...I'm very fond of him, but I definitely don't love *him*." She realized with dismay that she had emphasized the last word. She could only hope Craig hadn't noticed.

"Good. Perhaps I should say, not so good for Frank. He loves you. You know that, of course?"

Megan nodded. "I'm sorry, but...."

"Don't get a guilt complex about that, Megan. It's not your fault. Where was I? Oh, yes, there'll be a real reshuffle of the staff. I'll be consulting with the new headmaster and then...."

"And then?" Megan almost whispered the words.

"I'm off to South America."

"South America?" she repeated. That was thousands of miles away, she thought, dismayed. He would go right out of her life forever... but perhaps that was better. It might be less painful than seeing him every day and knowing he saw her as a young nuisance!

Suddenly she thought of something and her hand flew to her mouth. "What about Patrick?" she asked nervously. "I think he has...well, I think it was the meanest...."

Craig looked amused. "Your brother is weak and easily influenced. Gaston Duval has a smooth tongue and built up a wonderful future for Patrick with a minimum of work. I think Patrick realizes life is not as simple as that. He's been made a good offer for the dancing school, one I think will tempt him so that he'll sell it."

"And go back to England?"

"I doubt it very much. Actually I'm buying his dance studio myself and shall offer him the post of manager. I'm also going to arrange for the classes of older girls to go to his school for lessons. I shall arrange, or have arranged," he added with a smile, "for them to meet more people, lead a more normal life. Patrick could be of assistance in this way."

"You're very good..." Megan said slowly. "Not many men would be so kind." It seemed as if everybody's life was being wonderfully arranged—except her own, she thought sadly.

"South America is a wonderful continent," Craig went on, his face thoughtful. "I told you I was an archaeologist by preference? Well, it seems something interesting has turned up in Brazil, so I'm taking a six-months' holiday. That'll give Frank time to find his feet before I come back. I want him to be able to manage on his own, but this—" he waved his hand around expressively "—will always be my home."

Megan nodded. She couldn't tell him, but she would give anything for it to be her home, too, she was thinking when Craig startled her by leaning forward over the desk and saying, "Brazil is an ideal place for a honeymoon, you know."

The words sank into her mind slowly. For a moment

The Impossible Dream

she could only stare at him, but then, somehow, she forced herself to speak.

"So you're getting married?"

"I hope so. If the girl will have me," said Craig.

"The girl?" Megan whispered, for what girl would keep him waiting for an answer?

He picked up something from the desk, walked around and bent over her.

"This is the girl. Do you think she'll say yes?" he asked, showing her a photograph.

Megan caught her breath. It was a photograph of herself!

"But... but...." She looked up and found he was bending so close to her that his mouth was very near. "You love me?" She sounded startled.

He nodded. "Ever since my man in England sent me this. I think he took it when you were shopping in the supermarket. He sent photos of the three of you—you, your father and your Aunt Lily. I like to know everything about people I'm going to have to trust. I took one look at this photo of you and the strangest thing happened." He was smiling as he spoke. "Frankly, I've always been rather skeptical about love, Megan, particularly love at first sight. Yet, as I said, I looked at your photograph and knew you were the girl I wanted to marry."

"But...." Megan felt confused, for this was so unlike the Craig Lambert she had known. "You mean you fell in love with my photograph?"

He laughed. "I did. I don't mind telling you it was a bit of a shock. However, I knew I had to meet you and get you to know me—for I felt I knew you already."

"Then it was because of me that poor Miss Pointer was sacked?" Megan asked.

"Yes and no. Miss Pointer would have been sacked much earlier but for you. She was always a bit of a rebel, grumbling about the school, making the girls discontented because of our stringent rules. I had, for some time, been thinking of firing her, and then you turned up and when I learned you were a dance teacher, it seemed the answer. So I went and met your Mrs. Arbuthnot and told her I needed a teacher. I managed it so that we talked about you. I asked if I could see some of her teachers at work and she was only too willing to show me. I said I thought your youth and originality were what we needed...."

"They weren't really?"

He smiled. "Actually, they *were* really, but at the same time I wanted to get you out here so that you could get to know me. I could hardly ask you to marry me when you hadn't even seen me, could I? Anyhow, your Mrs. Arbuthnot agreed you were a good teacher and she said frankly that she wished you could have the job as she was very concerned about you. However, she told me it was unlikely that you would ever have a chance of accepting such a good job because of your loyalty to your father. That seemed to block off all my efforts. Still, I refused to give up hope. Your father wasn't all that old, maybe he'd marry again. You were young and I would have to wait. So I let Miss Pointer stay on. Then I heard your father was selling the house and that you were looking for a job."

"Craig...." Megan stopped him, her eyes narrowed as she thought. "You didn't deliberately make Patrick...?"

He looked startled. "You don't really think I'd...?"

"I don't think so, but they said...."

"If you'd rather believe what they said." Craig sounded hurt and turned away.

"Craig, please," Megan said quickly, "I didn't think that, only it seems such a coincidence that Patrick should ask dad for money and dad sell the house so I was free and—"

Craig turned around again, smiling. "Not a coincidence but fate, Megan." He pulled her gently to her feet and clasped his arms around her loosely. "I jumped at the chance I was offered and got you here. Tell me—" his arms tightened slightly "—tell me the truth. Do you love me, Megan?"

It was difficult to think properly when she was so close to him. She shook her head slowly. "I can't believe you love me, Craig. It was just one of my dreams that I knew could never come true." Somehow her arms found their way around his neck as she looked at him. "Surely you can see!" she said with a smile.

"I still want you to tell me," he insisted.

"I can't realize it, Craig. I just can't believe it. You... well, I had no idea you felt like that about me," she almost whispered.

"I couldn't let you know in term time, could I? I was waiting for the holidays. But, like Anarita, I refuse to wait any longer." His arms tightened. "Megan, will you be my wedded wife?"

"Oh, Craig, of course I will!"

"You still haven't told me."

She laughed happily. "It's like a fairy tale. My dream of an island with palm trees and blue lagoons and a house with a thatched roof and the darlingest man in the world...."

"Megan...."

Megan stroked his face gently. "Of course I love you, Craig. I love you very much indeed."

"That's all I wanted to know," Craig said as he tightened his arms so that she could hardly breathe.

At that moment, the phone bell shrilled impatiently.

Craig laughed. "Let it ring. I've more important business to do," he said, and then he kissed her.

FREE
*Harlequin Reader Service Catalog**

A complete listing of all titles currently available in Harlequin Romance, Harlequin Presents, Classic Library and Superromance.

Special offers and exciting new books, too!

*Catalog varies each month.

Complete and mail this coupon today!

FREE CATALOG

Mail to: *Harlequin Reader Service*

In the U.S.
1440 South Priest Drive
Tempe, AZ 85281

In Canada
649 Ontario Street
Stratford, Ontario, N5A 6W2

YES, please send me absolutely FREE the *current* Harlequin Reader Service catalog.

NAME:_____
(PLEASE PRINT)

ADDRESS:_____ APT. NO._____

CITY:_____

STATE/PROV:_____ ZIP/POSTAL CODE:_____

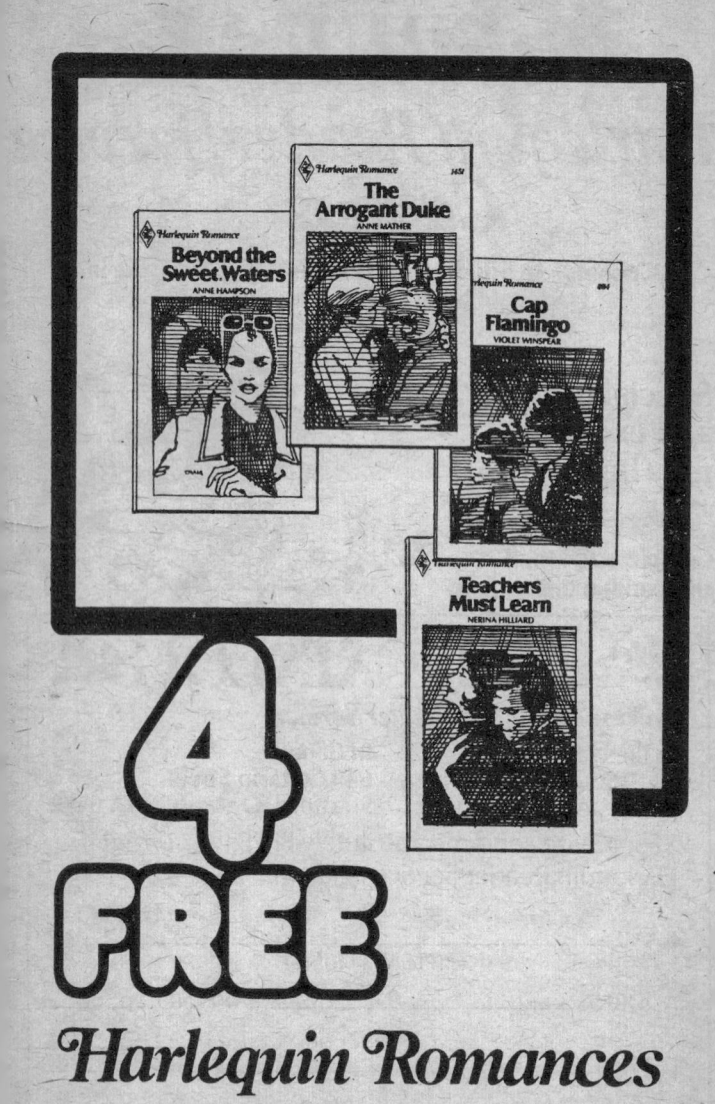

4 FREE
Harlequin Romances

TAKE THESE 4 Harlequin Romances FREE

as advertised on TV

Thrill to romantic, aristocratic Istanbul, and the tender love story of a girl who built a barrier around her emotions in ANNE HAMPSON's "Beyond the Sweet Waters" . . . a Caribbean island is the scene setting for love and conflict in ANNE MATHER's "The Arrogant Duke" . . . exciting, sun-drenched California is the locale for romance and deception in VIOLET WINSPEAR's "Cap Flamingo" . . . and an island near the coast of East Africa spells drama and romance for the heroine in NERINA HILLIARD's "Teachers Must Learn."

Harlequin Romances . . . 6 exciting novels published each month! Each month you will get to know interesting, appealing, true-to-life people . . . . You'll be swept to distant lands you've dreamed of visiting . . . . Intrigue, adventure, romance, and the destiny of many lives will thrill you through each Harlequin Romance novel.

Get all the latest books before they're sold out!

As a Harlequin subscriber you actually receive your personal copies of the latest Romances immediately after they come off the press, so you're sure of getting all 6 each month.

Cancel your subscription whenever you wish!

You don't have to buy any minimum number of books. Whenever you decide to stop your subscription just let us know and we'll cancel all further shipments.

Your FREE gift includes
- *Anne Hampson* — Beyond the Sweet Waters
- *Anne Mather* — The Arrogant Duke
- *Violet Winspear* — Cap Flamingo
- *Nerina Hilliard* — Teachers Must Learn

FREE GIFT CERTIFICATE

and Subscription Reservation

Mail this coupon today!

In the U.S.A.
1440 South Priest Drive
Tempe, AZ 85281

In Canada
649 Ontario Street
Stratford, Ontario N5A 6W2

Harlequin Reader Service:

Please send me my 4 Harlequin Romance novels FREE. Also, reserve a subscription to the 6 NEW Harlequin Romance novels published each month. Each month I will receive 6 NEW Romance novels at the low price of $1.50 each (*Total–$9.00 a month*). There are no shipping and handling or any other hidden charges. I may cancel this arrangement at any time, but even if I do, these first 4 books are still mine to keep.

NAME (PLEASE PRINT)

ADDRESS

CITY   STATE/PROV.   ZIP/POSTAL CODE

Offer not valid to present subscribers
Offer expires September 30, 1982   BP058

Prices subject to change without notice.